CREATURE FROM HELL

She was halfway down the stairs when she realized something was wrong. For no apparent reason, she felt she was no longer alone, that something or someone had intruded upon her home, something that was waiting for her to walk in unawares.

Cautiously she descended the rest of the way to the ground level and moved slowly to the archway leading into the kitchen. She extended her left hand, slid it along the wall, found the switch, and flicked it up. The room beyond was flooded with light and she heard the faint, familiar hum of fluorescent tubes.

Nothing seemed amiss. The cup of tea was still sitting on the table, steaming slightly, an appetizing golden color.

She walked to the table.

Just as she reached for her cup, the gargoyle stepped out of the pantry into clear view.

Not for a moment did she believe she was dreaming. Her only thought was to kill, to destroy this monstrous evil thing—before it destroyed her. . . .

THE BEST IN BONE CHILLING TERROR
FROM PINNACLE BOOKS!

Blood-curdling new blockbusters by horror's premier masters of the macabre! Heart-stopping tales of terror by the most exciting new names in fright fiction! Pinnacle's the place where sensational shivers live!

FEAST (103-7, $4.50)
by Graham Masterton
Le Reposir in the quiet little town of Allen's Corners wasn't interested in restaurant critic Charlie McLean's patronage. But Charlie's son, Martin, with his tender youth, was just what the secluded New England eatery had in mind!
"THE LIVING INHERITOR TO THE REALM OF EDGAR ALLEN POE"
— SAN FRANCISCO CHRONICLE

LIFEBLOOD (110-X, $3.95)
by Lee Duigon
The yuppie bedroom community of Millboro, New Jersey is just the place for Dr. Winslow Emerson. For Emerson is no ordinary doctor, but a creature of terrifying legend with a hideous hunger . . . And Millboro is the perfect feeding ground!

GHOULS (119-3, $3.95)
by Edward Lee
The terrified residents of Tylersville, Maryland, have been blaming psychopaths, werewolves and vampires for the tidal wave of horror and death that has deluged their town. But policeman Kurt Morris is about to uncover the truth . . . and the truth is much, much worse!

Available wherever paperbacks are sold, or order direct from the Publisher. Send cover price plus 50¢ per copy for mailing and handling to Pinnacle Books, Dept. 096, 475 Park Avenue South, New York, N.Y. 10016. Residents of New York, New Jersey and Pennsylvania must include sales tax. DO NOT SEND CASH.

Blood Beast
Don D'Ammassa

PINNACLE BOOKS
WINDSOR PUBLISHING CORP.

PINNACLE BOOKS

are published by

Windsor Publishing Corp.
475 Park Avenue South
New York, NY 10016

First printing: October, 1988

Printed in the United States of America

PROLOGUE
1933

"If I were a superstitious man, I'd say this job had been cursed from the start." Sean Kelly collapsed onto a folding chair in the corner of the construction shack.

Andy Mathewson glanced up from the desk where he was reviewing a seemingly endless stream of bills, materials receipts, requisitions, work vouchers, and other correspondence linked with the current job. "You *are* a superstitious man, Kelly—possibly the most superstitious man I've ever met."

Kelly closed one eye and folded his massive arms tightly around himself, regarding the younger Mathewson steadily through his open eye, "And with good reason, too." Mathewson suppressed a smirk, noticing that Kelly's voice had acquired the Irish lilt that appeared only when the older man wanted to make a certain impression, although he denied categorically that this was in fact what happened. "When you've lived as long as I have, Andy my lad, and seen the things I've seen in this life, you'll learn to have considerable respect for what moves behind the scenes, so to speak. Don't let them educate you out of touch with the real world. It's a dark and mysterious and sometimes frightening place that we live in, I'll tell you, and those that don't recognize that fact and try to explain everything away by waving a book at it are doing themselves and others a disservice."

"I've known you to read a book or two when you had nothing better to do." This time Andy could not restrain the smile; the two men had been through some variation of this conversation so many times that they had it down to a ritual. Kelly, despite his pretense to the contrary, was not an uneducated man, although he had picked up his learning by individual study, never having had time or funds to pursue a more formal education. Having left school at fourteen to support an impoverished family, Kelly had soon displayed an obvious intelligence that had allowed him to progress rapidly despite his Irish background in a profession that was coming to be dominated by second-generation Italian–Americans.

Not that Andy Mathewson came from any more exalted a background. His family had been slightly better off than the Kelly clan, but except for a few quick business courses, he had nothing better than a high school education, although he knew enough to hold down a job as general accountant and paper pusher for the Cardonella Construction Company. Unfortunately there was not enough to qualify him for a better position with a more prosperous firm. Not that CCC was doing badly; they had landed the Sheffield job not by underbidding the competition, but by holding a reputation as the most competent, trustworthy, and best-equipped firm in the state. Although Rhode Island was too small to contain much competition, he reflected.

Kelly had both eyes closed now, but he appeared tense

and preoccupied, and Mathewson suddenly dropped the bantering tone. "More problems? Anything serious?"

The older man's eyes snapped open, but he didn't seem to be looking at anything in particular. "Lots of problems, problems everywhere. The generator is down again and the back-up is missing. The riggers just arrived and they were supposed to be here hours ago. That missing crate finally turned up and they even delivered it on time, but the ground is so soft from all this rain that we're not sure it'll support the crane. Sheffield has been all over the lot, complaining about the weather, about the cost, about the quality of the materials, and he gets in the way and slows us down further. Sometimes I wish we'd never bid on this job, or that someone else had beaten us out."

"At least he doesn't keep changing his mind." Their last job had been for an elderly man who kept altering the layout of the ground floor of his office building, then complained interminably because they were behind schedule.

"No, you're right. That I will grant him. There's been nary a deviation from his original drawings. Sometimes I wish there had been. Some of the tolerances he insists on are tighter than I'd expect from the government, and he comes out and checks them himself, often as not. A very peculiar man is Mr. Paul Alan Sheffield, if you're asking me."

"You're right about that." Mathewson leaned forward onto his elbows, ignoring for the moment the mass of paperwork with which he still had to cope today. "Why anyone would want to build a mansion this size in a hick town like Managansett is beyond me. The architecture doesn't blend in, he'll never be able to sell it, and there's nothing in this town to attract him, as far as I can tell. It doesn't make sense."

"To say nothing of the problems he's going to have maintaining it," replied Kelly, shifting his weight and scratching at his scalp with one hand. "There aren't enough fireplaces to heat the house properly, and the shelving in every room is built in so solidly that it will take a major refurbishing to convert it to normal use. Every bleeding room in the place has floor-to-ceiling shelves, no less, with specific instructions on the intervals. The stone walls will keep the heat in, I suppose, but we're having a devil of a time matching up the pieces he brought in from overseas to the ones he had cut here."

"I know." Mathewson sighed and sat back in his chair. "And the stonecutters he used locally weren't all that careful, either. We've sent four blocks back for recutting, and three were cut too short and had to be done a third time. I have a letter here complaining that Sheffield never told them about the bias on the stone for the southwest corner. They're refusing to do another without payment."

"Not our problem. Let them take it up with him. He buys the parts of the puzzle; we just put them together and hope we come up with what he wanted in the first place."

"He does seem to know what he's doing."

Kelly straightened up and his voice became deeper, the lilt gone. "Mechanically, you're absolutely right. But there's something wrong in that man's mind. The separate parts of this house of his work fine, but together, they just don't seem to add up. There's different styles of architecture on the interior and exterior, the facia don't match from side to side, and the layout of the rooms is impractical and wastes space."

Mathewson had nothing to add; he agreed with everything the crew boss had said. Sheffield had spoken to him briefly on a couple of occasions, and if ever there was a man with a warped obsession, Sheffield was that man. Wealthy beyond anything Mathewson might ever aspire to, Sheffield was a reclusive man without family or friends, insofar as Mathewson could tell. He was living at the Managansett Inn during the construction, and the owner, Mr. D'Angelo, had told Kelly that Sheffield never left his room unless it was to come to the construction site. When he did leave, it was always by horse and buggy, hired from one of the nearby farmers. Sheffield apparently never traveled by automobile unless there was no alternative. D'Angelo considered it an interesting and amusing idiosyncrasy, but Mathewson viewed it as just one more indication of the man's aberrations.

"Is he here now?"

"Just arrived." Kelly shook his head. "Wants to supervise again, I suppose. Now that his precious gargantua has shown up, he'll want to make sure we handle it gently and stick it up just right."

"Gargoyle, not gargantua," Mathewson corrected. "A gargantua is a giant of some sort; a gargoyle is one of those goblin things they carve on the sides of cathedrals in France. This is a gargoyle."

"Well, it's one gargantua of a gargoyle, then," Kelly answered, sliding forward on the chair and rising to his feet. "Why he wants the damned thing mounted right over his bedroom window is beyond me. Statues belong down low where you can see them and clean the bird shit off, not up near the roof line.

"Well, that's how they do it in Europe," Mathewson explained. "Some buildings had whole rows of them."

"Then let's thank our lucky stars that Mr. Sheffield here only wants one."

"Has it been uncrated yet? I'd like to take a look at it."

"Be my guest. They should have it done in another few minutes. Sheffield's watching to make sure they don't scratch it. I had them dump a load of crushed stone out by the site so the crane will have a firmer base."

"Doesn't that mean we'll have to clean it up? There's no provision in the costing for that."

"Don't worry about it. Over there the grounds are going to be made into a small garden and he specified crushed stone walkways. We'll just sweep it around a bit or dump loam right on top for the flowerbeds. It won't cost the company anything to do it this way and it'll be a lot safer. That damned thing is going to be heavy and awkward; the weight isn't distributed evenly."

Mathewson rose and joined the other man, donning a light jacket. It was late May and normally warmer, but there had been a cold breeze for almost a week. The incessant drizzle, punctuated by an occasional downpour, had made the air chilly and unpleasant. Mathewson zipped up and followed Kelly out of the shack.

As ugly as it was, the Sheffield mansion was certainly impressive, an imposing stone building five stories high, with flying buttresses, fake battlements, stained glass windows, wrought iron trim, elaborately carved embellishments, and even an ornate tower at one corner. The building was nearly complete now, with only a few minor items to be taken care of before emphasis could be switched to getting the grounds into shape. Sheffield had specified a series of gardens and paths to surround his new home, but they were to wait until the main house was completed. Even to Sheffield, these were apparently an afterthought, and he had easily acceded to a few changes

10

suggested by the landscape people, whereas he had absolutely refused even to listen to suggestions for alterations in the layout or specifications of the main house. The only obviously incomplete aspect of that building was the vacant space on the south wall where an enormous stone block needed to be inset directly over a narrow window.

The European components of the house had trickled in over a period of months during the previous summer. Many of these had had to be held in storage until they were called for in the assembly of the mansion. But Sheffield had fretted noisily about a single shipment which had gone astray after the vessel carrying it had developed mechanical problems and returned to the Danzig. Alternate arrangements had been made, but during the transshipping, three crates had been misplaced, and two had subsequently turned up in Istanbul, of all places. Sheffield had successfully recovered these, but the third crate had eluded all efforts to locate it. Then, just as it appeared that Sheffield would have to make do with some native substitute, he received a letter of inquiry from a shipping agent in San Francisco, he acknowledged that he was in fact the same Paul Alan Sheffield whose name was stenciled on the crate, and the missing piece had arrived belatedly a few days earlier. Now all that had to be done was to install it, and the last major component would be in place.

The two men walked single-file, Kelly leading, along wooden planks that had been laid across the muddy ground. To the right Mathewson could see the crane slowly assuming position beside the south wall of the mansion. A flatbed truck had been backed up close by and several men stood in a group aboard it, apparently preparing the last piece of the mosaic for the final leg of its journey.

Even from this distance he could see the broad outline of the block, which from this perspective looked far larger than the breach that had been left for it up above. Knowing Sheffield's penchant for precise detail, however, the young man had no doubt that the stone would fit that gap perfectly.

A handful of men stood by, hoping to watch the operation. Kelly would normally have ordered them back to work, but he was curious himself and could hardly fault the crew for their own interest. As a matter of fact, despite all the setbacks, construction of the mansion was actually almost a week ahead of schedule, and he could afford to look the other way from time to time. Kelly took very good care of his men, and they responded with loyalty and affection—even those who'd once angrily insisted they'd never work under the supervision of a "goddamned mick." Kelly was a man who seemed to rise above circumstances, triumphing where others would not even make an effort, and his evenhandedness and obvious concern for the safety of his work crews had made him the most popular and successful crew boss in the company.

As the two men drew near, they could make out more detail. The long awaited final stone lay on its flat backside, what would eventually be the interior wall. Protruding into the air was the gargoyle itself, carved from the front half of the stone block, for the most part obscured by the bodies of the men moving about it, preparing it for installation. Mathewson saw glimpses of gnarled limbs, half-folded wings, the irregular curve of the head, a foot with splayed toes—all carved from an unusually dark stone.

"Colors aren't going to match," he remarked, glancing up at the open space.

"That's no surprise," Kelly answered tersely. "Nothing else does. Why should this be any different?"

Sheffield himself was on the truck, a clear violation of Kelly's safety rules, and Mathewson looked to see if anything was going to be said about it. Kelly glowered, obviously having just made the same observation, but finally simply turned away, glowering. Unless Sheffield did something dangerous, Kelly would remain silent. Their current employer had promised a substantial personal bonus to every member of the work crew if the job went as planned, and Kelly knew better than to alienate the man and endanger his crew's bonus unless there was absolutely no alternative. But that didn't mean he had to like the constant interference, the infringement of his safety rules, the upsetting of established work schedules.

The crane operator dismounted and approached Kelly, giving him the thumbs-up. He was a new man, someone Mathewson had never met; their normal operator was down with the flu and they'd had to borrow someone from Pontiello's crew.

"How's she sitting?" Kelly was speaking to the crane man, but his eyes were fixed on the mixture of mud and crushed stone a few yards away.

"Square. Shouldn't be any problem. Whenever your people are ready with the rigging, we can lift."

Mathewson thought he detected a tinge of impatience, the wrong tack to take with Kelly, who was a stickler for procedure. He stood and watched while Kelly walked completely around the crane, eyeing the ground speculatively, his mouth set firmly in an expression of distaste. "Looks firm enough," he conceded, "but his load is off balance. Are you sure you can compensate if you have to?"

The crane operator looked as though he were going to

take offense, then thought better of it. Kelly's reputation was known throughout the company, and the industry, for that matter. His reply was firm but not belligerent. "I can handle it. It's only tricky toward the end, while your men are guiding it into place and releasing it. I can handle my part of the job. The weight distribution won't matter because it's a straight lift-and-carry. If you've left enough space above, it'll go in just like a cork."

"Kelly turned away and crossed to the truck. Mathewson gave the crane operator a sympathetic look, but the man had already started back for his machine. Kelly scrambled up onto the back of the truck, obviously planning to conduct his customary final inspection of the rigging lines, but he was intercepted by the tall, spindly form of Paul Alan Sheffield. Curious, Mathewson moved closer so that he could overhear the conversation.

"I know we've been over this before, Mr. Kelly, but I want to emphasize again that this is a priceless, irreplaceable object, one which I spent several years acquiring. I trust you'll take care to ensure its safety during this operation." Sheffield's voice was high, reedy, but there was no indication of a whine. It was clearly a voice used to making people jump. More than once Mathewson had noted people flinching when addressed by Sheffield, even the self-confident and imperturbable Kelly. There was something about the quality of Sheffield's spoken words that just pierced one to the core.

"Not to worry, Mr. Sheffield. We've done jobs like this many times before without any problem. I'd caution you against remaining up here, however. These are experienced men, and they know how to deal with a situation should anything untoward arise. Your presence here at the wrong moment might interfere with their performance, particularly if we have an emergency of any kind."

"But you assured me there would be no emergency." Mathewson would have sworn that Sheffield was deliberately taunting the other man, except that there'd been no indication of a sense of humor, sarcastic or otherwise, in anything Sheffield had ever said or done in their presence.

"Yes I did, and it's extremely unlikely that we'll have anything to worry about. But I believe in safety, sir, and in preparing for even the most unlikely of circumstances. I've trained these men to respond to an emergency in very precise ways, and I would hate to see your property damaged because you happened to be standing in the wrong place at the wrong time."

Good for you, Kelly, thought Mathewson. Let's see him get out of that.

But Sheffield merely smiled thinly and nodded. "Point taken, Mr. Kelly. I will dismount, then, and let you get on with your business. You'll forgive me, I hope, for unnecessarily burdening you with my concern, but as this project nears completion, I become increasingly worried that some happenstance at the last moment will intervene to prevent me from achieving my goal. One does not have to be Irish in order to be superstitious."

Mathewson would have liked to have seen Kelly's face at that point, but it was turned away from him. Sheffield moved to the ladder mounted on one side of the truck and turned to descend, his impossibly long limbs making him awkward as he groped about for secure footing. He was in his early forties, Mathewson remembered, the sole heir to a large fortune managed by a firm of accountants. There'd been an article about him in the Providence newspaper when it had first been learned that he was moving to

Rhode Island, but the details had been sparse. Sheffield, it appeared, actively disliked publicity, and little was known of his life other than that he had spent most of his adult years touring the world, searching for specific kinds of art. And someone had told Kelly a few months before that there was a warehouse full of books, statues, and the like waiting in Cranston for installation once the mansion was finished.

Kelly inspected the rigging and jumped back down from the truck, disdaining the ladder, as did all the members of his crew. Mathewson was wryly amused by the efforts of the construction workers to avoid looking soft; it was an affectation that he did not share, although he often tailored his own actions to conform to their inclinations just so he'd be accepted by the men. As the only man assigned to this job who had no duties involving physical work, he was often the butt of crude remarks and even practical jokes, so he had taken to occasionally stepping outside and helping with the cleaning up or other light work as a diplomatic move. It had worked; a few of the men had become openly friendly, and if the crude remarks continued, they at least had the decency not to say them in his hearing.

Kelly waved to the crane operator and then moved to an advantageous spot in order to watch the operation. There was a roar from the motor as the engine was gunned briefly, then the arm and cab made a graceful turn to the left, the dangling hook slowly lowering until it was about ten feet above the heads of the men who remained on the back of the truck. The operator waited until the line was positioned directly above its cargo, then honked his horn and started to slowly let out cable so that the hook dropped to a level where two of the men could grab it. When they had as much slack as they desired, they waved to the crane, and the horn sounded once more in acknowledgment.

Mathewson crossed to stand by Kelly, even though the ground there had turned a blackish mud. Sheffield had moved around behind the truck and was standing near the mansion wall, right at the rope line Kelly had had erected to cordon off the danger zone, what he called the "drop area." "That is one peculiar man" he said softly. Kelly glanced his way but didn't respond.

There was another wave from the back of the truck, and another hoot as the slack began to disappear very slowly. The sound of the crane's engines changed at the last moment, since for the first time the weight of the stone block had become a factor. Kelly had six men aboard the truck, arranged evenly around the block. As it rose from the flatbed, they would guide it around the guardrails until it had risen above them, after which everything was up to the crane operator. There was a metallic creak as the weight was lifted up off the truck's protesting springs, and the vehicle lurched slightly, bringing one guardrail perilously close. The man nearest the tailgate of the truck jumped nimbly out of the way; he would not have had the slightest chance of altering the outcome of the situation if the dangling load had moved any further, but the driver had positioned his truck correctly and there was ample room. A few seconds later the stone was safely clear, and the crane was slowly rotating back to bring it into position for the final lift. The five men who remained stood attentively in the truck, watching from relatively dry footing.

For the first time Mathewson could see the gargoyle clearly, in profile at least. The carving was roughly the size of a large man, which he thought rather unusual. Certainly the pictures he had seen of gargoyles on cathe-

17

drals had appeared to be comparatively small. Maybe Kelly had been correct that this was a gargantua among gargoyles. Certainly it was an impressive piece, in size as well as in basic design.

The knees were bent, as though it crouched, the clawed toes splayed outward, each joint exaggerated by a swirly knob. The legs seemed to be incredibly well muscled, the thighs disproportionately large for the trunk, which appeared striated from this distance, as though designs or shapes had been carved into it. The arms were similarly muscled, the fingers tipped with daggerlike claws, and there seemed to be two elbows rather than one. From behind the lift of one upper arm, rose the swell of a breast, almost female, though its shape seemed somehow slightly wrong. From beneath its body came the smooth lines of a half-folded wing, which expanded as it passed up the body, forming almost a cowl above the head. That last feature was the most prepossessing of all, even though it was currently turned almost completely away from him. An eye that was too big for the face peered out from a protruding brow ridge. The nose was not in sight, but he could see the corner of the mouth, from which a single fang was extruded. The ears appeared to be tufted, large and animalish, and a small, curved horn originated in the head slightly to the rear. The shoulder came to an unnaturally sharp point, a reflection of the wing tip. All in all, particularly carved as it was from a peculiarly black stone, it was a daunting, repulsive figure . . . hardly the face Mathewson thought he would like to have peering down from the side of his home.

The crane was parallel to the mansion now, its burden shifting just slightly as it dangled less than a yard from the wall. The man who had earlier leaped from the truck,

Ed Caldarone, approached, checked the alignment and the rigging to be certain it had not shifted, and then waved to the crane. Two faces had appeared and peered down from the opening on the top floor.

"Nice and easy, now," muttered Kelly, but he didn't seem to be speaking to anyone in particular. Almost immediately the crane engine altered its tone once more and, with a slight jerk, the stone cable began to retract and the stone to rise. After a few seconds, the carved figure could no longer be seen from below, but Mathewson found his eyes drawn hypnotically upward in any case. It was up to the fourth floor now, nearly all the way, and Caldarone had walked over to gauge the gap between it and the target area.

A few seconds later there was a sound like a gunshot, but impossibly loud. Something whipped whirring through the air. One of the men posted above had reached over to grab onto the cable and help guide the stone in, and he drew back now with a shout, bright red spurting into the air. The snapped cable had slashed through his wrist as though through water, and the severed hand would later be located over one hundred feet away. But he had been lucky. Caldarone had not. As the severed cable gave way, the stone started to roll in mid-air, and to the onlookers it appeared to be in slow motion, the gargoyle's body turning in their direction and then passing out of sight as it rolled underneath. The remaining cables snapped as well and the stone dropped even faster, resuming something like normal motion. Caldarone stood below, transfixed, his eyes fastened on the growing blur above. Even had he been able to move, he could never have gotten out of the way in time. As it was, the plummeting block hit him, carving first, and one outstretched gargoyle arm struck the

19

man squarely in the chest, impaling him before the greater weight smashed him wetly into the ground. He was dead before the cables had stopped swinging.

For a few seconds everything seemed frozen in place. Then the onlookers were galvanized into action. Kelly had drilled them on emergency procedures and they rushed out purposefully, but there was little to be done for Ed Caldarone. Fortunately, Oliver Pantell had used his belt to put a quick tourniquet around the wrist of Frank DeSimone, his partner, and he was already helping the man down the interior stairway. Both men were white with shock, but DeSimone had remained conscious. A stretcher team took charge as they emerged, and the injured man was en route to a hospital in minutes.

Mathewson did not follow Kelly when he approached the dead man; only one arm was visible, protruding from the near side of the stone. The shape of the gargoyle was likewise barely visible, for most of its form was similarly pressed into the mud. But even from a distance Mathewson could hear Sheffield's piercing voice, now raised in anger. "Mr. Kelly, I thought you assured me nothing like this could happen! There's a very real chance that there's been irreparable damage to the statue."

Kelly's head swiveled in Sheffield's direction, but he remained silent. Sheffield leaned down, one hand braced on the side of the stone, and peered underneath. If he felt any uneasiness about the presence of the corpse, it was not apparent. "How soon can we get this up so that I can examine the statue?"

Kelly moved abruptly, caught the other man by the shoulder, half-lifting him as he turned him around and stared into his face. His words were delivered in a cold, even tone. "Sheffield, you get your goddamned ass out of here right now! There's a good man lying there dead under your fucking statue, and the damage to him is irreparable, too!"

Sheffield seemed undaunted and made no move to free himself from the man's grip. "Your man is dead and nothing can be done about it now. The disposition of his remains is your concern, Mr. Kelly, not mine. But the condition of my property is very much my business." The voice emerged with a squeak of excitement. If not for the gravity of the situation, Mathewson would have found it all laughable.

"I will move your property as soon as I safely can," said Kelly quietly, but with every bit as much steel as before. "When that time comes, I will notify you so that you may examine your property. But until then you will get out of the way and stay out of the way."

Sheffield regarded the crew boss levelly for long, silent seconds, his mouth opening once or twice as though he wished to make a retort. Finally his shoulders slumped, or perhaps just relaxed, and he took a step backward. "Very well, Mr. Kelly, I can see that perhaps it cannot be helped. I trust, however, that you will inform me *immediately* when you have done what is necessary." And without waiting for an answer, he turned and walked back toward the front entrance to the mansion. Kelly turned and followed Sheffield with his eyes, and then said something so softly that no one heard. "I hope the goddamned thing is smashed to bits, Mr. Sheffield; I really do."

Mathewson made no attempt to talk to Kelly for the remainder of that day. Kelly supervised the shifting of the block. The Managansett police had arrived along with an ambulance to take charge of the remains. The body had reportedly been smashed beyond recognition, although

Mathewson didn't know for certain; he had not chosen to view it and test his own squeamishness. Kelly had been present throughout, though, showing no emotion at all. Mathewson arranged for new, tougher cables to be delivered and installed the following day, then waited in the shack after the crew had been dismissed, hoping to talk to Kelly.

When the Irishman finally arrived, he showed no inclination to talk, but crossed to the desk and removed the bottle of whiskey he stored there. Each evening, his last official act was to down a shot of it, an unofficial sign that the workday was over. But tonight he sat down and nursed his drink, staring into the distance. Mathewson made a few desultory efforts to converse with him, but Kelly ignored him so completely that, under other circumstances, the younger man would have been extremely offended. As it was, he sighed, wished him a good evening, and hoped the older man would make it home all right.

Kelly never left the site. Mathewson didn't hear the full story of what happened later that evening, nor did he ever learn how much of it was true and how much fiction, but it was certain that Kelly never went home at all that night, and that the nearly full whiskey bottle was completely empty when Mathewson reached the site the next morning. He was rather surprised to find the shack unlocked, as Kelly normally did not come in this early and no one else had the key, but obviously today had been an exception. He was just settling down to sort through the previous day's paperwork when the sound of high-pitched shouting interrupted him. Curious, he put his jacket back on and stepped outside, where the first rays of dawn now illuminated the grounds of the Sheffield mansion.

Several members of the crew were running about, calling to one another excitedly, as he walked toward the crane. They'd managed to bulldog the stone block over the night before, and the gargoyle was once again lying on its back, staring up into the infinite sky. But even from this distance and in the murky light, Mathewson could see that something about its profile had altered. He was walking down toward the statue when he ran into a rigger coming in the opposite direction.

"Arthur, what's going on?"

The man slowed but didn't stop. "It's Kelly. He's dead down there, lying on the statue. I got to get the police."

Mathewson froze on the spot, unable to take the next step, unwilling to move any closer, a sudden freezing chill passing through his body. And so it was that he never personally saw the body of his friend. He heard the official report, of course: death caused by heart failure. The coroner theorized that Kelly had gone down to the statue the previous evening in a drunken rage, furious about the death of his subordinate, somehow blaming the inanimate object for the disaster, unwilling to accept that it could be human error or a failure of equipment. He had been found, after all, draped across the statue, a sledgehammer lying where it might have fallen from one limp hand. Fortunately for Mr. Sheffield, the heart attack seemed to have come before Kelly could strike the first blow, which explained why there was no damage to the statue. And the force of Kelly's fall explained why the outstretched claw of one gargoyle hand had penetrated up under his chin and into the brain. After all, the autopsy had proved conclusively that the man had died of heart failure; no explanation was necessary.

But none of that explained the other thing, the thing that only Mathewson knew and had seen. Mathewson never told anyone, had not even told Kelly, that when the cable snapped on that terrible day, releasing its load, he had been quite certain that one clawed hand had reached up to the cable, taken it between two stony fingers, and snapped it cleanly in two. Mathewson never told anyone, and he quit his job that very same week and moved out of Rhode Island, out of New England, in fact; but he never moved far enough away to expunge that memory from his mind—or from his dreams.

CHAPTER ONE
1950

Jimmy Nicholson was eight years old the first time he noticed the gargoyle on the mansion wall, not far from the tower. It was the Fourth of July, a sweltering, humid day, the first year he'd been old enough that the older kids were willing to sell him a few strings of salutes of his very own. Jimmy had already been all over town looking for the best places to use them—behind the police station; in old Mrs. Rawdon's garden while she sat rocking on her porch only a few feet away; outside Mr. Winslow's bedroom window so that he would shout futilely from the bed to which he was confined permanently, impotent to do anything else. He had tossed a couple over the stockade fence into the Boones's yard as well, hoping to hit their aging beagle, but apparently the dog had been brought inside the house for the day, judging by the frenzied barking after the explosions.

It hadn't been as much fun as he'd expected, though. People jumped at the sound of the explosion, and there'd been a satisfying sense of power at that; but they all seemed resigned to the annoyance and quickly returned to whatever they'd been doing. Even Mrs. Rawdon had simply given up and gone indoors to do her knitting. Jimmy found this transient use of power unsatisfying; there was no way he could come back on another day and view the results of his actions. They'd be washed away on the currents of time. It was important to him that he find a way to exercise power on a more permanent basis, that he discover a way to alter people's lives against their will, for good or ill. Frankly, it didn't matter to him which of the two alternatives he accomplished, and he frequently ran errands impulsively for the same people he tormented on another day. It was the impact that counted, not the nature of the actions. Jimmy was determined to make an indelible mark on the world, to provide an imprint that could not be denied, that would always ratify the fact of his existence, both to himself and to others. And the only way to leave a lasting mark was through the exercise of power.

Jimmy considered the dwindling supply of salutes, one full string and part of two others. He thought about setting the untouched string aside for use later in the year, when people weren't expecting them, but even at eight years old, he knew enough about himself to realize he'd never be able to resist the temptation to set them off sooner. He chafed at his own weakness even as he recognized it. If I can't even make an impression on what I do myself, he thought, how can I ever expect to affect the acts of others? He didn't phrase it quite that way, of course, never really put it into words at all. But nevertheless he realized the conflict he faced.

Most of the other kids in town were heading over to the Managansett Volunteer Fire Station. The local company was going to show cartoons and have a cookout for the entire town, then set off real, professional fireworks after it became dark enough to show them off to best advantage. It had become an annual custom these past few years, and the kids looked forward to it all summer. The other kids, at least. Somehow the elaborate skyrockets and roman candles and everything else seemed too gaudy and remote for Jimmy. He preferred the immediacy of a salute, the crisp, clean bang. Some of the kids even carried sparklers, shedding their tears of light on all sides, but Jimmy didn't think sparklers were much better than toys—there was no power to them. He wouldn't be caught dead carrying a sparkler; that was for little kids. And if Jimmy Nicholson had ever considered himself a "little kid," it was too far in the past to be recalled now.

So as the afternoon slowly yielded to evening, Jimmy wandered around an increasingly deserted Managansett seeking worthy targets upon which to expend what remained of this year's supply of firecrackers. All of the local dogs and cats, both pets and strays, seemed to have disappeared for the duration of the holiday. Most of the town's adult population had followed the children over to the fire station by now as well. Jimmy grew increasingly frustrated by his inability to locate a suitable victim.

The Sheffield mansion stood back from the road in a large, undeveloped piece of property on the outskirts of the small commercial district, at the opposite end of Main Street from the fire station. It was an unusual building. Its mix of architectural styles clashed internally, as well as with the countryside in which it sat. It had been left to the town as part of the settlement of the estate of a rich recluse, he knew, who had died in some sort of mysterious riding accident back in the 1930s. The building had apparently been closed up ever since, and certainly had never been opened during the years when Jimmy had been alive.

In one corner of the building a short tower stood above the roof line. The outer surface of the tower was a panoramic view of human history and imagination, the stone cut and shaped to illustrate one or another scene, randomly arranged without regard to chronology. They were sculpted by several different artisans hired by Sheffield during the three years in which he lived in the mansion prior to his death. There was Joan of Arc burning at the stake, adjacent to the Trojan Horse; Galileo and Archimedes stood contemplating wildly divergent models of the solar system; Socrates orated to a group of young Greeks. Caesar lay bloody at the feet of his assassins and only inches away the gods enjoyed a festive meal atop Mount Olympus. There were unicorns and werewolves and pyramids, ghosts and leprechauns and skyscrapers, gods and goddesses and wigwams, the exploits of Ulysses and Thor and Christopher Columbus and Leif Ericson and Perseus and Hercules and Queen Victoria. It appeared that Sheffield had tried to capture every time and period, every field of human endeavor, and every significant culture.

A small picnic grove stood on the hillside behind the library, converted from the original garden, which sloped down through a denser stand of trees to a low-lying area of boggy sandflats and swiftly moving water. Watersnakes were common here, and persistent rumors that some were venomous had worried enough parents that the area was generally considered off-limits to the local children, although the restriction was ignored almost as much as it was observed. Today Jimmy felt suffused with power, an inner strength emanating from the strings of explosives concealed in his pockets. It was a good feeling that surged through his body, allowing him to feel older and stronger and more powerful. At that moment he didn't care in the least about the rules that other people tried to make for him, even the rules of his parents. He was in control, the master of his life, capable of and willing to make decisions for himself.

Unsurprisingly, he found himself completely alone. Lily pads floated sluggishly on brackish backwaters, stirred only slightly by the fast-moving currents in the main stream a few feet distant. There was green scum in many places as well, and the air stank. A small animal of some sort splashed off in the distance, but Jimmy was unable to identify it. The only living creatures in sight were spindly skating bugs flitting about on the surface of the pools, and occasional frogs crouched half in, half out of the water.

Jimmy lobbed a few stones and stray pieces of wood at concentrations of skating bugs, which made very unsatisfactory victims. They either skittered aside at the last moment or were utterly destroyed by the missiles. In either case there was no surviving evidence of his exercise of power, no visible proof of his potency, his ability to alter the world around him. It wouldn't be so bad if the victims were of more substance, were obvious animals; insects almost seemed like tiny animated machines, and Jimmy was convinced they could feel no pain. He had spent considerable time on one occasion pulling wings and legs off one insect after another that summer, and insects just kept right on struggling to escape until some critical point of missing parts caused them to break down entirely and stop.

Jimmy squatted beside the pond, drawing deeply upon his own resources, searching for inspiration. And, as he knew it always had before, a spark came at last, the beginning of an idea that grew into a plan, and which he would ultimately turn into a reality. His thoughts racing, he looked quickly around for the means by which to implement his plan, and he spotted an old five-gallon can; one end had disintegrated in flakes of rust, but it was otherwise sound. He retrieved it, propped it against a stump, then closed off the opening with a piece of an old wooden sign held in place with a brick. Satisfied that it would serve his purpose, Jimmy then set out to capture himself a few frogs.

It took surprisingly little time to snag ten fine specimens. He imprisoned each in the makeshift prison, their bodies piled one upon another. All he had to do was lie quietly by the edge of a pool for a few moments. Sooner or later a head would pop up nervously from the surface of the water, and Jimmy would bring his hands sweeping down from opposite directions so he could compensate for whatever leap the frog might choose to make. Naturally the operation was not kind to his clothing, which was thoroughly soaked and stained, but he considered the results worth the punishment that would inevitably result. With any luck, he could return before his parents left the festivities at the fire station; in any case, he'd change clothes and conceal the evidence in his hamper.

There was an abandoned tractor not far away, crumbling with rust, its padded seat split and leaking stuffing, tires long since gone. Jimmy ripped the stitching out of the seams, then cut six-inch lengths with his pocketknife, placing the results carefully in one hip pocket. Everything was working out perfectly.

He carefully extracted one of the frogs and held it firmly so that he could wrap a length of string around its body, then around a salute, then a second time around the frog so that the firecracker was fastened firmly to its back. He lit the fuse and set the frog on the ground, quickly stepping back. It blinked twice, not certain yet that it was free, but made no other movement before the sharp report of the explosion signaled the end of its life without leaving any recognizable fragment behind as evidence of its passing. There was still no tangible residue, no proof of his power, but at least he knew he was terminating the life of a living being, and there was some satisfaction to be derived from that fact.

Pleased with the success of his experiment, Jimmy spent the next half hour executing the rest of his captives. Sometimes they were caught in mid-leap, but most of the time they squatted stolidly until their obliteration. He liked the leapers best, kidded himself that he was giving them a fair chance to reach the water and extinguish the fuse. None of them made it, of course; they carried their fates with them, as we all do in one fashion or another.

Having exhausted his supply of firecrackers in a reasonably satisfying way, Jimmy decided it would not be beneath his dignity to stop at home, change clothes, and put in an appearance at the fire station, maybe have a couple of hamburgers. But as he made his way back up past the mansion tower, he paused a moment to glance up at its summit. Along the south wall, just to the left of the tower, a narrow slit window opened beneath a carved figure which arched out and away from the comparatively shallow curve of the wall. It was a gargoyle, he knew, a gnarled figure with exaggerated, knobby joints, protruding claws, a grotesquely smiling face full of teeth, bulging eyes, oversized ears pointed like a wolf's, and a lumpy, misshapen skull. The gargoyle was mounted so that it stared down at anyone passing below. Jimmy supposed it was meant to be frightening, but the curve of its toothy smile, the way one

31

eye was half-closed as if in mid-wink, the angle of the head—all seemed to him indicative of a sly camaraderie, almost as though it was looking at him, Jimmy Nicholson, personally, and not with disapproval. Although he knew it was just make believe, he waved familiarly at the frozen figure and, just before he turned away, thought he caught the hint of a movement out of the corner of one eye. But when he turned back the gargoyle was as motionless as ever, and he figured it must have been just a shifting of the shadows as the sun disappeared behind the surrounding hills.

It must have made more of an impression than he realized. That night he dreamed that the gargoyle came and spoke to him, fully animated, asking him some incomprehensible question which he could not remember when he awoke. When he thought about the content of the dream, he wondered if he should label it a nightmare. He never had nightmares, though he dreamed from time to time, and he often wondered if the omission of them from his perception indicated the strength of his character, or just that he was on better terms with himself than most of his contemporaries. He had read a book about dreams once, or most of it, anyway—the parts he could understand—when he realized that the scary dreams the other kids talked about never happened to him. He had a vague understanding that dreams were a method by which the mind processed things that happened in life, but he had lost interest after a while and never pursued the subject further.

July turned into August, but the sweltering heat never really went away. Tempers were short, and his father's allergies acted up, worsening his temper. Nicholson chose not to spend any more time at home than necessary even at the best of times, which these were not, and he generally was gone by the break of dawn even though he didn't have to attend school at this time of year. He returned only for meals until bedtime. He had never developed a television habit, although he did watch occasionally, but there was never any blood and everything was so obviously make-believe that he just lost interest.

Neither did he have any close friends; although he did sometimes play with the other children his age, he preferred the younger kids. They were more willing to follow his directions. Occasionally, of course, it was necessary to use his superior size and strength to enforce his will, and this was no difficulty. Even in his own age group, Nicholson was above average in height, stocky, and muscled, and his unwillingness to accept anyone as his superior made it possible for him to influence most others and get his own way.

One weekday afternoon late in August, Jimmy had recruited three of the younger kids for one of his scenarios. Barbara Howell and Tommy Baker were both six, Billy Cruzeiro was only five. The three younger kids were the good guys, members of the French Foreign Legion trying to make their way across the desert to bring help to a beleaguered fort. Jimmy had watched *Beau Geste* on television a few days earlier, and it had made quite an impression. Jimmy was the leader of an Arab army; he almost always cast himself in the role of villain, because that was the more interesting part and allowed him more freedom of action. The good guys always had to abide by an implicit code of behavior that was too restrictive, and they were never able to use their power to best advantage. Villains, on the other hand, could do anything they wanted; they had all the fun.

33

The rules were quite simple. Jimmy established the limits of the desert, the unsettled regions between the commercial section of western Managansett and the swamps, bordered by two widely separated roads. The kids could hide anywhere they wanted within that area. If they remained undiscovered until Jimmy tired of the game, they won; otherwise, he was the victor. After giving them a head start, Jimmy set out to systematically search the woods, although he knew that if the kids kept moving, they could stay out of his sight indefinitely. He counted on their getting bored and stopping someplace, and on them staying together. He was right in both instances.

He spotted them sitting under a tree on the Sheffield grounds after a disappointingly short search, but unfortunately they noticed him at the same time. Running as hard as he could, he angled to cut them off as he headed downhill in their direction, but this time they did scatter and streaked off in widely diverging directions. Jimmy chose the closest target, Barbara, and tackled her as she tried to disappear into a patch of wild raspberries. Short of breath, he lay on top of her for a moment, holding her down while he recovered.

"Jimmy, get off! You're too heavy!"

"You're my prisoner now, legionnaire. I'm not going to let you escape me. You have to tell me where your two friends are hiding."

Barbara sounded more annoyed than amused when she answered. "I'm not going to escape and I don't know where they're hiding. I want you to get off of me."

"All right, but you stay right there while I tie you up."

When Jimmy rose, Barbara rolled over but stayed down. "What happens now, Jimmy?"

"My name isn't Jimmy. I am the Sheik Ali Waru, gen-

34

eral of the Arab army, and I have captured you. Where are your friends?"

Barbara sighed and lay back. "Okay, I'm your prisoner, but I still don't know where Tommy and Billy went, so you're going to have to go after them."

Jimmy considered the situation, then started to remove his belt. Barbara sat up and watched him. "What's that for?"

"I have to tie you to a tree with this so that I can go after the others without you escaping."

Barbara shook her head. "I don't want to. Pretend tie me."

This time Jimmy shook his head. "No way. Last time we did that you ran away and said you untied yourself."

"Well, then take me prisoner and I'll go with you. It's boring sitting here by myself all day while you and Tommy and Billy play."

"You shouldn't have gotten caught, then. Come on, back up against the tree."

"No." She set her lips firmly. "I don't want to. I'm not playing any more."

"Too late for that now." He grabbed her by one wrist and started pulling her across the grass to the nearest tree.

"No, Jimmy! Stop it! I'm not playing this game." She turned and twisted, pounding his wrist with her free hand, heels seeking purchase in the soft ground. "Let me go or I'll tell!"

Struggling to maintain control, Jimmy stepped across her body, catching her flailing arm, pulling her to her feet. She relaxed them, assuming that he was going to let her go, and he took advantage of her relaxation to spin her around and regain his grip on her arms from behind. He pulled Barbara's slim wrists together and held them in one hand while he tried to loop the belt around them with the other. Unfortunately, it was easier in theory than in practice, and Barbara did not remain quiet for long. She kicked back at his legs, scoring his shin painfully, and he was unable to secure the belt around her wrists. Infuriated with the pain, frustrated with the failure to have things as he wanted them, Jimmy closed his fist and punched Barbara in the side with all the force he could muster.

The girl cried out in pain and stopped struggling, and Jimmy took advantage of her shock to loop the belt around both wrists, run the free end through the buckle, and draw it tight, slipping the tongue of the buckle through the eyehole. Barbara was furious now, crying as she shouted at him.

"Jimmy, you let me go right now! I'm going to tell on you! I'll tell my mother and I'll tell your father and I'll never play with you again and neither will any of my friends! You hurt me, you big pig!"

Unimpressed, Jimmy dragged her forcibly, grabbed her shoulder, and pressed her back up against the tree. Barbara's round face was puffy with tears and distorted with rage, and something in Jimmy's mind told him to be careful, not to let the game get out of hand. Adults still had the ability to control him, he knew; he was not yet at the point where he had the power to do exactly as he wished. The loose end of the belt went around the tree and back, wrapped around itself, and with a little effort, could just barely be tied into a knot holding her in place. Jimmy stepped back.

Barbara calmed a bit when he stood away, but she was still furious. "Let me go right now! I don't want to play this stupid game any more!"

"It's not over yet. You can't quit in the middle. That's

not fair. You're just quitting because you lost. You're a poor loser is what you are."

"No, I'm not!" But her voice wavered and Jimmy thought he might have her now. "And it hurts."

"You're my prisoner and it's supposed to hurt a little. That's how Arabs get their prisoners to tell them where their friends are."

"But I don't know where they are," she whined. "If I did, I'd tell you. Can't we just pretend I'm tied up? I won't run away, honest injun. And you hit me too. Arabs don't hit!"

"They do too. Sometimes they beat up their prisoners until they talk."

Barbara looked dubious. "You're not going to beat *me* up, are you?"

"Not really, no, but we have to pretend like I do." And he took a couple of pretend swings at her, just brushing her clothing with clenched fists. Barbara played along that he was hitting her and it almost worked for him that time, but not quite. There was still something missing. This was the kind of thing he wanted, he knew, this ability to completely control other people, to make them do what he wanted them to, but it was still too much make-believe, not enough reality to be completely satisfying.

What he wanted was to bend her to his will, to make her do something she didn't want to do, to acknowledge him as her superior in every day. It would be even better with a guy, of course, because women weren't as good as men anyway, weren't as powerful, but it was still the idea of it, that he could control someone else, that was important.

"You have to tell me the secret code word," he said at

last, having had an idea. "Tell me it and I'll know where the secret entrance to the fort is and I win anyway."

Barbara looked at him in puzzlement. "You didn't tell us any secret word, Jimmy."

"It's a swear word, but I won't tell you which one. You'll have to keep trying until you figure it out."

Barbara looked honestly shocked. "I can't say swear words, Jimmy. I'll get spanked."

"You'll get worse than spanked if you don't tell me the code word, prisoner," he said, pitching his voice as low and menacing as he could. But it was the look on his face that was truly frightening, and this time Barbara read his expression clearly. She began to cry again.

"Jimmy, let me go! I'm tired of this stupid game and I want to go home!"

But Jimmy was past listening to her now, and he no longer feared the consequences of his actions. Entirely submerged in the part now, the evil Sheik Ali Waru approached the prisoner and grabbed her by the hair, pulling her head sharply back. Barbara cried out in surprise and genuine pain, then tried to kick his legs. Jimmy eluded her flailing legs this time and punched her for real, right above the waistline of her dungarees. The air whooshed out of her lungs and Barbara began to feel real fear along with pain.

"Tell me the code word!" he yelled at her. "Tell me the code word or I will have you tied between two horses and torn apart." He had stolen the idea from a movie; he could no longer remember the title. But Barbara had slumped, eyes closed, and for a second he realized he might have gone too far. When he bent close to her face, Barbara struck out with her right leg again, kicking him painfully in the shin. Jimmy skipped back, hopping on one leg, shocked to his core, enraged, and promptly moved forward again, swinging his fist wildly at her face. He hit something soft, and the impact shocked him back to sanity. Barbara slumped against the tree, blood pouring from her nose where his fist had struck. He stood transfixed, uncertain what he should do, caught between fear of discovery and punishment, and a longing to hit her again and again and again, until there was no doubt in her mind or his as to who was the boss, who called the shots, whose will would prevail. But then he heard Tommy and Billy calling out in the distance, moving in their direction, so he quickly untied her hands. Barbara fell to the grass sobbing, and he hesitated only a moment before turning and running off, oblivious now to everything except escape.

He never did find out what Barbara told her parents, if she ever told them anything. There were never any repercussions from the incident, so far as he knew, except that none of the three were willing to play with him anymore, and some of the other younger children who used to join his games watched him warily and seemed less interested in doing so, although he was never sure if this was really true or if he was just imagining things. In either case, the lack of discovery actually served to reward him, and retrospectively he was rather pleased about the incident. He had not actually managed to make her say a swear word, of course, and that was a shame; but the principle had been established that he was in control, that she would do as he directed or be punished for her refusal. And he had not been caught. That was the important thing, the single most important fact which he had learned from watching villains on the occasional television show or movie. The villains had all the fun until they were caught and punished; the important thing was not to get caught.

That was a lesson Jimmy carried with him into the new school year. Jimmy Nicholson was not the only bully at Managansett Elementary School, and his aversion to fitting in with other people's wishes made it difficult for him to join one of the existing power cliques. And so it was that during the second week of school, Jimmy ran afoul of Mickey Palatto and his "gang," although that was an overglorified term for the small group of admirers that hung around the older boy.

Mickey Palatto was ten, two years older than Jimmy, but age wasn't really the source of his power. Mickey stood five-foot-six and weighed almost one hundred and fifty pounds. He was the kind of boy who would be the star of the high school football team, make only second string at college (if he went at all), and be balding and overweight by thirty. But at the moment, if he wasn't king of the school, he was certainly king of the Grove Street bus stop.

It was Tuesday, and a steady drizzle kept the kids hiding under a tree until the bus arrived. Intent upon boarding the bus, Jimmy didn't even notice that he had cut directly in front of Mickey until a rough hand grabbed him by the shoulder and spun him away. That might have been the end of it, except that Jimmy was not used to being the target of other people's power; even his parents were careful not to push him too far. So when he swung up into the bus in turn and walked past the seat where Mickey sat, the word "asshole" slipped out almost on its own.

The bus jerked into motion just as Jimmy sat down, but he found himself immediately looking up into the face of the older boy, who had risen and followed him. "You got a problem?"

Jimmy felt a momentary hesitation, and a mild reply moved toward his tongue. At the last minute, however, a more brusque retort rushed out instead. "Buzz off, Palatto."

The older boy looked both shocked and pleased at the implied challenge. He ignored the shouts from the bus driver to be seated, continuing to stand over Jimmy's seat. "You want to make something of this, Nicholson, or are you scared?"

"I'm not scared of you, Palatto." The bravado in his voice felt good, but something in the back of his mind told him he was being foolish, getting in too deep.

"I'm glad, Nicholson. I'm glad you're not scared. How about proving it after school today?"

Jimmy knew he was in over his head now, but even if he'd seen a graceful way out, he was uncertain whether he'd have taken it. There was something in him that refused, absolutely refused, to be overpowered. "I might be able to fit you into my schedule."

"That's cute, Nicholson." Palatto smiled. The bus driver called back again, angrily this time, and Mickey waved at him, half-turning back to his seat. "I'll see you behind the old mansion, Nicholson, half an hour after the bus lets us off. You be there or I'll have to come looking for you."

Jimmy nodded.

That was the shortest school day of Jimmy's life, and as it came to an end, he finally began to regret the impulse that had gotten him into this situation. He was no match for Palatto in a fight; he rarely fought at all, as a matter of fact. Jimmy had always preferred the company of

41

smaller, younger kids, those who would not physically challenge him. But there was no way to back out now. At least a dozen kids on the bus had heard him accept Palatto's arrangement. Better to take his beating and get it over with than back out. No one would pay attention to him anymore if he turned chicken, not even the little kids, and he knew Palatto would tell everyone what had happened. He might be able to get in a few good blows before he went down; Palatto always showed a grudging respect for anyone who managed to mess him up a bit during his frequent fights. But he sure wished he could find an alternative solution.

Palatto showed up with a couple of admirers—one kid named Petey something-or-other, and a fat little kid whose name Jimmy didn't know. They were sitting on one of the benches on the grounds behind the mansion, idly throwing pebbles at the windows. Palatto looked up with what almost seemed like genuine warmth when he saw Jimmy approaching.

"Let's get this over with, Palatto," he said, looking around for a grassy spot. "I have important things to do when we're done." Jimmy cursed himself for his hasty tongue, but it still felt good standing up to the older boy.

"Your funeral," said the other lightly, moving to follow him into an open space.

The fight went pretty much as Jimmy had feared. He managed to belt Mickey a few times at the beginning, because for all his greater strength, the older boy was slower. But after a minute or two, Mickey connected with a direct blow across the side of Jimmy's head that made his ears ring, and he was never quite the same after that. Mickey moved in with a series of punches to his ribs, knocking Jimmy's hands aside whenever he tried to protect himself. Finally he caught a fist on the edge of his diaphragm and the air rushed out of his lungs. Jimmy doubled over and fell to the grass, gasping for air. Palatto stood over him, assured himself that his opponent was no longer interested in fighting, then nodded to his two friends and walked off.

Jimmy lay there for a long time, even after he had regained his breath and was physically able to rise. He hurt all over, but it was a dull ache, not really so bad. Palatto hadn't wanted to hurt him seriously, just dull his pride and establish his own superiority. Jimmy understood that desire; that was exactly how his own mind worked. He respected power, and in a certain way he respected Mickey Palatto more now than ever before. But at the same time he hated the older boy, and with an intensity beyond anything he had ever known. A higher will than his own was intolerable, and must be subdued, soon and effectively. No other choice was available; the only question was how.

Jimmy rolled over and got painfully to his feet, then began to walk slowly around the corner of the Sheffield mansion, the tower corner he noticed. His back ached as well, stiff from the long period he had spent on the ground. As he stretched back to ease the muscles, he noticed the gargoyle, still at its perch atop the building.

That's what I need to be like, he thought. Made of stone. No pain. No weakness. Invulnerable. Fists that would smash flesh aside. He stopped, staring up admiringly. Let's see Mickey Palatto stand up to something like that, he thought. And that reminded him that he had to find a way to get even. Standing there, staring at the carved figure imprisoned on the mansion wall, Jimmy had a thought so perfect, so elegant a solution to his problem, that he began to laugh despite the pain, laughed for quite a while, in fact, all the way home, and sporadically through the night.

It was almost three weeks before he could put his plan into action. His parents were accustomed to his being absent in the evenings, so they didn't find it unusual that he went out every night immediately after supper. They stayed out of his room for the most part, so they never noticed that one particular piece of his athletic equipment was gone every evening as well.

Jimmy crouched behind the foundation shrubbery at the Palatto home, waiting quietly in the dark. He had peeked in the kitchen window and knew that Mickey was still in the house. Several nights he had waited here, thwarted sometimes because Mickey stayed home and watched tele-evision, sometimes because he left with other kids. On those occasions Jimmy waited around until he returned, hoping the boy would be alone, but Mickey would not dismiss his followers until he was done with them, and he never arrived home unescorted. But eventually the opportunity had to arise, he knew, and tonight turned out to be the night.

The screen door swung open and Mickey walked out onto the porch, whistling something as he fitted his baseball cap over his longish hair. Jimmy waited tensely, watching to see if any of the other kids were going to show up, but apparently tonight Mickey was going it alone, or was meeting them elsewhere. He stepped jauntily down the steps and turned toward the street.

Jimmy rose from the bushes like the wrath of God, baseball bat rising behind his shoulder, slicing through a short arc with a rush of displaced air. Mickey never saw the blow coming, and the bat cracked against his skull with a sickening thud. The boy folded up and hit the ground without a sound. Jimmy waited for a moment until he was sure that the other boy would not rise before he slinked off into the night, content.

They never did discover who it was who'd assaulted young Mickey Palatto, inflicting a skull fracture that kept him hospitalized for a week and bedridden for considerably longer. In a way, it took much of the pleasure out of the victory for Jimmy; he didn't want the world at large to know what had happened, of course, because he knew what the consequences would be. But he had to be certain that Palatto knew, so that he realized he could not impose his own will on Jimmy without retribution. And then he hit upon the solution.

Eventually Mickey was cleared by the doctors to return to school, although he still seemed pale and drawn, and had obviously lost quite a bit of weight during the period of enforced inactivity. Jimmy waited until one day at recess, while an informal baseball game was in progress. Normally Mickey would have joined in, but the doctors had barred him from all such activity for some time, so he merely sat on a bench and watched solemnly, all alone. Jimmy casually walked over to him and sat down.

"What's the matter, Palatto? Don't you play ball any more?"

Mickey looked up at him, but his recent recuperation had sapped much of the feistiness from his personality. "Not yet. The doctors say by the end of the year I'll be okay." There was a long silence. "What about you? I never see you play any sports. What's your problem?"

"Me? I got no problem, Mickey." He smiled broadly and got back to his feet, preparing to leave. Then, with sarcastic emphasis on the appropriate words, he said smoothly, "I already had *my* turn at bat." And he looked significantly at the back of Mickey's head.

The older boy's eyes flickered with sudden realization, and for a second he half-rose off the bench. But the fire died and he sat back down. "Yeah," he said, looking away. "See you around, Nicholson."

And Nicholson was never bothered by Palatto or any other school bully again.

But he did have a new dream, one that recurred several times that winter, though it eventually became less frequent and finally disappeared altogether. He dreamt he was standing in a high place, looking down at the ground below, where an animated version of the gargoyle statue stood looking up to him. He would slowly turn his head to realize that he'd taken its place, that he was anchored to the wall, and that his body was now made of stone.

CHAPTER TWO
1953

Peter DiPaoli looked upon visits to his grandparents with a mixture of happy anticipation and nervous anxiety. His father's parents owned the farm they'd bought when they'd emigrated to the United States at the turn of the century, but when their only son, Edward, completed school, he found a good job in New Hampshire and moved out of Rhode Island, and the strong family ties that might otherwise have endured were rent asunder. Since his father had disappointed the elder DiPaolis greatly by this move, he was at great pains to return three or four times a year so they could see their grandson, Peter. There was an open invitation for them to visit New Hampshire, which they would never take advantage of; indeed, they didn't seem to travel at all. The truth was, his parents frequently embarrassed Edward, for they clung to the primitive superstitions of their mountain village in Italy, as well as some peculiar variations of their own invention.

The earliest visits Peter could remember clearly were those from the summer of 1953, when he was five. He and his parents would drive down from New Hampshire early in the morning, planning to spend the entire day, then heading back late in the evening, arriving late at night. The trip was not new to Peter, but all the previous visits tended to blur into one single impression of his grandparents hovering over him, speaking their heavily accented English, the only concession they'd ever made to the conventions of their adopted homeland.

That particular Saturday they arrived early in the morning. As they drove up, Peter's grandfather was using a hose to clean off the side of the house, raising and lowering the stream with a steady rhythm, using his thumb to close off part of the nozzle and increase the water pressure. He paused when he saw them arrive, and slowly crossed to turn off the water faucet above the basement window. Carefully he rolled up the hose and placed it on its hook before coming to meet them, opening the gate set into the picket fence and smiling gently.

"How are you, Mr. DiPaoli?" asked Peter's mother, standing on tiptoe to kiss his cheek. Helen DiPaoli, born Helen Treadwell, stood barely five feet tall and looked like a child when she stood next to her father-in-law, who was two inches above six feet. Nor were the two particularly intimate, although they had never openly quarreled. Peter's parents seemed to feel that his decision to move to northern New England had been at Helen's instigation, which was not even remotely true. Orphaned at the age of eight, Helen had always felt a void in her life when she saw other people interacting with their families, and if anything, she would have preferred to live closer rather than farther away. But she was also a very stubborn woman. When she realized what the source of tension was and, after several attempts, could not persuade them to the contrary, she began to reciprocate the coolness they showed her. Edward, their son, had never been able to deal effectively with interpersonal problems and chose to pretend the tension did not exist, which only exacerbated the situation. Even young Peter detected a hint of strain between his mother and his grandparents, and occasionally during visits, he would break into tears for no apparent reason.

Whatever their feelings toward their son, the DiPaolis were devoted to their grandson, although their taciturn nature and strange mannerisms frequently confused and sometimes even frightened the young boy. Arturo DiPaoli had decorated his farm with a variety of symbolic wards and good luck signs that would not have looked out of place in a Pennsylvania Dutch community—carved wooden plaques, paintings, tiny inhuman figures fashioned from straw and bits of wood and string, even occasional words of power inscribed in the right places to make the chicken lay, the fruit trees bear, the house remain safe, and whatever other desires he wanted fulfilled, requesting them from a blend of Christianity and animism which satisfied his religious urges. It was not clear how fully Maria entered into this activity, but certainly she appeared not to object, not even to the carvings he insisted she keep in her kitchen. On several occasions Arturo had taken Peter by the hand, pointing out the various charms and attempting to explain the significance of each in its turn.

They all went inside after the two men had shaken hands and Peter had had his hair tousled, and Maria greeted them in much the same fashion, although she insisted on hugs from her son and her grandson. She started to speak in Italian, then caught herself and switched to English; Edward remained fluent in the tongue of his parents' homeland, but Helen had difficulty just getting through high school Spanish, and certainly had no chance of ever picking up enough colloquial Italian to communicate with her in-laws.

Peter found himself sitting at the big, scarred wooden table eating homemade snickerdoodles and peanut butter cookies with a large glass of milk while the adults went off to sit in the living room and catch up on what had happened since the last visit. Although he was not yet old enough to be properly cognizant of the intricacies of the adult world, he would later recognize these conversations to be continuing exercises in miscommunication. Edward had specialized in electrical engineering, a field completely alien to his parents, and his single-minded interest in his chosen field had resulted in sharply delineated intellectual horizons. Helen did social work on a sporadic basis and worked as a temporary clerk–typist when she could find work. Her background was very much that of a urban dweller, and her inability to find anything of interest in the everyday doings of a small farm made prolonged conversations difficult, if not impossible. So they exchanged polite nothings, often repeating the same stories they'd told on previous visits.

The cookies disappeared quickly and Peter downed the last of the milk, then wandered into the other room and crossed to where his mother sat at one end of a couch, attempting to look interested as Arturo described the changes he was planning to make in the henhouse during the next few months.

"Mommy," he said quietly, pulling at her arm. "Can I go outside?"

"Hmm? What? Oh, I think so, Peter, if Grandma thinks it would be all right."

Maria was rocking slowly a few feet away and she nodded immediately. "Not outside the yard, okay? No play in the street, no have accident."

Peter shook his head solemnly. His mother reached over and patted his arm. "Go ahead and play. Try not to get too dirty."

The yard was completely fenced with neat white pickets which Arturo painted every second year to keep them bright and cheerful looking. His grandmother had planted flower gardens, lining the foundation almost all the way around the house, except for two doorways and where a storage hut had been built to store tools and old furniture. There were four decorations on the fence, hung around the exact centered pickets on each of the four sides— elaborate patterns woven from straw, horsehair, thread, even catgut, each supported by a framework of wood bent into whatever shape was desired. Each was unique unto itself. Peter examined them for a while, trying to remember what his grandfather had said, and considered removing one or more to play with, but something about the way they were arranged seemed purposeful, and for reasons he did not quite understand, he left them untouched. There was also a complex pattern painted in a circle on the rear wall of the house, high enough that he could not make out the details.

Peter played outside for a half-hour or so before his grandfather came outside and beckoned to him. "You like eggs, boy?"

Peter shrugged, uncertain what the proper response might be, still somewhat uneasy in the presence of this tall, dark-complected man with the deeply-lined face and hands.

His grandfather smiled and turned away. "Come. I show where come the eggs."

Peter followed his grandfather into the henhouse, although the dark, nearly silent figure made him uneasy. After a few moments, however, he became thoroughly enthralled by the skill with which the man withdrew eggs from beneath his layers, usually without disturbing the hen perched above. One particular chicken whose nest had been empty flopped down from her roost and began following them around, pecking gently at Peter's pants leg, where some of the stitching had come loose and was twirling about with his every movement. There was a peculiar patch of brown discoloration along one wing that was quite distinctive. Peter had been tempted to lean down and try to pet her, but somehow it had not seemed appropriate to do so in his grandfather's presence.

They spent at least half an hour gathering eggs, then another few minutes while his grandfather showed him how to spread feed for the chickens, who promptly half flew, half fell from their roosts to peck at his offering. Peter began to laugh now, amused by their antics as they scrambled about to be the first to catch each bit of grain that dropped. Eventually Peter tired of the game and the two of them left the hens, returning to the house. The women were in the kitchen, planning the midday meal, while Edward stood in the living room, examining a row of small wooden carvings displayed on a shelf in one corner of the room. There was no television; the DiPaolis didn't own one and never had.

Peter went back outside a little later and was standing in the yard when his grandmother came out, screen door slapping shut behind her, to disappear into the henhouse. A few minutes later she emerged, a squawking bundle of feathers, held firmly by the feet, dangling at her side. In retrospect, it was only logical that her sacrifice for dinner should be the chronically unproductive chicken, and there was no way she could have known Peter would recognize her captive. But recognize it he did—the brown patch on the wing was unmistakable. As she casually draped its head over a low, flat branch on a stunted peach tree, he still did not realize what was going to happen. But a second later, there was a flash of light from the broad-bladed kitchen cleaver as she cleft its head from the body and dropped the corpse to the ground.

As if that had not been shock enough, the hapless chicken didn't even know it was dead: the body staggered up against the trunk of the tree, leaving a bright red arterial smear on the bark, then half-ran, half-flopped across the short distance to the side of the house. It struck the wall and rebounded, rolling completely over, then convulsed and writhed its way across the grass to Peter's feet. Rigid with shock, he was unable to move as a pulse of blood stained his white sneakers. The body then flip-flopped over his feet, made unsteady progress across the grass, and pumped up against the picket fence separating the front yard from the sidewalk. There, it ran around in hysterical circles for a moment or so, wings flapping in a parody of flight, crashed into the fence once more, then staggered a few feet away and collapsed, still quivering and jerking spasmodically until it finally accepted the fact that its life was over.

Peter remained motionless, unnoticed, still in that same frozen pose when his mother came out later to find him staring in horrified fascination at the now motionless body. He had been so deeply disturbed by the incident that his father had spoken to his parents about it so it would never happen again. Grandmother DiPaoli had thereafter executed chickens by quietly breaking their necks with one quick twist, then hanging them from the peach tree until they stopped moving.

The situation had not been without its humorous side. On one visit later that summer, a neighborhood friend had come along to keep Peter company. The friend had later reported to all and sundry that Peter's grandmother grew chickens on a tree in her sideyard. But the humorous aspects had not erased the shock from Peter's mind, remnants of which remained even in his adult years, when he was far more familiar with the unpleasant side of human existence.

That particular visit was probably the most vivid in his memory but there were a number of incidents which engraved themselves in his mind during the ensuing years. One took place the day he was left alone with his grandfather while the other three adults went for a walk. Arturo had twisted his ankle badly the previous day and was walking with the assistance of a cane. For the most part he'd parked himself in his favorite chair in a corner of the living room, whittling tentatively at a block of wood with a set of knifes he kept in a drawer nearby for that purpose.

Arturo was a wood carver, an artisan, and had supported himself and his new wife in Italy with that skill when the crops from their small farm had proved insufficient for that purpose. His gnarled hands moved deftly, turning the wood this way and that, the knife flicking in to remove a tiny piece here, a strip there, as he struggled to find what he told the boy in no uncertain terms was the true shape hidden within.

Peter found it fascinating to watch those sure-fingered hands moving back and forth around the wood, which seemed to be in a perpetual motion of its own. At the same time, his grandfather kept urging him to look at the pieces displayed on the nearby shelves, to touch them. But Peter would not dare to handle even one of the ornate, minutely carved figures, all of people or farm animals in lifelike poses. There was a man cutting wood with an ax, another pushing a plow, and others working with pitchforks or shovels, milking cows, women washing clothes against primitive washboards, a horse pulling yet another plow, figures pitching hay, driving a horse and buggy, chopping down a tree, and a score of other poses. Each was carved so that it stood on an amorphous base, its contours suggesting the rocky New England soil.

Peter never knew how long he was left alone with Grandpa DiPaoli that day—he had not yet been taught to tell time—but it seemed as though an entire step in his maturation was completed, that he ended the afternoon with a kind of appreciation for those who worked with the soil and with animals and who brought forth food for everyone else. He would never be able to explain the method by which that knowledge was imparted to him, certainly his grandfather spoke only at rare intervals and haltingly and on trivial matters, but even his parents noticed that he was unusually silent on the way home, and his mother kept checking to see if he had fallen asleep in the back seat of the car. But he hadn't . . . it was just that so much new information seemed to have been implanted in his mind that he needed some time to sort it all out.

There was at least one more visit that year, later in the summer, or perhaps even early in autumn, he could never recall which. He remembered it because his parents had argued in the car during the trip down, the first strong disagreement between them that he'd ever been witness to. It was about his grandparents and their unfriendliness, at least as perceived by his mother, though she concentrated on the monotony of the visits. It was perhaps for that reason that Edward suggested they ride downtown and do some window shopping after they'd all eaten lunch.

Maria begged off; she'd already done all the shopping she cared to for one week, and she had too much left undone around the house to spend time on such fruitless pursuits. But at the last minute, surprisingly, Arturo agreed to come along, suggesting that he and Peter wander off by themselves so they wouldn't interfere with Edward and Helen. Peter had grown considerably more comfortable with his grandparents these past few visits and put up no fuss about the arrangements. His parents were all too glad to get a short reprieve from his presence for a while. Even as well-behaved a child as Peter wore on one's nerves after a time, and they looked forward to being without responsibility for an hour to two.

Edward parked in downtown Managansett so he and Helen could walk around town, peering in the shop windows, with Edward perhaps indulging in a bit of nostalgia as they did so, while Peter and his grandfather headed toward the western end of town, where a large tract of land was being cleared near the cemetery in anticipation of a housing boom. There were three tractors moving back and forth, pushing down trees and such, while a small group of men picked up the detritus and loaded it into the back of a large dump truck. It looked to Peter very much like some of the games he played with his toy trucks in the vacant lot next to his home, and this larger version struck him as enormously entertaining. Arturo watched silently, hands clasping and unclasping behind his back, while they stood at the side of the road. He'd been even more taciturn than usual and struck Peter as being restless, uneasy, and unwilling to hold still for very long.

Eventually the man touched his grandson on the shoulder. "Come, Peter. I show you something." He turned away without waiting for an answer, and Peter had to scramble to catch up with him, totally unprepared for this abrupt departure. They crossed the main street, then turned back east, opposite the side of the road they'd taken on their way out. The pair proceeded for several blocks, then turned into the grounds of an enormous stone building with boarded-up windows, an unkempt lawn, gardens gone completely wild, litter piled up behind the shrubs and in odd places. Even to Peter's unsophisticated eyes the place seemed dead, deserted, unwelcoming, and he couldn't understand why his grandfather had led them here.

"Where are we going, Grandpa? There's nothing to see here."

"Wait, you see ... something special." And the old man continued, increasing his speed, if anything, moving quickly enough that Peter almost had to trot to stay abreast of him.

They reached the corner of the building and turned, now moving along the side toward a bulge at the end which, Peter could now see, turned into a truncated tower as it rose toward the sky. But as his eyes rose, he caught sight of something else, something which he initially thought was a man climbing up the side of the building. His grandfather reached a point directly under the figure and stopped, peering upward.

It wasn't a man, Peter saw at once. It was a statue of some kind of monster, something with claws and fangs and bulging, staring eyes in a sinister, frightening face. And there was something else about it, a liveness, a feeling that this was a living being imprisoned in the stone or on the wall, capable of feeling and wanting and hating all those who had the ability to move about while it was forever locked into a single pose. He knew he should be a big boy and not be afraid, but almost immediately he felt the urge to cry or run away, and he tugged at his grandfather's arm.

"I don't like it here, Grandpa. Let's go someplace else."

But the old man stood like a statue as well, chin elevated, staring raptly at the shape that had hovered twenty feet above. "This is special place, Peter, a place of power." He paused and his mouth moved silently, as though he were chewing something ruminatively. "Someday he choose. Not me. Your Grandpa is too old." For a moment he looked away, and if Peter had been paying attention, he might have detected the glitter of tears. "Maybe someday he choose you."

Peter didn't know what his grandfather was talking about, but the idea of this threatening figure choosing him for anything was so repulsive that he began to shake. He pulled again at the man's sleeve, digging his fingers into the material. "Let's go, Grandpa! Let's go now!" And when there was no response, he jerked as hard as he could, hard enough that he pulled Arturo's body slightly about, and eye contact with the statue was broken.

The old man shook himself as though waking from a dream, looked down, and recognized dimly that his grandson was genuinely upset.

"All right, boy. We go. Come again some other time, though. You see."

But they never did come again, at least not together. During the next few visits, the rift in the family grew by leaps and bounds, and on at least two occasions there were shouting matches between Arturo and his daughter-in-law, and once between Edward and his mother. The visits became less frequent, the tension more tangible, and eventually, after one particularly stormy session ended with the younger DiPaolis departing hours earlier than had been planned, they stopped entirely. For a while Peter missed his grandparents, but he had reached the age where children viewed everything as transient that they did not see every day, and he more or less forgot about them as time unraveled in its usual manner.

Arthur Kaplan was working as a maintenance man for the town of Managansett the same year that Peter DiPaoli first saw the gargoyle on the wall of the Sheffield mansion. Arthur was an unusually quiet, withdrawn young man, perhaps because of the string of tragedies that had marked his life, so incredibly terrible that he was avoided by some as a harbinger of ill news. Arthur was a foundling abandoned in front of the First Baptist Church on the east side of Providence, and his maternal parents had never been identified. He was placed in an orphanage in Cranston, and a year later, when he was about two years old, the building burned to the ground, killing twenty residents and a staff member. Arthur had escaped with a few burns, but one had left a permanent discoloration on the left side of his neck which looked white most of the time, except that when he was angry or excited or nervous, it flashed a red that verged on violet.

The loss of the orphanage had strained the resources available to support him, and his subsequent adoption by Ted and Nora Heinz had not been handled as meticulously as might otherwise have been the case. The caseworker had overlooked the repeated drunk and disorderly charges which had been lodged against Ted over the years; he had never, after all, been convicted, and Nora's frequent fluctuations from depression to rage were not really common knowledge, although a little bit of judicious investigation in the neighborhood might have confirmed any suspicions. Nevertheless, it was fortunate that Nora was so close to the edge, because when she used the kitchen knife on her husband one evening shortly after Arthur went to live with them, the final papers had not been signed and the state had little difficulty regaining custody prior to her indictment for murder.

Perhaps in compensation, the authorities were particularly strict in reviewing all potential homes for Arthur thereafter, though there were few prospective foster parents interested in adopting a boy with such a notorious background, and disfigured besides. But eventually Murray and Nadia Kaplan had turned up, and although the couple was a bit older than might have been desired, they appeared to offer the boy a good home, genuine affection, and the chance to turn his life around. They were in their fifties and childless, neither had any living relatives, and Murray had amassed a reasonable amount of wealth by operating a string of women's clothing stores.

Unfortunately Nadia Kaplan was diagnosed as having leukemia exactly one year to the day after the final papers were signed and Arthur Brown's name was changed legally to Arthur Kaplan. Murray spared no expense in trying to find an effective treatment, and even sold one of his stores when the cash ran low. It was all to no avail, and she died seven months later, after a very painful, drawn-out illness. Murray was despondent and paid little attention to the business, and when he finally had had enough, he decided to sit in his car, running the engine for a while with the garage door shut. The executors of his estate found that his net worth had dwindled considerably. What remained after they'd taken their commissions went into a trust fund, while Arthur went back to the orphanage, this time to stay until he turned eighteen.

He emerged a taciturn loner, theoretically quite bright, though his formal education never quite seemed to take. By the terms of the trust, he could not touch the principal of his inheritance until age twenty-one, although he did receive a monthly interest check. Combined with the income from his series of part-time jobs, he was able to find an apartment and subsist quietly for the next three years.

On his twenty-first birthday, a total of almost six thousand dollars was deposited in his personal account, and the final affairs of the late Murray Kaplan were completely resolved. The following weekend, Arthur spent most of the balance on a bright red sports car. Two weekends after that, he lost control of the wheel on his way back from a drinking spree and sideswiped a panel truck coming in the opposite direction. Arthur was the only one hurt, and what cash he had left was quickly exhausted by the hospital stay, from which he emerged with a very slight but permanent limp in his left leg. The doctors had told him that the limp was psychosomatic, in his mind rather than in the limb, but Arthur had no more faith in doctors than he had in anyone else in the world.

He seemed to have been changed by his accident, perhaps the culmination of a life of adversity. It resulted in a decision to rise above what life seemed to have planned for him. His drinking was cut to the minimum required for social occasions, and he managed to get a full-time job working for the town, first as a sweeper in the town hall, later as an assistant janitor at the school. At age 25, he was considered a good candidate for promotion, and was engaged to be married as well.

No one had ever quite figured out how Arthur and Edith Furness got together. Edith was the spoiled daughter of William and Norma Furness of Providence. William was a highly respected surgeon working out of Our Lady of Fatima Hospital, and Norma was a nationally known psychologist and occasional writer of rather intellectual murder mysteries. They freely admitted that Edith was often a bit much for them to handle, but less willingly acknowledged that they had not really planned on having children in any case ... too much interference with the pursuit of their respective careers. But Edith came along anyway, and was entrusted to a series of babysitters and nannies, and enrolled in the Wheeler School, judged by her parents to be the best of the local private educational institutions and capable of measuring up to their daughter's unquestionably high intelligence.

What William and Norma Furness failed to realize was that intelligence and good sense, both learning and self-discipline, did not necessarily go together. Edith was an intractable child, resorting to fits of rage when she was thwarted in her desires, uninterested in absorbing any of the knowledge offered to her. There were threats of dismissal because of her conduct, more tactful comments about the need for outside tutoring. Finally, after seven-year-old Edith physically struck a staff member, an ultimatum was issued to the Furness family: either Edith saw a private counsellor who specialized in behavioral disorders, or she would have to find another school.

Norma Furness was a brilliant woman, able to look into the mesh of group dynamics and quickly develop a workable plan of action which would result in the desired change. But she was totally unable to cope with the eccentricities of her own child and often didn't even seem capable of perceiving them. Fortunately she was intelligent enough to recognize this failing. She scanned her colleagues, reviewing their work, until she was satisfied that she had chosen the proper person to deal with Edith. As in most things she attempted, Norma was successful, and there were soon radical changes—some might call them improvements—in Edith's behavior. The rages came at greater and greater intervals and eventually disappeared entirely, although for a while they were replaced by a stutter, then by an incessant tapping of the fingers, and as adolescence arrived, by one of the worst cases of acne ever seen. Edith never became a particularly good student, but she did well enough to pass and eventually graduate from high school, though her marks were so mediocre that it was just as well that she had no aspirations to attend college.

Three months after her graduation, she announced her engagement to Arthur Kaplan, janitor in the Managansett school system. No one could explain how they'd met, how long they'd been seeing each other, or what the source of the attraction might be. Edith was not an attractive girl, but neither was she unattractive, and physically they did not seem particularly disparate. But their backgrounds were so foreign that those who came to know them well during the next few years confessed a total inability to guess what had drawn them together. Her parents had not been overjoyed with their prospective son-in-law, but their investigation revealed that he was hardworking, considered honest, and reliable, and the truth was that the difficulties they'd experienced bringing up Edith had just about worn out their patience. All things considered, they were just as glad to get the girl off their hands and get back to full-time concentration on their own careers.

And so Edith and Arthur were married, and to everyone's surprise, they seemed to get on quite well. Not that there weren't occasional quarrels, of course, but no more than with most other couples.

During the summer of 1953, now married, Arthur Kaplan had to deal with a real problem. For several years he'd worked for the school system, and had been laid off during the summer months, when there was only enough full-time work for the two senior members of the maintenance staff. When he was single, he had been able to find a few part-time jobs and survive until the fall; but now he had a wife to support, had moved into a larger apartment, and was determined not to live on the money that was periodically offered by his wife's family.

So Arthur talked to his boss, who was generally satisfied with the young man's work, and a place was found for him on the regular town maintenance crew for the summer. Most of the time he cleaned up litter from the roads, or substituted for the regular staff at the school or town hall, or was sent over to help at the fire station, or even to take one of the town vehicles and run occasional errands. But one particularly hot day in August, he joined a crew of men sent out to do a quick job of cleaning up the grounds at the Sheffield mansion.

Arthur, naturally, knew of the estate; no one who lived in the town could have failed to be impressed by the massive stone structure that loomed silently, anchoring one end of the commercial district. Originally it had been rather remote from the busier parts of town, but as Managansett had grown, fingers of commerce had run down Main Street in both directions. The eastern flank was moving steadily toward Providence even now, but the western expansion had stopped dead at the boundaries of the Sheffield property, ceded to the town in lieu of taxes years ago, a gigantic white elephant that no one quite knew what to do with. Even the housing development that was being planned a few blocks further along would eventually collapse, with only a very few units being constructed before the backers rolled over and sank beneath the waves of disinterest.

The work crew went over in two panel trucks, riding up front, with the heavy-duty lawnmowers, gasoline, rakes, hoes, and shovels in the back. They were to cut the grass, pull out the worst of the weeds, clean up the accumulated trash, and place everything that needed to be carted away in a large dumpster. Arthur knew most of the regulars in the crew, but two of them were college kids rented from a local placement agency just for the day. The Town Council wanted the job done in a single effort so that they wouldn't have to pay any more rent on the dumpster than was absolutely necessary. Since all the mowers were power driven, the senior men had already staked claim to that part of the job. Arthur was to supervise the two younger men on the general clean-up, equipping them with rakes and trash bags.

Arthur worked with them at first, in a somewhat desultory fashion. He noted with considerable amusement the earnestness with which they approached their work, perspiring heavily almost from the start. He considered advising them to slow down; after all, the work wasn't going to rush off if they didn't get to it right away, and no one was likely to come out from the Council to make certain they'd picked up every last piece of detritus. At the rate they were going, they'd be finished by the middle of the

afternoon. So after an hour or so, Arthur gave them instructions and casually mentioned that he was going to
check the opposite side of the building to see if anything
needed to be taken care of there as well. The two looked
at each other, and Arthur suspected that some secret message passed between the two, but he ignored his suspicion
and sauntered off.

He walked the length of the rear wall of the mansion,
waving to the four men mowing off in the distance. The
grounds covered several acres behind the building, despite
the encroachment of civilization, extending all the way
back to the boggy marsh that effectively marked the northern boundary of the Sheffield estate. Then he turned the
corner, rounding the curve of the single tower, eyes peeled
for a shady spot out of everyone's line of sight where he
could sit down for a while. Arthur was not afraid of hard
work, but he didn't exactly court it, either, and so long as
his temporary wards were willing to do the work of three,
he didn't see any reason why he should not take advantage
of their magnanimity.

He couldn't recall ever having visited the grounds before, though he must have cut across the land many times
as a child. There was no fence, merely an irregular line of
hedges along the front, but one of the adjacent property
owners had recently erected a hurricane fence along part
of their common border. Arthur was quite certain he had
never been this close to the building before, and he spent
some time now admiring the ornate carvings that covered
the surface of the tower wall as he made his way around
its circumference.

And that was when he noticed the gargoyle for the first
time. It was, as ever, in its perpetual half crouch, knees
bent, extra-jointed arms extended slightly outward, as

though to brace itself when it leaped to the ground. The malign face was thrust forward as well, and the look in its eyes was almost eager. For a moment Arthur could have sworn that they sparkled hungrily as they stared at him, but he blinked and looked away, mildly disturbed, and when he looked back, the entire body seemed more relaxed, resigned to its eternal imprisonment in the wall, and the eyes were dull, the face still ugly but now contemptuous, and it almost seemed to have drawn back slightly, a trick of the light and perspective, he imagined. But despite its aura of inhumanity, its grotesque horribleness, he felt a certain affinity for the beast, captured by the limits of its own existence as Arthur felt captured in his own.

When at last his two charges had finished their assigned duties and came looking for him, Arthur was still standing there, and he was really quite amazed to discover that he must have done so for nearly two hours. He accompanied the younger men back to inspect their work, having missed his chance to sit in the shade, and became convinced that he had missed something else as well, something far more important—that he had been cheated, perhaps.

This was also the year that Valerie Meredith moved to Managansett. Valerie was eleven years old that summer, but already a charmer, the kind of girl that people said would be the ruin of many a man before her career was through. She had been systematically spoiled by her wealthy, doting parents, wore designer clothing, possessed everything she had ever expressed a desire to own. Valerie was even allowed makeup, and if the teachers disapproved, they found it politic to look the other way and pretend they didn't notice.

Shortly after her arrival, Valerie made such a spectacular impression on Barbara Howell, two years her junior, that the younger girl became virtually Valerie's satellite, following her everywhere, running errands, carrying her books to school, hanging on every word of sophisticated wisdom, as she interpreted it, that fell from the older girl's lips. Valerie could not be said to be fond of Barbara, but it was convenient to have someone so slavishly willing to answer her beck and call, and it is quite likely that she considered Barbara little more than a new toy to be used, abused, and ultimately discarded.

Only the very last leaves remained on the trees as October threatened to give way to November; it had been an unusually blustery fall, in fact, and members of the farming community walked around dourly predicting the coldest winter in memory. Valerie's family was living in Managansett only as a temporary measure while her father did some consulting work for one of the larger jewelry firms, so they were renting a comparatively austere home not far from Main Street. On the particular Saturday morning with which we are concerned, Valerie had risen at her usual late weekend hour, had breakfast in bed, then set out, without a word to her parents, to indulge in a vice she had just recently acquired.

She was walking along Nitock Avenue when a small voice called to her from the distance. Valerie recognized her name, but she also recognized Barbara's voice; having no immediate intention of sharing her prize—a half-pack of forbidden cigarettes liberated from her mother's purse—she began walking more briskly, pretending that she hadn't heard.

Running was so inelegant that she refused to escape in that fashion, but Barbara was less reluctant and soon overtook her.

"Valerie, hi!" Slightly out of breath, Barbara walked alongside the taller girl without saying anything more for the moment. Valerie tossed her head with annoyance, her long auburn hair lifting in the strong breeze, and remained silent.

"Where are we going, Valerie?" Barbara asked at last.

With strong emphasis on the first word, Valerie replied, "*I* am going for a walk. I just wanted to be alone for a while, get out of the house. *You* know."

"Yeah." Barbara was oblivious to the snub. "I have to get out sometimes, too, like when Mom and Dad are fighting. We could walk down and watch them knocking down the trees."

"Why don't you? Little kids like that sort of stuff." Valerie found the operation boring and loud and dirty and rather common, as a matter of fact.

Barbara's brows creased; she'd been gauche, she knew now, to suggest such a childish thing. "I suppose you're right. Big kids have more important things to do."

Valerie sighed, interpreting correctly Barbara's total unwillingness to be slighted by anything her idol said just now. She was about to angrily order her away when an even better idea occurred to her: as tantalizing as smoking was (it was the only activity her parents had ever proscribed), it was even more appealing to subvert someone else, particularly such a transparently sweet girl as Barbara. In Valerie's vocabulary, "sweet" was about the worst thing that could be said about anyone. If Barbara wanted to hang around with a big girl, she was going to have to learn to do the kinds of things that big girls liked to do, and that included smoking.

"Barbara, you've lived around here a long time, haven't you?"

The other girl nodded. She kicked at a stone lying on the sidewalk, suddenly uncommunicative.

"Where would you go if you wanted to be all by yourself for a while?"

"My room," she answered, without a moment's hesitation.

"No, not like that." Valerie's impatience with her companion returned, but she cut off her anger quickly. "I mean somewhere that your parents wouldn't come in and surprise you."

"They never come in my room without knocking. It's private, they say, and I have to knock before I go in theirs."

"Well, other than that, then. If you were just knocking around town and you wanted to be someplace where you wouldn't see anyone and no one would see you and you could even ... oh, take your clothes off or something, if you wanted."

Barbara actually blushed and Valerie suddenly realized how much she really hated this little wimp. "Are you kidding?" she said, giggling. "Take my clothes off outdoors? I don't even like going to the beach."

Valerie couldn't stand it any more. "Damn it, I was just giving an example!" Barbara stopped dead in her tracks, disturbed by the profanity, and Valerie realized she might have overplayed her hand. But just at this moment, she really didn't care. "I've got something really secret I want to show you, Barbara, but I can't do it unless we go somewhere that's real private and hidden so that no one else will see what we've got."

Barbara looked simultaneously intrigued and suspicious, and a bit offended as well. "Well, we could go down to the swamp. There's supposed to be snakes and things,

70

and kids aren't supposed to go down there, but we all do."

"If all the kids go down there, it can't be very secret, can it?" Valerie stamped her foot suddenly and spun on her heel, moving off. There was no doubt about it; Barbara had about as much brains as her parents had money, and there wasn't much of either.

"How about the haunted house?"

This time it was Valerie who was startled. "What haunted house? I never heard anything about a haunted house."

"Oh, it's not really haunted, at least I don't think so. But we call it that, and no one plays near it. It's not too far from here."

And so it was that Valerie Meredith followed Barbara Howell through the small park and down the path that led in to the sideyard of the Sheffield mansion. They made their way close to the house, and it was Valerie who took the lead at this point, locating a spot of clear ground almost completely surrounded by the runaway ornamental shrubs. She surveyed their hideout with a clinical eye and noted that it was completely concealed from the street and from most of the yard as well. Someone in one of the upper windows could look down on them, of course, but Barbara had assured her that no one had lived in the house for years and years.

She was not, however, prepared for Barbara's reaction when she finally showed her the pack of cigarettes.

"Valerie!" Her voice was shocked, almost fearful, and she looked around nervously, whispering as she continued. "Where did you get those?"

Valerie leaned back against a white birch and slowly

pulled a cigarette from the pack. "Snatched 'em. No one'll miss them."

"I didn't know you smoked!"

"Sure, plenty of times. My parents pretend they don't want me to, but they look the other way. Want one?" As a matter of fact, she had smoked exactly twice before, and had yet to successfully finish one cigarette.

Barbara recoiled in absolute horror. "No, no, I can't. My mom would kill me, absolutely kill me. They don't even let Uncle Lester smoke in the house when he visits. They make him go outside, or in the garage if it's winter."

Her plans still seemed to be going awry. "Come on. If you want to be popular, you have to do popular things. Guys like girls who smoke; it's sexy. That's the kind of thing boys go for."

"I don't care, and I don't want to be sexy." Barbara set her lips and crossed her arms and at that moment, Valerie hated her with a completely mind-devouring passion. "Smoking is stupid. My mom says so."

Valerie decided she had had enough. "Your goddamn mother is stupid, then. Smoking is great. Here!" And she thrust the pack at the other girl. "You want to be my friend and stuff, then you have to prove it and smoke with me."

But Barbara was beginning to see the seamier side of her hero by now, perhaps an earlier disillusionment than most of us are granted, and she took a step backward. "No, I don't want one. You can't make me." Her voice was uncharacteristically firm, and Valerie rebelled against the idea that anyone, particularly this common little girl, could resist her will.

"You're going to smoke this, you little asshole," and she moved toward Barbara.

With a small squeak of terror, Barbara spun on a heel and bolted through the interlaced branches of two bushes, breaking through into the open at the cost of a ripped sleave on her new blouse. Propelled by rage, the older girl followed. Too large to move through the same gap easily, she snagged herself on one of the branches. As she turned, trying to free herself, she lost her footing and went sprawling out into the open, the pack of cigarettes flying from one outstretched hand.

Barbara was gone by now, of course, and there was no point in rising, so Valerie lay there for long minutes, cursing softly, thinking of horrible things she'd like to do to get even: thorns under the fingernails, lit matches burning flesh, hanging upside down from the branch of a tree while she lit a fire below, perhaps. She found this kind of thought amusing and indulged herself for quite a while and lay there until the pictures started repeating themselves in her mind and she finally rolled over and sat up. That was when she first saw the gargoyle.

Her first impression was of its muscles, bulging in all the right places, even if the arms did seem to have an extra bend in them. The face was craggy, even inhuman, but somehow sexy at the same time. And that bulge between its thighs was so obvious that she almost laughed, although something about its demeanor, its stance as it leaned forward suggestively, drove all thought of laughter from her mind. This is a magical thing, she felt, a thing of power and glory and fury. She rose to her feet and walked over to the mansion wall, the better to see the details of this wondrous discovery. Strangely, no matter where she stood, it seemed that the face was staring directly at her, the eyes following her every movement. And the expression, she was convinced, was one of thorough approval.

"How'd you get yourself stuck up there, fellow?" She saw no incongruity in addressing a statue, even though she expected and received no reply. "Let your guard down at the wrong moment and someone caught you and locked you up, I guess." Her expression became grimmer. "No one's ever going to do that to me. No one's ever going to control what I do. I'm free and I'm going to stay that way."

The gargoyle never said anything, of course, but Valerie stood there a long time before retrieving her cigarettes and walking off to find some place of her own to smoke them. But there was communication of a sort nevertheless, and it was not to be the last between the two of them. And frequently the gargoyle came to her in her dreams, and remained hard as a rock in all the right places.

CHAPTER THREE
1955

Alex Furtado rapped on the plastic window that opened onto the lobby of the Eblis Manufacturing Company, the largest single employer in the town of Managansett. A harried-looking woman appeared almost immediately, sliding the glass pane to one side.

"I been waiting for a long time. They gonna see me or not?"

For a moment it looked as though the woman intended to respond angrily, but at the final instant, she seemed to think better of it, although her eyes betrayed her real feelings. "I'm sorry for the wait, Mr. Furtado, but you have to realize there are several other people being interviewed besides you and it does take some time."

Furtado reached up and scratched at one shoulder. "Well, I'm a busy man, too. If they don't have time to talk to me now, they shouldn't have called me."

"Someone will be with you soon. We don't schedule regular appointments," she said with some sarcasm. "All we told the employment office was to send applicants over during the morning. We try to handle the interviews as quickly as possible."

"Yeah, well," he looked around the small lobby, lined with inexpensive chairs and artificial plants. Two other men and one woman also waited to be interviewed, but at the moment they were pretending not to be able to hear the conversation taking place only a few feet away. "I'm in front of these other people, though. I was here first," he finally said belligerently.

"I'm well aware of that, Mr. Furtado," she said coolly. "You mentioned that a while ago, if you recall. I did take note of it at that time."

Furtado's head snapped up, as though he suspected he was being made fun of. After a moment's thought he dropped his eyes and moved his head nervously from left to right. "Well, all right, I guess. But tell them to hurry it up, huh? I got things to do today."

"I'll be sure to pass on your concerns," she answered, but she was already sliding the window shut and turning away. Furtado shifted about and glanced at his fellow applicants, trying to determine if any of them was a potential rival. Furtado had been out of work for over a year, having lost his job as press operator at the Providence Machine Works when their main plant was destroyed in a suspicious fire and the owners had been unable or unwilling to start again. His unemployment benefits had run out long before, and he had never built up any savings, despite the reasonably good wages he'd been earning. He was very good at the job, having developed an ability to blend his movements in with the rhythm of the equipment so he never missed a stroke and produced as rapidly as possible, and without developing the bone-aching fatigue that was so often associated with repetitive work of this sort. Furtado was also quite adept at setting up punch presses with new dies. He had developed the ability by helping the trained set-up men, because the sooner they were finished, the sooner he could be back at work, losing himself in his job, consciousness completely subordinated. The fact that this meant higher earnings while he was on incentive made no difference; the money seemed almost unrelated.

He was pacing back and forth when the window slid open once again and the woman called his name. Displaying a degree of anxiety that he hated to admit even to himself, let alone demonstrate to others, he moved quickly to answer. As he did so, the inner door opened and a man with a short beard appeared, wearing standard work clothing but clearly a supervisor; the real workers rarely looked this clean. He nodded. "Right this way, Mr. Furtado. I'll take you down to Mr. Wilson's office."

Furtado moved quickly, darting a final glance around the room. The other man let the door swing shut, then led him along a narrow corridor and out through a set of double doors onto the manufacturing floor.

The noise level rose immediately as Furtado found himself passing between two double rows of turret lathes, most of which were currently in use. One man stood at each position, holding metal stampings of one sort or another against spinning cloth wheels, and the sound of cloth cutting metal was one of the most piercing of all. Furtado knew from experience that he would soon notice the sound only on rare occasion, that it would eventually blend into the background.

They passed through a holding area of some sort, rows of boxes locked behind a wire mesh wall, some of them coated with grease and dust. An office stood to the right, and Furtado thought that might be their destination, but his guide continued on without pause, turning right and restarting down yet another corridor. Eblis Manufacturing was housed in a sprawling complex of buildings, all inter-linked, evidence of its rapid expansion over the past twenty years, but its unplanned development had resulted in a basically inefficient layout and even from his relatively inexperienced viewpoint, Furtado recognized that there were an unusually large number of floorboys in evidence, moving work from one place to another on dollies or with hand trucks.

They passed a soldering department, four rows of benches outfitted with soldering torches, all serviced by the first conveyor system he had seen, which was currently carrying completed work down to a series of rinses. All of these benches seemed occupied as well. At this point, the rhythmic sound of a double-action press intruded, and Furtado smiled. He was coming home. A few seconds later he could hear a second double action, a couple of single actions, and what was probably a hammer press of some sort, perhaps performing a trimming operation. The two men passed through a casting department and turned left, and the area ahead opened up into a much taller, wider, and less congested building. This was the press depart-ment.

Furtado was brought up abruptly by a hand on his arm. "Right in here, Mr. Furtado. Mr. Wilson will talk to you first, then take you on the floor."

There was an office to the left that he hadn't noticed, one of the portable kind, with thin walls and lots of plastic windows that can be moved about easily. Furtado entered, expecting his companion to follow, but the other man dis-appeared. The office was cluttered with paperwork, file cabinets with open drawers, a desk overflowing with paper, a wastebasket that should have been emptied long ago and papers piled up in the corners, on shelves, and even on one of two chairs that stood in front of the desk. The man sitting there, currently staring at Furtado's application, was presumably Wilson, the production manager.

"Sit down, please. I'll be right with you."

Furtado nervously took the available seat, crossed his legs, then uncrossed them immediately, uncertain where to put his hands. There was a short, awkward silence, after which Wilson put the application aside and met his eyes levelly.

"You have ten years experience on presses?"

"That's right." Furtado felt more at ease immediately. "I started on singles and moved up to doubles right away. I've worked on Dennisons and Bradleys—"

Wilson cut him off with a gesture. "It says here that you did some set-up work."

Furtado started to describe the way he operated at Providence Machine, but Wilson cut him off again.

"We don't have a union, here, Alex. We don't want one. Eblis takes care of its employees and expects each of them to return that loyalty. I remember that Providence Machine had a union and you were presumably a member."

Furtado shifted his weight uncomfortably. "Everyone had to join. I didn't never attend meetings or nothing. Never had no use for unions. I handle my own problems." He was telling the truth; he had resented the stipend taken directly from the first paycheck of the month to support the collective bargaining unit.

"I'm glad you feel that way. I'll have Campbell take you out and show you the floor in a moment, but that's just a formality at this point. You're aware of our hiring rate, of course. We do have piecework here, and I'm sure that with your years of experience you'll pick up your earnings very quickly. At the moment we have enough set-up help, but if an opening comes up and you're interested, we'll talk again. Do you have any questions?"

Furtado had none. The job was his, apparently; that was all that mattered. He missed the interaction with machinery almost as much as he suffered from the lack of funds, and he was impatient to get back to work. He rose and waited to see if Wilson would offer to shake hands, but the manager had already turned back to the papers which covered his desk. Campbell came through the door, the same man who had guided him out here, summoned by some mysterious method not apparent to him.

"This way, Mr. Furtado. I'll show you the press you'll be assigned to and then take you back to Personnel." Furtado glanced at Wilson once more, but the man never even looked up as he left the office.

An hour later, Alex Furtado left through the front door of Eblis Manufacturing, having filled in a number of employment forms in the Personnel Office, at the direction of the same woman who had processed his initial application. He suspected that she rather actively disliked him, correctly as a matter of fact, but this failed to disturb him particularly. Alex had been unpopular with most of his co-workers in the past, but the tension was never overt enough that management had ever been required to address the situation, and he was easily one of their most productive workers. They were willing to make certain allowances for personal idiosyncrasies when it was to their benefit, and Furtado realized that his new employer would undoubtedly do the same.

Furtado was a bachelor—always had been, always would be. There was no room in his life for anyone else. His horizon was the mouth of a very narrow tunnel that was dark and without feature. During childhood, his parents had feared he was retarded, but their concern was unfounded, at least in any conventional sense. But all his life he'd been a loner, had in fact run away from home in Fall River at fifteen, lying about his age when necessary, without friends or family obligations to encumber him. A variety of jobs had proven unsatisfactory until he took a part-time position at a small jewelry company, operating a foot pedal punch press, at which point he began to recognize his affinity for machinery. When that job dried up, he applied at a number of factories and finally landed a training slot at Providence Machine. Had that company not ceased to operate, it was quite likely that he'd have spent the balance of his working career in their employ.

Now that he worked for Eblis, Furtado had to relocate. He'd never learned to drive a car, despite his fondness for machines, and he had no intention of doing so now. He could still commute by bus, but now that he worked in Managansett, the ride would be more expensive and time consuming, and the buses ran at far greater intervals than within the limits of the city of Providence. So on the first weekend following his being hired, he rode the bus to the Managansett depot and set off to find himself an apartment.

He had switched from his usual coveralls to a flannel shirt and dark pants, and a page of the previous day's classified ads was stuck in his breast pocket, the three listings for Managansett circled. Upon arriving, he realized that he had no idea how to set about finding the indicated addresses, however, and a lifelong aversion to the telephone dissuaded him from calling for instructions. Finally, he conferred with the ticket agent, who provided detailed directions to the two that were relatively close by.

The third was an address with which he was unfamiliar, and he theorized that it might be out at the west end of town, near the cemetery, where some new construction had been going on for the past several years.

With a very brusque "thanks" that resulted in an irritated glance from its recipient, Furtado turned and left the depot, orienting himself on the street outside and setting off for the twelve-block walk to the first house. It was almost a straight line north from the depot, then two blocks horizontally, right in the heart of Managansett's middle class residential section. As Furtado walked along the street, he attracted several curious and sometimes suspicious looks from the residents of the neighborhood, most of whom were sitting outside enjoying the first really nice spring weekend. It was partly because Managansett was such an isolated, provincial town that any stranger was automatically suspect outside of certain limits, but it was also because there was almost an aura of disrepute, even menace, that followed Furtado like a shadow. He moved with purposeful strides, hunched over, head thrust belligerently forward as he read the numbers on the fronts of the houses. The more attentive onlooker would have noted the tightly clenched fists, the tense muscles at the corners of the mouth, possibly even the cold, impatient glare of the eyes. There was something not quite right about Alex Furtado, although even those who recognized this fact found it difficult to put into words exactly what it was that they were reacting against.

Finally Furtado came to a stop in front of a prim, white two-story residence surrounded by well-trimmed shrubs. The front lawn was broken up by little islands consisting of two white birch tress planted in tandem, each of their bases surrounded by a circle of neatly tended flower garden. His eyes sought the black numerals mounted over the front door until, satisfied that he was at the correct address, he moved up the front walk and rang the doorbell.

The door was almost immediately opened by a diminutive middle-aged woman wearing an apron over her skirt. She blinked in the bright light and looked up into his scowling face through the closed screen door. "Yes? May I help you?" The disapproving expression on her face would have clearly indicated to most people that she preferred not to help at all. Furtado was oblivious to this, however, as he had grown accustomed to evoking that reaction in others.

"You got an apartment for rent?" Furtado stared directly at her, demanding an answer.

"Well, yes...." The woman seemed uncertain. "That is, I do have the top floor for rent." She made no move to open the door.

"I'm looking for a place. But I'll have to see it before I decide."

She looked even more confused, but retreated into the mechanics of the situation, opening the door. "Of course. Won't you come in? I'm Edna Howell, Mr. ..?"

Furtado stepped past her into a small hall, looking around without curiosity, ignoring the antique furniture with its collections of cobalt blue porcelain, tiny pewter figurines, and shelves full of intricately blown-glass cats. "Furtado. Alex Furtado. Which way's the place?"

"Right up these stairs." She pointed to the staircase leading directly up from the hallway. "But there's a private entrance on the side that goes up as well." She had planned to say more, but the man had immediately started to ascend, and she almost had to run to catch up with him. Her niece, Barbara, appeared from the kitchen, looking at her inquiringly. "I'll be back in a few minutes, Barbara. I have to show the apartment. Keep mixing the batter and I'll be back to help you with the rest of it." The girl shrugged disinterestedly and disappeared from sight.

There was a short landing at the top of the stairs facing a closed door. Furtado opened it without asking and moved into a corridor that extended the entire length of the house. Doors opened to either side.

"There are two bedrooms and a sitting room, a full bath and a kitchenette," Edna explained. "One of the burners on the stove doesn't work, I'm afraid, but the refrigerator is practically new. I can also give you some storage space in the basement if you need it, but the attic is quite full."

Furtado opened each door in turn, without speaking. As he looked around, Edna began to regret the impulse that had caused her to place the ad. The house was far too big for her alone, now that James had passed on, and it had occurred to her that making the top floor into an apartment would provide some companionship. But somehow she had expected a single woman, or perhaps a young couple to rent it, even if they had a child. Edna rather liked children, although she had never been able to have any of her own. Her niece, Barbara, had been in and out of the house all her life, almost as if it were a second home. But she had not expected a man such as this to apply—and if she could be guided by the lack of a wedding ring on the gnarled hands, a single man as well. It would not be a proper arrangement for a single man to take the apartment, and certainly not this particular one. She fought down a small shiver of revulsion and told herself that she must be more tolerant.

"How much?"

He had to repeat the question before she was fully recalled from her reverie. "Oh, how much? Well, I have to have a minimum of $100 per month, and your electricity and heat are extra, of course."

Furtado frowned, his dark, full eyebrows meeting when he did so. "Ad says $50."

"That was a misprint," she said hurriedly. "They got my ad mixed up with someone else's, you see, and I didn't catch it before it got printed. I really must have $100, you know, because—"

But Furtado interrupted her before she could elaborate with the lie formulating in her mind. "Too much." And he had brushed past her and down the stairs before the meaning had even penetrated. She was still standing there when the screen door slammed behind him. "What a particularly repulsive man," she said aloud, still standing there, and resolved to call the paper and remove her ad immediately.

The second address proved to be another private residence, but in this instance the homeowner was happy to say that she had already leased the apartment to an elderly woman who no longer felt capable of maintaining her own home. He did prevail upon the owners to give him directions to the third address, which was indeed at the far end of town. Unfortunately, the most direct route involved following a path through a substantial undeveloped tract of land behind the Sheffield property, and somewhere he took a wrong turn and became lost. When he finally emerged, it was into the overgrown gardens behind the mansion.

Furtado stood motionless for a while, knowing that this was not the way he should have come. But retracing his steps did not seem very promising, either, and finally, shrugging, he set off toward the enormous building ahead, hoping to find someone who could give him fresh directions, or at least to emerge onto a street and orient himself in that fashion. It was while he was walking along the southern wall of the mansion that he felt he was being watched. He paused, glanced all around, then slowly let his eyes travel up the side of the building. Near the roofline, perched directly above a narrow window, a kind of monster leered down at him.

It took a few seconds for Furtado to realize it was not in fact a living being; in his eyes the distinction between life and nonlife was not always clear, in any case. After all, machines were supposed to be dead things, but they moved of their own accord, functioned for specific purposes, subsisted on electricity or gasoline, even reproduced by manufacturing more of themselves. And the creature above seemed to partake of both worlds: in form it was roughly the same as a man, though the turns and twists of its muscles and joints were frequently bizarre. But the arch of the powerful right shoulder reminded Furtado of the sidearm of his press back at Providence Machine, and the columnar thighs and calves resembled plunging pistons, poised, full of raw power, ready to operate in a steady, rhythmic, relentless series of movements. It was an impressive figure, possessing strength, desire, purpose, and efficiency of design, and its imposing presence held him transfixed.

Furtado was never later able to determine just how long he stood there. He had never owned a watch, had no concept of the passage of time, and used two separate alarm clocks in order to be certain that he would rise in time to arrive at work on schedule, although most of the time he was far earlier than he should have been, often having to wait until the security people arrived to open the building. But when he finally noticed that the gargoyle's head seemed to have turned away, disinterested perhaps, releasing him from his invisible bonds, Furtado doubled over suddenly, cramps in his thighs burning fiercely. He crouched there for several moments until, finally, he was able to move freely once again.

He never did check out the third address. Emerging from the Sheffield property, he almost immediately noticed a sign indicating "Mom's Rooms," a somewhat dilapidated but basically sound rooming house across the street, a block or so away, and when he approached, he saw a smaller sign out front indicating there was a vacancy. An hour later he'd paid a deposit for a two-and-one-half-room accommodation and was heading for the bus depot. It would not take long for him to pack the few possessions he considered worth the bother, and he planned to move into his new place by the end of the weekend.

That night, his last in the old apartment, Furtado dreamed a most peculiar dream, a dream that would recur in one variation or another at irregular intervals over the years, but rarely allowing more than a week to pass without at least one occurrence. He was working at his new job at Eblis, operating the big, double-action press in one corner to which he'd been assigned, number seven, stamping out a shallow concave form which was known as the item's "first draw." He was just reaching up to press the operating button when two glittering, metallic eyes opened on the press and the die opening changed into a smiling mouth full of dagger-sharp teeth. It should have been a nightmare, but it was actually not frightening at all. The malevolent features into which he looked posed no threat, at least not to him. Even when the flywheel uncoiled into a long, muscular arm with an extra elbow and reached out to clasp his shoulder, Furtado was not worried. He would remain there, held by the steely fingers, until eventually the meter-wide smile faded, the eyes closed once more, and the arm withdrew, recoiling itself, signaling some subtle, obscure disappointment which Furtado could sense, but not really understand. As time passed, the dream would become more vivid, would sometimes last longer or shorter periods of time, but in all its basics, it remained unchanged throughout his lifetime.

Furtado settled right in at Eblis. Although certainly not popular with his fellow workers, his taciturn nature guaranteed that he would stay at his machine, keep his nose out of company politics and policies, and he was a first rate producer as well. Each day he would work himself into the pattern of the job he was producing, lift, load, withdraw, press the operating button, count one, insert lever, pry out the piece, lift and set aside, and then repeat. Although each operator was generally assigned to a particular press, they were occasionally switched to another to cover an absence or to work on a priority job, but the press foreman, a man named Rossiter, quickly learned that the only resistance he would ever receive from Furtado was if he tried to separate him from his assigned machine. The man had quickly demonstrated that he could handle all but the most difficult set-ups himself, which allowed him to remain with the double-action press even between jobs, and he was so anxious to get back into this normal rhythm that there was a small but measurable increase in the overall productivity of the department. Down time as it related to total available machine time decreased a couple of percentage points, and Rossiter was complimented publicly at a production staff meeting.

He also fell into a pattern outside of work, although it differed from that which he had practiced during his previous employment. Furtado had always kept pretty much to himself, had no significant social life, never went out for drinks or attended the infrequent company function. He occasionally visited a bar by himself and ate most of his meals at small diners. No one had ever suggested twice that he go bowling or shoot pool or see a movie or anything of that sort; Furtado always reacted to such overtures with derision or contempt. It could be said with absolute truth that Furtado had not one single friend in the world; Rossiter was perhaps the only person who would even have regretted his passing at all.

But he did have a friend of one sort, or at least that's what he might have labeled it if he had ever thought about things in those terms. There was a coffee and sandwich shop not far from the rooming house where he usually bought his evening meal. Mom's Rooms did not include kitchens, and he was generally unwilling to go to the trouble of cooking a meal in any case, lacking most of the knowledge necessary. So he would purchase a sandwich, usually cold cuts with lots of trimmings, and wander off somewhere to eat. While living in Providence, he had followed a similar pattern and generally retreated to his apartment to consume his meal, but here in Managansett, he had found a new haven: the grounds of the Sheffield mansion.

Each evening, if the weather permitted, he would slip through the hedges and wander over to the south wall of the mansion, where he had picked out a grassy spot from which he could sit and stare at the gargoyle. He never again achieved the sense of closeness which had occurred during their first encounter, and indeed, it seemed to him that the malformed but beautiful head was always turned away from him now, looking off into the distance for something that had not yet appeared. Furtado never spoke, never tried to impose himself on the consciousness of his silent host. He merely sat there, quietly eating, then carefully cleaning up any trace of the meal as the shadows of evening began to grow longer.

Furtado had been employed by Eblis for almost three months, and summer had arrived early and with unusual intensity. The entire factory was sweltering, of course, particularly in the soldering department, where each employee worked with a torch in hand for most of the day. The fans spaced strategically throughout the work area made little difference, the air was so heavy and moist. Wilson had spent almost the entire day in his office, the fan on his desk disturbing the papers as he worked, and still his forehead dripped with perspiration and his shirt clung to his back. He was in no mood for fresh problems when Harvey Rossiter knocked shortly after lunchtime and entered without waiting for an answer.

"Yes, Harve? What's up?"

Rossiter looked ill-at-ease, refused a chair, and began pacing slowly around the small office. "It's the new guy, Furtado."

"What now? Did he object to working another press again?"

"No, no . . . nothing like that, exactly. Or maybe it is— I'm just not sure."

Now Wilson looked up, his attention finally captured. "Come on, Harve. I haven't got all day—what's wrong?"

"He painted double-action seven."

Wilson frowned. "What do you mean, painted it? When would he have time? And why would he bother?"

"Not the whole thing. He just painted a sort of face on it."

Wilson could not understand why Rossiter was making such an issue of the matter. Other press operators had painted something or other on their presses, although usually it was words—their own names, or their girlfriends', something of that nature. One guy had painted a ghost on his, another a sports car. But they did it on their own time and the company really didn't object, although they drew the line at nude figures or anything obscene. "When did he do it? When he was supposed to be working?"

"No, he did it during lunch." Rossiter looked out the window at the production floor. "It might be easier if you came and looked. It's kind of hard to describe, but it's rather disturbing."

Wilson sat back, tapping his fingers rapidly on one knee. "All right," he said at last, rising. "But let's not make a big thing out of this. You get back to work and I'll take a walk through. I'll get back to you."

Rossiter looked relieved. "Okay, thanks. You'll understand when you see it."

He was absolutely correct. When Wilson walked through the aisle that separated double-action seven from double-action eight, he immediately understood Rossiter's concern. Furtado was apparently something of a frustrated artist. He'd taken the existing features of the press, augmented them with some dashes of paint in strategic places, and turned the entire front of the machine into a grinning devil's face, a demonic creature that seemed to glare threateningly at everyone who passed by. But it was a face that also possessed a quality of sneering humor, as though it were concealing some great, secret joke. There was no question it was unsettling, and Wilson considered ordering the press repainted immediately. But at the same time, he was reluctant to do so. After all, there was no specific rule against painting the presses, and it was hardly fair to penalize this man just because he was so much more talented than most. There had been no complaints, and he doubted there would be, even though he had to admit he'd have preferred not to have seen the face himself. He had the feeling it might return in his dreams, and he wasn't at all sure he wanted to face that visage in any situation where he could not turn and leave. There was also no question that Furtado was productive and valuable despite his rather unsavory appearance and uncertain reputation. Wilson was shrewd enough to figure out the real source of his productivity improvement, even if he was a good enough manager to attribute the credit to the supervisor in charge. No, he would tell Rossiter to leave things as they were ... if there were any complaints from other workers, he might have to do something about the painting, but in the interim, he'd let it remain. It had a certain horrible beauty.

So Furtado had emblazoned the visage of the gargoyle upon double-action seven, and despite their instinctive aversion, his co-workers were unwilling to appeal for its removal. The painting stayed, occasionally embellished when Furtado added a new feature. As the year progressed, as Furtado blended into the community as well as he ever had, his enthrallment increased.

The foliage was beginning to warn that the year was on the wane when Alex Furtado felt he'd settled in well enough to spend some of his carefully hoarded cash. His room was extremely bare; he'd brought to it only a few changes of clothes, toilet articles, cooking utensils he never used, and a handful of odds and ends he'd accumulated over the years. The room had come furnished with a bed, a small table, two chairs, and little else. He had no need of other furniture; no one ever visited him then. But he did need some fresh work clothes and some additional things to wear on weekends, and one of the alarm clocks had worn out and needed to be replaced as well.

He decided he needed to go shopping and made an unusual foray down Main Street to the center of Managansett, where he was able to pick up most of the things he needed in a relatively short time. Furtado hated shopping, particularly for clothing, because he always seemed to end up arguing with the clerks, and he really didn't need that kind of aggravation. After all, the thought, if I didn't come in and spend my money, they'd be out of work, wouldn't they?

His shopping completed, he discovered he was ravenously hungry, so he stopped at a small diner, stashed his bulging bags under the table in a booth, and wolfed down a hamburger plate. Since he had no intention of ever eating at this end of town again, he left without tipping the waitress, encumbered by the two bags, and inadvertently jostled a teenaged girl as he emerged onto the street.

The girl was tall and blonde, her hair elaborately teased and piled on top of her head. She was heavily made up and her clothes betrayed an obvious presence of money in her background to anyone perceptive enough to notice. But Furtado was not so perceptive, and when she staggered back and shouted, "Hey! Watch it!" he snarled a wordless reply and turned away, forgetting the incident almost as quickly as it happened.

But the young lady in question was not about to allow him to do so. When he turned his back on her and strode off, she flew into a rage, stooped down to pick up a flattened beer can from the street, and awkwardly pitched it at him. There was little force behind the blow, but the edge of the can caromed off his shoulder, stinging him enough that he almost dropped one of his bags. Snarling, he spun around with an alacrity that alarmed her, and she took a rapid step backward, uncertain, watching him warily but without fright.

"Fuck off, bitch!" he roared, and pedestrians who were pretending to ignore the interchange were startled into revealing their awareness of what was happening. "I got no time for you! Leave me alone!" With that Furtado turned to retreat once more. But the girl, barely into her teens, had never learned to surrender gracefully, and always, always made certain she had the last word in any argument, no matter what the circumstances or who her opponent might be. "Hey, you!" she screamed after him. "You little worm!" He was in fact a couple of inches shorter than she. "You come back here and apologize! You ran right into me!"

Furtado quickened his pace, vaguely aware he'd gotten into one of those confrontations he'd steadfastly tried to avoid all his life; he was unwilling to apologize, unable to figure out any way to smooth over the situation, but also unwilling to bolt for the safety of his room. Let the bitch shout, he thought.

When the short, ugly little man in the worn clothing didn't heed her cries, Valerie Meredith saw red. Her rage consumed her, distorting her vision so that she had no

94

time to perceive anything except the object of her hatred. No one treated her so cavalierly, not even her parents, and certainly not this repulsive little creep with the filthy mouth. Without thinking about what she was doing, Valerie burst into motion, striding rapidly forward. When she drew abreast of her quarry, she lunged toward him, elbow up, and clipped him in the side, just below the curve of his chest. He gasped and spun, the arm swinging down, the bag on that side tipping, then ripping in half as he made a frantic effort to grab it. A couple of cheap, solid-color shirts and a half-dozen pair of black socks, spilled loose, falling to the sidewalk.

"What the hell!" He was shouting now, still holding one full bag and the remains of the other. "You a crazy girl, you know that?" He clenched his fist, and for a moment Valerie thought he was going to strike her. During that split second, she hoped he would, hoped he would take a swing. If he did, she was going to duck under it and kick him in the balls, kick him hard, maybe cripple him for life, and no one would blame her; she was just a little girl, and he'd taken a swing at her first—she was only trying to protect herself, right? But although Furtado's eyes blazed and his fist clenched several times, he finally turned and began picking up his scattered possessions.

"What kind of an asshole are you, anyway?" she taunted softly, so that no one else could hear her. "You're obviously not a man and you look like an asshole, but I've never seen an asshole with legs before. You must be one of a kind." She made her voice mockingly sweet. "You don't have any balls, so you can't be a man, and you don't have any manners, so you can't even be a woman. I guess

95

that leaves only animals and assholes, and even animals aren't as ugly as you.''

Furtado busily stuffed the socks into the bag, then gathered the shirts up into his free arm. Valerie glanced around, noticed that they were relatively unobserved, then she darted in closer to him and whispered fiercely, "You get the fuck out of here, you queer. If I ever see you again, I'll pull your dick off, you understand? If I can stand the smell.''

It had never been easy for Furtado to deal with other people, particularly not when they were upset. This cold, calculating rage was totally new to him, totally beyond his knowledge, and he could dredge no correct response out of his experience with which to counter her aggressiveness.

He turned away defeated, but in possession of his purchases, and moved off again. This time Valerie let him retreat, standing with her hands on her hips, watching as he silently withdrew. Finally she shook her head, turned away in disgust, the incident almost forgotten. Or at least the specific details. But she remembered the feeling for several days, that sense that she was stronger than other people, and somehow special, that she could strike at them with impunity. It was a good feeling, and she resolved to experience it more often.

CHAPTER FOUR
1958

Managansett was no great social center, and the bimonthly dances at the local high school didn't do much to help pass the time for the younger population. There were no movie theaters in town, and since the local pool hall served drinks, anyone underage was barred from playing there. Providence was a half-hour's drive away, a haven only for those who had access to a car—a decided minority in Managansett. The infrequent bus service was being improved during the week, but so far it provided no real access to the city on weekends, particularly for those who wanted to return late at night—the last buses left Providence and Managansett at 8:30 and 9:00, respectively.

This left few options. House parties were common, but they were hardly popular with the older kids. The unattached guys spent a lot of time downtown, hanging out on street corners, browsing at Al's Record Rack. A few couples used the small park south of the town cemetery, or wandered through the wooded areas adjoining the waterway at the north end of town, but the most convenient privacy, the Sheffield estate grounds, were generally voided. There was no specific reason for this, but as younger children, the kids all heard one or another of the various ghost stories about the building that arose from the mysterious deaths during its construction, the owner's own demise just a few years later in a riding accident, and a few utterly fictional incidents which had embellished the legend in subsequent years. The aura of mystery, of something "not quite right," had carried over into their adulthood. Certainly there had not been any sighting, death, accident, or other event in living memory connected in any way with the estate to give its bad reputation a renewed lease on life. Nevertheless, the grounds were pretty much avoided by everyone in town, particularly after nightfall.

There had been talk of opening a small club in town for teenagers. Adults were uncomfortable with the sight of groups of boys standing on the corner or smoking in dark side streets, and parents were concerned that their daughters were going to pick up unfortunate habits or associate with the wrong kind of boy under the wrong circumstances. The individuals most concerned, the fifteen-to-twenty-year age group, were not consulted, and if they had been, their almost universal distrust of such a proposal might have killed the idea even sooner than its inevitable surrender to financial limitations and an almost complete lack of enduring interest.

Valerie Meredith was one of the lucky ones. She owned her own car, a present on her sixteenth birthday from her doting parents. Valerie's father had expected Managansett to be a temporary home, but Elbis Manufacturing had been so impressed with his consulting work for a local jewelry manufacturer that they'd offered to make him vice-president of sales. The straight-based salary offer was large enough, and the five-percent ownership of the business guaranteed to him if he remained for three years provided the pivotal inducement. So he set out to build what was going to be the most expensive private residence in town, down near the Managansett Inn.

It certainly could not be said that Valerie had a lot of friends, but she'd gathered enough admirers to make up for the lack. At sixteen she was easily the most striking girl at the high school, if not necessarily the most conventionally attractive, and she commanded a circle of envious acquaintances who hung on her every word and traded on their relationship with her to inveigle dates with the local boys. She had her choice of partners as well. Most were still in the stage where flashy make-up and an air of self-confidence seem vastly more interesting than a charming or an honest approach to life.

It was Tuesday night. Valerie and her mother were eating supper alone because Mr. Meredith was on the road, on a two-week selling trip that had become a ritual in their life twice a year. The new home was close to completion, and the house was littered with boxes and packing materials. The Merediths were going to be moved professionally, of course, but Helen Meredith was not about to trust her more prized possessions to the hands of outsiders who would really not care about them, and what did it matter that everything was fully insured? Some things were irreplaceable, the physical evidence of her lifetime of collecting.

Valerie rose from the table, her plate empty, and had started to leave the kitchen without a word when her mother looked up from her own as yet unfinished meal. "Valerie, do you have much studying to do tonight?"

Her daughter stopped in the doorway without looking back. Her tone was full of exasperation as she answered,

"No, Mother—I already told you that midterms were last week, and they're always easy on the homework after that." Lately Valerie's patience was growing thin. She considered her mother a rather silly, purposeless woman and avoided her company whenever possible.

"Well, Dear, I asked only because I wondered if you might be able to give me a hand with the packing tonight. I wanted to get all of the good china out of the way before the weekend, and it would give us a chance to do something together and talk." Helen Meredith had recently read a nonfiction bestseller stressing the importance of communicating with one's children, and it had struck her that perhaps she'd been somewhat remiss in the raising of her only child. If the truth be known, she'd never intended to get pregnant in the first place; the idea of being responsible for a child, even though it was a shared responsibility, had always terrified her.

Valerie turned to face the table but made no move to re-enter the kitchen. "Mother, we can talk another time. I have things to do tonight. I have to go out for a while. I'll be back before ten." She started to turn away.

"Where do you and your friends go every night, Valerie? You're out almost all the time lately, and your father and I never see you at all." The older woman looked up, her voice unusually firm. "You're never studying these days, and I don't even get to meet your friends anymore. The mileage is way up on your car."

Valerie spun on her heel, her eyes blazing. "Mother, we've agreed more than once that I have to live my own life. I've asked you not to spy on me, or try to find out where I go, and what I do, and who I do it with." Her voice was low but uncompromising. "We agreed that I have a right to my privacy, and what I do at night and on weekends is private.

"I realize that, Valerie, and I'm really not trying to pry. But your father and I *do* have an obligation, you know, to see that you don't get into trouble and that you know how to make a place for yourself in the world. We're responsible for you. You are our daughter."

"I don't want to hear any more about your responsibilities!" Valerie's voice rose, but she regained control at last and continued in a more moderate tone. "I've never embarrassed you, have I? I don't sell drugs or hustle men or get arrested or pass out drunk. I've never even had a traffic ticket!" She didn't bother to add that she'd twice been stopped for speeding, though—in both instances she'd been forced to resort to charm in order to avoid the citation.

The older woman recoiled physically from this onslaught. "Don't get upset, Valerie. I wasn't accusing you of anything unsavory. I'm just trying to take an interest in your life. I don't want the two of us to grow apart, now that you're becoming an adult. I want us to be as close as we were in the past, that's all."

"Close!" This time Valerie did move back into the kitchen, crossing the table and leaning down on the knuckles of both hands. The whining tone that had crept into her mother's voice never failed to infuriate her. "We've *never* been close, and don't you ever imagine we were! All my life, you've been poking and prying, trying to cover up your own failures by taking some kind of voyeuristic credit for my successes!"

Helen looked up at her daughter shocked. "What do you mean, my failures? I don't feel my life has been without success. Look at the home we are building here, and the beautiful things we have to put in it."

"Oh, yes, I did forget your one single success." Valerie spit out the words like tiny poison darts. "You did manage to bag Dad. And you've lived off his talent and skills ever since." She paused a moment to let it sink in. "Well, I'm not about to peg my whole life to a man, any man. I plan to make it on my own."

The shock on her mother's face gave way quickly to a long-suppressed rage. "Just who do you think you are, to talk about your father and me like that? *Just who do you think you are?*" She rose, then flinging the chair from the table, her hands fluttering nervously as she unconsciously acted out a desire to break something. "You have no right to judge us! What do you know about anything? We've provided everything you wanted all your life because *we* learned how to get around the obstacles the world put in our way! You've had everything served up to you on a platter!"

"Oh, Christ, Mother! Are trying for an Oscar?" She burst into a laughter totally devoid of humor. "Did you read those lines in the latest bestseller? You wouldn't know an obstacle if it sat up and bit you. You talk about having it easy? When did you ever have to do anything for yourself?"

Her mother's mouth worked, but for a few seconds . . . no sound came forth. Then she seemed to get a grip on herself and proceeded more calmly. "Valerie, I don't think there is any point in our discussing this further now. We're both upset and don't know what we're saying."

"Wrong, Mother. I know *exactly* what I'm saying. I want you to butt out of my life, as of right now. If it gets screwed up, it's going to be me that does the screwing." She laughed again. "In more ways than one, if need be."

"Shut your filthy mouth!" Helen had never heard such language from her daughter, though in her heart she knew she'd raised a distinctly different animal than she'd ever expected her own daughter to be.

"No, I will not!" Valerie straightened up and met her mother's stare. "Get it through your head, will you? You don't own me and you don't control me, and I'll do *what* I want *when* I want with *whoever* I want. It's none of your business, and I will not have you interfering!"

"As long as you live in this house, your father and I will have some say in your life, Valerie. You can't—"

"Yes, I can!" she interrupted fiercely, swinging one hand so that her empty dish went flying from the table, shattering against the wall. Helen was shocked into immobility by the crash, but Valerie continued without blinking. "This is the end of my being your sweet little baby! You will accept me the way I am, or—" and her voice dropped once more, "you can choose not to accept me and just stay out of my way. It's your choice, Mother. I really don't care."

Helen made one last-ditch effort to reassert her authority, but she knew that the cause was already lost. "I think you'd better go to your room, Valerie. We'll discuss this no further this evening. Your father will be home next week, and if you feel we've been unfairly restrictive—"

Valerie overrode her again. "Daddy will do exactly what I want him to do, just like he always does. He dotes on me. If you don't want to risk your soft berth with him, I suggest you keep that firmly in mind and do nothing to test his loyalty. If you force him to choose between us," and she smiled nastily, "you might be surprised at the

103

results." She turned again and walked to the doorway, then paused and looked back, smiling. "And I have too many things to do tonight to spend the evening in my room. Why don't you go to *your* room, Mother, and have a good long cry? It's one of the few things you do so well."

And she left the kitchen and the house without another word, slamming the front door behind her.

Helen Meredith stood motionlessly in the kitchen for a very long time, even after she had heard her daughter's car pull out of the driveway and disappear around the corner of the street, headed downtown. When she finally did move, it was to carefully sweep up the broken china and to wash the stained wall with a damp cloth. Then she went quietly upstairs to her bedroom, changed into her nightgown, and climbed into bed, but it was a long time before she successfully escaped into her dreams.

Despite the artificial calm which Valerie displayed even after leaving the house, she was seething within. The audacity of that hopeless travesty of a human being, she thought, to set herself up as a competent judge of my lifestyle! She tossed her head unconsciously as she turned the ignition key, trying to cast aside all memory of the conversation which had just taken place. Seconds later, wheels screeching in protest, she pulled out of their street onto the main connector to downtown and roared off.

Valerie picked up Lynn Hadley and Paula Fenton at the Hadley home and barely let them get settled in the car before she was pulling out into traffic again. Lynn whoofed as she was thrown back in the seat and Paula reached up and braced herself between the other two with one hand against the dashboard. "Jeez, Valerie, what's the rush?" she asked, breathless.

Valerie pressed on the gas pedal in reply and the other

two fell silent, recognizing her mood as one in which she was not to be easily cajoled. Neither really felt comfortable in Valerie's company; she was too intense much of the time, and drained those around her emotionally. But just being seen in her company was enough to raise their status in the eyes of their real friends, as well as in the eyes of some of the boys they dated, so they made concessions for the sake of their social standing. And an evening with Valerie was rarely boring.

Lynn was the quieter of the two, her long dark hair combed in two thick strands that framed her face and emphasized its sharp, narrow lines. She was the third of four daughters, and the size of the family had put a severe strain on its financial resources. Robert Hadley had frequently retreated to the bottle in the past several years, and although he was now a reformed alcoholic, the trauma attached to his earlier drunken rages had had a particularly devastating effect on Lynn, who had previously been his favorite. As a consequence, she was often morose, and uncommunicative, and occasionally she was prone to crying spells that seemed to have no direct relationship to anything going on around her. She had also developed a slight but noticeable fear, an uneasiness, around older men.

Paula, on the other hand, was a thoroughgoing chatterbox, though this aspect of her personality was generally suppressed in Valerie's presence. She was an attractive girl in an unfinished sort of way, with short blonde hair, an attractive figure, and an unusually clear complexion, but her face was just a bit too round, her muscle tone a bit too soft, and her color slightly too pale. She gave the impressions of hovering on the verge of a serious illness, and at one point she was even diagnosed as being latently hyperactive. Paula's parents preferred to describe her as "high-strung," not wanting to admit that perhaps there was a psychological problem.

They drove on in silence for a considerable time, turning up Main Street and starting off toward Providence. Most evenings Valerie and some combination of hangers-on would travel to the big city, wandering through the department stores, flirting with the boys near Union Station, occasionally stopping at a small drugstore where Valerie knew she could pick up fresh supplies of cigarettes without being asked her age.

After a few moments Valerie slowed down; the condition of the road as it twisted and turned through the unlighted woods made it impossible for her to maintain a faster pace. As the tension in the car gradually dropped, Paula reverted to her usual behavior, her voice slightly more high-pitched than usual, an indication that she was nervous.

"What're we doing tonight, Val? Are we going to Shepard's I think they've got the new dresses in—you know, the ones they told us about last time we were in. Mom says she's going to get me some new things this month."

Valerie shrugged. "I haven't decided yet. Shut up, will you? I'm trying to think about something." There was no emotion behind the words, just a deadly calm that Paula didn't detect right away.

"What's the matter, Val?" Paula turned to look at her. She couldn't imagine what could possibly be upsetting Valerie Meredith. She was rich, beautiful, and popular with the boys; she had her own car and great clothes; and she never had to worry about when her next date was going to be. To Paula it seemed an ideal life.

"Nothing." But there was such an angry undertone that

even her companions picked up on it and began to watch Valerie covertly.

"C'mon, Val." Paula was secretly pleased at this possible display of weakness on the part of Valerie. "I can tell something's bothering you. Why don't you talk about it? It always helps me to talk to my friends when I have troubles."

"I don't have anything to talk about." Valerie's voice was low, but this time Lynn became alarmed, sensitive to the emotion that could be hidden behind quiet words.

Paula started to say something further, but Lynn grabbed her arm lightly. "I don't think Valerie wants to talk just now, Paula. Let's leave it for a while."

Paula turned to Lynn. "Don't be silly, Lynn. We're her friends; she can talk to us about anything. That's what friends are for." She turned back to Valerie. "Right, Val? Isn't that what friends are for?"

Valerie turned and deliberately met the other girl's eyes. "Shut the fuck up, Paula. When I want to talk to you or hear from you, I'll let you know." And she turned her attention back to the road.

Paula sat there agape, contemplating a reply, balancing the pleasure of venting her anger against the very real possibility of being cut out of Valerie's circle of friends. Peggy Harper had been dropped from the group earlier that year, and the word was that any boy who dated Peggy or even danced with her was off Valerie's list permanently, just because Peggy had once laughed when Valerie slipped on an icy patch and fell into a snowbank. Finally Paula limited herself to an offended sniff and settled back into the seat.

Valerie's mood did not lighten. The threesome walked

from store to store, peering in windows, looking in each to see if the stock had changed since last time, but in every case, Valerie hustled her two companions out long before they'd had their fill. Nor was she interested in strolling over to talk to the boys who frequented the dimly lit park across from the railroad station. Although never as talkative as Paula, neither was Valerie so quiet as Lynn, and this evening it was Lynn who felt compelled to say something to break the awkward silence.

At last, Valerie grumpily announced that it was time to head back, even though it was barely eight o'clock, fully an hour earlier than normal. They walked back to the car where it was parked near the library. A red Ford in desperate need of repainting had pulled in behind them, its nose so close that only one person could walk between the two vehicles at a time, and even then only by paying careful attention. Valerie herself had pulled up close to the Chevrolet in front of her, and now she stood, arms akimbo, measuring the distance.

"Goddamn assholes," she said, peeved. "How the hell am I supposed to get out of here?" She unlocked the door, then paused again. "Lynn, get up front and guide me out. Paula, watch my rear end."

"I can't do that if you're sitting in the car," she answered merrily.

Valerie shot her a look that would have drawn blood. But Paula moved to a good vantage point, so Valerie swallowed whatever retort she had in mind and got into the car.

There shouldn't have been any real trouble. Paula guided her back, and Valerie cut the front wheels sharply forward, although there was not quite enough clearance for her to get out on the first pass. She reversed the wheels and backed up again, this time riding up slightly on the curb, but still safely away from the other car. But when she started forward again, Valerie depressed the gas pedal just a bit too suddenly and the car jumped. The corner of her bumper barely made it past, but the wheel jerked in her hand and she lightly scraped the other car as she pulled out. Lynn ran around to the passenger side immediately, and even in the dim lamplight, she could see a foot-long scratch in the fender where the fin of the Chevrolet had scored Valerie's car.

The door slammed as Valerie got out and stormed around to inspect the damage. She seemed momentarily stunned, then rounded on Lynn. "You stupid little bitch!" She stalked forward, her hands clenched into fists. "I told you to guide me, you asshole! Look what you've done to my car!"

Lynn shook her head disbelievingly. "But Valerie, I didn't—"

"Shut up, you little cunt! I don't want to hear anything you have to say, do you hear?" She moved so close that the smaller girl could feel her hot breath. "I don't want you to speak another word to me, ever again! *Not ever!*"

Lynn blinked tears of shock and anger. "I didn't do anything!" she shouted at last, her voice cracking with emotion. "You pulled out too fast, that's all! It's not fair to blame me!"

Valerie had started to turn back to the car, but now she rounded on the other girl, her arm moving with a will of its own. It was an entirely creditable punch, powerful enough, in fact, that her fingers hurt for several days afterward. Lynn staggered back, the blood spurting from her nose, until she backed into a parking meter. She raised both hands to her face, touched it where it dripped hotly, and looked up at the older girl.

"You hit me." She sounded puzzled more than hurt. "I'm bleeding."

Rage distorted Valerie's features as she charged forward, grabbed Lynn by the wrists, and pushed her away furiously, this time into the side of the parked Chevrolet. Paula overcame her momentary paralysis and ran forward, anxious that her friends were going to attract unwanted attention. "Valerie, Lynn, knock it off!" She was almost whispering. "There's not much damage. I think we should get out of here before the guy who owns this car shows up."

Valerie turned away from Lynn, who was now weeping openly, her nose beginning to hurt. "Who the fuck asked you?" For a second she hesitated, not knowing which of her companions to attack next, head swinging back and forth between the two. Finally she turned back to Lynn. She reached forward, caught one wrist, and pulled her close, staring malevolently into her eyes. "You're finished, Sweetie. From now on, you are dogshit with the guys, you understand? Anybody who dates you is off the party list; anybody—boy or girl—who is even nice to you is off. No one doubles with you, lets you come to their parties, or talks to you." She waited a moment for that to sink in. Lynn was still sniffling, struggling to regain control. "I guess," Valerie continued with mock sweetness, "you might as well start hitting the bottle like your old man. It's going to be the only friend you've got."

She released Lynn and pushed her away. "Get in the car. Paula. We're going home."

Inside, she reached across and unlocked the door. Paula climbed in tentatively, and held open the door for Lynn,

110

who had not yet moved, but still leaned against the Chevrolet, attempting to staunch the flow of blood from her nose.

"Close it!" Valerie was already starting the ignition. "Let her find her own way home. I don't want her in this car!"

"But Val, her parents don't even know she comes here with us nights. She'll get in a lot of trouble if she has to call them for a ride."

Valerie spoke calmly, enunciating each word as though dealing with a foreigner. "Paula, if you don't want to join her on the shitlist, you will close the fucking car door *right now*. I will not tell you again."

With a last look at her former friend, who had now straightened up and stepped onto the sidewalk, Paula did as she was told. It was a long, quiet ride home.

At fourteen, Barbara Howell was convinced that she would never be attractive. He limbs were too long, the lines of her body were too straight, particularly where her breasts barely hinted at femininity, and her dirty-blond hair refused to allow itself to be styled the way she wanted it. She judged her face too thin, the cheeks sunken, the nose too long, the eyelashes too short. And she absolutely hated her voice, which was so low-pitched that she'd been moved from soprano to alto in the school glee club. It wouldn't be so bad, she thought, if it was low and sexy, but it was just low and boyish. She'd have considered becoming a nun, but she wasn't Catholic, so her current career plan was to become a nurse. That way, at least her lonely life could be of use to someone. When she was being honest with herself, she accepted that this was perhaps a melodramatic way to look at things, but it did provide some consolation. Fortunately, she was just too fond of life to feel sorry for herself for any length of time, and her bad moods were generally brief.

Her own opinion to the contrary, Barbara was one of the more popular girls in her class, at least with those of her own gender. The rivalry for boys was just beginning in her age group, and Barbara's gangly awkwardness and firm conviction that she was out of the running resulted in her being a safe companion, one unlikely to steal away this week's steady boyfriend. Many of the boys enjoyed her company because they were not yet emotionally mature enough for the dating game. The were uneasy or even frightened by the changes in attitude of most of the other girls in the eighth grade, although for the most part, the girls of their own age group seemed more interested in the boys from the upper grades. Because of overcrowding, eighth grade had been moved from the elementary school to the high school, so the mix of age levels was wider than might otherwise have been the case. Even some of the older boys stopped and talked to her from time to time, simply because they somehow recognized that she was entirely different from the other girls. She interpreted this, naturally, as evidence that they felt sorry for her.

Although she admired many of her older schoolmates, Barbara did not count Valerie Meredith among them. There had never been another incident since that long ago day when Valerie had tried to get her to smoke out behind the Sheffield mansion, but Barbara had been utterly shocked on that occasion, and the two had never socialized since. Barbara envied Valerie her popularity, her expensive clothing, and her self-assurance, but somehow she knew there was a basic flaw in Valerie that was masked by a veneer of sophistication and popularity.

Barbara was hoping to make the girls' freshman track team next year, so she spent a great deal of her free time out running. When possible, she used the dirt track behind the high school, but there was usually a gang of boys playing basketball on the open courts nearby, and almost always they would call out suggestively or laugh among themselves when she ran. Generally she sought other places to practice—the old Reservoir Road, or the intertwined paths through the woods that abutted on it, or near the old dam. But her parents were constantly cautioning her not to stray too far from public ways, her father in particular much more conscious than Barbara of the perils of straying from well-traveled roads.

So most weekend mornings she was off in her shorts and sweatshirt to the large open area behind the Sheffield mansion, now recently reopened as a library of sorts, though actually open only three days a week and primarily for scholars interested in examining rare books. There was talk of making it over into a full-fledged public library, but Barbara's father had told her the town council was too cheap even to put a sign up identifying the building. Certainly they wouldn't authorize funds for the rather substantial alterations required, nor for the purchase of books. The most important consideration in all matters brought before the town government was the potential effect on the tax rate, so expending funds for public services, particularly relatively unimportant ones, seemed an unlikely result of their deliberations.

But the town had made an effort to clean up the grounds, although the maintenance workers were not too fussy about how closely they trimmed the grass, and no real effort had been made to restore the gardens to their former glory. Some of the ornamental shrubs had been trimmed back, but this simply resulted in smaller, more densely packed flowers. Nevertheless, a full three acres were cut down to lawn level, no one objected to her running there, and the old stories about the building being haunted had succeeded in making it pretty well shunned by the neighborhood children.

She had just finished her run one Saturday in July, when she realized she felt a bit lightheaded. It was hot, as it had been for some time, but it was also unusually humid. Barbara had skimped on breakfast—she wanted to get back in time to ride into Pawtucket with her mother later that morning—and the combination of events had left her uncharacteristically shaky. Drying her forehead with the towel she always carried along, she decided to sit in the shade awhile before starting home. It was then that she saw the man in coveralls standing at the tower corner, staring at her.

"Oh, hello. You startled me! I didn't see you standing there."

He looked to be in his late twenties or early thirties, not bad looking, she noticed, except for a funny sort of white scar on one side of his face. He was silent, staring at her until she felt uncomfortable. She glanced away and noticed a wheelbarrow full of lawn tools.

"I didn't know anyone was going to be working here today. I hope it's all right, my running here, I mean."

He moved at last, stepping away from the building. "It's all right, I guess. None of my business." He glanced toward the wheelbarrow. "Just came back for the tools I forgot. Didn't want them to get rained on." He seemed even less at ease than Barbara, and this realization made her feel better.

She glanced around, noticed that the grass seemed
114

freshly cut and the clippings removed. "Are you the gardener?"

"No, I work for the town—as janitor, over at the town hall." Arthur Kaplan had been promoted this year, and was quite proud of his new position, even though he knew it had little meaning or prestige for anyone else. "We help out here when we have the time. The place is real run down."

"It's very nice here." Suddenly Barbara felt awkward again. "I have to go. It was nice meeting you." She escaped quickly up the path, feeling his eyes boring into her back as she went.

Arthur watched until the girl was completely out of sight, then put the last of his tools into the wheelbarrow, steering it around the curve of the tower. He paused there, looking up at the figure frozen in a posture of resigned indifference. "What do you want?" The whispered question emerged without plan. But even though he waited a long time for the answer, none was forthcoming. Arthur's face reflected a depth of inner pain and desire that would have shocked Barbara deeply had she remained long enough to see it.

Most of the time, Barbara jogged home, usually following a wide, curving route that brought her around the swampy part of town, back behind the enormous concrete abutments that the kids had always called a dam. It had actually been designed to alter the course of several converging streams when it was first erected, though now it held them back. The water table had changed over the course of years, however, and now it served merely to cause some of the overflow to back up over a low-lying area that spread from the northern boundary of the Sheffield estate up to the north and over the town line.

But today she decided to take the direct route in order to save time, and because the brief encounter with the man at the mansion had disturbed her somehow. He hadn't done anything wrong, of course, but the way he'd looked at her made her feel unclean, and it wasn't even a sexual sort of look, more as if she were a plate of moldy food he'd found in the rear of his refrigerator.

As she made her way through the maze of streets, she made a mental note to stop by her aunt's house the next day. Her mother's sister Edna lived a few blocks away, and her health had been poor ever since her husband's death. Barbara tried to stop by at least once a week to be certain Edna didn't need anything, and she knew that her mother made a habit of stopping by to see that Edna was eating properly.

Barbara's run home was to be interrupted by one more incident: there was a deserted stretch of road that curved up and around the high school playing fields, dirt track, and basketball courts. Although some of the land on the other side of the road was slated for development, none of the building had been started yet, and there was a good half-mile stretch unbroken except for a small dirt road that wandered off into the trees and up to a burned-out farmhouse no longer in use. The road twisted at this point in an S-curve with an extra leg, the far side completely obscured by the intervening trees. There was a turnout there that served as a lovers' lane at times, and which was also a hangout for teenagers who wanted to smoke or drink undetected. As Barbara neared this curve, she heard an engine start and the squeal of tires catching hold on sand, then pavement. Then there was another, stranger sort of squeal and the roar of acceleration as the car sped off.

Barbara rounded the curve just in time to see the car disappear into the distance.

A few yards away, at the entrance to the turnout, a woodchuck lay in the road, surrounded by a growing smear of blackish blood, its head and front paws moving feebly.

Barbara ran forward, then stopped just a yard short of the creature, which snapped at her briefly before turning to gnaw at its own hindquarters. From this close, she could see that its back was broken, its hind limbs totally motionless. Frantic thoughts ran through her head, of carrying it to a veterinarian, or running for help. But she soon realized the impracticality of it all—no vet was going to drive out here to perform services on a wild animal that was almost certainly going to die in any case, and which would not be able to function again even if it survived as a cripple.

Her next thought was to end its pain, finish it off. Although the woodchuck was silent but for the scraping of its front claws on the ground, she knew it had to be in terrible agony. But what could she do? She began pacing back and forth, looking for a heavy stone or stout branch, but even if she found something, could she bring herself to bash the poor creature's brains in? For that matter, could she do it with a single blow? If not, wouldn't she be causing even greater pain out of a misguided sense of duty? But there was nothing to be found in any case.

She returned to the woodchuck, or at least as close as she dared go, just beyond reach of its snapping jaws. The frantic movements seemed slower now, but Barbara could see as well that the animal's teeth had drawn blood from its own side, where it had worried at the flesh, trying to kill the awful pain. Maybe she should just go on, try to forget about it. After all, there was nothing she could do;

she wasn't responsible. No one would blame her for doing so, even if anyone ever did find out. But even when it was snapping and snarling at her, Barbara fancied she recognized some kinship in the crippled animal's eyes, and she could not force herself to abandon it. Not in its final hour. She felt a kind of obligation that she was unable to put into words, but which bound her nonetheless.

It was a long time later, eternities later, when the frothy mouth stopped snapping, and the eyes slowly lost their glitter, remaining open and staring but without anything behind them, and the head lowered. The ragged breathing continued for a few seconds more, then stopped abruptly. There was the smell of blood and feces and the raw taste of pain in the air. When she was certain that it was finally dead, Barbara plucked some broad leaves from nearby trees, used them as shield for her hands as she pushed the body inside the line of trees and out of sight. She could not dig a hole, but she covered the tiny corpse as well as she could with small sticks and fallen leaves. Not once did she cry, at least not openly, not even when she was finally done and had set off to walk the rest of the way home.

But the most vivid memory of all, more vivid even than the dying struggles of the woodchuck, was the sound of the car roaring off into the distance, and the brief, fleeting glimpse she'd caught of its rear bumper.

She was absolutely certain that the car belonged to Valerie Meredith.

CHAPTER FIVE
1960

Jimmy Nicholson was a high school senior in 1960, a member of the football, baseball, and basketball teams, possessed of a tall, powerful body, with a complex and intelligent mind. He was egocentric, a consummate jock—good looking, and popular with the girls, with thick, wavy hair and blue eyes, and he was considered a first-rate prospect. He was also popular with the parents of most of the girls he dated, particularly those worried lest their daughters end up with some hippie or draft-dodger. The war in Vietnam was in its early years, not yet a serious concern of the United States, although already some suspected that it was a mire in which entire nations might find themselves trapped. But Kennedy was popular with the younger generation, and the later disillusionment was still to come.

To the surprise of most of his classmates, Jimmy rarely dated the girls with whom he was expected to associate. He did take out the Junior Prom Queen once or twice and had at least occasionally gone out with most of the more popular girls, but he seemed to spend more of his time with those whose looks were average at best, who weren't confident that they would be asked out almost every weekend, who dreaded the annual class dances for fear they would not be invited by anyone, or worse, be reduced to choosing between the real dorks and not going at all. He specialized in girls who were not confident of their appearance, or who measured their own personal worth in terms of their companions, who aimed for a specific social niche and suppressed all other considerations.

It was late in May, a Saturday evening, and Jimmy was walking along Crowley Street with Barbara Howell. They had just seen the early show at the Community Theater and had made no definite plans for the rest of the evening. At least Barbara was unaware of any; Jimmy had already planned the entire encounter in meticulous detail. It was overcast and appeared much later than it actually was. This was Barbara's first date in almost three months, her first ever with Jimmy, and she was determined to please him. She had blossomed somewhat during the past two years, and even developed a degree of confidence, but her appearance was still pleasing rather than beautiful, less flashy than that of the girls who headed Managansett's teenage social register.

Jimmy took her hand with studied casualness as they walked along the sidewalk. "Hungry?" he inquired.

She really wasn't—she'd eaten a light supper before he'd arrived to pick her up, and they'd shared a large order of buttered popcorn in the theatre . . . but he'd suggested it, so he must be interested himself. "Oh, I think I could manage to eat something—sure. What did you have in mind?"

A secretive smile passed quickly over his face, but he masked it before she could notice. "Well, I suppose we could eat at Grayson's Diner or the Inn, but they'll both be crowded by now with people from the movie. How about we pick up some clam cakes and fries and go find someplace to ourselves?"

"Sounds good to me."

His car was parked at the curb a block away. In a few moments they were on their way to the outskirts of town, the newly developed section of fast-food places, used-car lots, bowling alleys, and a few small shops. Jimmy picked up a double order of clam cakes, some fries, and a couple of drinks, stuffing them all in the back seat.

"There's some picnic tables around back," she suggested.

"No, not for us—there's always a bunch of kids running around or screaming and arguing about who gets how many pieces. I know a place that's better." He pulled out abruptly into the traffic, ignoring an irritated glare from a passing motorist.

Barbara felt a twinge of nervousness. Her mother had told her countless times that it was important for her to maintain control on a date, and she already knew that her control was starting to slip away. Not that she'd had much practice at this sort of thing, she reflected ruefully. It was a little bit exciting at the same time, though. The enrollment at Managansett High was running about sixty percent female at the moment, and even some of the better looking girls couldn't expect a date as a matter of course. The more daring ones took the bus to Providence and hung around Brown University, trying to meet interesting guys. Barbara's recent luck had been pretty dismal; the last two dates she'd had, months before, were both unmitigated disasters. Barry Larson was a real creep, and Ray Bognoni hadn't worked out much better. She'd been quite startled when Jimmy had asked her to go to a movie with him, seemingly out of nowhere. She'd even wondered at the time if it was all just an elaborate practical joke. He wasn't the single most desirable boy in the school, but he was easily in the top ten. He'd dated Valerie Meredith and Dolores Fontina and Paula Fenton and Milly Pierce, and everyone knew they were the most attractive girls in the school. Barbara had tried hard to cultivate a friendship with most of them, Valerie Meredith excepted, but she just didn't seem to fit into their clique—so she contented herself with avoiding their attention. It was not a good idea to get on the bad side of certain people. Poor Lynn Hadley's breakdown last year had been attributed by many to the consequences of her falling-out with Valerie. The lesson had not been lost on the rest of the school.

Jimmy drove back through downtown and out toward the west end. Barbara began to feel actively nervous now. There was nothing much in this area except for a few scattered farmhouses, the aborted development near the cemetery, and the beginning of Reservoir Road, which ran out past the DiPaoli farm to the west. There used to be a picnic grove along the way, but people left too much trash around and the town finally closed it down, took away all the tables and equipment, and put a big hurricane fence up around the place. Reservoir Road ran all the way to the Connecticut line, and even there you didn't run into much unless you went way up toward Hartford. Certainly they wouldn't be going anywhere near that far this late at night, but she needed to know what Jimmy had planned.

"Where are we going?" She flushed at the tremor in her voice.

He picked up on her uneasiness immediately . . . he had to be careful now. It was important to keep her on the defensive, slightly on edge, excited, without pushing her over the limit into fear. He'd worked this gambit with

122

other girls and it almost always worked, so long as he didn't rush things.

"Not far. I know a place where there are some tables outside we can use without anyone objecting."

"But there's nothing out here any more. Where are we going, really?"

"What's wrong? Don't you trust me? We're staying right here in town. There's no problem. I want to surprise you."

Barbara's anxiety changed form now; Jimmy genuinely felt hurt, or at least that was how he sounded. But there was still a line of tense muscle in the back of her neck. She tried to force herself to relax, but with little success. They passed a couple of cars headed in the opposite direction, then turned to the right and stopped at the curb. She looked around.

"There's nothing here except the library and a car lot, Jimmy." She was genuinely puzzled.

"Leave it to me, Barbara. Everything is under control." But whose? He was already easing his way out of the car and maneuvering the bag of food from the back seat. He held the food in one hand as he walked around the car and opened the door for her. After a momentary hesitation, she stepped outside and he closed the door firmly. After all, they were right in town, practically. It must be all right.

Jimmy put his free hand on her elbow and guided her across the library lawn and around the side of the building. When the Sheffield mansion had been converted to a library two years before, the grounds had been cleaned up somewhat and a modern parking lot was added. In an uncharacteristic mood of exuberance, the town council had also authorized funds to build a small children's playground. But all their plans had gone awry: the library was closed for lack of funding and interest by February of 1960, and the children of Managansett continued their tradition of shunning the estate. The playground equipment had rusted ever since. A swingset and slide stood just at the end of the parking lot, which was closed off from the road by a chain strung between two trees. Jimmy led Barbara through the lot, around the back, and to a spot near the tower corner where two picnic tables, disintegrating from the weather and ill use, stood off to one side. "See what I mean? Lots of tables, no waiting." The closest streetlight provided enough illumination for them to see what they were doing, but not enough to dissipate the atmosphere of privacy that Jimmy considered essential. He had used this spot several times in the past, and quite successfully.

Barbara felt an uneasiness that had nothing to do with her companion. Her last experience here, many years earlier, had never quite left her memory, but she shook her head impatiently, telling herself that she was being silly and immature. She began opening the bag and sorting out the contents while Jimmy straddled a bench and folded his hands in front of him on the table, watching her intently. She found his intense stare disturbing and tried to break the mood by starting a conversation.

"I sure enjoyed the movie, Jimmy."

He shrugged the remark aside. "It was okay. I don't pay much attention to movies, except westerns, sometimes."

She offered him a paper plate heaped with clam cakes, fritters actually, more batter than substance. "They're all right, I guess, but they're not very real," she said. "The

124

guys are always really good or really bad, and the women just stand around and look pretty and helpless."

"That's what they're supposed to be. Women are just incidents in the life of the hero; there's no lasting significance. Life goes on after they're gone. It would be pretty silly to have a married hero, wouldn't it?"

"But isn't that unrealistic? Most men settle down with a woman at some time in their lives ... even cowboys."

He smiled. "Not the really good ones. Maybe when they get too old, they look for a woman to settle down with, but when that happens, it won't be the flashy kind they find in the saloons, the singers and stuff like that. A hero wouldn't want to have to compete with her. They have to be careful and pick a wife as carefully as they pick the right gun to carry. And not until they're ready."

There was a silence. Barbara couldn't think of anything to say, so she attacked her french fries. Jimmy's words had annoyed her on one level, but they'd also implied that appearance wasn't everything. He seemed to be saying that the kind of woman whose looks turned men's heads lost out in the long run; she'd always secretly believed the same. Someday the guys would realize that people like Valerie Meredith were eye-catching but cheap, with no staying power. Then they'd recognize that what they really wanted out of life was a reasonably attractive woman with intelligence and loyalty and skills, one who could hold their interest and share their lives. Like Barbara Howell, she thought. I hereby nominate myself.

Jimmy had made a couple of perfunctory attempts to eat, but he was soon sitting quietly watching her again. She still felt uneasy, but flattered at the same time, twisted nervously in her seat.

"You know," he said at last, "I never really noticed
125

you until a couple of weeks ago. You're really quite pretty. Did you change your hair or something, or have I just not been looking in the right places before?"

Barbara nearly choked. It was almost as though he had been reading her mind. Unused to compliments, she stared at him suspiciously. His eyes sparkled in the light, but he seemed sincere. She wanted so desperately for him to be sincere.

"I suppose I'm just growing up," she ventured at last, then looked away. "And maybe you're starting to look for something different, too."

This time it was Jimmy who had to look away, but rather than hiding embarrassment, it was to conceal his amused smile. There was only one thing he wanted from every girl he'd ever dated. He wasn't looking for a wife; that would come later in life, when he'd worked out which career was best for him and decided what kind of wife would be useful in its pursuit. He looked back toward her once control was re-established.

"Maybe you're right, Barbara. We're not going to be kids much longer. You just turned seventeen, didn't you?"

"Sixteen, really, but I know what you mean." She looked down at the table and began pushing french fries around on the rough wooden surface with the tip of one finger. "It doesn't seem possible that you're graduating this year. It seems like we were little kids just a few weeks ago."

Jimmy slowly stood up and started walking around the table, his hand clasped behind his back. "I know what you mean. I'm going to be joining the army in a couple of months. I was thinking about college, but I don't think I'm ready for it, not mature enough. Last year I was playing soldiers; next year I might be using real bullets." As a matter of fact, Jimmy had absolutely no intention of joining the Army.

Careful not to look in her direction, Jimmy tried to measure the progress he'd made. He knew Barbara to be fairly inexperienced in dealing with men, but what with television and movies, most of the girls were wise to the more obvious lines. Before he made his move, he wanted to be certain that she thought he was genuinely fond of her, and that there was a chance for a long-term relationship. If he could affect a romantic or tragic image, chances were she'd come across for him. He usually worked his way up over the course of three or four dates, but Laura Mroz had panicked when he had her half-undressed a few nights earlier, and he was still frustrated and tense. Barbara was a bit more self-confident than most girls he was used to—noticeably quieter and less willing to please, and he didn't want to push her too fast. At the same time he wanted badly to score tonight, to wipe out the bad taste of the earlier failure. It was unhealthy to get all excited as he'd been and then have no release. Everyone knew that. And besides, Jimmy hated failure, hated it with an intensity beyond all understanding.

He passed behind her now, but kept moving. She half-turned her head as though to follow him with her eyes, but then shifted her attention back to the cooling, tasteless clam cakes. She picked one up and bit into it nervously, but it tasted like cotton in her mouth and she set it aside. Conflicting emotions warred within her. Jimmy passed her and continued his slow circumambulation of the table.

"Do you want some more clam cakes? They're starting to get cold." Her voice was unsteady.

"No, not right now. I was just enjoying being alone at night with a pretty girl. And we seem to really hit it off together. I don't click with a lot of people. That's why I never have a steady girlfriend. None of them seem to really want to get to know me, to understand me. There never seems to be any real communication.''

Barbara had heard a different, less complimentary explanation. Most of the girls who had dated Jimmy had little or nothing good to say about him afterward. She knew several stories about his small cruelties, how selfish he was, how he was interested only in necking—or worse. Some of the girls wouldn't talk about him at all, and Muriel Bates had broken down in tears one time when his name came up. Barbara figured the stories were exaggerated. A lot of it was probably jealousy. A girl who lost such a good-looking guy as Jimmy would want people to think the problem was with him and not with her. He certainly seemed nice enough; she wanted him to be nice.

"I like you too, Jimmy," she offered at last, her eyes still downcast. "You're the nicest guy I've ever been out with." Which, considering how few he was competing with, was not much of a compliment.

Jimmy felt a little thrill of anticipatory victory and forced himself to continue his slow pacing. "No, I'm not. I make a lot of enemies. I've dated a lot of girls the last couple of years. Some of them were really nice, smart, pretty, a lot of fun to be with. But sooner or later I'd realize that they just weren't what I was looking for." He stopped and turned to face her. "I don't mean it was their fault or anything. But I'd say or do something foolish because I was mad at the situation, and pretty soon we'd split up. It was my fault most of the time, Barbara; I have to warn you about that right now. I can't say that I'm a great guy who's simply misunderstood by the world, but my life seems to be going by too fast and I keep looking for something I can't find. Sometimes I get so upset that I hit out at everything around me, and sometimes I hurt whoever's with me at the time."

He leaned on the end of the table, his own eyes down now, but sneaked a quick look from half-closed lids to measure the set of her shoulders, the tremor of her chin. Things appeared to be going quite well.

Barbara felt a rush of sympathy for the tall, broad-shouldered young man who now seemed so completely vulnerable. Can I really be what he's looking for, she wondered. She almost rose and went to him, but something rang just slightly untrue and she held back. It seemed there was a script for this evening, and she balked at acting predictably. She was still willing to be convinced of his sincerity, but the votes were not yet all in.

Jimmy had expected her to rise and come to him. When she didn't, when the silence extended too long, he felt a flash of rage. What was the bitch waiting for? His thoughts raced furiously while he regained his composure, then decided to turn the anger to his advantage.

"Damn it! Why am I this way? Why can't I be like the other guys and just look for fun on dates? Why do I always want something more, something serious, something that will last?" He spun around and rose, afraid that Barbara might see his half-smile. Carefully measuring his pace, he walked over to the wall of the building, placed his hands against it, head turned to look out across the darkened grounds. The moon had come out from behind a cloud and shadows flowed through the bushes and trees.

He waited, confident of his power over the girl, relishing the inevitability of her surrender. He felt her rise from the table and move to his side. With an enormous effort of will he refrained from turning when he felt her hand on his shoulder.

Barbara stumbled mentally as she sought the right words to bridge the gap between herself and what she believed to be a lonely, tormented soul. "I don't think there's anything wrong with you, Jimmy," she said, "although she did, in a way. Something still seemed not quite right about the situation. He turned his head toward her. "A lot of girls feel the same way, you know. They want dates because they get status from being seen with the right guys. They really don't care about him personally or what his problems are because they're too involved with their own. They're using the guy."

Although he'd rushed through his normal approach, Jimmy, growing even more impatient, decided to speed things up. He turned completely around and caught her firmly by the upper arms. "Barbara, I like you. I mean it; I really like you. But I don't want to be hurt, and I don't want to hurt you, either. If there's a chance you and I could get to mean something to each other, then I want us to take it, but I'm afraid of another disappointment. I'm tired of girls who want to stay girls all their lives and don't know what it is to be a woman. I'm tired of playing childish games with adult bodies. I want for us to mean more to each other than that."

Barbara felt giddy. It was happening exactly as she'd dreamed it might. A strong, attractive man was exposing his weakness to her, asking her to help him be strong, offering to share all that he was with her. The small alarm going off in the back of her brain was just a carryover from being a little girl, listening to scary stories, and she ignored it. "I don't want you to be disappointed, Jimmy. I like you . . . I like you a lot."

She swayed toward him, overcome briefly by her own romantic notions. And that's when he made his mistake.

Misjudging her mood, he moved one hand to gently caress her breast. He recognized his error almost immediately, could tell by the sudden tension, the change in her breathing, that she was frightened. He quickly reviewed his options. A stammered, guilty apology might result in another date, another opportunity, but all hopes for this evening would be shattered. He decided to press on; he could always insist that he'd been overcome by her presence and the poignancy of the moment. Later he could either promise never to see her again in expiation of his guilt, or arrange another tryst to prove that he loved her. He would have to play it by ear.

Leaning forward, he pressed his lips over hers, found her resistance was passive. He closed his hand more tightly on the breast, moved one leg forward, and started to slide his free hand to the small of her neck. Suddenly she shifted in his grasp and a burst of incredible pain flowered in his groin. The entire world seemed to grow fuzzy and recede from him. As if in slow motion, he fell backward, striking his back against a wooden bench, sliding down onto the ground. Barbara had driven one knee up sharply between his thighs.

Barbara stepped back, her hands clenched tightly together. Tears ran down her face, and she wasn't sure if it was fear or hurt that caused them . . . perhaps both. "You bastard," she said softly. "You filthy bastard!"

Jimmy caught his breath as he sat there, blinking away the pain, hands clutched on his kneecaps. "Stupid bitch!" he gasped, all hopes of seduction now dashed. "What the hell do you think you're doing? Who the hell do you think you are?"

She took two steps back. "Everything you said was just a line, wasn't it? You were never really interested in me at all, were you, except to get me to give in to you?"

Blind fury made even his pain seem insignificant. "Of course not. Why would I be interested in someone like you? I just didn't have any other pussy lined up for the night and yours was available. I was pretty hard up, obviously, or I wouldn't have given you a second look, but I thought you might like being a real woman for one night. I didn't realize you were still just a *kid*." He made the last word seem like a damning insult.

She opened her mouth, but what emerged was half-cry, half-growl. She glanced quickly from side to side, then rushed to the table, picked up the remains of their meal, and threw it at him.

"What the hell?" He threw up his hands to ward off the fusillade of clam cakes and french fries.

"Everything they said about you was true! More than true!" She backed away again. "You're a monster!"

"You're really a jerk, you know that?" he answered. She turned and started to walk rapidly away and he raised his voice, determined that she'd not escape unscathed. "You might as well have had the fun. Everyone knows you went out with me tonight, and everyone knows what happens when I have a chance to operate. And you can be sure that I'll tell everybody you were a lousy lay, even though, much to my surprise, you turned out not to be cherry after all." But by then she was gone and there was no point in going on.

It was quite a while before the pain had subsided enough for him to raise himself to his feet and walk unsteadily back toward the library. He felt lightheaded and he stopped for a brief rest, leaning against the cold stone of the tower. With one hand against the wall for support, he made his way around the curve, glancing up, curious to see if he could locate the carved gargoyle that he suddenly remembered from years past. Sure enough, there it was, just to one side of him, crouched against the wall below the narrow window. It didn't seem to be quite in the same position as he remembered it, but then it had been a good number of years since he'd been here last, and it was so dark that he really couldn't see much. Jimmy had never even been in the library when it was open. Books were for people who were willing to let others tell them about life; Jimmy planned to find out all those things for himself. That was the only way to know whether or not they were really true, to experience them directly and personally.

The gargoyle stared lifelessly down at him, barely visible in the darkness, a smug, contented smile on its distorted face. "How're you doing, old buddy?" Nicholson called. "Get laid lately?" He chuckled thinly while the gargoyle remained predictably silent. "Yeah," Jimmy said at last, becoming more serious as he turned away. "Neither did I. Let's hope we both have better luck in the future."

He wanted to leave at that point, but something held him on the spot and he looked back up. Funny, he thought, how that damned statue seemed to be staring directly into his mind, and how he could sense that vision even in the darkness. Don't be silly, he told himself, and turned away once more, heading back toward the parking lot.

"See you around, buddy," he muttered under his breath.

That night, Jimmy tossed restlessly in his bed, finally dropping off to sleep quite late. As the hours stretched

133

toward dawn, he began to dream, an erotic scene in which he was courted by a bevy of beautiful women while Barbara Howell remained in one corner tied to a tree, begging Jimmy to take her as well, to strip the clothes from her body and ravish her. But he merely smiled and occupied himself with the other women, even when she wept piteously and begged him to make love to her. And all through the dream, the gargoyle, freed from its imprisonment on the mansion wall, stood to one side, observing it all with grave satisfaction. He sensed that it wanted to join in, but couldn't. At least not yet.

Ron Joslin had transferred to Managansett High during his freshman year, when his family had moved from Wallingford, Connecticut, because of his father's promotion and transfer within the Executron Corporation, a medium-sized conglomerate which had purchased several companies in the Providence area over the years, enough of a concentration that they had moved their general headquarters from Reading, Pennsylvania, up to Boston a decade earlier.

Ron was a quiet boy, a bit of a bookworm, but he was also moderately if unenthusiastically athletic. Now, as he looked ahead to being a sophomore, he planned to try out for the track team. He had few friends in town, and most were considerably younger. The seniors, the juniors, and even the boys in his own grade seemed a coarser lot than he was used to—louder, less disciplined. Ron was intelligent enough to suspect that a part of this was his perception of strangers, a group of which he was not an integral unit, rather than an objective difference, but he nevertheless felt it difficult to warm up to even the occasional slight overture that had been made in his direction.

But during the course of the summer, while out running behind the high school, he had met Barbara Howell. Despite their mutual shyness, they had quickly become good friends, though they had yet to do anything together that they actually might have called a date. The two of them had started running together on a regular schedule, each planning to try out for the school track team when classes resumed. Ron found Barbara to be quite talkative once she had gotten used to him, and he usually let her carry the conversation. Although he had to admit that she wasn't the prettiest girl he had ever seen, her appearance was pleasant, her smile was definitely infectious, and even a short time in her presence was enough to bring him out of his occasional gloomy moods. For her part, Barbara thought that Ron was the greatest thing that had ever happened to Managansett High, a quiet, intelligent, studious boy who wasn't a complete dork, good-looking in an intense, dark fashion, and possessed of the singular virtue of finding her interesting company. She had decided by their third meeting that she was in love with him and was already planning their eventual wedding and family.

They had their first date on the last weekend before school was scheduled to resume. It had taken Ron a long time to work up the courage, and he had stammered out the invitation just as they were about to separate after their routine morning run. "Listen, Barbara, if you're not doing anything, do you want to see a movie tonight?"

"Sure," she replied without a pause. She had been waiting for this moment for weeks, had rehearsed replies for an enormous variety of situations. "What's playing?"

Ron hadn't really thought about that and strained to remember what was written on the Community Theater marquee. "I think it's a scary one. *Plan Nine from Outer Space,* or something like that."

"Sounds like fun to me—I like the creepy ones. What time?"

Greatly relieved, Ron made arrangements to call her after he'd checked the starting time. They each lived within a half-dozen blocks of the theater, so they agreed to walk, even though Ron was certain he could've borrowed the family car.

Their date went quite well, despite the ineptness of the film, so bad at points that they were doubled over with laughter, whispering to each other as particularly cogent criticisms insisted upon being expressed immediately. Things didn't turn bad until the movie had ended and they were on their way out of the theater.

A tall, muscular boy stood in the lobby, talking to one of the ushers. He looked familiar to Ron—probably someone at the high school whom he had yet to meet. The figure was more familiar to Barbara. She had not seen or heard from Jimmy Nicholson since school had ended, and had no intention of seeing him now.

"Come on, Ron ... Let's go."

Ron could tell that Barbara was upset, although he had as yet no hint of the cause, and he followed her toward the front doors. But Jimmy had spotted them as well, and he stepped forward and called out to them.

"Hey, Barb—who's the stud?" His mocking tone was obvious, even to the strangers who surrounded them in the lobby.

Ron paused, puzzled by the animosity in the other boy's tone, but Barbara caught him by the sleeve and pulled him toward the door. "Ron, I want to leave, right now."

"Okay," he answered, but he watched the other as long as he could until they were outdoors.

Standing on the sidewalk, Barbara relaxed slightly but still looked upset and worried to him. "What's the matter, Barbara?" he asked.

"Oh, nothing really." She was lying, he knew it; and she knew he knew it. "We don't exactly like each other," she gestured with a toss of her chin toward the theater. "It's a long story. I'll tell you about it sometime."

Ron might have asked more, but at that moment Jimmy Nicholson left the theater, saw the two of them, and crossed to where they stood. Barbara moved closer to Ron's side, and he decided that he didn't much like Jimmy, though he rather enjoyed being cast in the role of a protector.

"Barbara, why'd you run off?" Jimmy looked back and forth between the two. "Don't I rate an introduction?"

"I'm Ron Joslin," Ron said, moving to interpose himself more completely between the two. He did not offer to shake hands. "Nice to have met you. We're in a bit of a hurry." And he took Barbara's arm and started to lead her off.

"Yes, I can imagine you are," Nicholson called after them. "Barbara's often in a hurry; she's quite fast company, in fact." He grinned unpleasantly, then winked, as though implying some secret knowledge between himself and Ron. "I've had some trouble keeping up to her in the past myself, and I've been around."

Ron glanced quickly at his companion, saw the hint of a tear shining on one cheek. Furious, not really sure what was going on or why, he stopped and turned back to the older boy. "I don't know what your problem is," he said levelly, "but take it somewhere else, all right?"

Jimmy just looked amused, but Barbara pulled Ron

137

away. "Just ignore him, please. He's bad news and he's not worth the effort."

The two turned off Main Street and started north, heading toward Barbara's home. They had only gone two blocks when a car moved up to pace them, the driver's window rolled down. "So long, Barbara," Nicholson's voice called. "Remember what I taught you." And the car began to pull away.

Without a moment's hesitation, Ron stooped, picked up a loose stone, and flipped it sidearm after the car. With a faint crack, it bounced off the rear window and caromed into the darkness. Nicholson immediately hit his breaks, stopped, then pulled to the side of the road. He was standing there, having checked his unbroken rear window carefully, when Barbara and Ron reached that point a few seconds later.

"Okay, sport." Nicholson stepped forward, lifted his arms, and pushed Ron sharply in the chest. "You want to be a hero, you got to pay the dues."

"Go away, Jimmy Nicholson!" Barbara was ashamed of the panic in her voice, apparent even to her. "You started it. Now it's finished. Just leave us alone!"

"Oh, no. It's never finished until the credits roll up. You just came from the movies; you should know that."

"Listen, Nicholson," Ron moved to interpose himself once more. "I don't know you and I don't want to know you. Let's just forget we ran into each other and save both of us the hassle."

Nicholson's eyes shifted back to Ron. "I never forget, hero." His voice was cold, uninflected, firm and confident. "And I never lose." He glanced meaningfully at Barbara. "Sometimes it takes me a while to even the score, but I always end up ahead before the game is over." And with-

138

out further warning, he turned and swung a fist that caught Ron on the side of the head, knocking him sprawling over the curb and into the street.

Ron rolled over onto his hands and knees and rose quickly, his own fists ready now. Nicholson danced forward, his arms moving rapidly, caught and deflected a couple of unskilled punches, and swung again. Ron doubled over as one blow pounded his ribs, but never saw the second one directed straight at his chin. The next thing he knew, he was lying on his back on the sidewalk, trying to catch his breath.

Barbara reached forward and grabbed Nicholson by the arm, but he brushed her back, then raised a fist as though to dispose of her in the same fashion. At the last moment his anger cooled and he contented himself with kicking his fallen opponent lightly in the thigh.

"She's all yours, hero," he said finally. "I already had her, and she's not good enough to fight over." With a last glance in her direction, Nicholson climbed into his car and roared off into the night.

If Barbara Howell had never quite forgotten the day her idol had tried to get her to smoke forbidden cigarettes over at the Sheffield mansion, then neither had Valerie Meredith forgotten the little twerp who'd refused to do as she was told that day. But Valerie had ambitious plans for herself, and a busy social group to keep in order, and she rarely spared thought for her enemies so long as they kept well out of her way. From time to time she'd been forced to take drastic measures, as in the case of Lynn Hadley, for example, but she was patient. There would be a time and a place, she knew, in which she could exact her revenge on Barbara Howell ... just as she would even the score with everyone else who had displeased her.

The opportunity appeared to have arisen during this, Valerie's final year at high school. Barbara seemed to have acquired a boyfriend over the summer, a new boy at school. He was only a sophomore, but tall for his age, and good-looking. Valerie set the standards of conduct for her set rather than having to abide by them, so she knew she'd lose no status by showing interest in the younger boy. He'd probably be boring, but she planned to drop him as soon as she'd made her point, in any case.

For the first two weeks of school, Valerie contented herself with observing the situation, making plans, laying the groundwork. She watched how the two of them acted together, even casually, noticed that while they didn't exactly avoid each other, they rarely touched, and certainly not with the possessive intimacy that she'd have expected if they were actually having sex together, or even doing some heavy petting. That's about what she'd have expected from Barbara, anyway. Miss Virtue of 1960, thought Valerie. Probably thinks her shit doesn't stink.

The humiliation must be total, she thought—incontrovertible and public. Most of all, it must be public. There had not been an opportunity for Valerie to demonstrate her power lately, and some of her cohorts were a bit restive at times. If she could break up this little twosome, she'd get her revenge and whip the troops into shape, all with a single move. And the kid wasn't half-bad-looking besides, she thought.

Two days later, Valerie began spreading the word about a party she was going to throw in celebration of the beginning of her senior year. It was going to be catered, with a live band in from Providence, and it was the first party she had ever given at her parents' newly completed home. There were going to be written invitations, and a very limited number of invitees. Everyone was put on notice that only those most loyal to Valerie Meredith would be asked to attend.

Valerie let a week go by without any further information, just mysterious references to the elaborate preparations. She'd had no difficulty talking her father into it. Not only did he consider his daughter the greatest person in the world; he was determined to compensate for what he interpreted as her mother's embarrassing weakness, her dependency on drink and tranquilizers. Helen Meredith was currently "taking a vacation," her father's euphemism for her increasingly frequent trips to a refuge for alcoholics.

The date of the party was set for two weeks after when the invitations went into the mail. Valerie hadn't bothered to request RSVPs; she knew no one would decline the invitation. With great care she had invited only established couples. Now only the final step needed to be taken.

During the previous weeks she had arranged to be introduced casually to Ron Joslin, had subsequently taken great pains to occasionally show up where he was likely to be, though avoiding approaching him when Barbara was around. So far as Barbara knew, Ron and Valerie had never even met. But now it was time to lower the boom.

School had just ended, and everyone who walked home migrated en masse to the front lawns, where plans for the evening were generally made. Valerie knew that Ron and Barbara met here almost every day, walking home together or occasionally taking a side trip to the Friendly's across from the school. That's where they were today, talking to a small group of their friends, when Valerie walked over to Ron, pretending not to know that he was with Barbara.

"Hi, Ron. I was looking all over for you."

"Hi, Valerie." Ron broke into a silly smile. Fond as he was of Barbara, he felt quite flattered that the most popular girl in school would come looking for him, although he hadn't the faintest idea why. "What's up?" He failed to notice the venomous look in Barbara's eyes when she turned in their direction.

Valerie raised a slender hand and placed it on Ron's arm possessively. "It's the silliest thing," she said, leaning forward, hoping he would be quick enough to look down the front of her dress and clumsy enough that Barbara would catch him at it. "You know about this party I'm giving?"

Ron nodded, unsure what was coming next. "Sure. Everyone's been talking about it."

"Well, I've been so busy with the preparations, sending out invitations, arranging for the band, doing up the decorations, that I forgot one very important thing." She put her free hand on her hip and angled her leg away from him, the skirt riding up over her knee. She watched covertly to make sure his eyes moved appropriately, allowed him a second or two of voyeurism, before shifting so that his eyes came back to meet her own. "I forgot to get myself a date."

This was the crucial point. She had to rush him into answer before he had time to think, and before Barbara had a chance to become a factor in his decision. "It occurred to me that you're new in town and haven't had much of a chance to meet people, and you're kind of cute, too." She moistened her lips with her tongue. "So I thought you might be willing to come along to keep me company, and I could introduce you to the gang. It'll be a lot of fun, and you'd be doing me a good deed." She gave him a blatantly sly look. "I'd owe you a big favor if you'd do this for me—and I always pay my debts." She allowed Barbara to catch her eye as she said this last, hoping she'd know it was intended for her benefit.

Ron looked distinctly uncomfortable, and she could see his eyes veering off to where Barbara stood, shocked into silence. Valerie was pleased with herself. Ron would have to accept right in front of Barbara; there was no way out. Even if he tried to defer his answer, even if she'd let him get away with it, Barbara would eventually know he'd gone to the party as her date. It never occurred to Valerie that Ron might turn her down. She'd never been faced with refusal, and she had no intention of starting now.

"Uh, I'm really flattered, Valerie, but I already have plans for that evening ... you know how it is."

She was ready for this. "Can't you change them, Ron? I mean, if you have a date or something, you can put it off, can't you? This party is going to be really special for me, and I want you to be a part of it."

Ron looked to Barbara before continuing, and now his voice was stronger, less hesitant. "I'm sorry, Valerie, but I just can't do it. I'm sure there's lots of guys who'd want to go with you. You don't need me."

Valerie felt the situation beginning to slip away from her. "Ron, I don't understand ... are you going to let some sophomore date for a movie and a soda keep you away from my party? I think I'm being insulted, don't you? I mean, I'm trying to help you get to know people here in town and fit in with everyone, and you don't seem to appreciate it at all."

"I'm sorry, Valerie, but I just can't come to your party.

I'm kind of going steady." This time he looked quite openly at Barbara.

Valerie wanted to hit him, to claw out his eyes, to pull every hair from his head, to rip off his balls and stuff them in his mouth. but it would not do to lose her temper here, not in public, not in such a way that it would confirm that she'd been thwarted ... better to save her revenge for another time and place.

"All right, Ron," she said softly, but with unveiled menace, and now she cast a glance in Barbara's direction as well. "But I won't forget how you snubbed me. You remember that. You remember it real good."

And she spun on her heel and was gone.

CHAPTER SIX
1963

Arthur Kaplan stumbled over the bucket of water he had placed conveniently to one side, lurching off balance. One arm rose to ward off the sink, but he misjudged the distance and struck the rim with his elbow rather than with the palm of his hand. A brilliant pain lanced up his arm, piercing the alcoholic fog that he felt helped make this boring job a bit more bearable.

"Shit!" he screamed, grabbing his forearm as though to squeeze away the sensation. He regained some semblance of equilibrium, straightened up, then lashed out with his foot. The bucket jumped away, some of the soapy warm water sloshing onto the floor, but the wheels on the bottom kept it upright and it skittered across the floor, banging against the cracked tile wall of the Managansett Town Hall men's room.

It had become his habit these past few years to eat his lunch at the Main Street Grill, one block from the hall, a bar and game room that offered a limited variety of sandwiches. Most of the time he had only a beer or two, but sometimes he just had to have something stronger, something that could make him forget his dead-end job. Even as recently as three years before, with his son Keith only two years old, the promotion to full janitor had seemed a significant change in his life. But now Keith was starting school at the age of five and his sister Jeri was three. Arthur had come to the realization that this was it, this was all there was in his life. Although he received a small annual raise from the city, there was effectively no place for him to go in his job. His immediate superior was Edgar Catterall, assistant to the town manager, an appointed position to which Arthur could never hope to aspire.

The pain subsided into a numb ache and he flexed the muscle slowly. "The hell with this," he muttered, retrieving his mop and quickly spreading the spilled water about so that it wasn't quite so obvious. Leaving the rest of the floor pretty much as he had found it, he pushed the bucket into the hall, allowing the door to swing shut behind him.

The corridor seemed to sway as he moved a bit too quickly, and he extended a hand to the wall to steady himself, his eyes closed as he tried to regain control. That was a mistake as well, for with his eyes shut, the entire world seemed to start to spin around him, accelerating quickly. He snapped his eyes back open and the feeling dissipated, but it left him shaking. The two brandies at lunch were not responsible; it was the bottle he had brought back and hidden in the utility room in the basement. For some reason this had been a particularly arduous day, and he'd felt the need to sneak back for a bracer a bit more often than ever before. Now he was having difficulty physically getting through the workday.

"What's the problem, Kaplan?" Arthur's head snapped around. Edgar Catterall stood directly in front of him, his lips set firmly.

"Sorry, sir." He struggled to stand erect unaided and

managed to do so with only the slightest hesitation. "I'm not feeling very well today. I think I'm coming down with some kind of virus. Feel kind of dizzy."

Catterall did not look sympathetic. "I'd say the problem was a lot more specific than that, Kaplan. I don't want to hear any more complaints about you, understand? You're skating on thin ice around here lately. Do your drinking after hours and we'll both be a lot happier."

More than anything Arthur wanted to lash out at that smug, disapproving face. Catterall had recently replaced Bill Rhine, who had taken a job working for the city of Cranston. Arthur and Rhine had an understanding of sorts; Rhine was more interested in the appearance of an efficient organization than in the actuality, and he was willing to overlook the occasional lapses of concentration or sobriety of an employee who would cooperate in the unofficial requisitioning of certain supplies, the diversion of selected small discretionary funds, and similar practices. But Catterall was a strict taskmaster, believing in ironclad policies and schedules, and a bear for discipline.

"I do my job. No one complains about my areas."

"That may have been true once, but it certainly hasn't been the case lately. There have been several comments about the cleanliness of the rest rooms, the conference room was not swept in time for the council meeting last month, and the lawn should have been cut last week."

"I wasn't told about the meeting, and the grass at the library took the crew all week."

"The meeting was posted, as you well know. The bulletin board is there for your benefit, too. And the library grass could have waited. Now that it's closed again, it only needs to be kept reasonably well. Once a month is sufficient."

147

Arthur felt his hands clenching into fists and tried to rein in his growing anger. "If we only go out there once a month, it's going to look like hell!"

"Then let it! Damn it, Kaplan, you don't set policy around here. You're the janitor, not the town manager. And if you don't control your drinking, you won't even be that for much longer."

Catterall turned away, apparently wanting to disengage from the conversation, but Arthur was less inhibited than usual, eight shots of brandy having loosened his tongue. "I don't drink except on my own time, at lunch," he lied. "You've got no business dictating what I do in my personal time."

Catterall stopped and half-turned in his direction. "I don't care whether you drink at lunch, on your coffee break, or as part of your breakfast. What I care about is your job performance, and your performance lately has been piss-poor. Maybe it's related to your drinking and maybe it isn't, but whatever the cause, you'd better solve it and solve it quickly, because there's no room in this organization for drunks. If there are any more complaints, I'm going to have to take steps, understand?" And he turned away once more.

It's not certain what Arthur planned to do. Certainly he moved forward as though to follow his boss, perhaps to argue further, perhaps even to actually strike him. Even Arthur didn't know for certain. He was angry enough that a physical attack was not out of the question. But whatever he had planned, consciously or unconsciously, was thwarted by his own unsteadiness and the presence of the unlucky bucket. This time, when his foot struck its side, he was unable to regain his balance. The bucket flew in one direction, spraying soapy water in a wide swathe that soaked

Catterall's pants legs from the ankles halfway up the calves, while Arthur himself fell heavily onto his back, stunning himself, arms and legs spread wide, the breath exploding from his lungs, the dizziness returning with a vengeance.

He was not in the best of moods when he returned home that evening. Although he'd avoided his secret bottle for the rest of the day, the look of contempt in Catterall's eyes as he'd stalked off silently had burned itself into Arthur's mind. Immediately after punching out for the day, he'd made an unusual extra stop at the Main Street Grill, tossed down two quick whiskeys, then set off to walk the six blocks to the small apartment he and Edith had rented shortly after their marriage. Edith had been after him to move to a bigger place ever since the birth of their daughter, Jeri. Keith was in the spare bedroom now, and the baby's crib was in their own room, but soon other arrangements would have to be made and Edith was opposed to having siblings of opposite genders sharing a room.

He slowly climbed the stairs to the second floor, one hand firmly gripping the bannister. Despite the alcohol, or perhaps because of it, his head hurt fiercely, and this frightened him. Whenever he suffered a headache in the evening, whenever he was angry or upset or worried, the dream would come, almost the very same dream he had experienced for the first time in his early adulthood, after seeing that strange statue out at the Sheffield mansion, now known as the library. He would be attempting to accomplish something, climbing a mountain or cutting down a tree, or performing some other relatively easy task, and he would fail, fail miserably and inexplicably. When he looked around, that hideous figure would be there, staring at him with utter contempt. It was then that Arthur would think of himself as a failure, a hopeless incompetent, a lost

149

and pitiful soul beyond all hope of redemption. Each time he woke from the dream incredibly depressed, often feeling that suicide was his only option, although to date he had managed to resist its blandishments. But the recurrent dream had a compelling power over him, and since his position required that he schedule maintenance to the grounds of all town property, he had used this authority to ensure that the library grounds received priority treatment whenever possible. It was a form of propitiation, although he would never have recognized it as such, or admitted to it had it been brought to his attention. To Arthur, it was simply something that felt right, appropriate, necessary.

He reached the door to his apartment and hesitated. Even from outside he could hear a thin wail as young Jeri complained about something or other. Straightening his back as best he could, he grasped the doorknob, opening the door and entering the apartment.

"Oh, *there* you are!" Edith did not sound pleased.

"I got tied up," he growled. "Had some things to do before I could leave work."

Edith sat in her bathrobe on their badly worn couch, a half-filled glass of beer in one hand. Jeri was standing in her playpen, angrily demanding to be taken out. Keith was nowhere in sight; he had never quite adjusted to the presence of a fourth member of the family, and while not exactly hostile, he seemed ambivalent about the existence of a sister, and he was uncertain how he should act.

Arthur closed the door and tried to walk casually into the kitchen to see what had been done about supper. He thought he'd handled it quite well, but Edith must have picked up on something, a lack of rhythm in his step, or perhaps the slightly unfocused look in his eyes, because she called to him.

"If you have to drink, you could at least do it at home. It costs less."

Arthur froze in mid-step, then deliberately continued. Edith had changed during the ten years of their marriage, had become stronger as he had weakened—more dominant, more willing to challenge his authority as head of the family. Lacking a strong role model during his own youth, he was uncertain how he should be reacting to this, but everything he thought he knew about the relationship between men and women said that it should be him calling the shots, not her. But more and more frequently it was Edith who decided what would and would not be purchased, what they would do on weekends, how the children would be disciplined, and where the furniture, such as it was, would be placed. She had named both the children, and while he had no objection to Keith, he thought Jeri was a stupid name for a girl. But Edith had been adamant about it.

Two hotdogs lay half immersed in oily-looking water in a shallow pan on the stove, their sides burst open from internal pressure venting itself. The burner had been turned off and the hotdogs were lukewarm to the touch. A package of rolls and a bottle of yellow mustard stood on the counter.

Arthur sighed, his stomach churning at the thought of greasy food, and he turned to the refrigerator instead, extracting what appeared to be the last can of beer.

"You can heat up the dogs if you want." Edith stood at the doorway, glass of beer in one hand. "You ought to let me know if you're not going to be home on time. It is just simple courtesy."

"Look, Edith, I don't want to hear it, all right?" He found that if he talked very slowly and distinctly, he did not slur his words. "I had a bad day. You don't know what's it like," he paused, "what it's like having a bad day at work. You don't have to put up with some bastard like Catterall who doesn't understand priorities, doesn't know how much work there is keeping everything done on schedule." He popped open the beer can and drank deeply. "The bastard's always on my case about one thing or another. I think he's trying to find an excuse to fire me."

"Well, then you'd better be real careful about what you do, Arthur," she said without the slightest indication of sympathy. "We can't afford to have you out of work right now. When we didn't have the kids to worry about, I might have gone out and found a job of my own, but now I have to stay here with them. Unless," she added contemptuously, "you'd rather stay home with them while I go out and make a living."

Just at that moment, Edith's face almost seemed to writhe and change like a malevolent demon, took on the appearance of that face out of his own dreams and memories, and for a few seconds the gargoyle stood at the kitchen door, an expression of sarcasm etched in every feature. Arthur's arm moved of its own volition and the beer can flew across the room.

"Get out of here!" Arthur waved his arm, dispelling the vision immediately. Edith stood as before, but now her expression was one of shock and growing anger. The can had gone over her shoulder into the room beyond, but a wide stain across the front of her robe indicated where the missile had discharged its contents.

"What the hell is wrong with you?" She shouted at him

finally, violating her own admonition that no harsh language be used in front of the children. "You almost hit me with that goddamned can! What the hell do you think you're doing?"

Arthur wanted to say something, open his mouth twice, but no words came. How could he explain to her, to this stranger he had married but never known, and who had changed so completely in the intervening decade, in any case? How explain the growing sense of dread, of hopelessness and helplessness, that was becoming more and more a factor in his life? They remained in a silent tableau for quite some time, communicating no more now than they had in the past, two utter strangers who had discovered that they were married to each other.

In June 1963, Barbara Howell married Ron Joslin. Theirs had been the kind of relationship that was generally believed to exist only in the movies, a meeting of souls and minds that seemed to slide through all adversity effortlessly. Despite the ostracism of the high school in-crowd and of their contemporaries, most of whom wished someday to join the elite, their friendship had flourished, and finally developed into what they both concluded was true love.

Ron worked part-time and attended a small business college in Providence taking a reduced credit load. Barbara lived at home and worked full-time in the order department at Eblis Manufacturing. The job paid the minimum wage and wasn't particularly demanding, but it was the first time she'd ever had access to so much money of her own, and she told herself it was really just temporary.

Their engagement was a mutual agreement, the acting

out of an inevitability, and one evening they informed both sets of parents that they were tentatively setting a wedding date. There were expressions of mutual delight on all sides, and the truth was that the Howells had been very nervous about their daughter's future ... not that there was anything really wrong with her, they assured themselves, but she was so withdrawn, unsocial, and wrapped up in her own insecurities. It was only with Ron that she seemed to open up, and they could not have been happier with the proposed arrangement. Ron's parents were almost as enthusiastic. Barbara had never been shy in their presence, and Ron's father had secretly decided that when the boy really grew up, he would go into business and become an executive. He believed Barbara would make the perfect executive wife, even more so than his own partner of thirty years of marriage.

The college required that all freshmen live in the dormitories, and the wedding was to take place just after classes ended. Ron and Barbara had found an apartment in Managansett, not far from the Sheffield library, so that Barbara would be close to her job and Ron only three blocks from a bus stop that would take him into the city for classes. It was, in fact, the same apartment that Alex Furtado had been unable to rent some years before. There had been some talk of their moving into the vacant rooms at Barbara's aunt's house, but Edna Howell Mackey had become very ill that year, so ill that a permanent live-in nurse had been settled in those rooms. Barbara's mother had told her quietly that Aunt Edna would probably not live more than a couple of years.

Barbara was obviously intelligent and willing to help out wherever necessary, so from time to time she was loaned to other departments when people were absent or unusual fluctuations in workload caused difficulties. Frequently this meant that she was assigned to work directly with the office manager, Henry Wood, who used her as a floating clerk. On one such occasion, she had an unpleasant encounter in the factory.

"Barbara, could you do me a favor?" One thing she liked about Henry Wood was that he always phrased his instructions as requests, occasionally asked her opinion about how things were to be handled, and generally gave her a free hand to accomplish whatever tasks he assigned her in whatever manner seemed most efficient to her. Although Barbara was polite, even friendly, to everyone she had dealt with in management, Mr. Wood was the only one she honestly liked.

They were working in his office. The company fiscal year had ended in June and now, two months later, they were sorting out the previous year's files for retention, storage, or destruction. There seemed to be an endless supply of invoices, memos, reports of actions taken or reports indicating that action was necessary, and a lot more that should never have remained in his office in the first place. Henry Wood seemed always to save everything until the last possible moment, and his usual reorganization of the filing system usually resulted in boxes of paperwork being transferred to other offices that should have had them in the first place, to people who would now be faced with arranging their ultimate disposition.

"I just came across the original contract with Mancini Metals that the quality control people have been looking for. Can you run this up to them now before I misplace it again?"

Barbara looked dubious. "I've never really been out in
155

the factory before, Mr. Wood. I don't have the faintest idea where their offices are."

"One office, way in the back, on the mezzanine level. It's easy to find; all you have to do is follow the lines painted on the floor." He proceeded to give her directions.

It was certainly easy enough to find if you had some idea of the layout of the manufacturing floor. What Henry Wood did not realize was that, faced with painted lines forking in two directions, Barbara would make the apparently logical assumption that the wider lane was the main route. In this case she was wrong; the wider travel space was to accommodate material handling equipment delivering coils of brass or copper to the appropriate punch presses, or removing completed skids of stampings.

She walked directly past a blank section of floor space which had formerly been Mr. Wilson's office. A series of heart attacks had forced Wilson to take early retirement a year before, and his replacement, Frank Cataldo, had taken a far different approach to management. One of his first acts had been to tear down the glass-lined office and replace it with a roughly finished but more private one located near the loading docks. Cataldo considered that the most strategic location; if he could watch everything coming into the factory, it would provide a feel for the workload that was every bit as important as the facts and figures provided by the fledgeling production control department that management had recently added, taking advantage of the transition between factory managers.

Barbara still had no idea that she'd taken the wrong turn, but when she reached the far wall, she was faced with yet another decision: the pathway now branched to her left and right, with no indication of which route she should travel. Either Mr. Wood forgot to tell me about this place, she thought to herself, or I took a wrong turn somewhere along the way. Undecided, she glanced in each direction. The lane to her right seemed to end at a set of overhead doors; surely that was wrong. To her left, it passed several punch presses, most of which were currently in operation; the noise level was so loud that she couldn't imagine how the operators could stand it. But further along there appeared to be another intersection, and perhaps that was the way she should have gone. In any case, it looked promising, and perhaps she would at least find someone who could give her fresh instructions. If all else failed, she'd ask one of the workers, even though there was a kind of unwritten rule that the office people didn't speak to anyone in the factory except people in management.

It was just as she was passing the first press that she noticed something peculiar ahead. The next press in line was one of the bigger ones, a colossal mass of metal dominated by a pair of solid columns to either side, much of the operating machinery open to view. But as she drew near, she could see that it had been painted heavily in sombre colors, unlike most of the others, which were antiseptically bright and cheery. There seemed, in fact, to be some pattern to the browns and dark greens and black, and she moved to the other side of the aisle as she drew abreast so she could see the entire painting. It was a monstrous face, she saw, a grinning, leering caricature of a human visage, with various features of the press itself emphasized or camouflaged to increase the resemblance. It was, as a matter of fact, a masterful job, well conceived and executed, totally frightening, almost seeming to be a living thing.

She stopped, mesmerized, and moved to stand directly

between the two columns. Although the press was not in operation, it almost seemed to her that the face changed somewhat as she stood there, the smile becoming more knowing, the eyes narrowing in a slight increase of malevolence and wry amusement. For reasons she could not explain even to herself, she felt utterly terrified, personally threatened, in fear for her very life.

"Whadda you want here?"

Barbara jumped at the sound of the voice, for a split second almost believing that the press itself had spoken to her. But it was instead a short, heavy-set hirsute man in filthy coveralls who'd emerged from the back of the press with an enormous crescent wrench in one hand. His face was smeared with grease, his hands and forearms so black that the looked as if they'd been plunged into paint.

"I said, whadda you want?" He glared at her, demanding an answer.

"Oh, I'm sorry . . . I think I'm lost. I'm looking for Mr. Paruti's office. You know, quality control."

The man held her eyes for a moment, then looked away, grabbing a filthy rag and wiping his hands, probably picking up as much additional grease as he was cleaning off. "It's not around here," he said at last, his tone sullen.

"I know. I think I got lost. Can you tell me where it is?"

"I don't know." He turned back to the press, ran his hand along one column for a moment, almost caressingly. Barbara found the action disgusting and was annoyed at herself for what she imagined to be a snobbish reaction. After all, this was one of the men who did the real work, made the product. She had no right to feel superior just because she worked in the office and kept herself clean.

"Is there any office around here? Somewhere I can get directions?"

But the man was already disappearing at the rear of the press and whatever mysterious duty he was taking care of in that dark recess. Barbara shrugged and turned away, almost running into the tall, dark-haired man who'd approached from her blind side.

"Oh, I'm sorry." She stepped back, hoping that she was not really blushing.

The tall man seemed amused. "That's all right, but you ought to be careful out here. Why *are* you out here, as a matter of fact?"

The friendly tone reassured her. "I'm trying to find Mr. Paruti's office. I'm supposed to deliver this and I think I got lost." She showed him the packet of papers she was carrying.

"Lost is right. You're headed almost directly away from him. Come on, I'll show you the right way. You are ... ?"

"Barbara, Barbara Howell. I mean Joslin. I just got married." She cast one look back at the press as they moved away, and at that horrible face, and shivered just a bit.

"Sure is ugly, isn't it?" The man still seemed amused. "Alex takes better care of that press than most people take care of their families, though. Won't let anyone else touch it, and he's the most productive man we've got. He's not any too charming, but he's harmless." He led her to the first intersection. "Follow this straight across until you can't go any further, then turn left. Keep the wall to your right and you'll eventually come to a staircase that leads up to the mezzanine. John Paruti is in the third office; the name's on the door."

Barbara thanked him and disappeared. Frank Cataldo watched her go. A nice kid, he thought, kind of cute. Too cute to be wandering around the factory. She wouldn't come to any harm, but it was a distraction to have attractive young women walking about on the production floor. He started back the way he'd come and stopped in front of Alex Furtado's press. Furtado was crouched behind it, tightening some of the settings, ignoring Cataldo's presence.

Cataldo had thought about having the press repainted on more than one occasion. There had been a number of unofficial complaints about it, and while not a superstitious man, Cataldo had to admit a certain degree of uneasiness when he stood in front of it. The operators assigned to nearby presses regularly requested transfers to other equipment, sometimes even other departments. But none of the complaints had been made officially; most of Furtado's fellow workers seemed slightly uncertain of him, even afraid at times, and without an official reason to do so, Cataldo was unwilling to chance a confrontation with his most productive employee. But sometimes he wished he could think of a valid reason to order the painting's removal. It just didn't seem healthy.

"Are you all right, Peter?" Uncle Bill had walked silently over and placed a hand on Peter DiPaoli's shoulder in a gesture that was meant to be reassuring, but which only served to emphasize to the teenager how much his situation had changed.

"I'll be okay." He didn't sound like he believed it, he wasn't certain that he could, any more than he could really believe that his parents were gone, both killed almost instantly when a drunken driver jumped the curb and hit them head on.

His uncle's hand moved away as he walked into the back bedroom, looking around to see that everything had been taken out. By the terms of their will, Peter's parents had made his mother's brother and his wife Peter's legal guardians. They were childless, and he was sure that they felt this to be an imposition for which they were not ready, but they had shown no resentment toward Peter. The truth was that in some ways they actually looked forward to his company. Uncle Bill had flown out the day after the accident, transferring most of his cases to other members of the law firm of which he was a senior partner, rearranging the others as best he could. Aunt Jeanne had followed two days later, but had to get back on Monday because of the hectic workload at the advertising firm where she'd worked her way up to copy chief.

Peter had remained in a daze as arrangements were made for the wake and the funeral. Uncle Bill had lost his composure only once, briefly, when a telephone call to Peter's paternal grandparents had resulted in their uncompromising refusal to attend either event. Peter could have told him it would happen; the elder DiPaolis had not spoken to their son or daughter-in-law in six years, and only once or twice very briefly on the phone to their grandson. There had been a quarrel the last time they'd visited Rhode Island the nature of which had never been explained, although he knew it had something to do with an objection by his grandparents to something his mother had said or done. Whatever the nature of the rift, it had grown wider during the intervening years, until it had become an absolute chasm, and he knew that the assignment of his custody to Bill and Jeanne Sherman had been a direct result of that argument.

"Peter, we're leaving for the airport in about ten minutes. If there's anything else you want to take, you'd better decide now."

Peter looked up. Uncle Bill stood leaning against the door, a look of concern in his eyes. "No, nothing . . . I have everything I want."

"All right, then. I'm going to make a couple of quick phone calls and then we'll go."

Peter was not really sorry that he'd be moving to the midwest. He'd never quite fit in anywhere in his life, not in Marlboro, New Hampshire, where they'd first lived, nor in Bennington, Vermont, nor in Montpelier. He was withdrawn and intensely introspective and did not make friends easily. Close friends he didn't make at all. Neither was he attached to material things. Uncle Bill had told him to decide which of his parents' belongings he wanted to keep, because the balance of the furniture was to be sold along with the house, the proceeds to be added to the insurance money which his uncle was setting up as a trust fund. But somehow, nothing in the house seemed real anymore, no more real than the death of his parents, his imminent move to another state, the grandparents he never saw. There was only one thing in Peter's life that seemed real: the monster.

Peter had been visited by the monster throughout his life, ever since that first day when his grandfather had introduced it to him. The monster was the size of a man, but not really manlike. It had claws on its hands and feet, a horribly smiling face, tufted ears, batlike wings, and an extra elbow in each arm. The monster came to Peter virtually every night for the first few years, less frequently of late, appearing in one guise or another in his dreams. Sometimes it would be a playmate from school, another time it would come in the form of his father of mother, but most often it appeared with the sober, brooding face of his grandfather. No matter what disguise it wore, it would pose as a friend—reassuring, helpful, suggesting things that Peter could do with his life, or with some dream problem that might or might not relate to something in the real world. And each time, just when it appeared that the advice was working, the figure would strip off its mask, revealing the monster within, the covering flesh torn aside bloodlessly as the monster stepped out fully revealed, and whatever course of action Peter was taking would then take a disastrous turn.

He would be mountain climbing and the rope would break, or he'd be engaged in a swordfight when his blade would snap in half. He might be asking a girl for a date at the urging of a classmate, and the girl would lash at him, pointing him out as an object of scorn to her friends. No matter what the action, it would be ultimately turned against him, and his adviser, his friend, would be revealed as the duplicitous monster, triumphant once more. It was no surprise then that Peter had no real friends, no one to whom he was close. Consciously or not, he always half-expected them to rip off their own masks and reveal the monster within, and the border between dream and reality grew increasingly thin as the years passed.

Peter rose from the chair he'd occupied for several hours. As he walked through the house, he glanced around, noting intellectually that this was certainly the last time he would be inside these walls; the house had already been sold. He knew that he should feel some emotional impact, some significance to the moment, but all was muted, distant, indistinct. Uncle Bill believed that he was still in shock from the loss of his parents, that he would eventually break down into tears, resuming his life after accepting their death. He was partly right; Peter was in shock. But Peter had been in a kind of shock for a full decade now, and it was caused not by the death of his parents, but by the entrance into his life of the creature his grandfather had so admired, the gargoyle mounted on the side of the Sheffield mansion. It was a force from which he had never been free and never would be.

Alex Furtado bundled his worn jacket tightly around him, trying to keep out the chill November wind. He'd picked up some sandwiches on his way home from the factory; it was too blustery today for him to eat on the mansion grounds, so he was retreating to the privacy of his room. Actually, it was almost unnecessary for him to visit the gargoyle now; he was completely attuned to it.

Once inside the rooming house, he moved more quickly, climbing the stairs with an alacrity that many a younger man might have envied. Within seconds he was at the door of his small apartment, fumbling the key with stiff fingers until he had unlocked the door and stepped inside.

No one else, not even the rooming house manager, had been inside his room in many years. Mrs. Hagerty still owned the building and was theoretically in charge, but her arthritis was steadily worsening and she almost never left the lobby or her own first-floor apartment. Alex had had a plumbing problem once, but he'd fixed it at his own expense rather than allow anyone else to enter his sanctum. For a sanctum was what it had come to be.

One entire wall, an interior wall with no windows, had been stripped bare of furniture and wallpaper. Alex had painted over the plaster with an off-white base, then painstakingly created a faithful rendition of the gargoyle. It was hard to know in what position to pose the limbs and face; they often seemed subtly different to him when he gazed up at them from his favorite spot. But after he'd completed his painting, the work of almost a year, he noticed that this rendition also seemed to alter slightly from time to time. Surely he had painted the wings rather more furled than they were now, and he had attempted to give the face a more approving, tolerant expression. Perhaps it was a failure of his ability, but for whatever reason the face now reflected supercilious contempt and sometimes utter loathing. There were times when Alex felt genuinely ashamed in its presence and would kneel on the floor in front of it for hours, his head bowed, in silent contrition, hoping that when he finally glanced up, the figure would have forgiven him. But not once had he ever seen a softening of that hard expression.

Undaunted, he had turned to other media. A clay figure two feet tall stood erect on his bureau, with wings completely outspread, as though ready to jump into the air and fly about the room. A less successful, only half-completed wood carving in smaller proportions lay on the table beside his bed, along with the various knives he used to work at it. There were piles of smaller drawings stacked on a chair, piled in the bottom of the closet as well as on its shelf, and scattered about the floor. Some were pen-and-ink, some pencil, some crayon; the best was in charcoal. In one corner of the room stood a mansize assemblage of scrap metal parts, technically the least accurate version, with pieces of jagged metal, nuts, bolt, screws, machine parts, and such, assembled to suggest rather than represent the hunched, satanic figure that so completely dominated his life. Even in this case, the expression of the face was hostile, but Alex felt that it was less so than any of his other attempts to capture the spirit of his god.

Alex threw his coat over a chair and sat down on the foot of his bed to eat, consuming the three identical sandwiches with a solemn, monotonous sense of duty rather than any actual pleasure. When he'd finished he bundled the wrappings up and threw them into a paper bag that served as his wastebasket. He extracted this week's paycheck from his shirt pocket, then rose, crossed to the bureau, and opened the top drawer. The uncashed check went into the disorganized pile of similar ones collected there, some of them two years old. Vaguely he remembered that his boss had been after him again to cash them or bring them in so that replacements could be issued; he never really understood what it was that they wanted him to do about them. All he knew was that whenever he ran out of cash, he would draw one at random from the pile, sign the back, and turn it in at the bank. Money no longer mattered to him.

It was always warm in his room. Mrs. Hagerty kept the heat turned up right from the first day it turned chilly, because her arthritis bothered her much more when it was cold. Since Alex's room was directly above the furnace, and several heating vents passed through his walls on the way to the other apartments, his was generally the warmest in the building. In fact, it might have been uncomfortably warm, but somehow the heat seemed right to him, and he'd never complained about it. For that matter, Alex never complained about anything, so long as no one bothered him and no one interfered with what he wished to do.

Stripping off the dirty coveralls, Alex considered the

166

walk down the hall to the showers. It had been a while. He washed up cursorily before leaving work each day, but he had not had a really thorough scrub in about two weeks. He had once gone almost two months without showering, back when he'd been experimenting with different courses of action to see what might cause the gargoyle's expression to lighten, to express even the slightest approval. But it had been to no avail, and he'd finally given in to the rather unsubtle hints of his department supervisor. From that point on, he'd reverted to showering weekly, each Sunday night. But last week the hot-water heater had been inoperative, and his schedule was thrown off. It never occurred to him to shower on a weeknight.

He crossed to the dresser, pulling off his torn undershirt and throwing it on the bed. His nearly hairless chest, lean and muscular, tapered down to his comparatively narrow waist. Alex stared at himself in the mirror for several moments, a sudden formless thought manifesting itself: an observer would have noticed that his eyes remained fixed upon a spot in the center of the mirror, while the brows rose and fell repeatedly and the jaw muscles clenched and unclenched, tugging at his lips, as though some bizarre battle was being waged within his head—as indeed it was.

The twitches and spasms quickly died away, and Alex crossed to the small sink and toilet which made up his bathroom. He took up his safety razor, carefully extracting the blade, rinsing it clean of hair and shaving cream before walking back into the room. Taking up a position in front of the larger mirror there, he raised his arm and, with long, shallow cuts, began carving the likeness of the gargoyle's face into his own flesh, from breastbone to navel. This time, he thought, this time I'll make it come out right.

CHAPTER SEVEN
1965

There was no longer a Jimmy Nicholson; he had shed the diminutive of his name shortly after high school graduation. By 1965 he was James Nicholson, and not even his intimates called him Jimmy or even Jim. James was a trainee expediter at Eblis Manufacturing, working out of production control to ensure that the right jobs were given the proper priority, that all subcomponents were scheduled to be completed in a timely fashion so that the next highest level of assembly could be started on schedule. There were a lot of bugs to work out in the system, but since the company was starting from a position of having no scheduling methods, anything he accomplished by its very nature was impressive, and James was already one of the darlings of upper management, although his immediate supervisor, John Bullock, found him to be erratic in his performance, preferring confrontation to cooperation in an environment where it was important to provide incentives for factory supervision to view the system as a boon rather than a new set of restrictions.

Nicholson also seemed to find excuses to turn up under the eyes of top-level management with astonishing regularity, and Bullock was not naive enough to believe this coincidental. There were times as well when the young man was subtly insolent, and the quiet unassuming Bullock recognized that his was not the kind of personality which could keep an energetic, politically astute employee in check. It could not be doubted, however, that Nicholson did an excellent job, never backed down when faced with resistance, and had an encyclopedic memory.

Nicholson was married as well. Although only twenty-three years old, he had a two-year-old son and another child "in the oven," as he was fond of saying. He had married a hometown girl shortly after graduation, apparently a rather rushed affair. Their son, Eric, had been born only seven months after the ceremony, and at nine pounds, eight ounces there was no question of his having been premature. Although a few people still remembered the stories of his wildness and cruelty, it was assumed that the intervening years and the responsibilities of married life had taught him to moderate his behavior. He had become engaged to Dolly Pantell even before taking the full-time job at Eblis, while still working as a part-time stock clerk at a grocery store.

The Nicholsons had moved into a small house in one of the developments that had sprung up along the periphery of downtown, a three-bedroom ranch with wall-to-wall carpeting, a carport, a tiny lawn, and virtually nothing to distinguish it from the scores of similar houses that surrounded it. Nicholson liked it that way; he fit well into his community, and the neighborhood was advantageously located adjacent to one of the older, more genteel parts of town. The down payment had come from a small inheritance his wife had received from a spinster aunt, with enough left over to provide enough basic furniture to cover their needs. Nicholson joined the local bowling league, attended church regularly, went hunting occasionally with some of the guys from work, and had season tickets for the Red Sox.

One evening in early June, he was spending a typical if not restful night at home with his family. The union election at work had been held earlier that day. Although the company had originally tried to keep the expediting positions part of management, a majority of Nicholson's fellow workers had voted to join. Nicholson carefully expressed the opinion that he really saw no need for union representation, so that his superiors might view him as a potential ally, but he had also been careful not to alienate himself from the rank-and-file. This year he'd decided to run for vice-president of the union, but he'd lost to Big Ed Nelson and was more than slightly annoyed at the outcome.

Ed was a backslapper, a "regular guy" who during the couple of weeks that preceded the election bought drinks for just about everyone who could be expected to vote. Nicholson had never been very good at that, and was basically a loner; most people could tell that there was a fundamental insincerity concealed beneath his social overtures, but he knew that he was sharper than Nelson, that he could, if so inclined, strike a better deal in the upcoming negotiations than the other man. He was certain, too, that the elected position would only serve to put him in a more appealing light to top management. Many of the current midlevel managers and supervisors had come out of the union; Eblis believed firmly in promotion from within, one of the reasons why Nicholson had been so interested in securing a job with the firm. Increasingly the other major companies were expecting college degrees of all those in higher-paying and more powerful positions, even when experience was far more important than formal training. The election loss was a slap in the face to James Nicholson. He fumed about it, vowing never to run for a union office again. His co-workers had rebuffed him; that was their loss. Somewhere along the line he expected to be able to return the favor. Nicholson had a remarkably long memory for offenses both real and imagined.

Dolly could tell that he was preoccupied, but knew better than to ask about his mood. As a matter of fact, he had never even told her that he was running for office. He was careful to keep his work life and his home life separate. When (not if) he moved on to a job in management, it would be time for her to know something about his job, because it would be then that she could be of some use to him in the pursuit of his career goals. The incipient birth of their son Eric notwithstanding, James could never have been induced to marry Dolly had she not fit his image of what the wife of an up-and-coming businessman should be.

He finished up his monthly budget while Dolly was putting the finishing touches on dinner. The evening meal was always served precisely at six o'clock. Nicholson placed a lot of importance on regularity and predictability in his life. He liked reliability. Dolly was not the most organized person, but she was a good cook, a fine hostess, and considerably more attractive than most of the girls he'd dated in his younger days. He'd selected her with great care and judged her to be adequate to his present and future needs, reasonably intelligent, and capable of following instructions without being so independent that she'd insist on her own prerogatives at inopportune times. He had even been reasonably faithful to her. Sex for him was an exercise of power, a method of domination to be used when circumstances required it, but not an activity to be pursued for its own rewards. He'd never resorted to prostitutes, however; if he paid for sex, it would imply some degree of equality, an exchange of money for services rendered, and he would be unable to interpret the subsequent act as a demonstration of his authority and strength.

There was a dull thud and an outburst of crying from the far bedroom. "What the hell is it now?" he yelled over his shoulder toward the kitchen, remaining seated at his desk. Methodically he continued to replace checkbook, unpaid bills, budget book, and other paperwork in their appropriate places.

Dolly swept past him, wiping her hands on a dish towel, a resigned look on her face. "Don't worry about it, Dear. I'll take care of it. Supper will be ready in ten minutes." She disappeared down the hall and within seconds the crying had subsided. Nicholson swiveled around on his chair and reached up to turn on the television. The local news was still on, so he turned the volume all the way down but left the picture on so that he would know when the sports coverage started.

Dolly reappeared, heading toward the kitchen. "Nothing serious, he just fell off the bed again." He nodded absent-mindedly, walked over to the bar, and mixed himself a drink.

"Bring me some ice, will you?" He bent and started searching the shelves inside the bar. "Dolly, where the hell are the good glasses? You aren't washing them again, are you?"

"No, Dear—I just put them in the cupboard in the pantry. We almost never use them. They just get dusty in there and have to be washed every time we have company and want them out."

Nicholson straightened, picked up a bottle of gin as if to read the label but actually to concentrate his thoughts, then set it down a bit too forcefully. "I know they get dusty in the bar. How many times have I told you not to move things without asking me first? If you weren't here, how would I ever find them in the damned pantry cupboard?"

"But I'm always here, James." Her voice was starting to acquire the whine that always drove him to anger. "Every once in a while I like to move things around a little. It gets monotonous here. I always talk to you about anything important; you know that."

"It's not monotonous." He quickly finished mixing his drink. "It's orderly." He turned and saw her standing in the kitchen archway, compulsively wiping her already dry hands with a dish towel. "My mother used to move the furniture every couple of weeks during the day while my father was at work, and it kept him in such a disorganized state that the rest of his life got sloppy and he never amounted to anything. That's not going to happen to me. I'm going to *be* someone one of these days, someone with the power to control other people's lives. If you want to succeed in life, you have to decide what your goal is, chart your course, make your decisions, and stick to them in an orderly manner."

'Yes, but—"

"Don't interrupt me, Dolly." This last was said in such a cold, threatening voice that she jerked as if he'd slapped her. "We've been through this before. Things belong where they belong. We can't keep changing our lives because some little thing seems boring or repetitious. That's instability. Life is boring. My job is boring. But I can't decide today I'm going to work on a punch press because

173

that would be more interesting than what I'm supposed to do, or that I'm going to work on the assembly line Wednesdays to relieve the boredom. Running this house and raising my children are part of your job, and that includes providing a stable environment for Eric to grow up in. If you teach him bad habits at this age, it's going to take years to train him out of them later on."

Dolly's eyes glistened and he knew she was close to tears. "I know that, James, but sometimes it's just so hard. You don't understand—"

He interrupted her again. "Oh, I *understand*, all right. I know it's not *your* fault that your parents spoiled you all your life, but somewhere along the line you have to learn to accept the responsibilities of being *an adult and a wife and a mother.*"

Her head snapped up, and for the first time she met his eyes with her own. "My parents did not spoil me. I've asked you before not to bring them into our arguments. They have nothing to do with this."

Nicholson felt the blood pounding in his temples. The only time Dolly ever questioned his authority was when he was critical of her parents. She'd been quite close to them, and they'd died in a plane crash only a few months before she'd met him. The desire for a new source of strength in her life had made her natural prey for a man like Nicholson. Now that he had secured what he saw as possession of her soul, he'd set about making her over into the image of his wife that he carried around inside himself, but had never been able to drive a lasting wedge between Dolly and her parents. It was her only serious flaw, the only vestige of her previous life that he'd not been able to restructure . . . yet.

"Oh yes, your perfect parents." He turned away from

her and walked slowly across the living room. "I suppose you didn't turn out so bad from your mother's point of view, and your father didn't have one, of course. He wasn't allowed."

The sharp intake of breath was audible but he pretended not to have heard it.

"My father was a very loving man." There was a tremor in her voice, but it was as much anger and sadness as it was fear. "Just because he wasn't ambitious like you and never made a lot of money doesn't make him any less a man."

"Well, I suppose he did as well as he could." His tone was deliberately casual. He turned now to face her again. "But you and I both know that he held a second-class job all his life. He let your mother make all the decisions, and maybe that was best; she seems to have had a lot more common sense. But there are some things in life that a man has to decide for himself. I don't tell you how to cook, how to clean your kitchen, how to do the things that are important to your job." He drained his drink, paused, them made his voice sterner. "But I don't expect you to ignore the things that I consider important, either. I won't tolerate sloppiness in this house. I expect you to live up to your responsibilities. How would you like it if I decided that I was bored with my job and took a couple of days off and then we didn't have enough money to pay for the groceries? That'd be pretty irresponsible of me, wouldn't it?" He moved back to the bar, started to mix another drink, noticed out of the corner of one eye that her head was already tilting in defeat. "I don't want to have to talk to you about this again." He said it quietly, but each word was loaded with menace. When he turned to face her again, she had disappeared back into the kitchen.

Their meal was a silent, awkward one. Even young Eric seemed affected by the tension and was on his best behavior. Nicholson decided to be magnanimous and pursued the matter no further. He had a third drink with his meal, and a fourth directly following it. Dolly mixed one for herself as well.

"You should have told me if you wanted a drink," he said. "I'd've made one for you."

"That's all right." She didn't look in his direction, didn't tell him that she knew he deliberately mixed her drinks with as little alcohol as possible. And right now she felt the need of a very strong drink."

"Don't sulk. All is forgiven."

"I'm not sulking. I'm just tired, and I have to finish cleaning up and get Eric to bed. And the baby is getting restless and probably needs to be changed."

Nicholson considered forcing the issue, annoyed at even this token rebellion, but it had been a tiring day for him as well. What right did she have to make his home life uncomfortable? Particularly today, when he'd had so much grief at work. Not that she knew anything about it, of course, or would understand. When they were first married, before Eric was born, she'd worked part-time at Deitchman's Market, but he had soon put a stop to that. Women with independent careers didn't make good wives; they had a conflict of interest. The extra money was nice, but it was more important that Mrs. James Nicholson not work for a living. Besides, with the second baby due in another couple of months, she'd have been forced to quit in any case.

He recognized that there were certain jobs women had to do, because no self-respecting man would be a secretary or a nurse, for example, but that was for the wives of weak, unsuccessful men. Dolly was going to keep his house and raise his children and do the things that women were really good at, and not insult him by implying that he couldn't support his own family adequately. She hadn't wanted to stop working, had talked about babysitters and such, and for months afterward whined to him about how she missed her friends from work, and how she wanted to help him by earning money. Her mother had worked most of her life, which was obviously where she'd gotten the idea. Although he'd never met them, Nicholson despised her impertinent mother and spineless father and was determined to eradicate what he interpreted as the more pernicious aspects of their influence on their daughter's personality.

But tonight he just didn't have the energy to push the matter. He was furious about the election defeat, a bit lightheaded from the gin, and slightly tired as well. He'd had difficulty sleeping the night before. It was hot and muggy and they couldn't afford an air conditioner yet. Fortunately there was a cool breeze tonight.

Maybe a brisk walk would be a good idea. Nicholson always preferred to be alone when he was working things out in his mind. Dolly wouldn't know if he was mad or not, either. Yes, a walk was definitely the right move. "I'm going out," he said to her back. "I'll be home later."

It was surprisingly pleasant outside. The sky was clear, the temperature had dropped to the high seventies, and the humidity was down. A slight breeze from Narragansett Bay made whispering noises in the leaves of the Japanese maples and birches Nicholson had planted. There was little traffic in this area, though he could hear an occasional distant horn from the commercial zone.

He considered walking along the state road toward the

reservoir, but there were no streetlights in that direction and, although he refused to admit it even to himself, Nicholson was uneasy in the darkness. He didn't believe in ghosts or vampires or werewolves or any of that kid stuff; his feet were solidly planted in rationality and logic. But there was something about a dark, silent street, something primitive and lonely and isolated, something that made him uneasy and sometimes even panicky. He could rationalize his feelings, people the dark with lurking muggers, teenage gangs, perverts, criminals, and psychotic killers armed with knives, pitchforks, and other implements. He told himself that it was not blind fear, but a rationally determined avoidance of dangerous situations. But deep down inside, where all pretense and self-deceit were unmasked, he was terrified of being alone in the dark with no one but himself for company. That fear was part of the reason he so frequently did go for a stroll after nightfall, mastering his own fear, forcing it to respond to the strength of his personality.

But there were limits, and unlighted roads were beyond those boundaries. So he turned instead to the well-lighted road that led to Main Street. In due course he found himself passing the boarded-up shell of the Catterall Realty Office, gutted by a fire a month before; Rhein's Bar and Grill; Ace New and Used Cars; and finally the town library, which stood dark and silent, well back from the road, closed now, apparently for good. Part of the surrounding estate had been sold off by the town and new businesses were encroaching on the grounds. There had been talk of reopening the library at the last town meeting, but no one was seriously willing to advocate a tax increase to pay for the alterations which would make it practicable.

Standing in front of that ponderous stone building,

Nicholson was reminded of that long ago night when he had been thwarted by Barbara Howell. Dumb bitch, he thought. Now she's married to the wimp Joslin, with his half-baked job and no future, a management trainee at a hardware store somewhere in Providence. He'd always thought Joslin was queer anyhow. Maybe he was and she'd married him so she wouldn't have to put out. If she'd played her cards right, she might have ended up married to James Nicholson, who'd just embarked on a career that he knew, deep within, would not stop even at senior expediter. He had set his sights on the top, or at least as close to the top as he could get. Briefly he entertained a fantasy in which he encountered the Joslins at a social event somewhere, finding Barbara sitting there talking to her wimpy husband, suddenly seeing him appear and realizing what she had thrown away.

But the fantasy was less satisfying than he'd expected. Dolly's insolent resentment had put him in a bad mood. Just at that moment, he wanted to be back home so he could straighten things out, bring them to a head, force Dolly to acknowledge her gratitude. What does she expect, anyhow? He shook his head in bewilderment. I work hard, make a good home for her, tell her she doesn't have to work any more, and she's pissed at me when I try to help her grow up.

Just like Barbara, he thought. I might have married her if she'd been the right type, if she'd treated me right. But then he admitted to himself that it could never have happened ... she was much too independent. But that didn't make her own loss any less significant, he thought. She might have thrown away the best opportunity she'd ever have for her future. He walked onto the library grounds, looked up at the unlighted windows, wondered if the picnic tables were still out back. He hadn't been here since that night; the defeat had rankled him too much.

He started to walk around the building, noticed a broken window on the ground level. The swing set was gone, and most of the rear yard had become overgrown. Even the pavement was cracked in places by grass growing up wherever a fault line offered itself. There were a couple of wire trash barrels scattered in among the stand of trees, and there was still a single bench over near the fence, but the tables had been removed. He walked halfway across the parking lot, remembered his last visit a little more distinctly than he cared to. Even now he felt a psychosomatic twinge of physical pain. "Stupid bitch!" he said aloud at last, then quickened his pace, turned to follow the curve of the tower wall at the corner.

The neon sign from the adjacent car lot flooded the side wall with garish red light, even through the screening trees and shrubs. Nicholson's eyes were drawn to a shape protruding from the side of the building, crouching there in the red glow. He moved to one side to reduce the effect of the glare, almost immediately recognizing his old friend the gargoyle, crouched in a dynamic pose about ten feet below a narrow window. Funny, he thought, but his memory insisted that the grotesque homunculus had been situated higher on the building years ago. Obviously it was just a trick his mind was playing on him. He'd been a couple of inches shorter when he'd been here last, and younger; the world had seemed a larger place than it did now.

Otherwise the figure was much as he remembered it— that knowing smile, the tongue protruding from one side of the fanged mouth, the comradely cock of the head, the sense that he and that stone figure were somehow in possession of a secret that had eluded the rest of the world, that they shared a private joke. "You and I have something in common," he said in a low voice. "We know when we have to be hard. The world's not a soft place, but it's filled with soft people. The only ones who get ahead are the ones who aren't afraid to push, who bend others to their will." He put one hand on the cold stone wall and looked directly up into the gargoyle's eyes. "We're two of a kind, you and I, but I've got something you haven't ... I'm not stuck here. I'm going to cut and slash and beat at the world until I've made my own kind of place in it. I'm not going to be stuck with a two-bit job in a two-bit town. You found your place; I haven't found mine yet, but when I do, the rest of the world had better look out, because I'm not going to let anyone or anything get in my way."

A car drove past and its headlights swept briefly across the wall. For a split second it looked as if the gargoyle had turned its head slightly and winked at him, but then it was motionless once more. Nicholson was amused by his own startled reaction. "Too bad you can't really move, friend. We'd be good partners, the two of us. But you can't. You'll be up on that wall forever, waiting for the world to come to you because you can't go out yourself and grab it by the throat. One of these days the world will come to me, but it'll come when I want it to, not just when it feels like it or wants something from me. You have to make people do the things you want them to do, or they'll just use you for their own purposes. It's a kind of game, you know, and the ones who win are the ones who learn the rules and then change them to suit themselves. And I intend to be one of the winners."

The gargoyle offered no reply but continued to meet

his stare. Nicholson assumed that the face was supposed to be frightening—the grossly exaggerated features, the protruding fangs, the glaring eyes, the satanic horns rising from each side of the head. But he was damned if he could understand why. It seemed almost ... friendly.

A few minutes later, Nicholson turned and walked back toward Main Street and home.

That day did not work out exactly as Arthur had planned. On some level he still felt affection for Edith, although the same could not be said of his feelings toward the two children. Keith was a very quiet seven-year-old, recovered from his jealousy of young Jeri, but not adjusted to his father's frequent drinking spells. There had been little violence, it must be said; physically Edith was almost a match for her husband, and emotionally she was far the stronger of the two. There were occasional overreactions to Keith's or Jeri's mischief. As a child of five, Jeri had proven to be obstinate enough to try her mother's patience on more than one occasion. She would knot her fists and set her chin and refuse to be moved by cajolery, threats, or even minor physical punishment.

It had not helped when Arthur lost his job working for the town. His dependency on alcohol had grown rather than diminished over the years, and he had courted termination for nearly two years before he was finally caught too far under the influence to perform his duties. He had been allowed to resign rather than be fired, so that he was subsequently able to find a job as a floorboy at Eblis Manufacturing, and for a while he even limited his drinking to the evenings. But the money hadn't been nearly sufficient in this new, even more menial position, and Edith had finally been forced to find a job as well. Keith was in school now and Jeri was just starting kindergarten; a neighbor picked Jeri up after school and watched her until three o'clock, when Edith's job at the Main Street Diner ended and she could pick up Keith at school and take the two children home. But Edith had resented the change, not so much the work itself as the absolute necessity of it, and particularly after a difficult day, she would sit silently at home, ignoring Arthur completely.

On one such occasion, desperate to break the silence that had grown between them, Arthur decided to tell Edith the most important secret in his life. He waited until the children had been put to bed, Keith helping with Jeri, toward whom he had grown quite protective, perhaps as a way of expiating some guilt he felt about his earlier aversion to having a sister. Shortly afterward, he was sent off to bed as well; the two children were sharing the same room until an apartment with an extra bedroom could be found in their price range, an eventuality which Edith considered little more than a daydream.

She returned to the living room, plopped down into her favorite chair, and began leafing through one of the magazines she had borrowed from a co-worker. Arthur went out to the kitchen, opened another beer, and found excuses to take as much time as possible to return. Although he'd already decided at this point to tell Edith, it was hard to actually start . . . not that he expected her to disbelieve him; to Arthur the truth was so self-evident that he was surprised other people did not recognize it already. But it was difficult to talk about it, to put into words what he felt so deeply.

"Edith," he said at last, returning to their living room. "I want to tell you something."

"Can't it wait?" She did not look up from her magazine. "I'm reading something interesting here." She emphasized "interesting" in such a way as to leave no doubt that she didn't believe anything Arthur had to say could possibly be worth the distraction.

"It's important, Edith. It's kind of a secret thing I know about, that I wanted to tell you about."

She glanced up at him this time but did not raise her head. "What kind of secret?"

He licked his lips and began pacing. "There's someone in this town who's not really the same as the rest of us," he ventured, then stopped, knowing that that wasn't really what he wanted to say.

Edith stared at him impatiently. "Everyone's different in their own way, Arthur. What are you talking about?"

"It's not exactly a human person—that is, it's not even a person, really ... I'm not sure." Now that he'd started, Arthur wasn't sure he could go on. This wasn't working out at all well. He'd never put his feelings about the gargoyle into words, and now that he was trying, the right words wouldn't come. "It's someone bigger than human."

Edith dropped the magazine to her side. "Arthur, the only person in this town bigger than human is Mrs. Winters over at the school, and she's on a diet. Is the booze you're always drinking finally rotting your mind? Are you having the DTs?"

"No!" he shouted, surprised at the intensity of his own words. "This is real! It is no illusion!"

She looked up alarmed. "Arthur, keep you voice down. You'll wake the kids." She paused a second, listening, but there was no sound from the second bedroom.

Arthur took several deep breaths and regained some semblance of control. "I don't know how to explain it, Edith, but there's someone in town who's looking us all over, choosing among us, looking for those fit enough to serve him. And I'm one of the ones he's considering."

"You?" Edith laughed and this time set the magazine down beside her chair. "No one in their right mind would choose you for anything. Look at yourself—you can't even hold a steady job, your kids are afraid of you, you even despise yourself most of the time." The look of contempt on her face just then was almost exactly the same as the one he had often seen on the gargoyle, and suddenly he was frightened. Should he have talked about this to her? Had he made a mistake? What would be the results of his misbehavior, if that's what it was? He drank heavily from the can of beer, then resumed his pacing.

Edith watched him, then sat back in the chair and continued in a softer tone. "Listen, Arthur, I know you're not entirely to blame, and I know that sometimes I make things harder on you than they already are. I get tired and frustrated and angry, too, and maybe I should be more understanding and patient. But damn it, you're ruining your health and your life and our marriage! I loved you once, Arthur, and I still like you some of the time, but I don't know if I love you any more, and I don't have the faintest idea whether you love me or the kids or what. You've become a stranger living in the same apartment with me, and the kids are afraid of you. Sometimes I am, too. And now you start talking like a crazy man."

"I'm not crazy!" Arthur stopped pacing and turned, facing her squarely. "I know what I'm talking about! I've seen him. I see him often."

"Who is this person, Arthur? Who are you talking about?"

Arthur opened his mouth to speak, closed it, then fin-

185

ished the can of beer. "Come on," he said at last. "I'll show you."

Edith looked slightly alarmed. "What do you mean?"

"He's not far from here. We'll walk over and I'll show him to you."

Edith glanced toward the back bedroom. "We can't go now, Arthur. We can't leave the kids alone."

"It's not far and it won't take long. They're asleep anyway."

"But what if something happened while we were gone? We'll go some other time, maybe take the kids with us."

"No!" He raised his voice again. "We'll go now. We won't be gone more than ten minutes. Nothing will happen here."

They argued for a few more moments, but for some reason Edith felt a compulsion to go with him, to see what he was talking about. She felt this strange revelation was more than just a drunken tirade, that it somehow concerned the entire range of problems in his personality. If she could know what was really causing him to resort to the bottle, maybe she could help him overcome it. Despite all the unpleasantness that had taken place in their marriage, Edith Furness Kaplan still loved her husband, loved him very much, and her bitter reaction to his drinking was just her method of dealing with a deeply felt hurt.

Eventually she let herself be talked into it. She could always turn around and come home if it looked like their excursion would be too lengthy, after all, and if it helped her understand Arthur's obsession, it might be a chance to salvage something of their relationship, a chance which might never offer itself again.

They left the building shortly afterward, and Edith followed Arthur quietly as he led her several blocks through the back streets and into the grounds of the old Sheffield mansion. The encroachment of commercial establishments on both sides had marred much of the wild beauty of the place, and she wondered how much longer the building would stand as it was. The library was closed now, and the town still owned the property, though there had been talk again recently of seeking a buyer for what remained of the estate. Several smaller lots had already been split off and sold, although the bulk of the remaining land, which bordered the swampy northwestern part of town, was probably not as appealing as that which had already been disposed of.

Although the grounds were unlighted, the reflected glare from the surrounding businesses was great enough that they had no difficulty picking their way through the bushes to the side of the building. Edith had never been inside the grounds before, had never noticed the rear corner, which had been capped with a circular tower that extended ten feet above the roofline. Someday she would have to come back here during the day, she told herself— perhaps bring the kids along and have a picnic.

They made their way almost directly to the tower, and when Arthur finally came to a halt, Edith was more perplexed than ever.

"Is this where you wanted to bring me, Arthur? Where is this friend of yours?"

"He's not a friend, and he's right there. Can't you see him?"

He gestured toward the towering wall and, when she looked up, Edith could vaguely see a human shape, right at the roof level, looking down from the eaves. It was a statue of some kind, she saw, but the light was not sufficient from this angle for her to see much more. She moved off to one side, caught it in partial silhouette. "It's some kind of stone monster. Is that what you're talking about?"

"Yes, that's him . . . but he's not a monster. He's more like a kind of god." And he stood there, staring up raptly.

Now Edith felt a wave of despair. Bad enough that Arthur was an alcoholic and could not be counted on to hold a steady job, but now he was delusional as well. She tried to speak several times before she could actually force out the words, and when they came, it was in a torrent.

"You absolute idiot! You're standing there worshipping a goddamned hunk of stone! That's no god! At best, it's some kind of demon, and not even a real one! This is make-believe, Arthur, it's all inside your head! You can't stand the reality of your life, so you look in a bottle. When you can't find it there, you look at a fancy carved wall and decide that must be where the real truth is. Well, it's not there! The truth is you and me and our children, and your job and the bills that have to be paid and the small amount of money we have to pay them with. The truth is that you're a hopeless alcoholic and that you might be losing your mind!"

"No," he said quietly, turning to her. Then again, more loudly, "No!" He clenched his fists and moved threateningly in her direction. "I won't have it that way! You're wrong! You don't understand! You *can't* understand!" He lowered his voice. "This is the biggest, the greatest thing in my life. Don't you scoff at it. *Don't you dare scoff at it!*" He took another step in her direction and she felt a faint thrill of fear. "He is power and ability and everything that I want and don't have," Arthur said, turning to stare back up at the gargoyle. "He has all these things and he can give them to those who please him."

"And do you please him, Arthur? If you do, why don't you have anything? Why don't *we* have anything?"

"No," he answered softly. "I have not pleased him yet, but I hope to. I hope to find the way to do what he wants, so that I will be worthy. But I haven't found it yet, not yet. I keep looking and asking, but I can't find it and he won't tell me. He even turns his face away from me." These last words seemed despairing.

Edith stepped forward, raising one hand toward her husband, wanting to go to him and reassure him and drive the madness and self-doubt from his mind. But as she stepped forward, he turned with a speed she no longer believed he could manage, and his arm flashed up and at her face. He still held a beer bottle, empty now. She never saw it coming, but she felt it, felt it smash against her teeth and nose. She fell back and away, startled and off-balance rather than in pain. The pain didn't start until she lay on her back, trying to decide what had happened, where the hurt had come from, and the bottle rose and came down again and again. Blood spurted from her nose and from her smashed teeth and she tried to scream but instead choked on her own blood, which flowed down her throat and into her lungs. She was still alive when Arthur ripped open her clothing and raped her: but when he was spent, he rose and picked up the bottle and his arm went up and down several more times, until what lay there could no longer be recognized as Edith Kaplan. And perhaps it was the neon sign from the car lot and perhaps not, but the eyes of the gargoyle perched high above glowed a brilliant red in the night, and for the first time ever in Arthur's presence, the face seemed to smile approvingly.

Somehow Arthur knew what to do after that. He dumped the body in the swamp, then returned to their apartment,

189

where he changed his clothing and showered thoroughly. Then he made a quick trip down to the supermarket to dump a garbage bag of trash and bloody clothing in the dumpster before returning home to report his wife missing. The police had some suspicions about Arthur's story— he claimed she had taken a walk over to the package store and not returned; Arthur was generally known to be drunk and unreliable and had had more than one run-in with the authorities in the past.

But the following morning, Edith Kaplan's body was discovered lying in the swamp, and for several days the town was electrified by the story of a mad rapist prowling the dark streets. Edith had been an attractive woman, and Arthur never wavered from his story, so whatever private doubts the police might have held, they kept to themselves. There was, after all, no physical evidence linking Arthur to the body or the scene of the crime, identified by analysis of the blood on some fragments of glass. The Kaplans were not considered an ideal couple, but neither did they have a reputation for loud or frequent fights; Edith kept their personal troubles religiously private.

Eventually the case was relegated to the "unsolved" stack, despite Chief Dowdell's personal conviction that there was more going on beneath the facts than was readily apparent. For several weeks there was a sharp increase in the number of reported prowlers, and many teenage girls found themselves unofficially grounded, but as the days wore on and nothing further happened, people forgot about the murder. After all, no one had really known Edith Kaplan very well; she wasn't important in the town and it was unlikely that anyone outside her immediate family much regretted her passing. As it happened, the police would never learn the real truth.

CHAPTER EIGHT
1967

After four years of marriage, Ron and Barbara Joslin decided that things just weren't working out the way they had originally hoped. It wasn't because they fought, though they did, for they didn't disagree even as much as most relatively happily married couples did. But their interests had changed, their personalities had altered, and they had grown apart. They still liked each other, in some ways still loved each other, but it wasn't the same anymore, and they continued to drift apart until it was obvious that the marriage would have to end before they became bitter and started to quarrel in earnest.

One evening they sat down to discuss the situation, and it was the most involved they had been with the details of their lives together in months. They concluded that it was best to end things now, while they could still be friends, without animosity, without recrimination. Fortunately, they had fallen out of romantic love as simultaneously and completely as they had originally fallen into it in the first place, and the biggest problem appeared to be finding grounds for a divorce. Then more problems arose: how would they deal with their friends? What would happen if their acquaintances felt compelled to choose sides? They resolved to think about this awhile, consult a lawyer, and do things in an organized manner.

Grounds were eventually found, more or less manufactured, and a date was set for the final termination of their partnership. It was Barbara who ultimately came up with the idea of the party, but Ron adopted it immediately, embellishing it beyond her original conception, and it was the best time they had had together in almost a year. They even made love that night, one of the last times they would ever do so.

Barbara's idea was simple: they would throw an enormous party to mark the end of their marriage, inviting all their friends and everyone who had attended their wedding. Instead of receiving presents, they would give a present to each of the guests. There would be two small wedding cakes, with the figure of a woman on one and a man on the other. They would announce their formal disengagement, their intention of going steady for a while, then just dating. They even considered reciting their marriage vows in reverse, but then decided that some people might be offended at the implicit sacrilege. Their obvious friendship and goodwill toward each other at the party puzzled many, but it did ease the transition and avoided much of the tension that would inevitably have existed in a town as small as Managansett, where each of them still planned to live and work. Many remarked afterward that it was the most civilized divorce they'd ever seen.

Ron was now assistant manager of Hasty's Hardware Store, working long hours for mediocre pay, but having a great time doing it. Barbara, now Howell again, was looking for a new job. She still liked Mr. Wood and enjoyed working with him, but her permanent assignment was changed to the sales department, interpreting order trends, working with the forecast, and summarizing the results for the production control department. In some ways it was very interesting work, but if she were ever to get to a better position with Eblis, she would have to become involved in the incessant office politics, and her gender put her at a disadvantage right from the start. Old Mr. Eblis was still the titular head of the company, but he was increasingly willing to turn over all the decision-making to his top-level managers, who frequently indulged in territorial battles, fights over precedence and procedure. Some were healthy arguments, such as how to balance the sales department's desire for massive inventory against the financial department's insistence that the carrying costs were excessive. But more and more the arguments hinged on lines of reporting within the hierarchy, the power of various departments to make binding decisions for the company, and even the number of employees who were to be assigned within each functional responsibility. Barbara found it depressing at best, infuriating most of the time, and saw no place for her own future to mesh with the working-out of this power struggle.

Barbara still ran every morning before work, and twice as long on weekends and holidays. She had never been overweight, never needed to diet, but she felt better, healthier, more alive when she exercised regularly, and running was something she could do almost any time, almost any place, and she didn't have to depend upon anyone else. For that matter, she really didn't care to run with company most of the time, although occasionally Ron had gone with her, even after the breakup of their marriage. It was pleasant to periodically match herself against someone else.

She had one particular route that she followed almost all the time, the details worked out precisely, but occasionally she would feel the need to try something different. She would then run up to the northeast, through the nearly deserted roads that wound through the undeveloped forest, or down to the southeast, past the Managansett Inn and into farming country, or out west and along Reservoir Road, toward the DiPaoli farm and the Connecticut border. It was on one such exploratory run that she decided to take a shortcut through the Sheffield estate.

Although she'd seen James Nicholson on more than one occasion at work, she'd not spoken more than a casual word to him in years. He was part and parcel of the infighting she'd come to detest at Eblis and had worked his way up to assistant manager in the production control department. He was considered hot stuff within the company.

Her dislike was more deeply rooted than that, however, going back to that night seven years ago when he'd nearly assaulted her behind the Sheffield mansion. Now as she jogged across the worn paths, she was struck by a kind of fascinated nostalgia. As much as she'd been horrified and offended by Nicholson's attempt to manipulate her emotions, she was also rather pleased with the way she'd handled herself. It was one of the few interpersonal encounters from her teenage years that she remained proud of, and now she wanted to relive it briefly, even if somewhat vicariously. The amicable end to her marriage notwithstanding, Barbara felt that somehow it had marked a personal failure for her, reflecting her inability to form deep, lasting relationships. Even now she had no close friends, no

194

confidants, no one with whom she could have a good cry or a heart-to-heart talk about her personal anxieties. So she veered from her path toward the tower corner.

The area had changed drastically, almost beyond recognition. One rickety bench remained, perhaps from the original equipment, but the tables were gone and some of the surrounding trees had been cut down to make way for the light poles and hurricane fence of the car lot next door. All things considered, the grounds had been kept up quite well, although she could see the first indications of neglect and decay here and there.

Curious about the mansion itself, she examined it for the first time in the full light of day. Naturally she had seen it before, had even visited the library once or twice when it was open, but she had always come and gone through the front and had never really been interested in the architecture or its appearance. Now she examined in detail the carvings in the tower, the representations of various achievements, both heroic and dubious in nature, that covered its outer surface. And subsequently her eyes lit upon the gargoyle crouched high above.

It was extraordinarily hideous, and the sight of it reminded her of that long-ago day when she and Valerie Meredith had played here. Something unpleasant had happened, something about cigarettes. Valerie had always been fast company, and Barbara had not seen her since graduation, though she was still living in town somewhere, still single, still reputedly living it up in nightclubs and bars. Barbara shook her head and told herself not to be so judgmental. But the statue fascinated her, its inherent evil so apparent now that she was amazed no one had ever seen it before. It glared down at her with an expression of appalling bellicosity and hatred. For a moment she even fancied it was a living thing, ready to spring down from its perch and tear her limb from limb. But that was a passing fancy, and she blinked the thought away and forced herself to examine every detail of the statue's distorted body.

It was a remarkable piece of work; there was no doubt about that. The sculptor who'd created such embodied malevolence must have been a genius of unparalleled talent ... but a warped genius. Barbara found herself wishing that the statue had been mounted lower, within reach. For the first time in her life, she had a powerful urge to vandalize something, to desecrate it, to scrawl graffiti on its chest, break off its stony claws, draw a mustache over the snarling lips. But at last she recovered her composure, laughed at herself for reacting so savagely, and turned away, resuming her run. It had been a disquieting encounter and she had no intention of ever returning.

"Good morning, Mr. Colbert. How are you today?" Barbara waved cheerily to her next-door neighbor, who looked up perfunctorily from the hedge he was clipping. Three years of determined amiability had not elicited a single friendly gesture from the taciturn couple next door, but Barbara steadfastly refused to surrender her own good disposition.

Knowing better than to wait for a reply, Barbara checked to be certain her house keys were zipped into the pocket of the gray sweatsuit as she walked out to the sidewalk. She could hear two lawnmowers growling somewhere nearby, but the neighborhood was otherwise silent. It had become increasingly the home of older couples these past few years, and even on a Saturday morning such as this, there were no children about.

Sometimes it seemed as though the entire week was just preparation for the weekend. Managansett was a sleepy little town with a low crime rate, but she was not so independent or foolhardy that she would wander about alone after dark. Thus the time she could spend running was limited to those daylight hours in which she had no prior commitments.

Barbara paused on the sidewalk in front of the house she'd inherited from her late aunt and stretched a bit to loosen up her muscles. Months before, she'd mapped out the route that provided the optimum combination of slopes and hills, the least traffic, the surest footing. It began here at home and threaded its way through the residential areas north of Main Street, crossing the commercial district only once, down through the cemetery, around the low-income housing development, then through a short wooded section in a loop that brought her back above Raynor's Pond and toward home.

Drawing a deep breath, she set off, her pace slow at first. Gladys Dowdell came into sight from around the side of her house and paused. "Lovely morning, Mrs. Dowdell," Barbara called, slowing as she passed. The older woman gave her a tentative smile and a wave. Although she had never said so explicitly, it was obvious that Gladys considered jogging unladylike at best and was vaguely uncomfortable whenever she saw her younger neighbor decked out in her baggy sweatsuit. Barbara had once given in to impulse and suggested that Gladys accompany her some morning, and the woman had positively stuttered her demurral.

She turned left on Olney Street, her muscles starting to loosen up now as she made her way past a depressing row of identical ranch houses, differing only in color and in the variety of cars parked in their uniform driveways. This street marked the border between the houses built before and after the war, and although Barbara thought her home a bit ugly, and definitely too big for her, now that Ron had moved out, she still preferred it to the sterile conformity of Olney Street.

Three blocks further she would turn right on Le Croix Avenue and follow it to the high school playground. The houses here were just as characterless, but through some fortunate combination of events, the contractor who had developed this area had chosen to leave standing many of the immense oak trees that had formerly covered this part of town. Their shade would be very welcome in the warm months to come; as it was, there were times in July and August when she was forced to cut short her run, or at the very least take brief breaks which interrupted the continuity of her exercise.

It was just after she'd turned onto Le Croix that she first caught sight of the other runner. Although jogging was starting to catch on throughout the country, the addiction was largely unknown in Managansett, conservative in this as in so much else. During the past three years, Barbara had never once seen another runner within the town limits except when Ron had been with her, and even after all this time, she still received strange looks from others who shared Gladys Dowdell's opinion. That was another reason she preferred to maintain the same route; most of the people she was likely to encounter were accustomed to her presence by now, and weren't quite as likely to stop and stare as she ran by.

But today things were different. There was another figure running along Le Croix, a woman with hair cut as short as her own, similarly clad. The woman was at least a block away and moving in the same direction, running with practiced ease. It must be a newcomer to the area; certainly Barbara would have encountered her long before this if she ran regularly.

Le Croix ended at the high school, and since the grounds were fenced, the runner ahead would have to turn to her left or her right, or return along Le Croix. Barbara considered picking up her own pace and overtaking the woman, but her shyness caused her to hesitate: perhaps if the other runner reversed her course, she could greet her as they passed, possibly starting up a conversation. She was still rehearsing opening gambits in her mind when the figure reached the far end of the street and turned right.

Well, thought Barbara, that delays but doesn't necessarily prevent the meeting. She's still on my course.

The ground sloped gently upward as the fence turned and curved around the back of the school. Generations of childrens' feet had formed a firm, well-delineated pathway. On the other side of the building, Laurel Street led through one of the older parts of town. Barbara's route led down Laurel to Jackson, which ran parallel to Main Street. As she rounded the back of the gymnasium, Barbara had a clear view of the other runner from the rear, predictably having crossed to the shadier side of Laurel Street.

Great minds run along the same paths, she told herself, pleased that their two routes appeared to coincide so closely. The two of them might have a lot more in common. More determined than ever to meet this potential companion for her running excursions, and possibly for more than that, she began to pick up speed. Laurel sloped very gently downward, which helped, even though Barbara felt the jarring in her knees. Unfortunately, the grade helped both of them, and the woman ahead was moving more rapidly as well, still maintaining her one-block lead. Barbara tried to accelerate again, but almost immediately felt the strain. The soft office job was taking its toll; she had gained nearly five pounds during the past year. She began to feel winded and slowed resignedly, annoyed with her own weakness.

A few minutes later the woman turned abruptly right and started down Jackson. Barbara suddenly realized that if she turned immediately and followed Monroe Street, she would be following a straight course that cut across the curve of Jackson and would stand a good chance of over-taking her quarry where the two roads met. Impulsively she made the turn, even though it felt distinctly wrong to be leaving her prescribed route. It was the first time she'd stepped outside the routine in almost two months.

Adrenaline gave her an anticipatory lift. There were three cross streets, she remembered, before Jackson. She was already perspiring heavily, much earlier than usual, but it would be worth the extra effort to find a running mate. She smiled at the pun. It also occurred to her to wonder about the depth of her excitement: was she becoming bored, or even lonely? Though not unattractive, Barbara was far from striking, and she had been out on only one or two casual dates since the divorce. There just didn't seem to be any eligible men her age in her social group. And although she had become more self-confident and even somewhat extroverted as she grew older, she just didn't seem to fit in with most of the women's circles, either, perhaps because she'd not gone through a more typical adolescence nor learned to make the kinds of social adjustments that were necessary in that milieu.

She forced her mind back to the task at hand. The first block passed quickly, but she was laboring slightly and wasn't certain how long she could maintain this pace. Perspiration rolled down her forehead and, when she could no longer blink the moisture from her eyes, she tossed her head from side to side, eyes closed. But when she looked ahead once more, her unknown companion was back in view, running about one block ahead of her on Monroe. The other woman had apparently taken one of the cross streets back up to the straightaway.

Well, thought Barbara, at least I know we don't have identical routes ... that would really have stretched the limits of coincidence. But now the one-block gap seemed just as insuperable as ever, and just as infuriating. It was almost as if the woman were keeping the distance intentionally. Barbara missed a step and stumbled, but regained her balance with practiced ease. It was hard to believe that the other runner was still unaware of her; they had covered nearly two miles together by now.

Monroe ended at Pond Street, so it was unsurprising when she turned left, down in the general direction of the Sheffield property. Barbara squinted and tried to pick out the woman's profile, but intervening trees masked the view so thoroughly that she saw little more than an occasional patch of the gray sweatsuit. Determinedly, Barbara turned to follow.

They were working their way along one of the paths now, off the road, and as the rear of the mansion loomed closer, Barbara reviewed the options facing both of them in the moments ahead. Normally she skirted the property and crossed Main Street into the cemetery, but it was quite possible to turn left and head toward downtown, or right and out toward Route 13 or even Reservoir Road. The western part of town was a bit too deserted for her taste most of the time, and except for a brief shortcut

201

through a section of it on her way back, she usually avoided the area.

She watched intently as they followed a branch of the path that veered away from the building, down between it and the used car lot, and out toward Main. The woman took a quick glance in each direction, followed by a sprint across the street and in through the cemetery gate. Barbara sighed with relief and a few seconds later duplicated the movement and was making her own way in among the gravestones.

The two of them had the graveyard to themselves, although there was a distant sound of childrens' voices from a playground next to the housing development. Barbara's lungs labored now, and the muscles in her calves and thighs stiffened. She knew from experience that this would soon pass, that she would start to get her second wind on the backstretch.

Once again Barbara tried to shorten the intervening distance, this time angling across a grassy hill that crested near the Coleman family vault. But she slowed down considerably on the upslope, and when she spotted the elusive figure on the other side, she had lost ground rather than gained. A few moments later the gap had narrowed to its former distance, and Barbara began to suspect that the other runner had slowed intentionally, was toying with her for some mysterious reason of her own.

They ran on. Almost in synchronization they left the cemetery through the southern gate, then made their way up through the rows of duplexes the state had financed some ten years earlier. They crossed Reservoir Road and took the well-marked path that wound through a wooded hillside, then down through a meadow to Route 13. They passed two teenagers on bicycles and a barking dog and

disturbed some squirrels, but their run was otherwise un-
eventful until they reached the high ground above Raynor's Pond.

The pond was artificial. Years before, Carl Raynor had
built a concrete retaining wall across a section of swamp-
land where it drained between two high banks. Although
the water had backed up behind it, as expected, it had
eventually found other outlets and had never deepened as
was intended. Raynor died soon after, and the legacy he'd
left the town was a deteriorating, blocky mass of concrete
attractive to the town's children, which they referred to
incorrectly as "the dam," attractive despite or perhaps
because of its accompanying dangers. The current ran
swiftly and the banks above were eroded and unsafe.

The two figures ran along one of those banks now, about
twenty feet above the water, bearing down on the dam
site. And now, for the first time, the woman in the lead
began to falter, the even rhythm gone from her feet. Just
about goddamned time, too, thought Barbara, whose own
legs were decidedly shaky. Under normal circumstances,
she'd have stopped for a time rather than push on in this
condition. But she had no intention of allowing her silent,
mysterious companion to outlast her.

The other woman was swaying from side to side, showing signs of distress. Emboldened, Barbara actually picked
up a little speed and the distance began to shorten. She
concentrated on her breathing, and when she judged she
was within hailing range, she called out, her voice loud
but quavering with the effort.

"Hello, there! I've been trying—"

She stopped in mid-sentence as the woman half-turned
toward her, tripped over her own feet in the process, and
fell awkwardly, skidding to the edge of the embankment

203

and beyond. Barbara stopped suddenly, shocked and confused at what she'd seen in the other's face, then started forward again.

Both the woman's elbows were planted firmly in the soil, supporting her, but the soil itself was treacherous. It collapsed under her weight, disintegrating so suddenly that she just had time to look up into Barbara's face before dropping out of sight. And, for the second time, Barbara caught a glimpse of a frightening truth in that visage, which was an exact replica of her own. It was impossible! The shock rolled over her senses like a burst of flame. She had been pursuing some aspect of herself.

Barbara halted just short of where the other woman had disappeared, then edged forward gingerly to peer down at the concrete below. There was nothing there, no body, no sign of any impact, nothing to indicate she had ever existed . . . if she had.

Barbara stood there for a long time, staring down, not seeing. She tried to tell herself it had been a chance resemblance, that there was no possibility that the runner had worn her face, that her body had been carried away by the rushing water. She knew that none of this was true, no more true than the thought that she might have hallucinated the entire incident. It had been no hallucination, she was convinced, not in any ordinary sense of the word.

As she finally turned away, and brought her eyes and mind back to the present, she felt dizzy and her tentative step forward was uncertain. Overstressed muscles betrayed her at last, and she slipped, falling toward the brink.

She planted her elbows firmly in the soil, but it began to loosen and crumbled under her weight. Barbara glanced up, spotted a figure approaching, a figure in a gray sweatsuit much like her own, a youngish woman with short hair, moving as though she was very, very tired. And then she was looking up into her own face and, as the bank finally crumbled and she felt herself slipping away, the face changed, fangs growing from the lips, complexion darkening to a gritty blackness, eyes flaming red, and two enormous wings unfurling from the back of the Sheffield mansion gargoyle as it stared down at her pitilessly.

And she screamed and fell back and down . . . and woke up in her own bed.

Barbara lunged up, scrambling for something to hold onto, disoriented, drenched with sweat, every muscle screaming its exhaustion as though she really had run for nearly two hours. She sat on her bed, the light off, her body braced by the palms of both hands. She breathed heavily until the terror of her nightmare diminished and she could finally loosen her muscles enough to turn on the light and get out of bed.

There would be no more sleep for her tonight, she knew. Although she rarely had nightmares, they were always intense when they did come. And this was like nothing she'd ever experienced before. Barbara did not know how to articulate it precisely, not even to herself, but she knew that this was more than just a bad dream suggested by the events of the past few days. This was something sent to her from the outside, something important that she needed to understand.

But understanding was to be a long time in coming.

Although there had been some investigation into the possibility of taking custody of Arthur Kaplan's children away from him, neither the town nor the state nor the various governmental and nongovernmental agencies had ever found any concrete evidence that could be used as the basis for such an action. The children had not been physically abused in any fashion that they could detect, although they seemed unnaturally reticent of strangers, and diffident at best toward their father. Keith, in particular, seemed quite mature for his age and had taken much of the responsibility for Jeri's care on his own shoulders after the death of their mother. There was still some suspicion about that incident as well, but lacking any evidence to link Kaplan to his wife's murder, the police could certainly not use such speculation in any other application. And there were never funds available for even the obvious cases of necessary child care—so a borderline situation such as this did not even merit a second look. So the three of them continued to live together in their small, dingy apartment, and Arthur Kaplan continued to work as a floorboy at Eblis Manufacturing.

There were definite advantages to this job, despite the lower pay. The small insurance policy which his wife had carried, plus the benefits available through his employer, had taken the sting out the loss of her income. Eblis was a sprawling factory, built almost entirely on one level, expanded hodgepodge over the years to provide a plethora of places to hide. Management had created a centralized trucking department, which was supposed to eliminate waste by controlling all movement of materials from a single spot in lieu of having individuals assigned to each department. In theory, it made a lot of sense, but in practice, it only reduced the amount of supervision applied to each person within that department. The supervisor Charlie Colwell, was weak, disorganized, and unwilling to work hard at his new position. Bullock, the production control manager, was constantly chewing him out for not delivering materials as scheduled, and Colwell kept insisting that it was because he had insufficient manpower for the work that had to be done. And now that Nicholson kid had been taken out of production control and made a special assistant to Cataldo, the plant manager, to look into personnel utilization, and everyone was worried that they were going to be asked to cut back on staffing.

Kaplan had been careful of his drinking for the first few months following Edith's death, not out of remorse or even a sense of reform and responsibility, but only because he feared he might say or do something while under the influence that would lead to trouble or suspicion further on. But he had soon reverted to his usual state of near-constant inebriation, primarily because of his dreams.

With the death of Edith, he had felt that he had finally made the sacrificial act that would move the gargoyle to choose him as its representative. That night, for the first time in his life, he had felt a sensation from the glowering statue that was close to approval, and the warm glow of that feeling had continued for some time afterward. But soon the dreams regained their old tenor, the harsh disapproval, dissatisfaction, even disgust. More than once Arthur had been startled into wakefulness, crying out, "What more do you want of me?" Frequently, he woke with tears streaking down his cheeks. There had never been any answer.

His alcohol-befogged mind refused to provide him with any plan he could pursue to change the course of events, and it wasn't until the first snows of winter were beginning to soften the harsh outlines of Managansett that a new thought occurred to him, a new act of contrition. And when it came, it came suddenly, in a blinding, terrible flash.

Keith and Jeri were at home, and Arthur had gone out to replenish his supply of brandy before the nearby package store closed for the night. He was their best customer, but old Mr. McKenzie, the owner, hated to wait on him and wished he would take his trade elsewhere. Arthur had become increasingly repellent to him during the past two years, his physical condition deteriorating, his eyes less clear, his cheeks always red, his hair badly in need of washing and cutting, his clothes increasingly threadworn. Arthur was the picture of the classic alcoholic. Despite Mckenzie's years of selling the drink with which people destroyed their lives, he was a man with a great deal of sympathy for human self-destructiveness and would have refused to serve Arthur for his own good and that of his family if there were any legal way for him to do so. But there wasn't, so he handed Kaplan his change and the bottle of brandy and watched with open disapproval as the man left the store.

Unwilling to wait even the short time it would take him to reach home, Kaplan opened the bottle and took a long drink on a dark street corner, then closed the bottle and put it back in the bag. Chief Dowdell had warned him about drinking in public, so he had been somewhat circumspect, but there was also an element of daring in the act: what right, after all, did the police have to tell him what he could and could not do on a public sidewalk? Kaplan felt self-righteous and considered a second drink as an act of defiance, but he stumbled on the curb and decided it would be wiser to return to the apartment first.

He slipped once climbing the stairs, scraping his shin on the lip of the next step, and had to wait for several seconds while the shooting pains dissipated. Then he dropped the key while trying to fit it in the lock, pounded the door once, and called out, "Keith, open the fucking door," but his voice was too low to carry and the boy had already gone to bed. Mumbling to himself, Kaplan stooped and very carefully picked up the key, this time inserting it accurately into the lock and turning it. The apartment was nearly dark, lit by a single lamp in the living room, absolutely quiet except for the hum of the refrigerator in the kitchen and an occasional knocking as the hot steam coursed through the pipes, heating the building. Kaplan closed the door behind him and removed his coat slowly, switching the brandy from one hand to the other as he did so, then dropping the worn garment to the floor. Several deliberate steps brought him into the living room and he flopped down into the chair under the single illuminated map, the package in his lap.

When next he rose from that seat an hour later, the bottle of brandy was only half-full. He was clutching it in one hand when he arose, but it fell to the floor, spilling some of its contents, unnoticed. Kaplan shuffled into his bedroom, turned the light on, and looked down at his empty and unmade bed. He missed Edith after a fashion, particularly at night, partly for sex, partly for the simple fact of her presence in bed with him, a human weakness he had never quite overcome. Standing shakily in the doorway, it occurred to him as well that she used to check on the kids before coming to bed, and that he had never done so, not once, before or after her death. Arthur always thought of it in those terms, "her death," for his own actions seemed discrete from the fact of her departure from his life. It was, after all, a sacrifice demanded independently of his, Arthur's, wishes in the matter.

With one shoulder brushing the wall, Arthur made his way down the short corridor to the second bedroom, this time not turning on the light as he entered. Keith was asleep in the frame bed to the right, positioned directly under the room's only window. His breathing was regular, but the face seemed lined already beyond its years. Jeri lay in a trundle bed on the opposite side of the room. A restless sleeper, she had kicked her covers off and was lying on top of them now with her nightdress twisted to reveal her plump seven-year-old's legs. It occurred to Arthur that he should cover her up against the chill of the night, and with measured steps he crossed the room, endeavoring with moderate success to do so quietly. But when he reached down for the edge of the blankets, his knees gave way and he sank forward, out of balance, and half sprawled across the foot of the bed.

Jeri complained grumpily without waking up, turning over in her sleep, and one bare knee brushed the back of Arthur's hand as he struggled to push himself back to his feet. The touch was electrifying and he froze, then moved that same hand, stroking her bare leg. There was a faint stirring within him that was part affection, but mostly something much more powerful and terrible and he repeated the touch, more firmly this time, then moved the hem of the nightdress so that more of his daughter's flesh was exposed.

"Daddy, is that you?" Jeri's eyes had opened and she was staring at him levelly.

Arthur thought he saw accusation in that stare, and his mouth moved as though to answer. But something moved within him again, paralyzing his vocal chords, and instead he reacted by gripping one small thigh more tightly, so much so that Jeri cried out in sudden pain.

The sound wakened Keith, who struggled up out of unconsciousness. Arthur was blind and deaf to any other presence and grabbed Jeri by one arm as she moved to crawl away. Once more he felt a desire to speak, to explain, to plead with his daughter perhaps, or to plead with something else to free him of this compulsion. But as he hovered on the brink of two very different courses of action, a small flurry of fists about his head shocked him into a defensive reflex and he swept both arms around instinctively, knocking Keith sprawling. The nine-year-old was up again almost immediately, charging at his father, and this time Arthur met him with a closed fist. Keith's head jerked up at the blow and he staggered back, hitting the far wall with the back of his head and sliding senselessly to the floor.

Arthur Kaplan turned back to his daughter, who was now crouched at the head of the bed where it abutted the corner of the room. She was completely trapped. Her eyes flashed in the dim light and there was fear in them, but she didn't cry out then, or even later, not until her father had returned to his own room and she had crawled painfully out of bed and over to the recumbent form of her brother. When he regained consciousness in the small hours before dawn, she was curled up against the side of his body, asleep.

CHAPTER NINE
1970

"Nobody works on my goddamned press!" The words had been shouted loudly enough to penetrate the thin office walls despite the din from the manufacturing floor outside. Frank Cataldo tossed his pencil down on the desk and pushed the weekly labor reports aside. It was Alex Furtado again; he'd recognize that gravelly voice anywhere. The man was rapidly becoming more trouble than he was worth.

There were further shouts, inaudible this time, and then faintly the slow, measured tones of Calvin Scott, newly appointed press room supervisor whose appointment followed the resignation of the former man, Rossiter. Cataldo found himself almost cringing, awaiting the inevitable renewed outburst.

"Don't care what the goddamned contract says! I didn't sign no fucking contract!" The voice still agitated, rising and dropping, sometimes unintelligible.

With a disgusted sigh Cataldo pushed away from his desk and got to his feet. He had expected problems reorganizing Eblis Manufacturing and had looked forward to solving them, but some of the personnel problems were in a class by themselves. First he had that bright but vicious assistant assigned to him, Nicholson, who had almost singlehandedly brought about the demise of John Bullock, the former production control manager, by a systematic analysis and demolition of everything the man did. It had been helpful to Cataldo, who'd been locked in a power struggle with the man for operational control ever since his arrival, but what Cataldo had interpreted as overzealous loyalty had proven to be something entirely different. His first goal accomplished, Nicholson had set his sights on John Paruti, the quality control manager, planning to demolish his credibility similarly. But Paruti and Cataldo were close friends, and Cataldo had ordered his assistant to desist, only to find himself faced with stubborn refusal. It was then that he realized Nicholson was out to make himself look good, at the cost of anyone and everyone else. The man did not understand the meaning of personal loyalty and expected neither to give nor receive it. And he had been succesful enough already that Cataldo could not move against him without a good and sufficient reason to do so.

Alex Furtado was another case in point. The man was surly, obstreperous, and increasingly troublesome these past two years, with no interest in the opinions, rights, or authority of anyone else. Fortunately the man was not a union official—that would have made it a bigger political mess than it already was.

He opened his office door and glanced out across the production floor. The company owned about three dozen presses, about a third of them double-action giants, the balance made up of more limited single-action equipment. At any given time, about two-thirds of the presses were in operation, fewer than in the past because of the recent fall

213

off in business. Right now few of the presses were actually running, because most of the operators had stopped to watch the small drama playing itself out.

The oldest of the double-action presses, a monstrous piece of machinery from the Blair Press Company, number seven as it was known at Eblis, was nearing its final days. Although it was nearly obsolete and almost impossible to repair because of a lack of replacement parts, so many of the production die sets had been made specifically for this one press that phasing it out of service was a major undertaking. Alex Furtado was in many ways the perfect match for the machine; he was one of the company's more senior employees now, set in his ways, unadaptable, cranky, and less efficient with each passing week. He was also totally opposed to the new system Cataldo had ordered installed, where operators were rotated from press to press rather than working exclusively on one piece of equipment.

Almost from the first day of his employment, Alex had adopted number seven as his own, bullied his previous supervisor into catering to his whim, even learned to do all the set-ups of new tools himself, and during the past few years in particular, he'd virtually never worked on another press. No one had *ever* worked on number seven for more than an hour during that time. Bill Stevens had finished up a job one day years ago when Alex had been out sick, and at quitting time the following day he'd discovered that all four of his tires had been mysteriously slashed.

In the past, management had been lax, and by the time Cataldo was hired to improve the company's flagging productivity, Furtado had become an apparently insurmountable obstacle, one of the few that the new factory manager had to date been unable to circumvent.

The new union contract made it impossible to fire him or lay him off without due process, and they lacked grounds for either action. Any disagreement with Furtado, no matter how slight, became a major labor issue, requiring hours of argument and associated paperwork, because he would immediately file a grievance through the union, whose officials privately confessed an aversion to him as well. Fortunately, since Furtado was not an official himself, everything ran smoothly so long as he personally was pampered. The rest of the membership was considerably more cowed ... or cooperative, Cataldo thought with a smile. They're being more cooperative. But the effect on morale—particularly that of Calvin Scott, recently promoted to the position of press room supervisor—bothered Cataldo more than the occasional grievance in any case. Scott was his handpicked man, personally loyal, an ally in the unraveling battle for power within the company's volatile organizational structure.

Jameson, the time-study man, walked briskly past, clipboard and stopwatch hanging loosely in one hand. He glanced up at Cataldo, grimaced, and shook his head, but didn't stop to talk. Frank suppressed a grin: as much as he disliked Furtado, it was amusing to see how easily he could upset Jameson, who had never quite understood why there had to be people involved in the production process. It was so much more orderly and predictable and quantifiable without the human element to consider.

Cataldo waved to Scott, who seemed to have been waiting for him to appear. Scott said something inaudible to Furtado, who answered gruffly and began walking back toward his press. Scott watched the man for a second, then crossed the floor to where his boss stood.

"What now?" Cataldo stepped aside so Scott could enter the office.

"The same as always—Furtado doesn't want anyone else touching his precious press. He says they loused up its timing, this time. Christ, can't we do something about the guy? Retire him? Transfer him to another department? Promote him?"

Cataldo didn't bother to answer. The question was obviously rhetorical, a product of frustration rather than a serious suggestion.

"Why not let him run the job?"

Scott sat down without invitation and lit a cigarette. "It's that new seashell server. The first draw is the same as on the old style, and the only press we can run it on is good old number seven. Jameson studied the job on Furtado last time we ran it, and the rate is apparently too high."

"How much did he make on the last run?"

"Not that much. He never does lately. He and that press run at just one speed. But the pricing is apparently a real issue on this item, and Jameson wants a check study on another operator . . . any other operator."

Cataldo sat down on a corner of his desk. "What did you tell Furtado?"

Scott took a drag on his cigarette and exhaled. "Obviously I didn't tell him that the rate was too high. I changed the lubricant and reset the timing on the press and told him it was a method change. He wouldn't buy it."

"All right, let it slide, then."

Scott jerked as though hit, then glanced up at the older man. "Let it slide? I thought we agreed that we had to
216

meet this problem head on. If you aren't going to back me up with this man, I'm going to look pretty foolish out on the floor."

Cataldo smiled. "Don't worry; we're not backing off for long. A couple days, if all goes well. Davenport made a deal." Davenport was their new labor relations manager, a man who specialized in the kinds of labor problems that most companies chose to ignore. "He's worked it out with the rep from the union's international office. Some of the members have been complaining about the special treatment we've been giving Furtado, even though they're too chickenshit to say anything openly within the plant. The company is going to make some concessions on the retirement fund proposal, and in return Furtado finds his footing cut out from under him, so long as no one else is hurt. All very unofficial."

"So someone got paid under the table." Scott didn't look particularly mollified. "Rather than face him on the issue, we sneak around and stab him in the back?"

"You could look at it that way." Cataldo paused a moment, staring at the young man whom he thought of as his protegé, perhaps his heir-apparent in about ten years, if he moved up to replace the ineffective and largely ornamental vice-president of manufacturing, Oliver Moore. "There's something you have to learn about management, Scotty. You have to decide whether you want to win the battles or win the war. We could fight Furtado forthrightly and feel very noble about it, and the union would back him up because they're obligated to, and we'd probably win after a long, expensive battle. And along the way, we'd alienate a lot of a people who are currently neutral. Sometimes you have to swallow your pride, or your sense of

217

fitness, and be pragmatic. This way we win, so this is how it's going to be played. That's all there is to it."

Scott stubbed out his cigarette in an ashtray and rose. "All right, you're calling the shots. I don't particularly like it, but I can't suggest anything better." He crossed to the door, opened it, then turned back. "Have to admit, I'm looking forward to seeing his face. Maybe we can even repaint that damned press of his one of these days."

"Maybe we will, Scotty," replied Cataldo with some amusement. "Wait and see."

It turned out to be almost two weeks before the details of the clandestine agreement were worked out, and a day or two more before the first confrontation. Furtado was disputing a rate, one that had been studied the previous week. It was silly for him to be doing so, on the face of it; the company had been after him for years to cash his checks on time. But Furtado was shrewd in his way, and he knew that if he didn't maintain a certain level of production and earnings, he might be in serious trouble in his running battle with the efforts of management to oust him from exclusive control of his press. Jameson had refused to release this particular rate at first, because a speed rating below sixty-percent efficiency was considered too unreliable to use as the basis for setting a standard. Furtado had been deliberately speed-rated at fifty percent to force the issue.

Cataldo considered handling the situation personally, but immediately thought better of it—it was more advantageous to handle things routinely. The agreement with the union was fragile enough that he didn't want to risk puffing up the matter into something more than it should be. Besides, if he stepped between Scott and his own department, he'd be undermining his own supervisor. But as it happened, he ended up facing the situation himself.

He was reviewing the overtime listing when the office door was pushed open hard enough that it slammed the wall. Furtado stormed into the room, hair disheveled, coveralls badly in need of washing and mending, safety shoes so worn that the metal cap showed through. At the best of times, Furtado was not the most pleasant of sights.

"Goddamn it, Cataldo, what the hell is going on?" Furtado placed both hands down on the desk and leaned forward intimidatingly. "This goddamned jerk," he gestured back over his shoulder to where Scott had appeared in the doorway, "is trying to give somebody else my goddamned job! He can't do that! Tell him he can't do that! I got rights! It's my press and my goddamned job! Get'm off my back; I got work to do!"

Cataldo slowly raised his eyes to meet those of the other man, savoring the moment. "Get off my desk," he said in a low voice. He considered rising, using his superior height for psychological advantage, then discarded the idea. He doubted it would work with this man ... better to play this as low-key as possible, at least for now. "If you have a complaint about work assignments, you're welcome to use the grievance procedure. You've used it often enough in the past to know how it works. You don't own work in this factory, Furtado, and you don't own the press. No one does. This is a place of business, not a private club, and you will abide by the same rules as everyone else."

"But that's my goddamned press! It's always been my goddamned press! I got my rights, my seniority!"

"Yes, you certainly do." Cataldo opened his desk drawer and fished around for a copy of the union contract while still talking. "But the company has its rights, too, and reassignment of individuals within a department is at the discretion of the company so long as the employee in question retains the opportunity to make within ten percent of his normal piecework earnings." He tossed the small bound contract booklet down on the desk. "Article Five, if I remember correctly. If you believe that we're in violation, file a grievance with your supervisor." He nodded to Scott. "And in the meantime," and this time he did rise, and his tone deepened as well, "don't you ever come into this office again without knocking. Now get back to your job!"

The two men stared at each other, but it was Furtado whose eyes dropped first. He turned and started out the door, brushing past a clearly amused Scott. Halfway out, he turned. "You don't give my press to no one else, you understand?" His voice was low but menacing. "It's my goddamned press and it always will be. I'm warning you . . . don't mess around." And he was gone.

Scott waited a few seconds before speaking. "He'll see the shop steward during break and, if they don't tell him what he wants to hear, he'll be calling the national office during lunch."

"Let him." Cataldo resumed his seat. "The fix is in, as they say." Oddly, the scene had not been as satisfying as he'd anticipated. There was an air about Furtado, a frightening aura that persisted even after he'd left the room. Cataldo made a mental note to be careful not to go alone into dark corners for a while. He wouldn't put outright violence beyond the man.

Unsurprisingly, Furtado bolted straight for the pay phone when the noon bell sounded, not even bothering to wash up. He spent almost the entire half-hour there, feeding coins into the slot, and when he finally replaced the receiver, he was pale, his hair damp and matted. He never went to the cafeteria at all, but returned to the press area where he sat on a bench beside double-action seven until the whistle blew, not eating, not speaking, barely moving.

He stared into the painted eyes of the gargoyle, the curled lip that even in his own creation seemed to sneer at him, and he lost the last vestige of hope that had sustained him through the years. He had failed, failed utterly, and would never be able to enter proudly into the presence of the being he worshipped above all others. He had been abandoned, thrown aside like a piece of trash.

A few minutes later Cataldo was disturbed by a shout from outside his office, followed by another, then a general uproar. The rhythmic concussion for the punch presses became irregular, faltered, stopped entirely. Then someone screamed.

With a horrible feeling Cataldo rose and walked quickly out onto the floor. People were running around shouting, and one man was leaning over a trash barrel, holding on with both hands while he vomited into it.

There was a growing crowd at double-action seven, and as he approached, he seemed to know already what had happened. He pressed forward, almost losing his balance as one foot slipped in something sticky. People moved aside revealing the press, ram down, die set firmly locked, top to bottom. There were streaks of dark wetness that might almost have been oil. Alex Furtado had removed his safeguards, leaned over the bottom die, and waited calmly for the two-ton ram to descend. He would never file a grievance again.

The problems that had revolved around double-action seven should have started to clear up in the weeks following Furtado's death, but they didn't. The state and federal governments had sent investigators, and a seal had been placed on the press for almost a month before the company was exonerated of all responsibility in the matter of Furtado's death. Then it was discovered that a bearing had cracked, and the repairs dragged on even longer while a few other suspected faults were corrected.

Finally everything had tested out and Scott had the press set up to run a sample lot for a new water pitcher. Maria Cramer, one of the most experienced operators in the department, was just putting on the safety cords—cuffs around her wrists attached by a wire to the descending ram, so that when it met with the bottom die her hands were pulled safely out of the way—when she slipped on an oil spill and cracked her head against the front of the main housing, which had recently been repainted to remove the blood stains, as well as the hideous face that had long gazed out across this area of the press department. Maria was rushed by ambulance to the hospital, diagnosed as having suffered a mild concussion, and placed on medical leave of absence.

The following day, a newly hired set-up man named Walters was lubricating double-action seven when his sleeve caught on the main drive chain. He broke two fingers before Scott cut the power. Cataldo stormed into maintenance and the press was properly shielded two days later. The following week, another operator lost three fingers when one of the safety cords snapped and he didn't withdraw his hand in time. The state inspector paid another visit, and this time there were dour hints about citations and fines.

Scott was in Cataldo's office that same afternoon.

"If this keeps up, people are going to start saying Furtado is haunting the place. There's already a couple of people who say flat out they don't want to be assigned to double-action seven, ever."

"They'll get over it. It's just bad luck, all of these things happening close together like this. Give them time to forget it and things will get back to normal."

"Yeah, but in the meantime we're falling behind. There's a couple of jobs I can move to double-action six, and we can do all the trimming operations on alternative equipment, but too many of our biggest sellers were designed specifically for number seven. We're starting to fall seriously behind schedule, stock outs are up, and even overtime won't solve the problem if we don't get back into production soon. And we're short three operators now as well."

"We've been through all this before. Most of these tools should have been designed to be interchangeable long ago, but they weren't, and converting them all is going to be a long and expensive process. We're just going to have to make do with what we've got for now. Requisition some more operators through personnel; with the economy down, there ought to be at least a couple of experienced people in the market."

"So what's next?"

"The tool room people are building a screen to cover the front of the press. The operator inserts each piece through a small gateway, using a crimped bar to push it into place. It's slower, but it's as foolproof as we could make it."

"That's going to slow us down even further."

"Can't be helped. We don't want the state people shutting us down for safety reasons."

But the next day they fared no better. Irma Kalin, who was scheduled to run number seven, balked. The woman was plainly frightened rather than rebellious, so Scott changed her assignment and tried to get another operator to switch jobs. This man refused as well, insisting that number seven was bad luck. "She's gone bad, Mr. Scott. Old Alex was the only one who could get along with her."

Scott had nearly flown into a rage at that point. DaRosa from production control had just given him hell because the entire master schedule was going to have to be revised again, and he was in no mood to hear further talk of curses and ghosts and bad luck. He just wanted number seven back in operation.

Finally he hit upon what should have been the solution. He had started as a press operator himself and wasn't afraid of getting his hands dirty. "All right," he said at last. "Go back to your job. Today I'll run number seven, and assuming I survive the experience, maybe you'll realize how silly you sound."

It was later ascertained that he had completed nearly two hundred pieces before the accident occurred. As the ram began to rise, the brass stamping caught in the top die, possibly because of uneven lubrication. As it rose, the piece fell half-free, and since it was rectangular, one corner snagged in the mesh of the protective screen and began pulling it upward as well. Scott leaned forward to poke at the piece with his bar, and at that moment the screen pulled free with such force that it smashed through Scott's safety glasses, cutting across both eyes, destroying them.

For days following the accident, Cataldo felt irrationally guilty. Although he had set in motion the chain of events which had ended so tragically, there was really no way in which he was responsible. He felt an irrational rage as well. He hated double-action seven with a passion so strong that he felt a tremor pass through his body whenever he walked past it. But this latest incident had accomplished something else: old man Eblis was now reluctantly willing to admit that none of the press operators were likely ever to agree to run number seven again. They had hired two full-time toolmakers to convert the die sets for other presses. Double-action seven was headed for the scrap heap.

Removal of the press was a two-day job. All easily detachable portions were disassembled first while a hole was cut in the roof over the press room, not far from Cataldo's office. On the second morning, the riggers arrived with a crane and began attaching the cables with which the press would be lifted out and placed on a flatbed trailer for its final ride. Cataldo thought about watching her go up, but even in these final moments, he could not stand the sight of her ugly green sides, scored countless times over the course of decades of use. Instead he sat in his office, reviewing reports, reading his mail, trying not to think about Scott.

He did in fact hear the first cable when it snapped, although the sound meant nothing to him, a minor mystery not worth the time to investigate. He thought it might have been the ascending press grazing something on its way up, and he would not even have risen had he not heard the sound of men shouting excitedly. He had just opened the door to find out what was going on when the second cable gave way. The remaining strands held just long enough to change the angle of momentum as it fell. The flimsy office superstructure didn't even slow its descent. Neither did the fragile construction of flesh and bone that stood within it.

Valerie Meredith had never needed to worry about money. Even though she had moved out of her parents' home shortly after graduation, the death of her mother after an "accidental" overdose of medication had provided her with an inheritance so vast that she did not even need to remain on good terms with her father. Since it wasn't necessary, she made no effort to do so, and the string of live-in boyfriends which she had accumulated over the next few years first strained, then ultimately snapped the strong bonds of affection which he had always felt for her. Subsequently he had taken a job in Chicago, sold out, and left town, and she did not even have his current address.

Many people wondered why Valerie, an obvious beauty with income enough to provide her with a comfortable standard of living, should settle down in such a backwater as Managansett. The town was easily two decades behind the times, a conservative stronghold isolated even from nearby Providence, which was hardly on the cutting edge of culture itself.

When asked, Valerie would answer disingenuously, if at all. This was her home, so why should she move elsewhere? But the truth was that even Valerie didn't understand the attraction, at least not consciously. That was a bit of knowledge which she kept concealed even from herself.

Her current boyfriend was Eddie Bridges, two years her junior. Valerie's looks had not dimmed after high school, and the two made quite a handsome couple. But Valerie had yet to find anyone whom she could really consider an equal. The men she had slept with over the years had all been ridiculously simple to manipulate, either sexually or by other means. Eddie was no exception—intelligent enough to write copy for a local advertising agency, with a reasonable income, good looks, a lean physique, but with hair that was already starting to thin on top.

They had been together for three months now—close to a record for Valerie—but she felt it was time to bring it to an end. She was up before him and had never been able to remain in bed much past seven. Valerie was filled with a restless energy that she found difficult to satisfy, the kind that in a different sort of person would have resulted in great works of art, literature, a financial empire, political success, or some other outstanding human endeavor. But nothing in life had managed to hold her interest, and she subliminated any ambition with an endless round of drinking, partying, sex, and excitement. She drove fast cars, experimented with drugs, and had a genuine fascination for pit-bull meets. The closest she ever felt to real emotion lately was when one dog inflicted particular harm on another, a cracked leg or a gouge in the side, preferably with lots of blood.

But today she had decided to evict Eddie Bridges from her home and her life. The question facing her now was how to accomplish the eviction, and how to derive the most amusement from it. In the past none of her sexual partners had been allowed to be a part of her personal world again, and most of them had had no desire to. Valerie had a way of terminating her relationships that compelled others to keep the details of their parting a secret, although there were many rumors, some pervasive enough that many potential suitors attempted to resist her initial blandishments. But Valerie could be very convincing when she needed to be, and few had been able to remain outside of her grasp once she decided she wanted them.

She could hear Eddie stirring sleepily as she sat on the porch of her apartment, three stories above the ground, the only decent apartment building in the town so far as she was concerned. It had been built one block south of the Managansett Inn, set back from the road and shielded by a double screen of poplars planted along the property front. There was a clause in the rental agreement prohibiting children, so the complex remained quiet, and most of the units were occupied by single people or older couples whose children had grown and moved on. It would have been quite expensive closer to Providence, but the rates were actually fairly moderate, all things considered.

"Morning, Val." Eddie brushed past her and crossed to the small table where she had left the coffee maker and its accoutrements. She watched while he poured himself a cup, then added sugar and lots of milk. Another year or two and he would be drinking it black, she thought, in order to keep his boyish belly flat . . . not that such abstinence would do any good. Eddie was basically a soft person, soft in mind and soft in body.

He approached and sat in one of the chairs, half-facing her, looking out over the parking lot. "Sure is bright and cheery today." He sipped at his drink; she would not dignify the syrupy sweet mess by calling it coffee, not even in her mind. She always took hers black and strong.

As he sat there, striving to look charming and sexy despite his sleepiness, the bathrobe casually thrown over crossed legs to expose as much of one thigh as possible, she felt an almost physical churning in her stomach. Yes, today was the day, all right . . . he had to go today. If she had to spend another night with this jerk, she'd probably throw up all over him. The question was how to go about making sure the severance was complete. Valerie didn't like loose ends and wanted her affairs to end with a distinct finish. The idea of having some lovestruck, or luststruck, former beau clamoring for another chance struck her as both unpleasant and unnecessary. So in each case, she had staged some final act so that the separation was marked with a degree of permanence that would allow no rapprochement. Preferably there had to be an air of humiliation as well, not only because she enjoyed manipulating people, but because it made it very difficult for her ex-partners to spread the word about the dangers of forming a temporary alliance with her. And temporary was definitely the word in Valerie's case. She barely tolerated most people, was only mildly fond of the men she had bedded, and certainly neither loved nor admired anyone, male or female.

"What are we going to do today?" Eddie made it sound casual, but Valerie knew from experience that he was still captivated with her, not so much for the sex as for the opportunity to be seen publicly in her company. She boosted his prestige and his own self-image enormously and was clearly the most striking woman he had ever known, let alone dated. Her adolescent youth had flowered into a firm, mature loveliness that was daunting in its perfection and frightening in its coldness, in the calculating awareness of everything that took place around her. Valerie dominated any company she shared. She knew instinctively how to take control of a conversation, how to draw all attention, male and female, to herself. And her beauty was the kind that would remain unchanged for years to come. She was the kind of woman that caused people to make half-humorous, half-jealous jokes about the painting she must be concealing in her attic.

"Mess around, I guess," she answered at last, rewarding him with a brief smile. "But I want to go up to the Loft this evening."

The Loft had just opened this year, an oversized barn converted at great expense into a double-tiered nightclub, with a dance floor at ground level, and a bar and tables in an elaborate mezzanine along three walls. The fourth wall held an elevated stage for live bands, although most of the time the music was canned. The Loft was way out at the western border of town, up a long, unpaved road; the building was originally intended as the barn for a real farm, but the owner had experienced a series of financial and personal setbacks, dropped all plans for developing the property a few years before, and sold out for what he could recoup from his original investment. The new owner had spent a great deal on improvements, and many of the local people had considered him foolish, assuming that there would be insufficient business this far from the city to justify such an expensive club, but its remoteness, its atmosphere, and skillful management had turned it into one of the more popular and profitable clubs in the state.

"I thought you didn't like that place."

"It's not the greatest, but maybe I didn't give it a chance the first time." As a matter of fact, she *didn't* like it. The owner walked the floor whenever the place was open, and if he felt someone had had too much, he personally escorted them out. He seemed to have an uncanny knack of knowing exactly when someone had exceeded his or her personal limits. Neither would he tolerate having his club used by prostitutes or pushers, and he only gave one warning before calling the police. Valerie had even tried flirting with him once, with absolutely no luck. She thought he might possibly be gay; the wedding ring was probably just an affectation.

"Who're we going to bring along?"

She smiled seductively, but her mind was working furiously. "Oh, I thought we'd just go by ourselves. I have an idea for something really special tonight."

"Like what?"

"You'll see, Eddie. It's going to be my surprise." She

smiled at him, and even Eddie, overwhelmed by her beauty and her personality, noticed something in the look that made him slightly uneasy, enough to make him wonder just what she had in mind. "I'll drive," she added, almost as an afterthought. But it was not; she had had her inspiration.

They arrived at the Loft about eight o'clock and had three or four drinks in the mezzanine. Eddie asked her to dance, but she declined, pleading tiredness but actually too intent upon her evening's amusement. Valerie had copied his choice of drinks with each round, although the sombreros that he seemed to be fond of at the moment struck her as nauseatingly sweet. After the second round, he never noticed when she switched glasses, always arranging it so that he was consuming much more alcohol than she was. She had also been careful to make certain that they ate lightly and early, so that his body would have more difficulty than usual adjusting to the drinks. After the sixth round, she felt the time was ripe, and the look from the owner last time he'd passed their table had warned her that Eddie was judged to be at his limit. It was important that they not be thrown out before she could consummate the day's plans.

"Let's take a walk, Eddie. I need some air."

He giggled, positively giggled, and she wondered how she had managed to stomach him for as long as she had—nearly three months. Was he really always this disgusting when he had had too much to drink, or was she just letting it get to her more this evening because she wanted the affair over with? It didn't matter, in any case, and Valerie was not given to introspection.

"Come on!" She got up, grabbed his wrist, and tugged him to his feet.

"Okay! All right, already. I'm coming." He reached down and picked up his drink, drained it, and placed the glass back on the table with exaggerated care. She pulled at his arm impatiently.

Climbing down the stairs to the ground level was quite an accomplishment, and Valerie decided she should have made her move one drink earlier. But with judicious bracing, she managed to guide him down without mishap, then led him across the dance floor, sparsely populated this evening, and out the front door. The night was cool, but not uncomfortably so, and as the door slammed shut behind them, muting the noise from the speaker system, she felt a surge of adrenaline in anticipation of the events already unfolding in her mind.

She led Eddie past the corner of the Loft and into the woods that abutted it on three sides.

"Where are we going, Val?" Eddie glanced around nervously. He didn't like the dark.

"I've got something special planned, Eddie—something you'll really like." They walked down the far side of the building, about halfway, then turned and picked their way carefully through the trees. It was mostly pine here, and the ground was thickly matted with needles. Valerie stopped, looked around to make certain they were shielded from view, then dropped Eddie's hand.

She could just barely make out his face in the filtered light. He looked slightly puzzled but still smiled, his eyes unfocused. She'd take care of that pretty quickly. And with one fluid movement she grabbed the hem of her pullover and lifted it up over her head, allowing her breasts to spill free.

"Val!" He looked around nervously. "What're you doing that for?" He hiccoughed, he actually hiccoughed.

"Someone'll see us here!" Eddie had become quite agitated. Easily embarrassed at the best of times, he suddenly felt goose pimples break out on his skin, and they had nothing to do with the cool breeze.

"Come on, stud," she said playfully, tossing the blouse to the ground. "Get 'em off. We're going to fuck right here and no one's ever going to know a thing about it." She put her hands on her hips and swayed forward suggestively. "I'm going to give you a thrill like you never had before."

He still looked dubious, so she stepped forward and ran the palm of one hand down his chest, over the belt buckle, lightly stroking the inside on one thigh. "Let's go, Eddie. This is something special, you know. It's going to be our greatest night ever, I promise you."

"Shit," he whispered, starting to unbutton his shirt, his fingers clumsy and ineffective.

"No, let me do it." She did so, then helped him work it down over his arms. His belt and zipper came next, but he pushed her away when she tried to edge his jeans down over his hips.

"You too, Val," he said huskily, moving a step away.

She struggled to suppress an annoyed look, although he might not have seen it in the dark. "Sure, Eddie, I can undress faster than you any day."

Seconds later, both of them were naked, and Eddie was moving toward her. "No," she whispered, making it sound sultry and seductive. "A little further on." And she urged him several yards further from the building. "This looks good."

They both dropped to the ground and Eddie was reaching forward to grasp one pendulous breast when she pulled back suddenly.

"Shit," she said. "I forgot."

Eddie had to try twice to get intelligible words out. "What'sa matter?"

"Forgot to put in the damn thing."

"Well, do it now!" He sounded petulant.

"Can't see well enough here. I'll have to go inside."

"Wait—don't do that!" Eddie sounded nervous again. "You can't leave me alone out here! I'll come with you."

"Don't be silly." She was already on her feet. "It'll only take me a minute. I'll be back before you can get dressed anyway."

She ran to her clothes and started dressing. "You can lie right down there and make a warm spot for me to lie on. You wouldn't want me to catch cold, would you?"

Although he had half-risen, Eddie froze, now uncertain. Valerie finished dressing, still keeping up the patter, more to occupy his mind than anything else. When she was ready, she squatted, gathered Eddie's clothes into her arms, and rose.

"Eddie," she called sweetly. "Remember back when we first started going together, you told me you weren't ready for a heavy commitment?"

"Yeah," he sounded uncertain and probably could not see her at all.

"Well, I think you were right . . . in fact, I don't think you're ready for *any* kind of commitment. So I made a decision today, a decision for both us. It's time for this particular circus to fold up its tents and move on. You can pick up your clothes and things tomorrow; I'll leave them in the front hall." She had already arranged for the apartment lock to be changed during the day, while they had been ostensibly shopping for her summer wardrobe.

"Don't understand, Val . . . what're you talking about?"

234

And obviously he didn't. Her words had not penetrated at all.

"We're through, Eddie. This is the end. I don't like long, drawn-out farewells, and I don't like emotional partings. So let's just say this is for the kicks and let's go our own ways from now on."

Without another word she turned and left him there. He didn't even call after her; he was still trying to figure out what had happened.

Valerie opened her car door, threw Eddie's clothes through to the passenger side, and realized she had forgotten his shoes. Maybe that was best. The poor slob had a four-mile walk back to town, closer to five if he chose to take advantage of the darkness to sneak back to his own apartment house, although without a key, he would have to wake someone up to open the front door for him. She laughed as she started the engine. The only problem with this jest was that she wouldn't be around to see some of the best parts. But on the other hand, it wasn't likely Eddie would ever complain publicly about the way she'd broken off the affair. And it was extremely unlikely that he'd try to get her back.

All in all, it was a very satisfactory solution to the problem, and a more than satisfying evening.

CHAPTER TEN
1973

The Kaplan household had much of the feel of an armed camp. Keith Kaplan was not particularly large for a fifteen-year-old, but his father had allowed alcohol to diminish his own physical resources to a point where he was no longer willing to risk a test of strength with Keith. It would be too humiliating to be bested by his own flesh and blood.

Arthur was basically a coward, a man whose secret desire was to physically dominate those around him, even though he was hardly equipped to do so. There had been a few repetitions of the assault which had first taken place three years ago, differing only in detail—Keith trying in vain to defend his sister while Jeri grew to accept what she could not understand. But a year ago Keith had inflicted enough punishment on his drunken father that Jeri had been spared, and the boy had thereafter made certain that the two of them were never left alone together. For a year now, there had been relative peace, although it was a sullen one.

Business had picked up at Eblis Manufacturing, and some of the equipment was now operating full-time once again. In order to save production hours, maintenance work and cleaning had been rescheduled in the evening. Arthur's work schedule now commenced at three o'clock in the afternoon, and he rarely made it home before midnight. Keith would meet Jeri after school, and their father would be gone when they arrived home, and sound asleep when they rose the next morning and prepared for the day. After several months of this routine, Keith finally began to relax for the first time in far too long.

It was a Monday evening, and Keith and Jeri were poking around in the kitchen, looking for inspiration about supper.

"Isn't there any meat at all?" Jeri called from where she stood crouched, peering into the cupboard where they kept the canned goods. She had grown almost as tall as her brother now, but thin, her face in particular. The gauntness was exaggerated by her long, straight hair. Jeri Kaplan was not attractive in any conventional sense, but there was an intensity about her that imprinted itself on the memory of most who met her.

Keith had opened the freezer and was poking around. "Nothing worth the trouble to thaw. There's a couple of soup bones, some vegetables with freezer burn, and a few other things I can't even make out.

"He was supposed to do the shopping Saturday. He said that was why he didn't have any cash to give us."

"Spent it all on booze again, probably." Keith slammed the freezer door shut in disgust. "Anything down there?"

"Nothing to make a meal on." She pushed the packages and cans about aimlessly. "Unless you want to go vegetarian. We have canned peas and canned green beans

237

and canned cream of corn and four, count 'em, *four* different brands of crackers."

"I'll pass on that, I think." He considered the matter. "Tell you what, Jeri. I have a little bit of cash I, uh, borrowed from him once when he wasn't paying attention to where he left his wallet. I'll take a walk down to the Buy 'n' Save and pick up some hamburger and rolls. There's still some relish in the fridge."

"Sounds all right to me. I can heat up the beans when you get back, if you want."

"Sure, why not?" He disappeared into the bedroom they still shared, recovered a few dollars he had secreted on a shelf in their closet, and put on a light sweater. It was spring, but the weather hadn't turned really warm yet.

"Coming?" He waited at the front door.

"No, not if you don't mind. I have a lot of homework to do. Things weren't quiet enough this weekend, and I have to catch up." Arthur Kaplan had paced the apartment like a caged lion all weekend, roaring and complaining at every excuse. The night shift did not appeal to him, he was tired of the apartment, the kids were not properly respectful, Jeri's cooking wasn't fit for pigs, and so forth and so on.

"Nah, go ahead and get it done. I hope you're not starving. This is going to take half an hour anyway."

"Nope. I pigged out at lunch. See you when you get back."

As the door closed, Jeri gathered her school books from the bedroom, brought them into the living room, and scattered them on the floor. She seemed to be able to concentrate best lying on her stomach, with the work materials within easy reach. The first algebra problem went easily and the second was progressing quite well when the door opened again.

"Forget something?" She turned and looked up, expecting Keith. But it was her father standing there, the familiar brown paper bag clutched in his hand. Jeri's mood changed as though she'd been slapped in the face. "What's the matter?" The words implied interest, but not the tone. "Aren't you supposed to be at work?" For a frightening moment, she feared he'd been fired.

"Power failure," he explained after a long pause. "No work tonight." He looked around the apartment. "What's for supper?"

"We couldn't find anything, so Keith went out to get some hamburger." Her mouth snapped shut. How were they to explain where Keith had come up with the money? But how could they avoid having to make an explanation eventually? Keith would return with the evidence soon enough. Arthur seemed not to have picked up on the implication of her statement, though, and she hastened to change the subject. "I have to get back to my homework. It's due tomorrow."

She turned back to the book, but the numbers and letters and symbols blurred in front of her eyes. She could still feel his gaze burning through her back. *Keith,* she thought, *hurry home, please.*

Arthur sat down in the chair beside her, and she could hear him open whatever bottle of liquor he'd brought home this evening. He drank deeply, paused, drank again, then set the uncapped bottle down on the table. "You're getting to be pretty grown up, Jeri," he said at last. "Probably learning all sorts of adult things in that school." He wiped his lips with the back of his sleeve and his eyes

239

remained fixed on her reclining form. "Learn to drink yet, did you?"

She could not concentrate. Half-rising, she pulled her books together in a pile, then got to her feet. "I think I'd better get out of your way and do my studying in my room." But when she moved to pass his chair, Arthur reached out and grabbed her by the wrist.

"You'll stay here!" His voice was full of anger and something else, hatred perhaps. Jeri felt a thrill of terror and thought furiously, searching for a way to stall him. Half an hour, Keith had said, give or take a few minutes. Surely she could keep him under control that long. Keith had taught her a couple of things, if worse came to worse—things she could do to defend herself.

She turned and stared down into his face, taking in his bloodshot eyes, the uneven moustache, the long black hairs protruding from his nostrils, the puffy cheeks, the bright red complexion that should have indicated health but actually warned of something entirely different.

Arthur Kaplan smiled and it was anything but friendly. "You and I used to get along a lot better, didn't we, Jeri?" He laughed, but it was an ugly sound. "Guess your father taught you a few things along the way, didn't he?" Kaplan seemed to think this was truly hilarious, but his laugh was almost painful, a convulsive sound somewhere between a gasp and a cough. Jeri took advantage of his inattention to pull her wrist free.

With a speed she would not have suspected him capable of, he pushed himself up out of the chair, grabbing her by her upper arms. The books crashed to the floor and she staggered back a step, but he moved right along with her, more by inertia than by plan. "You little bitch," he said coldly, "just like your fucking mother. A tease is all you are, both of you!"

Jeri wanted to protest, to defend the mother she could only vaguely remember now, but her vocal chords seemed paralyzed. *Keith,* she thought, *where are you?*

Arthur released one arm, then slowly moved his hand over toward her chest. "It's gonna be all right, Jeri." His voice was low and even, what he probably thought would be reassuring, perhaps even alluring. "We're gonna be together again, is all, the way we used to be. You used to like it, didn't you, even though you never admitted it? But you were just a kid then, and now you're almost a woman, so you ought to like it even better."

That was when she made the move Keith had taught her, one knee driving up and in, aimed for her father's groin. But Arthur was standing slightly to one side, and Jeri was scared and overanxious. The combination was enough that her blow merely grazed the inside of his thigh, painfully to be sure, but not the disabling blow that had been intended. He never even lost his grip, although he froze for endless seconds, his face distorted by pain. Had Jeri been calculating enough, she could have repeated the blow more accurately, or at least have broken loose in that moment, but the actual commission of the act of violence had shocked her into immobility as well, and the silent tableau held until Arthur recovered first and slapped her head with the open palm of one hand.

Jeri fell back against the wall and turned away from him, her hand raised to her burning cheek. Arthur grabbed her right arm from behind and twisted it up behind her back, then pressed himself suggestively forward. "You like it rough, huh?" He jerked her arm further upward and she cried out. "You little bitch!" Spittle from his lips sprayed across the nape of her neck. "I'll break your fucking arm for you if you ever try to hit me again!" He jerked the arm up again and Jeri swung her other hand back, trying to strike at him.

Kaplan recoiled instinctively, then kicked at Jeri's ankles. Off-balance, she fell, but he still held her arm, and there was a sharp crack as her forearm was bent at a bad angle. When she landed on the floor, there was a flood of pain that at first was so great that it held her transfixed, but when it began to recede, it was as though someone had touched a red hot brand to her arm and she screamed. Arthur was beyond caring about the consequences now—whether the neighbors heard, whether they called the police, what damage he might be doing to his daughter.

He dropped to one knee beside her and flipped her over onto her back, and her right arm flopped awkwardly and painfully. She reached over with her left and he grabbed it by wrist and elbow, forced it down over his knee, and snapped the bone in that arm as well. "I warned you, didn't I? Let's see you hit me now!" This time the pain drove Jeri back down into some secret place deep within her mind, and even though her eyes remained open, she did not see anything further, didn't see or feel what he did to her during the next twenty minutes, didn't even see the door open, Keith's furious face, the lamp raised and swung, and then her father slumping forward with blood running down the side of his head.

In fact, it was a long time before her memory returned at all, and then it came only in bits and pieces. There was a hospital room for a long time, and a lot of strangers came and went. Some of them ought to have looked familiar, and of course there was Keith, who seemed almost to be living in the room with her, although they would not, of course, allow him to do so. But even after she left the hospital, there were the sessions with the hospital psychologist, to whom she was driven by her Uncle Robert. She and Keith were living with Uncle Robert and Aunt Marie then, her mother's younger sister and her husband. They were never to live with their father again.

Chief Dowdell had not been happy when Arthur Kaplan was released from the Adult Correctional Unit. He knew that the man had been drunk when the incident had taken place; he was in that state more often than not, so far as the Chief could tell. And he knew the public prosecutor was trying to spare the two children, particularly the daughter, as much public attention as possible. They had issued a restraining order forbidding Kaplan to so much as phone either child, let alone attempt to see them. But he viewed Kaplan as a tragedy waiting to happen, and all of his patrolmen were alerted to keep an eye peeled whenever they were in the vicinity of his apartment or near any of his favorite bars, and particularly if they saw him in any public place in the company of a child, any child.

Not unsurprisingly, Kaplan's name began to appear on the police blotter with surprisingly regularity. Public drunkenness, drunk-and-disorderly, resisting arrest—all were duly entered on his record. Kaplan had been fired the day following the assault, of course, but he would collect enough unemployment compensation to support himself for some time. Dowdell wondered what would happen when the benefits ran out. Certainly he would no longer be able to keep up the apartment, particularly if he continued to drink at his usual pace. If anything, he seemed to be drunker than ever.

As it happened, Kaplan lost his apartment sooner than expected. He came home one morning after sleeping all night on the picnic tables down near the low-income housing development, having gone there to drink his brandy undisturbed. When he arrived, all of his possessions were piled randomly on the sidewalk in front of the apartment building, everything except the furniture that had come with the apartment. Upstairs, he discovered that the lock had been changed—his key no longer worked. The lease had run out and the landlord had chosen not to give him the option of renewing. The eviction was not actually legal, but under the circumstances, no outraged voices were going to be raised in Kaplan's behalf, and the man had deteriorated so thoroughly now that it never even occurred to him to seek legal assistance.

Instead, he sought a new bottle, the euphoria of alcohol, and he walked off, never looking back at what remained of his possessions. And in due course, late that afternoon, he picked a fight in Donovan's Bar which resulted in the loss of two teeth, a black eye, bloody nose, and yet another arrest.

The following morning, Dowdell came in early, surprising Officer Vanelli, who had the morning shift.

"Chief!" Vanelli jumped to his feet. He was a bit of a sycophant, but not shrewd enough to carry it off. "What's up?"

"Couldn't sleep." Dowdell tossed his hat down on his desk and crossed to the coffee maker, drawing himself a cup. "Kaplan up yet?"

"Still asleep, last I looked, maybe an hour ago."

"Well, get him up. We can't hold him any longer without pressing charges, and the guy he tried to hit doesn't want to be bothered." He sighed, sipped at the hot coffee.

"I'll get him out of here right away, Chief." Vanelli was already on his way to pick up the cellblock keys.

"No, wait." Dowdell rubbed his chin thoughtfully. "Get him up, give him his things, but put him in the back room and tell him to wait for me. He's got no job here, no place to live. Maybe I can put the fear of God into him and get him to move on. God knows, I'd like to put him in the state prison rather than just let him go, but at this point, so long as he gets out of my town, I'll be content."

"Okay, Chief. Whatever you say."

But Arthur Kaplan was not asleep, had not been asleep even an hour earlier when Vanelli had looked in on him. Neither had he really been feigning unconsciousness. What he had been doing was attempting to extend his awareness. Something was utterly, completely wrong, and he needed to understand what it was. He had done everything he could think of to please that sardonic power whose presence he felt whenever he contemplated the gargoyle. But still his dreams were troubled. Still he felt that he was being branded inadequate, disloyal, a failure, utterly without worth. And there was literally nothing he could think to do to alter the situation.

When Vanelli opened the door, Kaplan followed his instructions without thinking, dressed, nodded as his meager possessions were returned to him, signed his name shakily on the receipt form, then went and sat in the room to which he was directed. He sat there for a long time, alone with his thoughts, alone with the acceptance that he was not, after all, the one who would be chosen. And then he did something else for a while, and then nothing.

At first Dowdell meant to keep Kaplan waiting just to put the man on edge. But then there was the report of a terrible automobile accident, and the ensuing knowledge

245

that the Caldarones were both dead. Dowdell had known them somewhat and he visited the accident scene personally, the presence of Kaplan in his holding room completely slipping his mind. It was only after he returned two hours later that Vanelli reminded him that the man was waiting.

Depressed, knowing it was not really the time for him to attempt this, Dowdell squared his shoulders and prepared to attempt to reduce a human being, no matter how pitiful and disgusting, to something he could manipulate and control, to drive him out of his town and away from that which he felt a duty to protect.

But when he entered the small room in the rear of the station, all words escaped him. For Arthur Kaplan dangled from the overhead light, his face purple, his tongue distended and discolored. Despairing and without hope, Arthur Kaplan had hanged himself with his belt, the final escape from the wreck of his life. But before he had done so, he had committed one final act that so revolted Dowdell that even he had difficulty controlling his nausea.

To judge by the evidence, Arthur Kaplan had, just prior to stepping off the chair and ending his life, pulled down his pants and emasculated himself.

James Nicholson enjoyed a long walk; it was one of the few innocent pleasures in his life that granted him perfect solitude. As a matter of fact, he had gone out of his way to avoid company in such instances, as they provided him with an opportunity to clear his mind, to reorganize recent events, to map out plans for the future. At the age of thirty-one, he was already a fairly big frog in what was admittedly a comparatively small pond, but he didn't have the advanced degrees or the family connections that could mark him as a "fast tracker" in the corporate world. Still, at Eblis Manufacturing, he was definitely a power to be reckoned with, even though his title ... factory coordinator ... wasn't very explicit and entitled him to a total staff of only one clerk and three floor workers.

When Frank Cataldo had died in a freak accident years before, Nicholson had entertained hopes of succeeding him, but neither Old Man Eblis nor Oliver Moore, vice-president of manufacturing, had been willing to even consider the possibility of appointing someone still in his twenties. But they had been unable to find a first-rate replacement for Cataldo, even after several months' search, and they had finally split the function into two parts. Nicholson was in charge of the paperwork aspect—systems, follow up, labor analysis, written reports, and miscellaneous projects. Harry Rollins, the best of the departmental supervisors, had been promoted to works manager, and took care of the physical aspects of the job—personnel problems, machine utilization, and direct supervision of the production floor. The split made some sense, but Nicholson remained dissatisfied. For one thing, he and Rollins had never gotten along, and their interaction now was as infrequent as each man could arrange. But the more lasting damage was that the position of factory manager, to which Nicholson aspired as the next step in his movement up the promotional ladder, was effectively eliminated. Oliver Moore was only about five years from retirement, but not even Nicholson believed that he could make the jump from his present job to that one without some interim position. He had even discussed the possibility of taking over the production control department, but Moore had pointed out quite correctly that he had no formal training and little experience of the disciplines of that field, and an outside man, Stuart Hansen, had been hired instead. Unlike his predecessor, Hansen was shrewd and a master of office politics; Nicholson had so far refrained from crossing swords with him.

It was Saturday morning and, as usual, James was the first to stir in the Nicholson house. The sun had barely risen and he knew that Dolly would not be up for at least another hour, and she would have to rouse the children. Ten-year-old Eric was a bit of a disaappointment to his father, a brooding, introverted child who periodically flew into fits of startling rage. His sister, Margery, was even more withdrawn, the mirror image of her mother in her less exuberant days, peculiarly joyless for such a young child.

James had dressed, downed two cups of coffee, and, since it was a pleasant morning, decided to walk for a while. He could head down to Main Street, and if he was hungry by then, stop at one of the diners for something to eat.

He stepped outside, pausing on the front porch to consider his surroundings. They had moved to a new home, closer to the factory, one with three bedrooms and a full garage in place of the earlier carport, a two-story house only six years old in a much more fashionable neighborhood. There was a full privet hedge surrounding the property, and Dolly was slowly breaking the yard up into a series of formal gardens. The new Buick was parked in the driveway; he hadn't bothered to put it in the garage the night before. Out in the yard, the doghouse stood brightly in its corner under the largest of their maple trees. On the opposite side of the house, the newly installed swimming pool was a light blue circle, ready to be filled as soon as the weather warranted its use. Nicholson was not a swimmer himself, but he considered the swimming pool a symbol of prestige, the means by which he would gain an excuse to invite certain of his neighbors over for a visit. He was quite aware of the uses of social events in the furtherance of one's career. The Colemans, for example, were close friends of the Moores. The Brocks were cousins of the Eblis family itself. Nothing might come of these connections, of course, but it certainly couldn't hurt his career any to be on intimate terms with people like them.

The dog, on the other hand, had not been his idea. It had been one of the few situations in which he had been met by united and firm resistance from his family, and the truth was, he still rankled at the thought of it. But Eric and Margery had wanted a pet, and Dolly thought it would be good for them, particularly as they didn't play with the other children as much as they should, at least from her point of view. Part of this was not their fault, of course; James had definite ideas about which children his own offspring could and could not associate with outside of school. Nor did he care for the idea of having a dog. Dogs barked and annoyed the neighbors, they left messy little surprises around the yard, they had to be fed and watered daily and kennelled when the family was away. Dolly had suggested a cat, for they were more independent, but Nicholson hated cats, hated them as intensely as they, in turn, seemed to hate him. He considered cats sneaky, effeminate, and disloyal, and if his son had to have a pet, he supposed a dog was the lesser of two evils. But he had made it clear from the outset that there were certain rules: Dolly and the children were to make all the arrangements for the dog's care. If a persistent barking problem arose, the dog would have to go. And above all

249

else, under no circumstances was the dog to be allowed in the house.

Nicholson had to grudgingly admit that there had been no problems the first week. The dog, a puppy, seemed perfectly content to sleep in its assigned quarters, with a chain anchoring its collar to a post beside the front door. It had not barked or howled during the night, not even when an ambulance passed with its siren wailing, and it appeared that it was unlikely to cause any serious trouble for the Nicholsons.

He might have walked on at that point, but something subliminally told him that all was not as it seemed. Intrigued, but not sure just what was wrong, he moved off to the right, picking up a small stone from the yard and shying it at the side of the doghouse. It bounced off with a small thud and rebounded out of sight. There was no other sound. Nicholson bent down, grabbed the chain, and pulled the loose end out into the daylight. There was no sign of the puppy.

Could it have escaped during the night? Nicholson didn't believe it. He rose and looked down the side of the house speculatively. The original owner had rented out the top floor and installed a staircase up the side of the building to the second-floor landing. Quietly Nicholson walked over to the stairway and mounted it, then turned at the top and eased open the door to the hall. Inside the house, he walked quietly to the closed door of Eric's room, then quickly turned the knob and opened that as well. On the bed, the puppy lifted its head at him immediately, eyes open, and yipped softly. Eric mumbled something without fully awakening, moved one arm over to press his pet down into the covers at his side.

Furiously, James stepped to the side of the bed, grabbed

his son's arm, and pulled him out from under the blankets. Eric fell to the floor with a cry, totally disoriented, his arms and legs flailing about for support.

"What did I tell you about letting this filthy animal into the house?"

Eric was still confused, struggled to sit up. James grabbed him by the hair and dragged him, protesting, to his feet.

"Young man, I told you that your *pet*"—he loaded the word with contempt—"was to be kept *outside* at *all times*. If you're so determined to sleep with him, then you can spend the night in the doghouse!"

"I'm sorry," the boy sniffled sleepily. "He was lonely and crying when I chained him up for the night, so I thought maybe he'd feel better inside with me."

James pushed him down onto the bed. "I don't give a damn how the dog feels. You'd better be concerned with how I feel, not that stupid animal. Dogs are destructive indoors. They chew things, they make messes, they pee in corners. I told you all this before." The truth was, he thought that any affection directed toward the animal was a sign of weakness in his son, a weakness that he could not tolerate. Feeling affection toward people or animals allowed others some leverage against you. Even a casual stranger could cause an upheaval in your life, by running the dog down in the road, for example. It was the way a woman would feel, and he didn't want his son to pick up any womanish traits from his mother.

"He didn't make a mess." Eric looked up into his father's face, trying to make contact. "I kept him right here in the bed with me all night, and he just snuggled up and slept."

"It doesn't matter what happened, it's what might have

251

happened that's important, to say nothing of the fact that you have directly disobeyed me." Eric shuddered at those words. James kept careful track of every infraction he and Margery committed during the week, and Sunday night they were confronted with a list of their sins and punishment, the number of blows of his doubled belt on their backsides dependent upon the volume and severity of their errors. Rarely did a week go by when Eric was not found guilty enough to merit at least a half dozen blows, and Margery was only slightly less culpable.

"Now get up and get it out of here, and I don't want this ever to happen again. Understand?"

Eric's head dropped sulkily and he muttered something under his breath.

"What was that?" James bristled at the slightest hint of disobedience or rebellion.

"It's not fair," Eric said in a low voice, then repeated it more loudly, looking up at his father. "All the other kids can have their dogs in their rooms at night." He thrust his chin out pugnaciously.

James saw red, quite literally, and could not have stopped himself if he'd wanted to. One open palm caught his son along the right cheek and the line of his chin, a sharp crack that knocked him onto his back across the bed. The puppy yelped and jumped down to the floor, out of sight. Eric lay there stunned, his face reddening where the blow had landed.

"Do what you're told, you little bastard!" James pushed the words through clenched jaws. "The next time I have to talk to you about this will be the last!"

He spun and left the room.

The incident had contradictory effects on his mood for the rest of the morning. On one hand, he was enraged that he had been disobeyed, even in so unimportant a matter, and furious as well when Dolly seemed diffident about supporting his action when he told her of the problem an hour later. But on the other hand, he had relished the confrontation. Solving problems, as he put it, was a reward in itself, particularly the intricacies that were created when human personalities were involved. He viewed the atmosphere at Eblis as a latticework of power, formal and informal, a spiderweb of responsibility and authority in which he planned to become the chief spider. By cutting one line here and installing another there, he could create a new structure, one which eventually would feature himself, James Nicholson, sitting fat and smug and secure at its center.

His family was a much smaller web, of course, and one in which he was already firmly ensconced in a position of command. But command withered if it was not exercised, and had his family been completely cowed and subservient, there would be no excuse to demonstrate the extent of his authority. At least Eric was showing some spark. He had not been completely dominated by his mother's lack of spirit. In another year or two, it would be James's job to set about molding his personality so that he would be a success in the adult world worthy of his father.

That evening, after the children had been sent to bed, Dolly seemed preoccupied about something. James noticed her mood right away, considered asking her what the problem was, and then decided that if she wasn't willing to bring the subject up herself, it was probably not important enough to waste time discussing with her. But when he tried to watch television, she kept wandering in and out of the room, nervously flitting from one place to another, ostensibly to wipe a spot of dust she had missed, or to rearrange the magazines in their rack, several times to ask James if he wanted something. Finally he could stand it no longer and rose, turned off the television, and told her to sit down.

"Dolly, what's bothering you tonight? You haven't been still since supper. If there's something we need to talk about, let's do it now so I can watch television in peace."

Dolly licked her lips nervously, looked as though she wanted to rise and pace again, then thought better of it. "It's Margery," she said at last, not looking at her husband. "Mrs. Victor called from the school last week and asked me to stop by and see her, and I did."

"She hasn't been misbehaving, has she?" Nicholson's interest increased immediately at the hint of miscreance. "Not skipping school or anything like that?"

"No, oh no, nothing like that." She met his eyes now, briefly, then looked away again. "It's nothing that she's done wrong, exactly. But Mrs. Victor says she doesn't interact with the other children. She stands in the schoolyard by herself at recess, doesn't talk to the other kids even at lunch, won't volunteer in class, and sometimes goes for the entire day without saying anything."

"So? Sounds like an ideal student to me. Margery has always been quiet. You're not exactly a chatterbox yourself, most of the time, Dolly, and there's nothing wrong with you."

"But there might be something wrong with Margery. At least, Mrs. Victor thinks we should take her to see someone trained for this sort of thing."

Nicholson's cheeks reddened and he felt a familiar surge of adrenaline. "What sort of thing exactly does this busybody think she's talking about? Is she implying there's something wrong with our daughter just because she's not willing to waste her time talking aimlessly to everyone in sight?"

"I'm sure it's not like that, James. She sounded really concerned. She thinks Margery may be too withdrawn, might have trouble later on interacting with her own age group. It isn't that she's mentally ill or anything like that. She was very firm about that. It's just that Margery doesn't seem to be happy or want to play at all, and she's not even particularly interested in her schoolwork."

"Have the teachers been complaining? I haven't seen any problem with her grades."

"No, she gets B's in all her subjects. But Mrs. Victor says she's capable of much better work."

"So what? She's a girl, goddamn it! Of course she's better at bookish things. So were you! What good did it do? How often do you have to think back to history or geography or English to figure out how to wash the dishes or plan meals or entertain at parties?"

Dolly was silent a moment, her thoughts racing. She considered confronting his narrow view of the role of women in the world, but finally discarded the idea. I'm a perfect example of what he wants women to be, she told herself, so I'm hardly in a position to lecture.

But she shared Mrs. Victor's concern about Margery, although she had not been able to admit it to herself until the other had called her with fresh doubts. "Mrs. Victor just wanted to suggest that we talk to someone who knows more about this sort of thing, that's all.

"You mean a psychiatrist? Is that what you're telling me?"

"No, not that. Mrs. Victor gave me the name of a couple of counseling services that she knows of. It wouldn't cost much to have someone talk to Margery, to see if there is anything wrong."

Nicholson shifted his weight but remained seated, consciously forcing himself to remain calm. "There is nothing wrong with our daughter, Dolly, and we don't need to give money to some jerk who can't even call himself a professional quack. I can't believe you're sitting there calmly telling me that someone from the school called our daughter crazy. You should have rung back the principal immediately and demanded that the woman be fired. You'd better believe I'll be writing a letter about it Monday!"

Dolly looked genuinely alarmed. "James, you can't do that! She was only trying to help ... that's her job!"

"Her job is not to stick her nose in other people's business, or to make sly insinuations about the children."

"It wasn't an insinuation, James." Dolly sat back and tried to calm herself. Already her voice was becoming shrill and unsteady, a weakness for which she hated herself, but one which she had never been able to master when faced with his displeasure. "She's supposed to notify the parents when a child is having problems at school."

"Listen, Dolly, and listen good." He leaned forward, raised one hand, and pointed a finger at her. "Margery gets adequate grades and doesn't present a disciplinary problem. If she's quiet, then that's in her favor. Maybe Mrs. Bloody Victor should take pointers. She'd do a lot better if she kept her own mouth shut more often. Margery will *not* be going to any counselor, and I don't want to hear about it again. I will take care of Mrs. Victor and her opinions myself. But the subject is closed otherwise. Do you understand?"

Dolly wanted to say something, but finally slumped back

without a word. James was not satisfied with mute surrender. "I expect an answer, Dolly. Don't sulk. You're acting like one of the children."

Her eyes flashed at his tone if not at his words, but she dropped her eyes, staring into her lap where her slim fingers were twisting the fabric of her apron. "I understand, James."

And she did. All too well.

It was almost a full month later when the tenure of the puppy, now named Max, came to an end. Eblis had shut down for inventory, and the lower production level this year meant that there was less to count. Except for a few odds and ends, everything was done early and any managers with vacation days left were urged to take at least part of the time now, before production resumed the following Monday. Nicholson had had a particularly irritating week. Paruti in quality control had spotted an error in one of his reports, and although the man's standing at Eblis had diminished considerably over the years, his enmity toward Nicholson was undiminished. He had used the error to embarrass the younger man at a staff meeting.

There had also been a procedural battle with Rollins which remained unresolved, but which Nicholson would probably lose simply because he could not muster good enough arguments to effect a change. One of his floor workers had quit for a better job the week before, he had picked up a minor intestinal disorder, and the Buick was stalling for no obvious reason. So Nicholson had decided to finish up his morning reports and take the rest of the week off, applying it toward his accumulated vacation days. Nothing much could be accomplished now anyway, since most of top management was already gone for the week.

Nicholson did not have the car today. Dolly had dropped him off at work and was supposed to leave the car at a garage in Providence, do some shopping, and pick him up on the way home. The kids were out of school, but since they almost always played in the house or in the yard, the Nicholsons had taken to allowing them to remain alone. Margery was already capable of cooking simple meals, and Eric could manage to put together a sandwich, if necessary.

After considering a taxi, Nicholson decided it would be a needless extravagance, and instead, he set off to walk the three miles. If he crossed through the Sheffield estate, or what remained of it, and up past the high school ball field, he'd be home in twenty minutes. He'd walked further than that even when the weather was not so pleasant.

But as he entered the grounds of the library, now owned by the prestigious Providence Plantations Historical Society, under consideration as a possible site for their new headquarters, but currently still closed and locked, it occurred to him that there might have been another, less obvious motive to his choice of routes. He hadn't come by in years, but he still remembered the raw sense of power that the statue of the gargoyle had evoked in him during those past exposures. Although not fond of the "science" of psychology, Nicholson recognized that the gargoyle had taken on some deeper relevance to him personally than simply its imposing physical presence, and he felt compelled to investigate further. Among other things, the idea that an object, a statue, could affect his behavior was to imply a certain element of weakness in himself, and Nicholson ruthlessly sought out such facets of his psyche and worked to obliterate them.

With firm steps he made his way through the knee-high

grass alongside the building. The grounds had not been kept up for the past two years, and the underbrush had completely taken over. But with some difficulty, he reached the tower corner and looked up. It was there, of course, just as powerful and impressive as ever, even more imposing because it seemed closer to the ground than before. Surely he remembered it being up near the roof line. Wasn't it always right above the narrow window two stories above the tips of its wings? But obviously his memory had to be playing tricks on him ... The gargoyle was a statue carved out of a single block of stone, one portion built directly into the wall. His memory was fading, and these less important memories were placed on standby as his brain rushed to file and catalog all of the new data being input daily.

The expression, too, seemed different. There was a sense of welcome, of expectancy, and even of hopefulness to the cast of the mouth, the angle of the head, the position of the eyelids. It was, he had to admit, a marvelous piece of work, although in general, Nicholson had no patience for supposed works of art. Paintings were imperfect reproductions of photographs, sculpture no more than woodcarvings in stone, literature and film for the most part pleasant lies designed to provide an escape for people who couldn't face the fact of their own inadequacy and failure. Poetry was the self-delusion of women; male poets were invariably queer. Abstract art was a fraud not worth discussing. Only music was sometimes truly artistic, he felt, because it could at times match and enhance one's personality and mood.

Afterward, he thought he had stood there for just a few minutes before moving on, but he arrived home a full two hours later than expected, an inconsistency that bothered him briefly, but which was soon overwhelmed by the crisis that developed shortly after his arrival.

It had been a warm walk, so he went directly to the kitchen and took a cold beer out of the refrigerator. The kids were nowhere in sight, either in their rooms or perhaps the backyard. He walked around, taking an occasional sip of beer, staring out the ground floor windows, and finally spotted Eric playing near the rear gate with Max, some elaborate hide-the-ball nonsense. Margery was not with them. James turned away and walked in through the living room, planning to flop down in a chair and relax, when he noticed the stain.

It wasn't a big stain, only about six inches across, a round dark splotch at one corner of the living room rug. Initially puzzled, Nicholson rose, crossed the room, and crouched down with the beer still in hand. Then the smell reached him and he recognized it instantly: the dog had been in the house while he was gone. There was no question.

He rose and his free hand clenched at his side. After a few seconds he turned, placed the half-empty beer bottle down, and walked briskly through the house, out the back door, and over to where Eric and Max were playing.

Eric stopped immediately and stood up when he saw his father approaching, while Max continued to frisk about at his feet.

"Eric, come over here."

The boy did so, instantly aware that something was wrong, tipped off by his father's tone. Nicholson was never cordial with his son, but there were degrees of disaffection that the boy could identify with the ease of long experience.

"Yes, Father." He did as requested, Max still jumping up and down at his feet.

Nicholson did not look at the dog. "Eric, I thought I told you that the dog was not ever to go into the house again."

"Yes, but it was an accident. I just opened the door to get something to drink and he got in past me. I chased him out right away." Eric made no attempt to lie. Probably he had not seen the stain in the rug, or he would have tried to do something about it, but he had learned the hard way never to assume that he could withhold knowledge from his father.

"Accident or not, you disobeyed me. Carelessness is at least as bad, perhaps worse, than disobedience. Both require punishment."

"Yes, Father." Eric's eyes dropped to his feet. He wondered if this would be one of those rare occasions where the enormity of his offense required immediate punishment rather than deferral to the weekly beltings.

"We also will have to dispose of the dog. I told you that his continued presence was conditional, that he would go if you couldn't take proper care of him, didn't I?"

Eric looked up sharply, his face red and angry. James waited, wanting to see the boy flare up, hoping he would show some sign of nerve, hoping also that it would provide him with a further excuse to exercise his sense of discipline. But the boy did no more than hold his father's gaze for several interminable seconds before looking off to one side. "Do we have to take him back to the pound? Even if I promise never to let him get in again?"

Nicholson suppressed his disappointment. "Oh, he's not going back to the pound. You've spoiled him now. Besides, he's going to serve one useful purpose in his life.

He's going to teach you how important it is to fulfill your responsibilities, and the consequences that are possible if you fail." He looked around, spotted and picked up the shovel that Dolly used for turning her compost heap. "Bring him back to his house, Eric, and chain him up."

Nicholson turned away and headed for the doghouse, confident that the boy would do as he was told. He waited there while the boy brought the puppy over, then affixed the end of the chain to his collar. Max sat back on his haunches, tongue lolling as he panted in the heat. Nicholson handed his son the shovel.

"It's your responsibility, Eric. He has to be destroyed. I think that if you hit him hard enough along the back of the head, you'll break his neck right away and cause him no pain."

The boy stared at the shovel in his hand, then up at his father; the look in his eyes was one of absolute horror.

"No," he said softly. "I can't—"

"You can and you will!" Nicholson rounded on his son violently, every inch of his tense body communicating menace. "This is your fault and you will take care of it! We all have to clean up our own messes. I've given you the chance to do it mercifully, to cause as little pain as possible. Don't presume upon my patience! If you don't do it, then I will, and I'll be a lot less careful about it. I might miss and lop off a leg or two before I finish him off. Is that what you want?"

Eric shook his head, tears glistening on his cheeks, but could not manage to say a word. Neither did he make any move to do as his father ordered, however, until the man grew impatient and moved to pull the shovel away. At this moment, Eric's face tightened and he raised the shovel above his head convulsively, closed his eyes, and slammed it down. There was a single yelp, then silence, but Eric continued to rain blows on the small, bloody form at his feet until he was absolutely certain there was no longer any capacity for pain remaining.

His father watched until the rhythmic blows stopped, then turned back toward the house.

"Bury it in the back corner before you come in," he ordered.

It had turned out not to be quite so bad a day after all, he reflected.

CHAPTER ELEVEN
1975

The staff meeting had been scheduled for nine a.m.; Oliver
Moore subscribed to the theory that most people were at
the height of their mental energy first thing in the morning. James Nicholson suspected this might be true only of
a small minority; Stu Hansen, the production control manager, and John Paruti, quality control, both looked as
though they were ready to slump over in their seats. Bob
Miller, newly hired to take charge of the maintenance operation from retiring Elmer Washington, was still unsure
of himself and was making a superhuman effort to appear
alert and interested. The last member of the group, Harry
Rollins, factory manager, radiated energy and compe-
tence. He was Nicholson's only serious rival for power
within the manufacturing organization, having been confirmed in his position just this year with a formal change
of title. Nicholson was now administrative manager within
the manufacturing division, a title which was both frus-
trating and helpful. It implied little in the way of actual
authority, which was a negative, but it also implied an all-
encompassing interest, which was positive.

The reorganization of the past two years had usually,

though not always, gone his way. He had not liked the loss of his expediters to the Production Control department, but Hansen was a persuasive man, and although Nicholson had never admitted this during the debates that preceded the change, his arguments made a great deal of sense. Nicholson had picked up new product development that same month, however, and although that brought no new employees under his control, it had eventually been supplemented when the toolmakers were transferred to his department. He was also put in charge of consolidating the various departmental reports into the monthly presentation at the president's review meeting, had even been asked to sit in from time to time, and this control over the flow of information had made it possible for him to shift emphasis from one area to another so long as he was careful about how much he manipulated. It was too soon to see any measurable benefits, but there had been enough indications that things were being interpreted as he wished to encourage him further. At times he was accused of misrepresenting what was said, and he generally retreated in these instances, insisting that it was a misunderstanding or an oversight, but he knew that Rollins, Hansen, and Paruti all disliked him particularly, even though the three of them were frequently at each other's throats as well.

"All right, gentlemen, I think we can get this under way. I want to start off by congratulating Harry for the improvement in the labor variance this past month. We've made some real strides there and the effect on the bottom line will be gratifying."

Moore made a point of complimenting at least one staff member at the beginning of each meeting, sometimes really stretching a point to find a way to honor whoever it happened to be. Nicholson considered this an unnecessary concession; he was as indifferent to praise as he was unlikely to offer any. One did one's job and received the appropriate amount of pay. No comment was necessary on that performance unless it was unsatisfactory and corrective action was required.

Moore ran through some brief items of news, a large order from one of their specialty accounts, delivery problems on the electrical units for the new line, and a job vacancy opening up in the press department, then turned to the typed agenda that had been provided.

There were only two items on the agenda that involved any discussion or controversy. The first was a review of the proposed company position going into contract negotiations with the union in two months. Nicholson had collected and organized suggestions from the various members of management, phrasing some to sound petty where he could get away with it, taking care with others to make certain they sounded reasonable and well-thought-out. He was determined to change the way some subsidiary departments reported their labor, for example, because once they were forced to be as accurate as the major departments, it would provide more leverage for him to prove there were problems in the production flow. On this particular issue he was allied with Hansen against Rollins, because Hansen wanted to install a more sophisticated scheduling system and could not do so when significant portions of the production process were, in a manner of speaking, invisible insofar as recordkeeping was concerned.

Discussion was lively but basically amicable; some points were settled on the spot, others deferred for further consideration at the next meeting. Then attention was turned to the next item on the agenda, the reporting responsibilities of the centralized trucking function.

All the material handlers, formerly known as floorboys, had been taken away from the individual departments some years ago and placed in a new, separate department known as trucking, under Charlie Colwell. Colwell had been little more than a floorboy himself; his organizational ability had been acceptable, but he was too lenient with his personnel, many of whom took every opportunity to hide. As Eblis became more cost-conscious and as the internal rivalries increased, the inefficiencies and waste in this department became a political football of some importance and the pressure continued to build until Colwell resigned, some said one step ahead of a nervous breakdown. To date Colwell had not been replaced, and one of the more reliable members of his department was doing an inadequate job of filling in. The delay occurred because Nicholson had proposed that centralized trucking report to his department rather than continue to be a floating position reporting directly to the vice president of manufacturing, even though Colwell had never been of staff rank.

Harry Rollins disagreed strongly. The movement of material was a manufacturing responsibility, he argued, and it would be far more efficient to have it operated directly out of his office. He proposed reorganizing the supervisory force reporting to him, freeing up someone to direct the material-handling function without hiring anyone new. Nicholson had planned to pirate one of the expediters out of the production control department to head this operation, a man he felt would be personally loyal to him. He was useless in his present position, because Hansen knew how close he was to Nicholson and was careful about allowing him access to anything potentially detrimental to his own position. Hansen preferred to side with Rollins because of his dislike of Nicholson, but it was unclear how much influence he had with Moore.

"I've read the proposals submitted by both James and Harry on the question of central trucking." Moore looked around the table, carefully keeping his voice neutral. "There is something to be said for each position, obviously, or we wouldn't have to make any decision." He paused, and Nicholson knew that he had already made up his mind; the question was whom had he decided in favor of.

"Prior to the creation of trucking as a separate department," he continued, "it was a part of the manufacturing process reporting to the production manager. The decision to change this procedure occurred because it was hoped that duplication of effort could be eliminated. You've all heard the horrible example of the hand trucks that always went from press to polish loaded and came back empty, while the ones from polish to press always went loaded and returned empty as well. Charlie Colwell had his faults, but he did eliminate a lot of this waste, and the decision to divorce material movement from the actual production people certainly proved itself a valid one." He stopped and looked at Rollins directly. "This is no criticism of you or your people, Harry, but I think you're already spread too thin in middle management. The efforts you've had to make to reduce the labor variance indicates that there are areas that need your attention that you cannot get to now, and it certainly won't improve if we increase that workload."

Nicholson controlled his face with no difficulty. It looked as if he'd won this time. He was already running through remarks he could make after the announcement, remarks which would have to seem conciliatory to Moore while communicating clearly to Rollins his glory in the victory. And then he would have to work out a way to get Baker out of production control and into position. But Moore was still speaking and he wrenched his thoughts back to the immediate.

"James here has made quite a reputation for himself in the years he has worked for us. He's the youngest member of this team, full of ideas, ambitious, thorough, and hardworking. His organizational ability is clearly among the very best in this company." He smiled. "Sometimes I think that steel-trap mind of yours should have sought a career in accounting. They're big on precision. Certainly trucking would be better organized and better administered if it reported to you, James, even if, as you mentioned, you'd have to train someone to do most of the scheduling. But I'm concerned here about the layers of management that information would have to pass through."

Nicholson frowned. Was Moore hedging?

"With trucking reporting to your department, James, we would have production reporting to you when goods are ready to be moved, the quantity and identification numbers of the lots, and their present location. You would then have to communicate this to production control," he nodded to Hansen, "where they would perform their magic and advise you where and when to move things, and in what order. Armed with this information, you go back to production and move the work. Then Harry comes to you, James, and says, 'Why are the widgets at press five ahead of the wadgets, which have a higher priority on the shortage list?' So you, James, go back to Stu, who tells you why and sends you back to Harry, and so forth. It won't work."

Everyone looked puzzled now, so Nicholson decided to

allow his irritation to show. "Well, it has to report somewhere, Oliver. Unless you're going to have it reverted to individual department control, and that makes the problem you just described even worse."

"I'm aware of that, and I have no such intention. What I plan to do, effective next Monday, is have trucking report directly to production control." He turned to Stu Hansen. "I know things will be a bit confusing at first, and you may have to hire someone to do most of the administrative work, but I'd like to give it a shot this way. If we're going to move toward more sophisticated scheduling and control, you're going to have to become more intimately involved in the mechanics of work flow within the factory, and I can't think of a better way."

Hansen was genuinely surprised, and obviously pleased at the windfall. Nicholson surreptitiously glanced in Rollins' direction, but if the man was upset at the loss, he gave no such indication. But Nicholson saw something else as his eyes moved around the table, something that drove him into a barely suppressed rage. John Paruti was staring quite openly at him, his mouth split into an enormous grin. It was fortunate that the man was such an incompetent infighter, because there was no question at all in Nicholson's mind that Paruti despised and hated him and was now basking in the glow of his defeat.

Enjoy it while you can, he told the other man silently. *I've lost the battle but the war is far from over.*

Back in his office later in the morning, Nicholson devoted some time to rethinking his strategy. Oliver Moore was sixty, due to retire in five years. He would be thirty-eight then, old enough to be an authentic candidate for the position. The question was, who would be making the decisions by then? Old Man Eblis was still president, but the title had become more honorary than anything else, and the founder's influence in the affairs of the company was steadily diminishing. At least the man had the grace to admit it, and was turning over more and more of the actual management to his top-level team. But he was close to seventy by now, and there was a good chance that he would have little or no say in the ultimate decision of choosing Moore's successor.

There were only two other people on the Board of Trustees at the moment. Wolf, the executive vice-president of sales, was one of the two minor partners Eblis had allowed to buy into the business about ten years before. He was only fifty, firmly ensconced in his position, and would certainly be one of the decision makers. Nicholson always went out of his way to ask after Wolf's family and was on a first-name basis with the man, but he could hardly count on his vote just yet. The third partner was an investor from Boston who derived most of his information, and his opinions, from the controller, Ed Zamaski.

Zamaski was as close to an open ally as Nicholson had. The man delighted in Nicholson's willingness to tip him off to any irregularity in the manufacturing accountability, often anonymously as well, and could probably be counted on to put in a good word when the time came. Eblis theoretically had the power to make this decision on his own, but it was likely by then that he would have turned things over to his two sons, neither of whom was interested in the business, and both of whom had indicated publicly that their potential share of the company would be up for sale as soon as it was theirs to dispose of. So the best Nicholson could do at this point was to solidify his position and look for opportunities to improve it, preferably at the expense of other departments run by potential rivals.

Thoughtfully he dialed Jim Baker and asked him to stop by when he had a moment. Baker would be upset by the assignment of trucking to production control, because that would effectively block his promotion. Hansen didn't care for him at all; his last evaluation had strongly hinted that remedial action was necessary to avoid an even less favorable report in the future.

His secretary came in and dumped a sheath of reports into his "In" box. "Did Jerry get his samples?" Kate Short, secretary for only the past two months, was startled by his tone, recognized immediately that the morning meeting must not have gone well.

"I haven't seen him yet this morning, Mr. Nicholson. Would you like me to check with him?"

"I wouldn't have asked you if I didn't want the answer, would I, Miss Short?"

She recoiled as if he'd slapped her. "I'll take care of it right away." She sounded angry rather than frightened, and Nicholson made a mental note to keep a close eye on her performance. Resentment often broke down the barriers of confidentiality which he insisted his employees maintain. If she could not be made afraid of him, she would be replaced. Nicholson always chose his employees from those who had been long without a job, who might be most desperate to keep whatever they could grab.

He made another call himself, this time to Ableman, the product manager in sales. "Fred? This is James. I saw your memo suggesting that we expand the candleware line and I'll bring it up at the next product development meeting, but I just wanted you to know we're going to have some resistance."

There was a pause as the other man expressed surprise. "Well, you know these people in manufacturing. Between you and me, Fred, the standards were set too low when the original items were costed, and that's going to inflate the cost of any new assembly we make. No one wants to admit the problem. Time study isn't going to say they screwed up, and the factory people who were present certainly can't admit they let the time standards go in wrong without saying anything." Nicholson paused again to let that sink in. "We may have to go overseas for the expanded line." He knew this was a sore spot with sales; imported items bore the stigma of low quality, even when it wasn't true, though it often was.

The conversation ended shortly afterward and Nicholson was confident he'd nurtured the seeds of discontent he'd been sowing on that front. He had to be careful in his criticism of time study, as that function reported to Ed Zamaski, a man he did not want to alienate. But Ableman knew how to keep his mouth shut. If he brought up the subject at all, it would be in a roundabout fashion.

Baker arrived a few minutes later and Nicholson pointed to a chair. He was minimally cordial, but his main control over Baker was through sheer force of personality. Baker was a younger man, one of those insecure people who cannot meet let alone hold the eyes of anyone. He had an annoying habit of playing with a paperclip when he was talking, and even now he was slipping one out of his pocket.

"You've heard about the reassignment of trucking, I imagine?"

"Only that it's going to be absorbed by production control. No one knows who's going to head it up."

Nicholson ignored his hopeful look. "I don't believe a final decision has been made in that matter, and frankly, it wouldn't surprise me if this morning's change wasn't reversed very soon. Hansen can't handle that department."

"He's very good, though." Baker turned and twisted the paper clip, slowly unbending it. "He's got some big ideas."

Nicholson looked up. "Anything worth mentioning?" It was an order phrased as a question.

"Well." The young man looked increasingly ill-at-ease. "He's supposed to be working on a proposal to move purchasing and warehousing out of the finance division and into his department. He's already recommending that they train one of his clerks, Cindy something, to do a lot of the scheduling that he's doing now. I think he's planning to expand the department."

Nicholson had already heard the rumor about purchasing, from Ed Zamaski himself, in fact, but the warehousing tip was new. "Has he talked to anyone about it?"

"I don't know. He and Moore went through the warehouse together the other day, and he's had two or three appointments during the last two weeks in Moore's office. Long ones, too. I think he's pretty confident about it."

Nicholson's mind raced furiously. He had been concentrating so thoroughly on discrediting Rollins that he'd been flanked. Something had to be done to mend matters ... or if not, to take advantage of the new flow of power. Things were starting to move very fast. "Okay, Jim. Let me know if anything changes, will you?"

The younger man nodded at the obvious dismissal and left. As quickly as he departed, Kate entered. "Jerry has three of the seven samples. He didn't know whether to bring them up today or wait until the others are done."

"What happened? All seven were supposed to be here

today." His voice was still harsh, and he could see a flush rising in her cheeks.

"Apparently they're behind schedule in the press department. One of the tools should have been sent in for sharpening after the last run and was overlooked, and they can't put it in the press until it comes back."

Which neatly placed the onus on his own department. Nicholson grinned, and his tone was considerably warmer when he replied. "All right, call down to the toolroom and tell them I said to give the job top priority—overtime, if necessary. Then call Jerry back and tell him I want a typed memo explaining why the tool wasn't ready and why the samples will be late. Tell him not to speculate on how long the delay might run." No point in providing any good news, that would go in Nicholson's own follow-up memo explaining what had been done to pull manufacturing's nuts out of the fire. It was the first thing that had gone right today.

Barbara Howell stopped at the Sheffield Library more out of curiosity than anything else. The Historical Society had reopened it this summer, not so much as a library but as a landmark of some interest, the only one in town. There were persistent rumors that the building was going to be made over into the Society headquarters, which would make more sense than the present arrangement. It had been open to the public now for at least two months, and Barbara couldn't remember ever seeing more than one car in the lot.

But she was curious to see if they had done anything with the inside, so one Saturday afternoon she stopped by on her way home from visiting her parents. They seemed to be aging so quickly lately, and she saw them so infrequently, even though they all lived in the same town. Her new job at Brown University took up a great deal of her time, and there seemed to be little left for anything else. Not that her life was all that interesting otherwise.

Barbara walked up the front steps. A small sign indicated that the Sheffield Library was open to the public as a service of the Providence Plantations Historical Society, listing its hours, and closing with the single word "Welcome." She opened the heavy wooden door and stepped into the dark interior. The hallway opened up into what would be a medium-sized room in most houses, eventually giving way to a very wide staircase that led up to the second floor. Narrower passages led to either side of the base of the stairway and off into the distance. There were doors, mostly closed, along both walls. Directly to her right, a woman sat at a small desk, an account book of some sort open in front of her. She looked up with artificial friendliness, and Barbara immediately had the feeling that she knew the woman from somewhere.

"Hello, welcome to the Sheffield Library." The woman paused and looked puzzled for a second. "You're Barbara, aren't you? Barbara Howell."

"Why—yes." She searched the woman's face for a familiar sign, then realized that it was the hair color that had misled her. "Aren't you Paula Fenton?"

"Well, actually I'm Paula Fenton Underwood Ingells. It has been a few years."

Barbara recognized her now. Paula had switched from black hair to blond and was wearing it quite short rather than shoulder-length. She also seemed to have put on a lot of weight. Her face seemed puffy and unhealthy. "Well, I was Barbara Howell Joslin for a while, but I dropped my married name."

"I kind of like mine. It's like a family history to me."
She giggled girlishly, but it was not an attractive sound.

"I thought you moved out to the West Coast."

"Oh, yeah. Bobby and I moved out there right after we got married. He thought he'd have a better chance if he made a complete break with his family, but it didn't work. I was making almost as much money as he was, and the bastard was cheating on me while I was in the office. So we split, and I met Allen kind of on the rebound, you know. Boy, was that ever a mistake. We had absolutely nothing in common. So when that broke up too, I figured I'd come back home and start over again, you know?"

Barbara didn't know, but she didn't particularly want to.

"So what have they done to this place?" She gestured toward the building. "Spiffed it up or anything?"

"This? Between you and me, Barbara, they didn't do beans. There's a woman who comes in once a week and vacuums and dusts the place, but they don't even have a security guard, and I'm the only staff member. I'm supposed to greet people and make sure there's no stealing or vandalism, and not let kids walk around without watching them. How I'm supposed to do all that at the same time is beyond me." She sighed. "And they don't pay much, either. But Ma is a member of the Society and she pulled strings to get me the job, so I have to make do, you know, until I find something better."

"Well then, I think I'll just take a look around. It was nice talking to you."

"Yeah, sure. We'll see each other again, probably."

Barbara turned, then hesitated. "Any place in particular I'm supposed to go or not go?"

"No." Paula seemed uninterested. "There's only a couple of rooms closed, and they're locked. Otherwise it's all open. Pretty boring though, just a lot of books and paintings and statues and things."

"Okay, thanks."

But before she could escape, Paula called out to her once more. "Barbara, do you remember Val Meredith?"

Barbara paused, her foot on the third step of the staircase. "Yes, of course I do." She didn't look back.

"Is she still living around here, do you know?"

Barbara turned around, one hand braced on the railing, and looked back down at Paula. "Yes, I believe she is. I don't see her much, but she's been around. I hear about her every once in a while." She refrained from mentioning the unsavory nature of the stories she had heard.

"Thanks, maybe I'll look her up, you know. She's not in the phone book, but probably she has an unlisted number or something. Or is she married, too?"

"Not that I'm aware of."

Her tour of the library depressed her and she almost fled from the building. Barbara could not explain precisely what had changed her mood from mild curiosity to an almost tangible feeling of ominous threat and the inevitability of death. Perhaps it was the somber colors, the obvious age of the books and other artifacts, or their very nature. There were statues and carvings in stone, glass, and wood, of monsters, demons, devils, cabalistic signs, and primitive religious symbols, many of which were clearly phallic. The books were in a variety of languages, and most were in locked shelves, so that only the spines could be read. The furniture was sparse and, considering the expense in constructing the building and collecting the arcane contents, it was surprising how simple the furnishings were. Unless the original furniture had been sold somewhere along the way, she realized. That might explain its sparsity as well.

Perhaps her depression was because of the encounter with Paula. Barbara rarely spent time regretting her adolescence, a period which she considered largely unhappy, at least until she and Ron had gotten together. They still saw each other occasionally, although it looked like he was pretty serious about his new girlfriend; Barbara couldn't even remember the name. They had not met. But Paula brought back a flood of the less pleasant incidents, primarily those involving Valerie Meredith and her single-minded domination of the high school's social activities. For whatever reason, Barbara cut short her tour as quickly as she could without seeming to openly panic, and left with no more than a nod and wave to Paula.

She did not escape the mood as easily as she escaped the building. As she drove off, something deep in her subconscious insisted that something was wrong in the library, and for the first time in years she wished that it were not necessary for her to sleep alone. Still, she had no recourse. Her house had always seemed a haven to her in the past, somewhere she could go and shut away the outside world, a micro-universe that belonged entirely to her. But tonight it seemed she was heading back toward a lifeless, empty shell, with walls too thin to hold back anything that might seek her out.

When Barbara went to bed that night, she firmly resolved never to return to the Sheffield Library. As chance would have it, only two weeks passed before she would have to return to that same building.

It was a Saturday morning, bright, sunny, and unusually warm, and she was out on her ritual run before breakfast. For some reason she was reminded of that long-ago dream this morning, and the memory was unpleasant enough that she decided to change her route. She would run along the south side of the high school today, avoiding the playground, then cut in through the trees that ran along Trapelo Road, follow them north to the brook, then take one of the curving paths that wound back down through the Sheffield estate grounds, but exiting back through the used-car lot to Main Street before actually reaching the building proper. At this hour there would be little pedestrian traffic, so she could head down Main Street for the short distance that separated it from the cemetery, cross there, and follow the back exit road from the graveyard as it curved around toward the Managansett Inn. Certain of her proposed course, she set off.

As her breathing steadied and the regular rhythm of her running restored to her a sense of normality, Barbara shed some of the strange feeling that had plagued her since wakening, but enough of it remained to distract her attention from the matter at hand. And so it was that a short while later, while picking her way down the path that paralleled the brook, she missed her footing, stumbled over a small bush, and went sprawling into a thicket. A maple tree was directly in her path and Barbara's forehead struck it a glancing blow as she fell, not knocking her unconscious, but certainly stunning her sufficiently that she lay there unmoving for several minutes.

When she eventually regained her consciousness enough to extricate herself, she discovered that her legs wobbled treacherously, a blinding pain accompanied every movement of her head, and her stomach was upset. Tentatively raising a hand, she ascertained that the damage was apparently superficial, a scrape and bump rather than a cut, not even the most serious accident she'd had while running. But head wounds were always worrisome, and she moved off the path to a worn tree stump and sat down while the effects of the blow wore off.

That was how she spotted James Nicholson walking in the woods. He'd come down the same path in the same direction, although his pace was considerably less headlong and more surefooted. Nicholson was whistling tunelessly, his eyes intent upon the path, and he never once suspected her presence. For her part, Barbara recognized him immediately, even though it had been years since they had last met. Time had been kind to Nicholson, who had managed to avoid developing the paunch that plagued so many of his contemporaries. His hair remained untinged by gray, though for all Barbara knew, he could have been coloring it. The sideburns were perhaps a bit longer, but Nicholson remained clean-shaven otherwise.

Intrigued, Barbara climbed to her feet, half-tempted to call out, but at the last moment something made it seem impossible. Instead she crossed the path, planning to resume her jogging, but her head still spun and she considered turning and going home immediately rather than risk a further accident. But some inexplicable motivation compelled her to follow silently in Nicholson's wake.

At first they followed the same route that Barbara had intended to take right from the start, but at one branching, Nicholson turned directly south toward Main Street. The tree cover was quite thick here, and Barbara was not immediately able to orient herself, but as they moved slowly in tandem, she caught the outline of the Sheffield mansion ahead. They were heading directly toward its rear wall, the tower corner. There came a renewed wave of dizziness at this realization, and a feeling of intense déjà vu caused her to stumble uncertainly and stop. Nicholson disappeared around a turn ahead and she resolved to go no further, having no desire to relive even in her memory that one occasion in the past when the two of them had been here alone together. But her resolution faltered as she was possessed by an immense curiosity: what could it be that brought James Nicholson to this lonely spot, and by such a roundabout route? Carefully she moved forward to follow him.

Although the grass had not been cut in months, the landscape opened up and Barbara finally stopped again, unwilling to expose herself in the open. Nicholson was several meters ahead, now directly adjacent to the wall of the tower. He stopped even as she watched, looked around, then moved to the rickety bench that was all that remained of the original picnic equipment. It was small, made of wood on a metal frame, and he bent over it, apparently searching for something. Then he rose slightly and she could see that he had lifted it and now carried it back toward the wall and set it down about six feet away. Apparently satisfied, he brushed off the surface of the bench with his hand before seating himself upon it, facing the wall. He leaned back, his hands clasped behind his head, and sat back, and Barbara suddenly realized what he was staring at. The gargoyle! The same one that had figured so prominently in her dream!

The shock broke the spell or paralysis or whatever had held her to this course of action, and she turned and fled back the way she had come, running despite the weakness of her legs. But it was a panicky run, and she began to stumble until reason finally took hold and she stopped herself. "Don't be an ass, Barbara," she told herself. "It was only a goddamned dream." But whatever it was, she wanted no further reminder of it. She walked the rest of the way home slowly, but her thoughts could hardly be described as calm.

It was only after she arrived that a fresh puzzle struck her: Nicholson had sat with his arms at his side, body angled slightly back, eyes staring up into those of the gargoyle. He and the statue had almost seemed nose to nose, although that was certainly a trick of perspective and distance. Certainly they could not have been separated by more than a couple of meters.

And that didn't make any sense at all. There were many things Barbara wasn't certain of in a world that contained her divorce, the deterioration of her parents' mental faculties, the recent war in Vietnam, assassinations, and such atrocities as the Kaplan case, which had actually taken place right here in Managansett. Much that she had always considered immutable turned out to be impermanent, and even transient or illusory. But one thing of which she remained absolutely certain was that when she had seen the gargoyle in the past, it had been situated high on the building, up near the roofline, certainly nowhere near where a seated person could stare directly into its eyes.

It had to be a side effect of the blow to her head, that's all ... there was no other possible explanation. Perhaps the entire walk through the woods was an illusion and James Nicholson had never even been there. Or perhaps her unsteady eyes had misinterpreted what she'd seen from her hiding place among the trees, interpreting some shadow as the statue itself. But somehow she could never quite convince herself of the truth of this rationalization.

But neither could she convince herself to return to the library to check for herself. She was terrified that she might have somehow seen correctly, and then all that remained of her faith in the nature of reality might be in serious question. If that were the case, she was happier not knowing about it.

CHAPTER TWELVE
1976

Paula Fenton Underwood Ingells was not able to locate Valerie Meredith for several months, and it was January before she discovered the whereabouts of her high school companion; companion only, because Valerie had never really had friends. To her, people were items to be picked up and discarded when no longer useful. They had no lasting value.

Paula made the rounds of the singles bars, but she had been out of touch too long. It was two months before she saw a familiar face, somebody named Bob whom she had met at one of Valerie's parties, but he hadn't seen Valerie in several months, and he seemed oddly reluctant to talk about her. Paula tried the surrounding communities—Pawtucket, Providence, Lincoln, and even Central Falls—without success. She had just about given up when she ran into Susan Hadley in the Grotto, one of the sleazier stops on the singles circuit.

It was the first time Paula had ever tried the Grotto, and she intended it to be her last. The dim red lights were still bright enough for her to spot the filth; she could feel the coating of sweat and grease on the bar; the Naugahyde seats stuck to her clothing; the air conditioning labored without much effect. She had come alone; a few of the men she had met since moving back to New England were adequate company, but none impressed her enough to interest her in developing a more casual relationship. She was frankly on the hunt, but her own looks were fading and she had little else to offer. Always having judged her own value in terms of how she measured up in the eyes of her male friends, she found herself now incapable of developing relationships with other women.

She was sitting at the bar sipping a Black Russian when a slightly younger woman with far too much makeup sat down next to her. "Excuse me, sweetheart, but aren't you Paula Fenwick?"

"No," she replied coolly. "I used to be Paula Fenton, but that was a couple of marriages ago." She gave the other woman the once-over—inexpensive clothes, a year or two behind the fashion. "Do I know you?"

"Prolly don't. . . ." The woman paused and literally shook herself. "Sorry about that. Should have eaten something before I started drinking. No, you probably don't remember me. I'm Susan Hadley, Lynn's little sister."

Paula frowned in concentration. Yes, Lynn Hadley had had a younger sister about four years her junior. She wasn't yet in high school when they graduated, she remembered. Looking closely into the other's face, she tried to pick out recognizable features, but any resemblance to Lynn was slight and she just could not remember what the sister had looked like. Kids that young had been almost invisible to her.

"I think I remember now," she lied. "How is Lynn? I haven't seen her in years."

"She's gone now—dead. Happened a few years ago.

Killed herself over some guy, at least that's what we all think happened."

"Oh, I'm sorry." Paula waited for details, but Susan seemed uninterested in providing any additional information.

"You living 'round here now?"

"I've got a place back in Managansett. Came home last year after the divorce."

"God, I don't know why anyone'd come back here. Town's about as interesting as the want ads. Gives new meaning to the word 'dull.'"

"I've been worse places. It felt good, coming home. Made me kind of feel young again, you know?"

"So what've you been up to?"

Paula told her briefly about her job and the apartment she'd found. The woman made her vaguely uneasy, but it felt good to have found someone from her high school years. She changed the subject as soon as possible.

"Where's the old gang, do you know? I haven't seen Valerie Meredith, Donna Dedzic, Gloria Lampert, or Vicky Johnson in years. I found a couple of the guys in the phone book, but they're all married by now."

Susan flagged down the bartender and ordered herself another drink, so Paula motioned to her own empty glass as well.

"Donna married some guy and moved out of state. I don't remember what his name was or where they went. Gloria married a real slob and has a couple of kids. I think they're still living in town someplace. His name was Morrow or Morrell or Morrison, or something like that. I even got invited to the wedding. I don't remember anyone named Vicky Johnson. Lynn didn't introduce me to most of your crowd, you know."

"What about Valerie? You knew her, didn't you?"

"Who didn't? Prettiest girl in the school. Biggest bitch, too." She said the last with considerable bitterness. Paula remembered belatedly that it was Valerie's ostracism of Lynn Hadley that had been blamed for her subsequent nervous breakdown.

There was a long, awkward silence and Paula had just about given up on learning anything when Susan continued. "I haven't seen her recently, but Valerie is still around. Still just as good-looking, too, even though she's what—about thirty-two or -three by now. I don't know where she's living, exactly, but I see her shopping in town every once in a while, and I'll run into her in a club sometimes. Not recently though, now that I think about it."

"Any clubs in particular? I'd kind of like to look her up, talk over old times, stuff like that."

Susan looked at her as though she'd admitted to a preference for raw meat. "Your funeral. She's poison, that's for sure. Doesn't have any friends any more. Lots of people don't like her. There's more than a couple of guys that'll throw you out on your ear if you even say a kind word about her in their presence. She can really get to them when she wants. And she usually wants, if you know what I mean."

"I'll be careful. I put up with her for years, you know. I can handle myself."

"It's your business, not mine. Let's see, she goes to Mindy's Tavern sometimes, and the Cavalier. And I never saw her there, but someone told me she goes into the Tarpit a lot. The crowd's too rough there for me."

Paula grimaced. The first two were tolerable bars, although neither had a good reputation. There'd been a lot of fights at Mindy's and the crowd that hung out regularly was supposed to be loaded with Mafia flunkies. Drugs were dealt openly at times at the Cavalier; the local police had supposedly been paid off to leave the place alone, or to warn people in advance if they were going to conduct a raid. But Paula had been in the Tarpit only once, when she had first moved back and before she was really up on the local scene. There was some pretty heavy involvement with prostitution, some funny kind of code at the cloakroom, from what she'd heard, and there'd been something particularly unsavory about the atmosphere. It was not something she could really put her finger on, but there was a hungry look in the eyes of many of the customers, and there was a cold, ruthless air about the waitresses that had disturbed her.

It wasn't a bad-looking place. The furnishings were expensive, the bar well stocked, everything clean and orderly, even the rest rooms. But she had felt soiled when she left early that one time, calling it a night, insisting on being taken home where she had immediately showered. She had not gone back.

She and Susan made small talk for another half-hour before Paula finally made an excuse and left. They made polite noises about getting together some time and doing the town, but neither was sincere.

Paula was unwilling to return to the Tarpit without male company, and there was none to be had at the moment, so most of the next few evenings she spent at either Mindy's or the Cavalier. She even got picked up once at the Cavalier, but the guy was so drunk that he passed out in the motel room, so she had taken a taxi back to the club to pick up her car and go home. But then she mentioned Valerie's name to one of the waitresses at Mindy's.

"Valerie Meredith? I wonder if that's the same Valerie that Julian Gay has been seeing."

Paula described her, at least as she had appeared years before.

"Well, it could be. She and Julian have been an item for a couple of months."

"I don't know him. Does he come in here a lot?"

"Not likely," she laughed. "He's the competition. He manages the Tarpit."

"Does she go there to see him? At night, I mean. I feel kind of funny going in there without a date, but I'd really like to see Val again."

"Sorry, I don't know. I worked there for a while, but I couldn't take the place. There's a lot of pressure there to...." She let her voice trail off without finishing. "It's rougher work than I really cared for."

"I think I know what you mean." Paula thanked her and left a larger than usual tip when she decided to go home. There was no alternative now; she would have to try the Tarpit.

As luck would have it, she spotted Valerie the very first night. The Tarpit was shaped like the letter "E", with the bar the central arm, tables and dance space spread along the main shaft, and the two end corridors divided up into several "function" rooms. There was a small, two-story house that seemed to have some connection with the building, as there was a lot of traffic to and from it.

Paula came early and found herself a table near the entrance so she could watch people as they entered. She was certain she would recognize Valerie if she showed up. As the crowd became more dense and the evening passed, Paula began to consider leaving. Already she'd had more than she wanted to drink, fended off two drunken advances, and danced with a guy who'd tried to sell her drugs while they were on the dance floor. She picked up her purse and rose, planning to use the rest room and leave, when she spotted Valerie crossing to the bar.

She had arrived either through another entrance or during one of the infrequent moments when Paula was not watching, because there was no way she could have missed Valerie, even had she not been wearing an absolutely scarlet dress. Perhaps the darkness was kind to her, but from this distance, she looked exactly the same as she had at high school graduation: hair perfect, full-featured face, red lips, long eyelashes. All at once Paula was acutely aware of her own fading features, the extra five pounds that stubbornly refused to disappear. But she pushed the unwelcome thought aside and made her way through the crowd, the scarlet dress a beacon in the storm.

"Hi, Val. Long time no see."

The other woman turned slowly, and at first there was absolutely no recognition in her face. She stared at Paula for five full seconds before her mouth relaxed just slightly. "I'll be damned ... it's Paula Underhill, isn't it?"

"Underwood, actually, although it isn't that anymore, either. How've you been, Val? You're looking good, real good."

"I take care of myself. I thought you moved out to Michigan or Ohio or one of those places."

"California. But things didn't work out. I've been back for almost a year now. Looked you up, and some of the other girls, but couldn't find anybody who didn't have a handful of kids and a husband."

"Yeah, most of the old gang bummed out. That's what time does to you. It's nice seeing you again, though."

Even to Paula, the voice appeared to deny the content

of the words. Valerie was already turning back to the bar, gesturing for a drink. Paula noted that the bartender complied quickly and didn't wait to be paid. Valerie picked up the drink and started to walk off without another word.

"Val!" She called, taking a hesitant step forward. When the woman stopped and half-turned, she continued. "Maybe we can get together some time. How do I get in touch with you?"

Valerie was silent for another awkward minute, seeming to consider the matter carefully. "Yeah, maybe we can. It might be kicks. What's your number? Mine's unlisted."

Paula told her the phone number. "If you can hold on a minute, I'll write it down for you." She stopped to fumble with her purse.

"That's all right. I won't forget it. See you around, Paula. Nice running into you." She turned and disappeared into the crowd.

It never occurred to her to wonder that Valerie had not offered her own phone number until much later, after she was home, but she dismissed it from her mind. Valerie always had been secretive about her personal life.

Paula had to arrange two more encounters with Valerie at the Tarpit before she finally heard from her former chum. On each of those occasions she had been dismissed with equal curtness. She had not really expected warmth from Valerie; her recollections from adolescence were not so clouded by the passage of time that she could not still differentiate between what really happened and what she would have liked to happen. But there had been the idea that Val would want to bring her back within the circle of people she carried with her through life.

But two days after their third hurried conversation, just as Paula was about to give up and seek company elsewhere, her telephone rang and the full, sexy voice of Valerie Meredith was in her ear, sounding as animated and purposeful as it had in her memories.

"Paula, it's Val. I have to apologize for not calling sooner, but I've just been so busy lately. Julian, that's my beau at the moment, has been very demanding lately, if you know what I mean, and I just don't seem to have the time and energy for anyone else most of the time. But in your case, I'll make an exception."

"Well, sure, Val. I know how it is. When Buddy and I first got married—"

But Valerie pushed right on. "Listen, Paula, I don't mean to be short, but I've got an appointment to have my hair done and I'm going to have to run. The reason I called is to see if you'd like to go out on the town with us, Julian and me, this Friday night. We can take you around and show you all the best spots, save you months of looking around on your own."

"Thanks, Val. But I wouldn't want to be a third wheel. I'm not really connected to anyone at the moment, sort of between boyfriends, if you know what I mean."

"Not to worry. Julian will get a date for you. And trust me, he doesn't pick losers for my friends."

Paula wanted to say no, but couldn't. For one thing, she hadn't had a real date in far too long. For another, she had never had the ability to deny Valerie her way, never once had mustered the strength to run counter to Valerie's wishes, desires, or commands. Tonight was not going to be the exception.

"All right . . . I guess so. When should I be ready?"

They made hasty arrangements and Valerie hung up. Paula held the receiver in her hand for a long time before slowly and carefully replacing it in its cradle. She knew she should be feeling happy, but for some reason she felt the opposite, as if something terrible were about to happen.

Things went quite well indeed. Julian and Valerie picked Paula up on schedule and introduced her to a tall, dark man about her age named Ted Wexler. Ted was extremely handsome, soft-spoken, and self-confident, a much better catch than she'd expected. He did speak with a slight lisp, and there was a sharpness to his eyes that made her somewhat uneasy, but she didn't object even when his hands began to wander a bit as the evening progressed.

Julian Gay seemed an appropriate match for Valerie and resembled her in some ways. They were of virtually the same height, although Julian was heavier and darker, with a Mediterranean cast to his features. He was the kind of man that some would describe as "suave," and others, contemptuously, as "slick." In either case, he was clearly smitten with Valerie, who manipulated him easily.

They spent a lot of time in the car, stopping at a variety of small clubs for a drink or two, then moving on. Ostensibly this was in order to show Paula where the best places were, but she had already been to all but one of their stops, and Paula recognized pretty early that it was Valerie's unceasing impatience that was at the root of their frequent moves. Valerie had always sought new sources of amusement, even as a teenager, and Paula didn't have to be particularly perceptive to discern that the trait had not mellowed with age.

The large amount of time spent in the back seat of Julian's car enabled her to become rather thoroughly acquainted with her date as well. Their friendship became rather intense shortly after midnight, and at the next stop, Ted and Paula had elected to remain in the car while the other couple went inside. Paula had not graduated from high school a virgin, but she had always arranged her assignations in some degree of comfort. The backseat tryst seemed even more inappropriate at her present age, but the effects of too many drinks, too many years without any sign of affection, and a growing longing for her own youth combined to overwhelm her reservations. When Julian and Valerie returned, they glanced casually into the back, then exchanged rather unpleasant smiles.

Although the evening had ended amicably, it was the last Paula was to hear from Valerie for quite some time. At first she thought she had done something offensive, and she would replay the evening over and over in her mind, trying to figure out what it might have been. But it wasn't until she made an appointment with a doctor because of an irritating rash that she had sufficient motivation to return to the Tarpit on her own.

"I'm afraid there's no doubt that it's syphilis," the doctor had told her.

She left his office in shock, went directly home, and sat in a chair in the kitchen for the rest of the afternoon. It wasn't until the sun had gone down that she rose in the darkness, turned on the lights, and carefully dressed herself.

"I have to tell Val," she said aloud as she pulled out of the driveway and started off toward the highway. "She'll have to let Ted know, too, if the bastard doesn't know already. If I know Valerie, she'll even the score with him for doing this. She always protected her friends. She won't forget what he's done to me."

She arrived at the club at half past nine, and there was no sign of Valerie. After an hour, she flagged down a waitress and asked her if Julian Gay was in tonight.

"He's here somewhere. I think he went over to the house, though. He'll probably be back later."

"What about his girlfriend—Valerie?"

The waitress looked around uneasily. "I haven't seen her. She's not here every night."

Gamely Paula waited, drinking much more than was good for her. Eventually the crowd began to thin, and reluctantly she counted out enough money to cover her tab and the tip, ready to call it a night. It was just then that Julian and Valerie walked past her table together.

"Val, wait!" She jumped up, almost knocking her chair away, suddenly aware of how much alcohol she'd consumed.

The pair stopped and turned in her direction. Julian's face was in shadow, so Paula could not see his expression, but the look on Valerie's face was that of someone who had just found a particularly unpleasant insect in her soup. It must be a trick of the shadows, Paula told herself.

She moved closer to the couple, then lowered her voice. "Hi, Julian. Val, can I talk to you a minute?"

"I suppose so. You're here, aren't you?"

Paula ignored the curt tone. "Listen, Val, it's kind of private. Can we go someplace and talk?"

"There's nothing you can say to me that you can't say in front of Julian. Come on, get it over with."

The snap in her voice almost sobered Paula. What was going on here? What had she done to deserve such treatment? But now her own anger was coming out, and she pushed on without her normal subservient tone.

"All right, I'll tell you. That goddamned bastard you fixed me up with had the syph! And now I've got it, too!"

Julian turned away, hand to his mouth, and Paula thought for a second that he might be laughing. Valerie remained with absolutely fixed features, then set her shoulders back, glanced up at the ceiling, and did laugh, loudly, deep wrenching sounds that were more masculine than womanly. Paula felt as though someone had slapped her.

"Fuck you, Valerie Meredith! It's not funny!" She shouted the words, and there was sudden silence from all around. The people sitting at nearby tables were all turning in their direction.

Paula was beyond discretion. "Two of your friends are in serious trouble and you can laugh at it? What kind of a person are you?"

Valerie cut off the laughter as though with a switch. "Friends? Who? *You?* That stupid jackass *Wexler?* Don't flatter yourself, lady. Wexler never rated going out with us in his life. We just picked him up because we knew he had a bad case and could be counted on to pass it along if he got the chance. He's nothing to us. Never will be."

Suddenly Paula was reeling and the room had started to spin, and it had little to do with what she'd had to drink. "I don't understand. What's going on? Please, Valerie—" Her voice had gotten small and girlish.

Valerie abruptly leaned forward, pressing her knuckles down on a table, spitting the words out angrily. "You're a pain, do you know that, Paula? You were worth shit in high school, and you're not worth that now! All I wanted was to get you off my back so you'd quit pushing yourself into my life. So I sent you a message you'll be able to read every time you look at yourself in a mirror. Can you read it? Is it clear enough now?"

Paula opened her mouth, wanting to say something, either to deny those words or to throw back something equally spiteful in the face of her opponent. But the spinning increased until everything was just a blur and the

297

floor seemed to be where the wall was before, and then she hit it and she couldn't hear anything else.

Valerie Meredith's relationship with Julian Gay lasted a lot longer than any of her previous affairs. It was not that he was particularly good in bed, or outstandingly attractive or interesting to be with, or even particularly inventive. But he was by far the most powerful man she had coupled with, and power was something that fascinated Valerie, the one thing in life that made everything else worthwhile. She admired him for the same reason that she admired the statue of the gargoyle over on the Sheffield house. There was a sense of strength under control, power held by discipline, an intense drive toward chaos controlled by force of will. But all good things had to end, and ultimately she discovered that Julian's manipulation of people through drugs, sex, fear, and money was basically cycling back and forth through the same forms. So it was time to break it off.

But this could not be a simple matter of embarrassing the man into avoiding her in the future. Julian had enough muscle to send someone around to anonymously even the score, and he was a strong enough personality not to be scared into leaving her alone. No, this would have to be done with some skill, and Valerie spent a long time, several months in fact, laying the groundwork.

She began taking notes, unobtrusively—names and dates, mostly. Who came and went to the big house, the location of the safes in Julian's office, one concealed but obviously, for show, the other cleverly hidden in the floor beneath the desk, where the real records were. Valerie was very careful not to jot down anything which might be traced back to her and put no information into her notes that was not verified by at least two other people to her satisfaction.

She rapidly accumulated a considerable store of information, much of which would be very useful to the authorities, but there was no kicker. There had to be one single item around which all the others would revolve, preferably something that, as far as Julian was concerned, she knew nothing about. And eventually the opportunity presented itself.

It was a chance in a million and she knew immediately that no better offer would likely ever arrive. A bad head cold had kept her home in bed for three days and nights, and Julian had dutifully called periodically to make certain she didn't need anything. But late Wednesday evening, she began to feel considerably better and, bored with remaining in her apartment alone, she decided to make a surprise visit to the Tarpit and talk Julian into coming back to her place after it closed.

With her own key to the back door she let herself into the office. The light was on over the desk and she was about to cross and turn on the overhead lights when she heard a sound from the desk. Julian was slumped forward, his head turned to one side, resting on his crossed forearms, and he was snoring. He had fallen asleep. More important, the black log book, the one he had never allowed her to see, was lying open on the desk in front of him.

Valerie tiptoed across the office, not touching anything, moving so that she could read the words on the exposed page. It was dated in the upper left-hand corner in Julian's incredibly legible handwriting, followed by three names she didn't recognize and associated dollar figures, each then followed by a code number. The book appeared to be about half-filled.

Valerie carefully extracted a pen and pad from her purse and set them down on the desk. She reached toward the journal, planning to leaf back to a date earlier than that on which she had first become involved with Julian. If she could leak some information to the press or the police, something that had occurred before she even knew him, along with the confidential information about the location of the safe and other matters that could not be attributed to her, she would be able to get out, free and clear. At the last minute, her hand stopped and she picked up the pen, using one end to page back until she found a date approximately one year earlier. She copied all the entries from that page, turned back, and this time spotted two names she recognized, one a noted underworld figure, the other a member of the state police. She copied this page as well, then, satisfied, turned the book back to the current date. With a last check to make certain she had left no sign of her presence, and after bending over to make sure Julian was still asleep, she stole off into the night.

Valerie mailed the incriminating evidence to the FBI rather than the local police. After seeing the name of a prominent police official in Julian's book, she wasn't certain that anything would be done on a local level. Then came a long wait. She had almost given up, and was trying to work out an alternative plan when the police arrived early one evening at the Tarpit, an organized raid, seizing all club records and placing a seal and an armed guard over the floor safe, which Julian steadfastly refused to open for them, even when served with a search warrant. Valerie did not have the combination, of course, or she would have included that information in the letter she'd sent. But it was only a matter of time until they had it open.

She couldn't cut things off right away, naturally, because Julian was out on bail almost immediately, and the trial might not come for a year or more. But she heard through the grapevine that the Mafia was not pleased at the complete, accessible, decipherable records Julian had maintained, so she was not surprised when he skipped town a month later and was never heard from again. From her point of view, that was even better than a jail sentence, and the only improvement in the situation that she could imagine was if someone discovered Julian's half-decomposed body in the swamps of Managansett.

Spring passed away and then summer, and Valerie made no effort to find someone to replace Julian. Sex was a commodity she was not presently interested in possessing, and she spent most of her time bored, doing some cocaine and finding drugs had lost their allure as well. As a matter of fact, she wasn't really sure what was missing from her life, but she knew quite well that there was in fact a void there. It wasn't until autumn that she had some inkling of what might fill that void, and her discovery was almost by chance.

Valerie was not a walker. Although she lived only two blocks from a convenience store, she almost always drove the car there and back when she needed to pick something up on short notice. She certainly would never have set out to stroll casually around town. But her Mustang had seen better days, so she parked at the west end of town and was shopping for cars at the three dealerships that had sprung up in that part of town. One replaced what had formerly been a used-car lot adjoining the Sheffield mansion.

The library had been closed again. When the receptionist, Paula Fenton, had committed suicide during the summer, it had been closed briefly, ostensibly while a replacement was being found. In point of fact, the historical society was dissatisfied with the lack of significant public interest and shelved the action, and for all practical purposes, it was closed up again more or less permanently. Valerie had just finished looking at the current year's offering of sports cars when she realized her proximity to the building and, struck by an uncharacteristic nostalgia, decided to walk through the grounds and revisit the spot where she'd been thwarted by that snippy little wimp, Barbara Howell, back, oh, at least twenty years ago. Even now, decades later, Valerie felt a rush of rage at the girl: Barbara was one of the few people who'd risked her wrath and emerged relatively unscathed, and Valerie considered it one of her few failures.

She made her way carefully through the tall grass, once frightening a small, unseen animal into panicky flight into the woodland beyond. She walked along the side of the building, stopping when she reached a spot directly across from the tower. Leaning back, she looked up into the eyes of the gargoyle.

It was just as impressive now as it had been during her youth, she realized—a remarkable piece of sculpture. Valerie had little time in life for any appreciation of art, but she had to admire such unrivalled power. In fact, she thought, with the knowledge of an adult, it is even more evident a manifestation of strength. Surely she had not recognized as a child the significance of that tumescent bulge between the thighs or she would have remembered it. The arch of the hips was certainly suggestive as well, and the fanged mouth was drawn into a sly leer, one eye half-closed in a familiar wink. The outstretched arms seemed to offer welcome. She reached up and, standing on her toes, could just barely brush the bottoms of the clawed feet, the stone strangely warm, perhaps as a result of remaining exposed to sunlight all day. She ran her finger lasciviously along the sole of one foot.

My fine, powerful friend, she thought. Would that you really could climb down off that wall and carry me off to bed. She thought it would be a mating that would be talked about for years to come. It would be a meeting of two great powers, and she might even consider bearing a child to such a worthy sire. But she sighed and slumped back down onto her soles. All that was just a dream, however pleasant.

"Sorry, old friend," she said at last. "It just wasn't meant to be. Another time, perhaps; another place." She smiled. "Another body. We could have been a great pair, you and I."

She tossed her long hair back over one shoulder, turned, and strode off. If she had chanced to look back at that moment, she might have seen that the gargoyle's head was turned in her direction, that the look on its face was more speculative than ever. But she didn't turn.

CHAPTER THIRTEEN
1978

Peter DiPaoli carefully slid his awkwardly long legs out from under the dashboard of Bob Doyle's Fiat Spider and stepped into the late afternoon sunshine. Although he stood considerably taller than his companion's even six feet, he felt oddly small and vulnerable as he stood there, displaced in time, staring at the rapidly deteriorating farmhouse his grandparents had called home for most of their adult lives.

"Does it look the same as you remember it?" Bob Doyle had come around the side of the car and was staring at the building with interest.

"Pretty much. It was in a lot better condition the last time I saw it, and I was considerably younger. I don't think it's been painted in years, though. It's still the same color."

"You never visited after your parents died?"

Peter bridled at what he thought was a critical undertone in the question, but he forced himself to calm down and speak evenly. "No. After the accident I was sent off to live with my aunt and uncle in the Midwest. My grandparents hadn't spoken to my parents in years, and I hardly knew them by then. They didn't write letters and never tried to get in touch with me. When I was a teenager, I tried calling them once, but they seemed almost to have lost some of their English. I don't think they even knew it was me on the other end of the phone, and my grandfather started to sound angry, so I just hung up. I never tried again."

"Not what you'd call a close family." Doyle glanced around. "Do you suppose we need to lock the car? Doesn't look like anyone lives within miles."

"It's not quite that remote. There's not as much room to spread out here as there is out in Minnesota, but we're still fairly isolated, particularly for this part of New England. I don't think you'll have to worry about someone ripping off your tape deck, unless you park downtown. We're not going to be here very long anyway; I just want to take a quick look around before we head over to the motel."

"You're the boss, Pete. In this context only, of course."

There it was again, that infuriating ability to say just the wrong thing in his presence. Peter and Bob had been business partners, and lovers, for almost five years, and each year seemed to equip Doyle with more methods by which to keep Peter on the defensive. He had ignored it for a long time, thinking it a juvenile game not worth calling to the other man's attention, but he acknowledged that as a tactical error that forced him always to defer to Doyle in these little personal interplays, sometimes publicly. As he had many times before, Peter dismissed the issue and turned to the matter at hand. But he had not forgotten it, not by any stretch of the imagination. It was there for him to ponder and grow angry about, a glowing coal in the fire of his indignation.

Peter felt a shiver of nerves as he opened the gate to the small front yard. He supposed his grandparents had been much like anyone else's, but all of the images left from his childhood were intimidating ones. He had never seen them in any other context than this farm; they had never once come to visit his parents, even during the period when the family was still on relatively amicable terms. For all he knew, they'd never left the property since purchasing it shortly after their arrival in this country. Their voices were deep and resonant, and their distorted version of English had always made him ill at ease, an alien in a foreign land rather than a young boy visiting his grandparents.

The house stood one story tall, without an attic, a rambling building of ten rooms arranged in an asymmetrical floor plan that conformed to some pattern that had existed only in the minds of the elder DiPaoli. Peter's father had been their only child, and the additional rooms had perhaps been an unnecessary anticipation of events that never came to pass. That son had left this home when he was sixteen, not returning until six years later with his wife and newborn son. The reconciliation had never quite taken. The elder DiPaolis had done most of the construction of the house themselves, in a blend of European and American styles, mixed in a very uneasy harmony. The outer walls were stucco except for the front, where there were white clapboards and dark green shutters trimming small windows of various sizes that broke into the plain walls in no apparent order. The roof showed signs of neglect, a few shingles missing here and there, a bird's nest tucked under one that was loose.

The yard and surrounding area were overgrown. The narrow strips of neat flower garden that Peter remembered from his youth had disappeared. The lawn had gone to seed, and tall grasses swayed as they passed. Off to one side, one of the vegetable gardens was delineated only by its crumbling stone wall. The closest of the chicken coops was also visible, one side leaning in, the roof completely collapsed. His grandfather had died first and his grandmother had buried him herself, somewhere on the property. Two or three years had elapsed before she died as well, and several weeks more passed between her own death and its discovery by the Managansett Police.

Peter reached the door, kicked some dead branches and leaves from the threshold, and fished in his pocket for the key. Doyle was somewhere behind him, still looking around the yard. "Sure looks like it's gone to hell."

As Peter turned the key in the lock, he tossed a comment over his shoulder. "So would you if no one had looked after you for a couple of years. I'm going to check out the inside. Coming in?"

"In a bit. I'll take a look around out here first. How many acres?"

"Only eight, but that's a sizable piece of land around here. Farmland isn't an abundant resource in this part of the country, you know." Without waiting for a reply, he pushed open the door and stepped inside.

Metaphysical ghosts fluttered in his subconscious as he entered the dark hallway. The kitchen was off to the right, a living room to the left, with the hall leading directly back to a small bedroom, a dining room, and the rest of the house. At the moment, all was obscured by near-darkness. The electricity had been shut off—Peter saw no purpose in having it turned on for the short time he would be in the area. He intended to make arrangements for the sale of the property as quickly as possible so that he and

Doyle could get back to their small printing business in Minneapolis. This trip was also supposed to serve as a short vacation for the two men, but Peter had begun to worry almost before they'd left the city. He knew Gwen was perfectly capable of running the shop in their absence, but he knew it in his head, not his gut. Bob, on the other hand, seemed almost to visibly relax as they left the city limits on their drive east.

He moved tentatively into the kitchen, over to the nearest window to brush aside the dusty drapes and let in the light. But even when he had opened the second set of curtains, the room remained half-lit, shadows close about him and hiding in unlikely corners. If he didn't have clear memories of his grandparents working outdoors, he might have believed them vampires, for they seemed to shun the sun much of the time, and the house had always seemed unnaturally dark to him as a child.

A quick glance around showed him that the house had not been obviously vandalized. His grandfather had filled almost every wall with shelving, and the kitchen was lined with pots, pans, dishes, glasses, cooking utensils of every sort, condiments, canned goods, moldy boxes of cereal and crackers, jars of homemade pasta, more jars of tomato sauce put up from their garden. There was probably still a good-sized supply of the latter; both grandparents had spent many hours canning vegetables, fruits, sauces, and other foodstuffs. But the stone-lined basement, with its population of spiders and earwigs and less identifiable insects, was not one of Peter's fonder memories of the household, and he decided that this brief visit did not require a venture downstairs.

There were many less practical items on the shelves as well—straw kitchen witches, an occasional photograph, several vases, empty now—as well as a selection of his grandfather's incredibly detailed carvings. There would be others elsewhere in the house as well, he recalled, figures of every kind, both prosaic and bizarre, ranging from familiar farm animals and human figures to elaborate abstracts. Peter remembered the many times he had watched that shiny blade cutting through wood with a relentless force, sending slivers of discarded pulp in a slow but steady rain to the floor, where his grandmother would later have to stoop and sweep them up.

He tried the kitchen faucet to confirm that the water was still turned on. There was no telephone, of course, and no electric power. He and Doyle had rented a motel room for the night in nearby Scituate, but if the house was at all habitable, he hoped to spend the next couple of nights here. It was warm enough still that they wouldn't have to worry about the lack of heat. There were a couple of woodburning stoves, and the lack of regular lighting would be the only significant inconvenience. It should work out all right and save some money in the process.

He stepped back into the hall and started suddenly as a hand tapped his shoulder. Caught in midstride, he twisted off balance, half-fell across the hall, and banged his shoulder on the corner of a shelf.

"Sorry there, Pete. I didn't mean to startle you." Doyle half-turned, then glanced into the kitchen and back to the living room. "Boy, this place sure looks like a museum on the inside! Wonder if this stuff is worth anything?"

Peter straightened and rubbed his shoulder, his momentary irrational anger pumping adrenaline into his system. "Damn it, why can't you be more careful?" The words came out more harshly than he had intended, but he drove on anyway. "I thought you didn't want to come in. You shouldn't spring up out of nowhere like that. I might have hit my head!" It sounded a puerile complaint even as he said it.

"Cool down, Peter. Mellow out. There's no damage done. I just wanted to check the place out. You never know; I might want to take it off your hands myself."

Peter forced himself to relax, but tension formed a tight knot at the back of his neck. "Come off it, Bob. You never in your wildest dreams wanted to be a farmer. You'd last about ten minutes with a pitchfork in your hands."

"Yeah," Doyle nodded, sauntering past his friend to enter the living room. "But I kind of fancy myself as the country aristocrat, a member of the landed gentry. You know, a gentleman farmer who never gets his hands dirty. All the scutwork gets left for the hired help while he sits out on the front porch sipping mint juleps and looking rustic."

"There's no porch on the house and they don't drink mint juleps in New England. Hot cider is more their style." Peter felt a little of the tension draining out of him. The trip, short as it was, had proven an even greater strain on the relationship between the two men than had their business partnership. He'd thought a leisurely vacation together might enable them to bridge the increasing gap between their personalities, but if anything, it had widened the rift. He followed Doyle into the living room, which seemed even dimmer than the kitchen.

"So I could be a trendsetter," Doyle said as he opened some curtains. He still envisioned himself as lord of the manor, and Peter knew from long experience that there was no likelihood of being able to move him from the subject until he was ready to leave of his own volition. Opposition just seemed to egg him on.

"More likely you'll be an Irish setter." His heart really wasn't in the quip, but he and Doyle had struck up their original friendship because of their mutual fondness for puns and sarcastic banter. They had become even closer when a tentative advance from Doyle had not been rebuffed, and the two had become roommates not long after.

"Weak," commented Doyle. "You're letting the atmosphere get to you, boy. Pity you never learned Italian. You could have punned bilingually."

"If I did, you wouldn't understand them anyway, and that particular form of antisocial behavior would soon be extinguished."

"You mean it would peter out, right?" Doyle moved quickly from place to place in the room, squinting to see into the shadowy corners where many of the woodcarvings stood under a thin layer of dust. Peter was curious, but at the same time, he didn't want to look too closely. Everything about his grandfather had put him off since the day they'd walked around downtown and he'd seen the old man . . . but he chased the thought away. Doyle was speaking again.

"Very unusual decor in here, to say the least. Where'd they ever buy all these things? Didn't you tell me they almost never left the farm? Did they bring them from the old country?"

"No, my grandfather carved them, or most of them, at least. He was pretty good at it."

Doyle picked up what appeared to be the figure of a woman sitting at an elaborate spinning wheel. He blew the dust from it and examined it critically. "Pretty good is right, although the face is rather ugly. These might be worth more than the house itself, Pete. Maybe we should have them boxed up and shipped back to Minnesota so we can spend some time finding out what they're worth."

"No!" The word slipped out laden with all the tension and resentment of a few moments earlier. Peter knew his reaction was entirely irrational, but somehow the idea of removing the carved figures from the house was as unthinkable as having his grandfather strolling around downtown Minneapolis to see the sights. And he knew that he didn't want anything from this place to invade the home he'd made for himself. He repeated the word, more softly this time. "I just don't have the time to get involved in a project like that. No one's going to pay a lot of money for a load of ordinary wood carvings by a dead Italian immigrant farmer no one has ever heard of. Let the new owners crate them up or leave them here, or sell them, or do whatever they want with them. I just want to be done with this and get back home." Peter felt the tension knotting the back of his neck as he spoke and wondered whatever had possessed him to get this worked up over so trivial a matter.

"All right, Pete, calm down." Doyle looked directly at him, as though equally puzzled at the depth of emotion he detected in his companion's words. "It's your property. You can throw them into the fireplace for all I care." He looked around. "That is, if there is a fireplace."

"No, there isn't." Peter ran his hand through his thick hair and was surprised to find his forehead beaded with sweat. "Just woodburning stoves in the kitchen and a couple of the other rooms, I think, probably the two larger bedrooms. There's not much of a fireplace tradition where my grandparents came from. No firewood to speak of. They copied the general looks of the house from their homeland and what they saw around them, but the interiors are patterned after whatever they were most familiar with."

The rest of their visit went without incident. Peter felt a living presence in the house, almost as if his departed relatives were somehow still there, waiting in another room for him to take a single step across the line of permissible behavior, ready to pounce with sharp, cutting syllables. Even Doyle seemed something less than his normal ebullient self as they glanced through the bedrooms, a pantry, what had apparently been a sewing room, a couple more rooms used only for storage, one obviously the site of the canning operation. Each and every room and every hallway was lined with shelves, usually draped with filthy sheets obscuring the contents. Doyle glanced behind a couple of these. "More carvings," he said each time. "Your grandfather must have had lots of free time."

The house was in surprisingly good condition, and one of the bedrooms was sufficiently free of the encroachments of dust, mold, and clutter, so that Doyle could be persuaded to spend a night or two rather there than at the motel. He complained more out of a sense of duty than out of any conviction about Peter's frugality, and the tensions had threatened to mount once more, but the discovery of a cedar chest full of clean linens provided enough ammunition for Peter's position to prevail. They would spend the first night at the motel, as they had guaranteed their reservations, but tomorrow they would pick up enough supplies to be self-sufficient for the two or three days they expected to have to remain in Managansett.

There remained enough uneasiness between the two that Peter made no objection when, after returning to their rented room, Doyle volunteered to drive to a local store to pick up food, a cooler chest, and a few other commodities to last through their visit. Feeling unnaturally tired and depressed, Peter went to bed early and did not waken when, two hours later, Doyle returned and slipped gratefully into the other bed.

Peter, who rarely remembered his dreams, relived that night a series of actual events from his childhood, although in some cases they were somewhat altered. The first of these was that day long ago when his grandfather had shown him that awful, terrible figure carved out of stone mounted on the wall of some building downtown. The figure still occasionally troubled Peter's dreams, even after all these years, and this time was no exception. As he stood there, his dream identity standing next to that of his grandfather, both staring up, the gargoyle leaned forward, providing clearance so that the batlike wings could unfurl. Peter, who was the stature of a child again, cowered as the gnarled form launched itself outward and down, its eyes gleaming readily as it reached forward with its iron-tipped claws. Peter lurched upward out of his sleep, rising from the pillow, almost wakening Doyle by the intensity of his reaction. But then he realized it had been just another of his bad dreams, and he sank back down onto the pillows.

He was back in his own past again almost immediately upon losing consciousness, this time witnessing the execution of the chicken in his grandmother's yard. This dream was almost a photographic reproduction of that original incident, and he watched the blade flashing and falling with just as much horror and disbelief as he had during the actual incident years before. The headless body reeling away, not realizing it was dead. It staggered against the trunk of a tree, leaving a bright red arterial smear on the bark, then half-ran, half-flopped the short distance to the side of the house. It struck the wall and rebounded, rolling completely over, then convulsed and writhed its way across the grass to Peter's feet. Rigid with shock, the boy froze as a pulse of blood stained his white sneakers. The body then flipflopped over his shoes, made unsteady progress across the grass, and finally bumped up against the white picket fence that separated the front yard from the street beyond. It ran around in hysterical circles for a moment or so, its wings flapping in a parody of flight, then crashed into the fence once more, staggering a few feet away to collapse, still quivering and jerking spasmodically until it finally realized it was dead.

This time Peter was not able to throw off the aftereffects of his dream, and lay shivering and perspiring for quite some time afterward, unable to sleep.

Doyle was up and around early the following morning, but Peter lay abed until Doyle finally lost his patience. After a brief but bitter exchange, Doyle stalked off to find breakfast alone. When he returned over an hour later, Peter was dressed but in no better mood than that in which he'd awakened. It seemed to take him an inordinate amount of time to accomplish even the most routine of tasks, packing up his clothing, arranging change, keys, handkerchief, and such in his pockets, even locking the door and turning over the key to the receptionist. It was nearly eleven o'clock when they finally pulled out of the parking lot.

The farmhouse, not surprisingly, looked very much the same, although the day was far more overcast and the light dim. Peter felt the same sense of his own powerlessness and was surprised that the impact had not lessened since their visit the previous day. He sat in the car for too long, staring at the chicken coop, the picket fence, the house itself, remembering his dream, unwilling to take any course of action that might cause sympathetic recollections during the daylight. Impatiently, Doyle came around the side of the car and rapped on the window.

"Are we awake yet, Mr. DiPaoli? Are we getting out? Or is this just a bus tour? Yes, folks, this is the house of the woodcarving grandfather of the famous Peter DiPaoli, entrepreneur extraordinaire."

Annoyed and then angry with himself for being so easily goaded, Peter jerked the car door open and stepped out quickly, banging his knee and twisting his ankle in the process. He slammed the door shut in frustration.

"Hey, it's not the car's fault you share Wilt Chamberlain's genotype. Go easy on it, will you? We're not making so much money that I can afford a new one just yet."

Wordlessly Peter swung open the gate, crossed to the front door, and unlocked it. He paused for long seconds, but Doyle's perceptible presence behind him finally compelled him to enter, even though the other man remained silent. Doyle followed, a bag of groceries in one hand, an overnight bag in the other. "Don't bother to help or anything," he complained as he sidled through the door, dropping part of his burden and then carrying the provisions into the kitchen.

Peter turned to the left, noticing that the light was better in the morning, probably because of the angle from which it struck the windows. The living room did not seem nearly so depressing, although the layer of dust was now much more prominent. His eye tracked along one of the shelves—a row of carved farm scenes, a tractor, a brace of cows, a chicken coop, a stooped old woman hoeing, a gnarled tree against which stood the figure of a man, scythe held at one side, blade resting against his leg. The last was one of the largest and most elaborate carvings, set in the far corner of the room. Peter started forward to examine it in more detail.

"Hey, Peter!" Doyle shouted from the hall. "I'm starting to get really pissed off. Look around to your heart's content after we unload the car, but right now, how about lending a hand? I'm along on this trip for a vacation, remember? You're the one who's supposed to be conducting himself as executor of the estate. I'm just the chauffeur."

Peter's hands clenched. This was definitely not working out as he'd hoped. Their partnership had never quite jelled. Peter was frugal and wanted to plow every available cent back into business or retire outstanding debt, while Doyle was fond of a flamboyant lifestyle and believed in spending money while it was available and worrying about tomorrow only when it became unavoidable. He was fond of quoting statistics about how virtually every investment fell behind inflation. You might as well spend your money now, he reasoned, while it still commanded full value. If he'd had the capital and if there had not been more personal connections between the two, Peter would've tried to buy his partner out a long time ago, or would've sold out to him if Doyle had been able to raise the money. But even in its present shaky financial condition, the print shop lent a stability to Peter's life that had been lacking during his late childhood and adolescence, and he would not willingly relinquish the sense of security it afforded him.

Peter shook off his stupor and helped Doyle bring in the rest of their luggage and the small store of supplies from the back seat. Doyle busily made a list of items he'd overlooked, which he would secure while Peter was seeing the lawyer who'd handled the estate and taking care of a few other items of business. They drove into town, stopping at a hamburger stand for lunch, where Doyle put so much catsup on his sandwich that it oozed out the sides and made tiny mounds all over the table. Peter was acutely embarrassed by Doyle's sloppiness, which had manifested itself more than once in the past. His feelings were apparent enough that the other man noted them and was amused. Peter correctly suspected that Doyle did it deliberately to get a rise out of him.

Peter was consequently in an unpleasant mood when Doyle dropped him off at the attorney's office, but he was treated there in such a businesslike, matter-of-fact manner that his ill humor quickly disappeared. With no other living relatives, the simple will was not likely to be contested. Outside of the house and property, there were effectively no other assets; his grandparents' small bank account wouldn't even cover the inheritance tax and other expenses, and there was no insurance. Some of the bills would have to be paid out of the proceeds of the sales of the property. Not even the land was completely free; there was a lien on it because of a loan that had been taken out several years previously. Peter would be lucky if he ended up with as much as $10,000 after all the expenses had been covered.

When he'd finished with the lawyer, Peter visited the bank, where he was greeted with understanding and patience, if not exactly affability. Since there was still over an hour before Doyle was due to return to pick him up, Peter visited a realtor's office and arranged for an inspection and appraisal. The agent would be more than happy to handle the sale for him, of course, and was he thinking of settling in the Managansett area?

He visited a second realtor and made similar arrangements, just as a check on the first. He was not going to be able to stay around for the sale, and he had already signed over power of attorney to a lawyer, but he wanted some assurance that he was not being cheated. Having completed his business with dispatch, he was in a fairly jaunty frame of mind when Doyle came screeching to a halt in front of him somewhat later.

"Let's get going," Bob said angrily. "I'm pretty sick of this damned town." His usually infuriating good humor seemed to have utterly vanished.

"What's up, Bob? Get everything we needed?" Peter carefully folded his legs under the dashboard and closed the door.

"Everything plus." Doyle gestured toward a rectangle of paper on the dashboard which Peter belatedly recognized as a traffic citation. "Would you believe I got a ticket for going thirty miles an hour? From the goddamn Chief of Police himself, no less!" Doyle raised one hand from the steering wheel and slapped it back down as they pulled away from the curb. "Who the hell still has fifteen-mile-an-hour zones? That went out with the horse and buggy, for God's sake!" He pulled out into the main line of traffic and turned west, in the direction of Reservoir Road and the farmhouse. For a few seconds the Fiat accelerated smoothly and steadily, but then Doyle thought for a moment and eased his foot back. "They're probably laying for me now. I made sure that cop knew I thought he was a candy ass."

"Don't get paranoid, Bob. This is a quiet little town, cut off from the rest of the state and a bit old-fashioned about things. Nobody's plotting against you!"

"Don't patronize me, Peter!" Doyle's snap was very

uncharacteristic. "It doesn't suit you, and it won't wash with me. I've been patronized by the best and they never got anywhere, and you're not in their league, not by a long shot. So shut up, will you?"

"Damn it, Doyle, it's just a lousy ticket. Don't get so upset. Mail them a check. Or don't do anything ... rip it up. You'll be out of state and beyond their reach long before the court date. They don't extradite people for doing fifteen miles over the speed limit."

"It's the goddamned principle of the thing. I've never had a ticket in my life! Twenty years of driving, and not one ticket—not even for parking. And then they go and give me one for going thirty miles an hour!"

"Come off it, Bob." Peter turned and looked out the window, tired of the argument. "This is the third sports car you've owned since I've known you, and you're trying to tell me you've never even been pulled over for speeding?"

"Yes, that's what I'm telling you! Not once!" Doyle clenched his hands on the wheel. "I've never even had a warning. Years of a spotless record are wiped out because one bored hick cop has nothing better to do than enforce a law that probably dates back to the eighteenth century. If I didn't have out-of-state plates, you bet your ass this wouldn't have happened."

"All right, all right. Everyone is picking on Bob Doyle today, obviously. What can I say, old man? You just have to circle your wagons when the enemy is attacking from all sides."

The Fiat suddenly swerved into the breakdown lane and came to an abrupt halt. "Get the hell out of this car! I'm not listening to any more of this shit!"

"Fine!" Peter felt his temper flaring. "I'll catch up to

320

you at the farm, or more likely along the way, when the state trooper who's out to personally nab Bob Doyle pulls you over and cites you for seventeen separate violations of the traffic code." He was barely out of the car when Doyle pulled away, the door slamming shut, crushed stone spewing out from under the tires to spatter against his pants leg.

Peter felt simultaneously the cleansing euphoria of having blown his top and a return of the melancholy that had oppressed him since the start of the trip. The problems with Doyle and their partnership had seemed to grow rather than lessen as the miles passed. Peter had hoped a vacation away from the day-to-day grind might rekindle their friendship, but Doyle had changed, had become more bitter and egocentric. And he himself had changed as well. He was less resilient, less patient, less tolerant. And what other faults was he too blind to see in his own image? He often wondered what changes others could see in him. The financial disappointment of his bequest, the emotional pressure of the visit to the scene of the less pleasant moments of his childhood, the growing sense of the passage of time and with it the passing of his life, and the opportunity to make something of it, all these had combined to make the trip more an ordeal than a vacation. He felt as if everything in his life was starting to come apart at once, his present, his future, even his past, all mixing and deteriorating just as the farm was slowly subsiding into decay and neglect. He started to walk along the highway with measured steps, but his pace was that of an old man, an observation that was apparent to him even in his preoccupied state. He knew he was feeling sorry for himself, allowing his moodiness to turn inward and feast upon itself, but at the moment he was deriving a perverse pleasure from his own misery and was unable to shake off a growing feeling of despair.

It was almost an hour later when Peter finally reached the farmhouse. The Fiat was parked neatly out front, but Doyle was nowhere to be seen. Not feeling up to another confrontation just yet, Peter decided to walk around the property. Behind the house he found an old storage shed he did not remember ever having seen before, roof half caved in, walls lined with shelves full of paint cans and other containers. The shed was incredibly cluttered, with glass jars full of screws, nuts, bolts, pins, paper clips, washers, corks, matchbooks, buttons, staples, and other odds and ends, all neatly sorted by type and size. There were coils of rope, wire, and string, an old crosscut saw, a box of hammer heads, a row of shovels and other small tools with broken handles, a hoe, a hand scythe similar to the one he'd noticed in his grandfather's carving, a box of knives, several boxes of assorted glassware, drinking glasses made from jelly jars, hurricane lampshades, small dessert bowls, a few plates, all mismatched and jumbled together. There was a pile of lumber, some copper tubing, a roll of black electrical tape, a rusted screwdriver with a chip out of its handle, an anchor, an electric fan with a bent blade, another missing its blades entirely, a chest of drawers half-rotted from rain that had come in through the roof, a bin of newspapers, and another of neatly folded and now mildewed grocery bags. A faded calendar hung from one wall, a map of the world adorned another. In one corner, an old radio lay with its back off, not far from a disassembled mantel clock. There were a few toys as well, some stray pieces of flatware, and six spare tires, the inner tubes of which were hung on the far wall. It was shadowy in the rear, and even in the full light of day he could not identify all the shapes, but he thought he could see a fishing rod, a bicycle wheel, and an old water pump. There also appeared to be a discarded kitchen or laundry appliance, but it was covered by burlap bags. There was moss and mold everywhere, and a distinctly sweet and unpleasant aroma that eventually discouraged him from further exploration.

Part of the backyard was now impassable, the surrounding woodland having reclaimed what his grandparents had wrested from its grasp so many years before. The new owners, whoever they might be, would have their work cut out for them beating this back, although upon reflection, he realized they would probably hire someone to just plow it all under rather than painfully cut it back by hand as had been done before. Peter felt a surge of directionless anger, as though all the effort the elder DiPaoli couple had expended was nothing more than a joke, a useless exercise that was foredoomed to failure, even trivialization.

Eventually there was no further excuse and Peter had to go inside. Doyle had thrown a blanket over the loveseat in the living room and was sprawled across it, legs crooked over one arm, reading a magazine that seemed inordinately involved with naked human flesh. Doyle had never dated a woman since the two of them had taken up together, but he claimed to be bisexual, though Peter suspected it was a token gesture toward "normal" sexual behavior rather than a reality.

He didn't look up when Peter entered. The kitchen had been further supplied, but it was certainly no cleaner and a lot more cluttered than it had been when they'd first arrived. Peter opened a bottle of lukewarm soda, looked for a place to set it down, and found a mustard spill and crumbs where Doyle had apparently made himself a sandwich. The contrast to the neat, orderly kitchen his grandmother had kept infuriated him. It was a desecration. The man had no right. Peter spun on his heel and stormed back into the other room.

"You know, I really don't understand why you have to be such a slob. It's bad enough at home, but they're going to have to show this house to people before they can sell it. You could at least try not to spill food all over the place."

Doyle looked up and was silent at first, then threw the magazine across the room in anger. "What the hell is it with you lately, DiPaoli? Ever since this trip started, even before we left, you've been finding fault with everything I've done, bitched about everything that happens. You've been about as much fun as a vegetarian at a barbecue. This isn't exactly a palatial estate, in case you hadn't noticed. It's a rundown farmhouse out in the middle of nowhere, and it hasn't been cleaned or lived in for months. Ease off, my friend. The bugs will take care of whatever tidbits we spill in the corners long before anyone sees the place. Besides, we have considerably more important matters to discuss."

Peter walked across the room, picked up the magazine from where it lay with its pages splayed open, and tossed it onto a chair. "What matters are those?"

"Our business, Peter. The Finger Print Shop. Never did like that name, did I ever tell you? But it wasn't worth arguing about." Doyle swung his feet down and sat upright. "Peter, the store is going nowhere. Our receipts aren't going up as fast as our expenses, and it's only a matter of time until we can no longer pay our bills."

"Our expenses keep rising because more and more of

your personal bills keep showing up on the company books. We're showing a steady increase in profit otherwise, even with the raises we gave ourselves this year."

"Don't throw that in my face again. I've told you more than once that you should put some of your living expenses on the company tab. My expenses have been going up faster than the five percent raise we allowed ourselves, and I have a right to expect a higher standard of living, too. That's what we went into business for, after all."

"Is it?" Peter began pacing back and forth as he spoke. "I suppose in the long run it was, but I also thought we mostly just didn't want to have to answer to anyone else ever again. We were going to be our own bosses, entrepreneurs, cutting out a little portion of the market for our own."

"Yeah, that too. But you've been sounding more and more like a boss lately, Peter, or at least a guilty conscience, and I didn't give up working for American Glassware just so I could work for you. I want to live like the bosses do. *That's* why I threw my money into this deal. But it isn't working out, and we aren't working together personally very well, either." He paused to let it sink in. "There's just too many people going into the printing business, and there's not enough market left to share. If we get out now, we might even make a profit on what we've invested in equipment. It's time to move on to something else. And I think for you and me, it's also time for a parting of the ways. This isn't working. You know it and I know it. Maybe we can be friends again when there isn't money involved, but all we're doing now is wasting ourselves in a company that's doomed to mediocrity and destroying whatever friendship we once shared as well. I want out while there's still something left of each."

"Bob, you don't understand." Peter was horrified to detect a note of pleading in his voice. "I know the equipment doesn't depreciate all that much, and we can probably get back at least what we've put into the company. But we'll end up right back where we were five years ago, a few thousand dollars in the bank, no prospects for the future. We don't even have *jobs* to go back to."

"God damn it, I'm tired of hearing about the future! I'm going to be old in the future; that doesn't mean I have to look forward to it or plan my entire life for my retirement. We're both young. We've got plenty of time to make our fortunes, find our places in the world. The printing business might be the right spot for you, Peter, but it's not right for me. Things move too slowly. By the time I make a pile of money this way, I'm going to be too old to enjoy it."

"If you pull up your roots and move on every few years, you're never going to." Peter's voice cracked with tension and he fought for control. He couldn't let Doyle dissolve the company now. Too much else in his life seemed insubstantial or transitory. If the inheritance had been larger, he might have been able to buy him out, but that was unlikely now. "Maybe we should give it another year, see how we both feel then. If you'd concentrate on getting new customers for a while and stop pulling money out to blow on fancy cars, expensive hobbies, and whatever else it is that you do with your money, you'd be able to start building your fortune now. There's ways we could expand our offering that would generate more income, but we have to invest capital first, and you're siphoning it all off."

"Peter, you sound like an investment counselor. Listen, I don't want to give it another year. I'm tired of customers who don't want to pay their bills for ninety days, and I'm tired of suppliers who demand to be paid in thirty. I'm tired of dealing with employees who sit down whenever your back is turned, but who can't be fired until they've been through the three-step warning system. I'm tired of the paperwork, I'm tired of having ink stains on my hands, I'm tired of paper cuts, and I'm colossally tired of the sounds of the presses and copy machines. I don't want to collate and staple anything again in my entire life. I'm tired of that cluttered little shop and the scruffy customers who come into it, and there are even a lot of times lately when I'm pretty tired of you. And I'm sure there are other times when you wish I'd fall down a well or worse. It's nothing personal, but we just don't click together anymore and it's probably better for both of us to end this now, before we end up hating each other."

Peter felt as if things were slipping away from him— that his grasp on the world was growing tenuous. He heard his own words as if someone else were speaking. "We don't have to be such ... close friends in order to be business partners. We could get separate apartments." The tone seemed flat and unconvincing, even to him. "Maybe you could just be a silent partner, withdraw from the business if it bothers you so much, and I could buy your share out over the next few years if you still feel the same way."

"No way, Peter ... sorry. I want out now and I want my money. No offense, buddy, but I'm not sure the Finger Print Shop will stay solvent even with professional Pete calling all the shots. As much as you criticize me for taking some of the money over and above my official salary, we lose just as much because you're such a soft touch. You're so damned desperate for clientele you give credit to anyone who asks for it, even the ones who never have any intention of paying us, even the ones who have stiffed us in the past, and whenever a big account wants longer payment terms or a bigger discount or some other little favor, you bend over so far to give it to them that you could kiss your own ass. Tannahill is willing to give us a good price for the business, and I think we should take him up on it."

"That's the only way to build up your customer base." Peter ignored the reference to Dan Tannahill, a rival printer who wanted to turn their shop into a branch of his own. "Most of them—"

Doyle pushed himself suddenly to his feet, interrupting Peter in mid-sentence. "Forget it, Peter. I've made up my mind. Made it up before this trip even started, figured it would be a good chance for us to go over the whole thing. You're not going to talk me out of it, and there's really no point in having you try."

Peter watched as Doyle reclaimed his magazine. Finally he felt as though he had to say something, break the silence. "All right, if you still feel that way about it tomorrow, I guess that's the way it'll have to be. Sleep on it, Bob. Don't throw away everything we've worked for just because you're pissed at me."

"I'm not pissed at you, Peter, but we don't have all that much to throw away. All we have is a half-assed business that pays the rent and the grocery bills, and that's just about it. And a half-assed friendship that just might be worth saving. I won't change my mind. This isn't sudden."

The two men met each other's gaze, but Peter soon dropped his eyes. Doyle had always been the stronger personality. After a few moments he got up and walked out, leaving Peter standing there.

He was never certain afterward how long he remained

motionless, the thoughts racing pointlessly in his mind as he tried to come up with the one uncontestable argument that would win his partner back to their original commitment. But all he could think of were variations on the same theme, and he knew already that he would be wasting his breath. It was not a clear-cut transition from his immobile stance to the examination of the woodcarvings around the room. Possibly his mind was seeking some neutral territory to which he might escape, and they were the first thing that came to hand, or to sight. *In any case,* he suddenly came to himself standing closer to the wall, half-crouched to examine the figure of a woman bent over a hoe. Oddly enough, each of her arms seemed to have an extra elbow, an inconsistency that could not have been accidental.

The next was a man sitting at a fishing hole, but when Peter looked closely, he saw a pair of satanic horns protruding from the sides of the head. Then came a grazing cow, the feet tipped with long, sharp claws. Another farmer figure sat on a tractor, but from his back rose the nubs of folded wings. And finally he reached the man with the scythe, except it wasn't a man at all, but an accurate rendition of the gargoyle mounted on the mansion wall. Peter recoiled in horror and quickly backed to the doorway. From this distance the figures all appeared entirely ordinary once again, and he wondered if possibly he had hallucinated the entire thing. But somehow he could not muster up the courage to move forward and find out.

Peter dreamed again that night. First he relived yet again the decapitation of the chicken, every detail engraving itself on his consciousness. Next he repeated the visit to the gargoyle's lair, but this time it was the gargoyle who led him by the hand, and it was the figure of his grandfather who was mounted on the wall, his body made of stone. Then came the final sequence. Peter found himself in the yard outside the farmhouse, walking around to where the stunted peach tree stood silently and alone. Its twisted limbs moved slowly back and forth, although there was no hint of a breeze. Scattered through the branches were several small peaches, rotted black in the sun, their skins burst open to reveal syrupy red interiors. Peter found himself drawing even closer to the tree, although his feet were no longer moving. As the distance lessened, he was able to discern tiny sets of features on the fruit, realizing in growing horror that they were the faces of his father, his mother, some of his childhood friends, and most prominently his grandparents.

With an enormous effort of will, he seemed to turn away from the tree, but now he was confronted by a gigantic version of the carving of the man with the scythe, except that naturally it was not a man at all. The smooth metal blade tapped rhythmically against the roped muscle of the leg, becoming more insistent with each stroke, and the tapping increased to a reverberant thunder that threatened to shake him to the ground. Peter fell to one knee, braced himself with his hand, and turned to look upward. The figure bent at the waist, head lowering toward his own, and the fang filled mouth opened, saliva glistening on the chin. . . .

When Doyle rose the following morning, Peter had already gotten up and left the house. Still in his underwear, he lit a can of sterno under a pot of water for coffee, then walked through the various rooms. He was not entirely awake, but it was obvious that he was alone. Shrugging, he returned to the kitchen, made coffee, ate a bowl of cereal and a couple of bananas, and finally returned to the bedroom to dress. Peter had still not made an appearance.

Never patient, Doyle was soon muttering to himself. Perhaps Peter had gone out for an early morning walk. It was not typical behavior for him, but he'd been under a lot of stress lately. Doyle felt a twinge of guilt with this thought, knowing he himself was responsible for much of the tension, but he suppressed the feeling. The jerk was only getting what he deserved, after all. Friends don't make snide remarks about each other, particularly to the hired help. He knew that Arthur frequently complained to Gwen about his partner's actions, and he knew because Gwen had decided she was in love with Doyle and had no compunctions about breaking what Peter certainly believed was a confidence. Peter wanted to use their print shop as a shield against the outside world rather than as a means to further his position in that millieu. Doyle had other plans for his life. They did not include Peter DiPaoli.

He stepped outside, and noticed that it promised to be a bright, clear day. No sign of Peter. Turning to the right, he started to make his way around the house. He noticed a rundown storage shed and wandered in its direction, idly curious. As he approached, Peter stepped out from behind its crumbling rear wall. Doyle barely had time to register the smooth shining flash as the scythe swept up from knee level in a broad swing that severed his head cleanly from the rest of his body.

The foreshortened body staggered up against the trunk of the tree, leaving a bright red arterial smear on the bark, then half-ran, half-stumbled the short distance to the side of the house. It ran into the wall and rebounded, toppling and rolling completely over, then convulsed and writhed its way across the grass to Peter's feet. Mesmerized, he was unable to move as a pulse of blood smeared his white tennis shoes. The body flip-flopped past him, rolled unsteadily through the grass, and bumped up against the white picket fence that bordered the front of the yard. Grotesquely it rose to its feet and ran around in hysterical circles for a moment or so, its arms flapping insanely against its sides, then crashed into the fence once more, stepped a few feet forward, and collapsed, still quivering and jerking spasmodically until it finally realized it was dead.

When the body was completely motionless, Peter dropped the scythe and turned away.

A few days later, Officer Vanelli of the Managansett Police Force reported finding Doyle's body after investigating the hysterically sobbed story of a pair of local teenagers. They claimed to have been casually passing by, although Vanelli frankly suspected they'd planned either to vandalize the farmhouse or find anything worth stealing that might have been left in it. But his investigation had turned up something else that the teenagers had not noticed at all. According to the report, he had also noted that an unusually tall man had apparently hanged himself from a peach tree behind the house. There was no other indication of a struggle of any kind.

CHAPTER FOURTEEN
1982

James Nicholson, who hoped to be known as J.T. Nicholson once he consolidated his position, had grown along with Eblis Manufacturing, which was now one of the leading manufacturers in the state. He hadn't progressed as far as he'd expected when he was younger, but then, his expectations had slimmed down somewhat along the way, for personal ambitions and the opportunities available to him had only coincided some of the time. He was currently vice president of manufacturing, having succeeded Oliver Moore in that position earlier this year after cleverly playing his cards to best advantage in the political battle that ensued when controlling interest in the firm was sold to Gordon Wheeler, a wealthy investor with too much cash for his own good, at least in Nicholson's view. It could not be said that Wheeler liked or admired him, but he did find Nicholson useful. It could not be said that his peers liked him, but they had been forced to accept the fact that he was skillful in interdepartmental politics, not a man whose bad side you wanted to be on. Neither could it be said that his subordinates liked him, but they feared him for the most part, feared his temper (which appeared to be spontaneous and violent, but which was calculated, controlled, an instrument of policy rather than emotion), feared the system of checks and balances that he was establishing to ensure that he always knew immediately when someone had screwed up. They knew that he considered them all expendable, that so long as they were assets and kept their mouths shut, they were safe, but that if they even appeared to be liabilities, either because of their performance or because of their lack of loyalty, they would be sacrificed upon the altar of J.T. Nicholson's career.

The accomplishment that had won him the vice-presidency had been his spearheading of the year-long legal and tactical battle to break the back of the union. Twice his windshield had been smashed, and he had finally invested some money of his own to arrange a serious but nonfatal accident for a particularly obstreperous union official. The effect had been worth the investment. His people were careful to arrive before him, and they rarely left until his car was seen leaving the parking lot. They rode their subordinates in turn, and though his turnover ratio was the highest in the company, he'd reduced the payroll so significantly that no questions were asked about his methods.

His secretary, Cheryl, quietly removed a dirty coffee cup from his desk as she dropped the overtime report in his "In" box. He pretended not to notice, but he could tell by the set of her lips that she was still angry over his decision to deny her leave time to visit a sister in Oklahoma. The woman was terminally ill with leukemia, if he remembered correctly, but there was no point in Cheryl's going out there before the disease reached its final stage. Company policy allowed her bereavement time at that point regardless of his feelings in the matter, and he was resigned to losing her for a few days. Besides, whether she acknowledged it or not, he was doing her a favor by preventing her from having to spend several weeks with the dying woman. A year from now she might thank him. Probably not, though. Even when you did favors for people, they were generally ungrateful. In any case, they had a business to run. One didn't work to make friends; one worked to earn a paycheck. If a few less stolid hearts got stepped on along the way, that was just the nature of things. You couldn't expect the lions in the world to eat grass simply because there were so many sheep. You needed a few carnivores to thin out the herds, to separate the incompetent from the acceptable. The outstanding people would take care of themselves.

He glanced at the newly arrived report and made a note to speak with Sheldon down in timekeeping. Just because there was some overtime in one or two production departments, some of the timekeepers were getting premium pay. He'd put a stop to that; the department supervisors could fill in the production cards and leave them on the timekeepers' desks for the following morning. Maintenance overtime seemed to be creeping up again, but he doubted he could do much about that. Installation of the new equipment required by OSHA and the EPA was an unavoidable expense. Nicholson was incensed that the new administration in Washington, for which he had held so much hope, had done so little to curb these meddlesome agencies.

He turned his mind to more pleasant subjects. Today was to be a day of triumph, not a day to become annoyed by petty problems beyond his control. This week a power struggle had been resolved in his favor, and he intended to savor the sweet taste of victory. His predecessor had been a weak man in Nicholson's opinion, indecisive, a man whose decisions frequently favored the loudest shouter, the last voice heard. Nicholson had manipulated the man for years, with varying degrees of success, aware that an almost certain way to win his point and bully the boss was to draw his chair forward, drop his pad on the other man's desk, and lean forward aggressively. Moore had often visibly drawn back, usually opening his desk drawer and pretending to stare at the contents in order not to meet Nicholson's eyes, particularly during the past three years, as Moore's health and vigor had steadily declined. Moore had become a living power vacuum and had taken retirement earlier than he'd wanted when it became apparent that his own staff no longer held any respect for him. And Nicholson had emerged pre-eminent during the power struggle that ensued.

During his decline, Moore had agreed to a partition of the manufacturing division, and the materials department under Stuart Hansen had been switched from manufacturing to finance, an arrangement awkward for all concerned, and one which Nicholson had been determined to rectify. The materials department scheduled all production through the factory, purchased virtually all raw materials, and was the primary interface between sales and manufacturing in all matters. Hansen had left shortly after the change for another job, and his assistant, Cynthia Rose, had been temporarily promoted from master scheduler to fill in for him and had performed well enough that her new position became permanent. She was currently the only woman in the company with any real authority, and her unique position at the hub of the company's activity had put the vice-president of finance, an ambitious but unimaginative man named Jennings, at a decided advantage in many interdepartmental skirmishes. The production scheduling function allowed Cynthia Rose to directly affect the production efficiency of Nicholson's departments and gave her an excuse to monitor and report on any inefficiencies as well. It was a hammer constantly poised over his thumb.

After six months worth of arguments, Nicholson had finally convinced Wheeler that Rose's department belonged in manufacturing. How much of that decision was based on the power of his personality rather than the pithiness of his arguments Nicholson did not know, and he cared even less. The end result had been that he'd gotten his way, and he figured it would take less than three months to force Rose out and replace her with Lundberg. He was one of her two assistants, a competent man, but one who resented working for a woman. He was not above making alliances outside his chain of command. Lundberg would be easy to control, and Nicholson would no longer have to watch his back quite so carefully. Admittedly he would not do as good a job as Rose, but he would serve until a better alternative offered itself. At least he was a man. Nicholson could accept differences with other men; after all, it was only fair for each male to do whatever he could to establish himself high in the pecking order. But Cynthia Rose had no business being there. Nicholson did not know how to relate to her and felt awkward dealing with her as a peer. She had a disturbing habit of frankness; she didn't play by the conventional rules. But all that could be taken care of now.

The last appointment for the day was with her, and he'd been looking forward to it for hours, deliberately delaying it until late afternoon so she'd have plenty of time to think about what might be in store for her even before it happened. At four o'clock precisely Cheryl indicated that the woman was in the outer office. Nicholson told her to have Rose wait for a few moments, then deliberately read an article from a professional magazine before asking her to send the woman in. He left the magazine open on his desk, then ostentatiously closed it when she took a seat.

"Well, Cindy, welcome back to the manufacturing division." He planted his elbows on the desk and intertwined his fingers. "I'm sure we will find working together to be both interesting and challenging."

"You don't have to be charming with me, Nicholson," she answered sternly. "We both know why this is all happening. We can at least be honest with each other about it. No one else is here to see the show."

Nicholson sat back. She was confirming his opinion already; she just didn't understand the proprieties, didn't know how to play the game. She was basing her actions on emotion, not logic. "All right, I know we've had our differences in the past. That's no reason to let it interfere with our working together in the future, is it?"

She remained silent, crossing her legs restlessly. Nicholson was uneasy, felt his control slipping in a situation where he had expected to hold all the cards. He could not deal with this woman as he would deal with, say, Dolly. Dolly was still there when he needed her; although she had gotten soft and puffy as the years passed, she had remained loyal. She was a good wife, if not a good mother. Her softness had infected the children despite his efforts to minimize her influence. Eric had left home the year before, unable to discipline himself and unwilling to accept discipline from his father; he called his mother periodically, but he hadn't spoken to his father since the night of that final argument. Margery had died of a drug over-

338

dose just before Christmas; she had retreated into the ultimate weakness, a chemical dependency, until it had claimed her. Nicholson would not allow her name to be spoken in his presence.

"I've never been fully briefed on the details of your department's operations, Cindy," he said, moving some papers about on his desk as though impatient to get back to some real work. "I know a lot of changes have been made since I was involved with production control and I'd appreciate it if you'd work up a complete job description on all of your people, along with employment records, compensation, and so forth, for me to review next week."

She uncrossed her legs and leaned forward. "Look, let's stop beating around the bush. Your track record around here isn't a company secret. Just what are your plans for my people?"

"I don't understand what you mean." It was a lie. He understood all too well what she meant, and he was looking forward to it. Materials was a parasite department; it did no real work, it was just a bunch of glorified clerks with delusions of grandeur. He expected to cut its staffing in half within the year. "I don't have any preconceptions. Certainly I feel as though I have something to contribute to the function of your department, but I don't have any intention of reducing your effectiveness."

Rose looked at him skeptically, opened her mouth to say something, thought better of it, then spoke in a more conciliatory tone. "Listen, I've spent two years building up a group of experienced, highly trained, loyal people. My staff feel obligated to work; they're not casual employees waiting to get a husband or a better job. They're used to working in an informal atmosphere with relatively lenient work rules, and I let them take as much individual responsibility as they can handle. I know your management philosophy is different, and some changes are inevitable. All I want to know is what the major impact is going to be so I can start to lay the groundwork."

"You sound like you're casting me as the heavy, Cindy. Any decisions I make with regard to your department will be for the good of the company as I see it. I don't engage in personal animosities."

"Who are you trying to kid?" Rose seemed honestly surprised. "Do you really expect anyone to believe that line? I know about your attempt to discredit Stu Hansen." She leaned forward, put her hands on her knees, and stared disconcertingly back at him, and he had to fight to avoid dropping his own gaze. "You are the most vindictive, manipulative person this company has ever seen. You are very, very good at it, I have to admit. Maybe right now you're what this company needs. But don't you ever try to hand me a line about your disinterested altruism. You're not a good enough liar, and I'm not a good enough actress to pretend I didn't notice. I didn't get this job because I'm tactful. I don't have time for tact. I care about my work, and I care about my opinion of myself. If you want someone to tell you how great you are, then fire me and promote Lundberg to my place. He'll tell you anything you want to hear, and he's a pretty good scheduler. But as long as I take money from this company, I'm going to tell you what I think is best for its future, whether you like what I say or not. You can act on my suggestions or you can ignore them. If you're as smart as you think you are, you'll value that."

Nicholson was amused and irritated. Her candor was disconcerting, but her frankness was her weakness as well. Already she had said enough that a case for insubordination could be made. He could set up a public confrontation and goad her into making similar statements. This would probably be even easier than he'd originally expected.

He decided a firm reply was called for, preferably a somewhat pompous one. She was obviously contemptuous of him; let her think him naive and she would be less careful about covering herself.

"Cindy, I am shocked that you'd think such a thing." He rose from the desk, clasped his hands behind his back, and began walking back and forth. "I resent the implication that my motives are for my own aggrandizement rather than for the good of my employer. All of our personal futures are dependent upon the success of Eblis, and I would certainly not engage in politics that I believe would have an adverse financial impact on the company. Certainly I look out for myself as well, but the two are not contradictory goals." He paused and rounded on her, feigning anger. "But there is more than one opinion of the proper way to run a manufacturing operation. You've been working under finance, which is concerned with balanced ledgers and manipulation of numbers in an unreal atmosphere. In manufacturing we deal with the practicalities of the real world, and sometimes that means dispensing with the luxuries of some record keeping, rolling up our sleeves, and getting the actual work done."

She met his stare levelly, then laughed and clapped her hands exaggeratedly. "You're good, Nicholson, you really are. If I didn't know you so well, I'd almost believe you meant all that. Cut the bullshit for a while, will you? What specifically do you want?"

For a second he was genuinely angry, but he calmed down and even considered answering her honestly. If she'd been a man, he probably would have, would at least have

341

been able to gauge where she stood. He could have told her that he wanted a substantial cut in manpower, so that the rectitude of the decision to transfer materials into manufacturing would be positively reinforced in Wheeler's mind. He might also tell her that he wanted longer production runs in order to increase his productivity, that she should adjust the direct and indirect labor reporting to cover up the ever climbing rework dollars. But she was just too frank, too unpredictable. She might well be capable of repeating the entire conversation to the wrong party; she could not be trusted to keep an unspoken gentlemen's agreement. If her action couldn't be predicted, she couldn't be controlled. It was essential that he remove her at the earliest opportunity.

"I don't think there's any point in continuing this conversation," he said at last, his voice cool and unfriendly. "Please get me those personnel summaries by Wednesday morning. When I've had an opportunity to review them, I'll discuss the matter further with you and your staff as necessary. Unless you have some specific question, I don't think we have anything further to say to each other today."

He turned back to his desk, sat down, glanced up, and was startled to see that she'd made no move to leave. When she was certain she had his attention, she slowly got to her feet. "That's okay, Nicholson. I think you've already told me everything I wanted to know." She moved to the door but still didn't open it. "You know something? I'm not even mad at you. I'm sorry about what's going to happen to my people, and I suppose things are going to be quite difficult for me until you find an excuse to dump me or I find somewhere else to move along to, but I just can't get mad. You are such a sorry excuse for a man, let alone a manager, that I can only think that there must be this big, rotten place inside you that's eating away at your guts. You must be in terrible pain all the time. It doesn't excuse you, and it doesn't make things any more pleasant for those of us who have to deal with you, but it makes it damned hard to feel anything other than pity."

And before he could say anything in reply, she was gone.

Infuriating woman! He seethed, his ulcer sending warning signals through his body. But let her have her day; he'd have his week, his month, his many years. She'd lost the war, so let her inflict a few token wounds on her way out. He could be generous in the moment of victory. All that remained now was to work out the details of her departure.

As it happened, it took longer than Nicholson expected to build a case against her. He kept a small notebook locked in his desk in which was inscribed dutifully every incident he thought might be of help. Each act of petty insubordination was written down in loving detail, although he had to admit that she carefully negotiated the line between sarcastic resistance and actionable rebellion. But it was a pattern that he hoped to establish, a series of incidents that collectively damned her; he knew she would be careful not to provide him with an overt reason for her dismissal. Gathering evidence of poor performance was more difficult. Nicholson had known from the outset that she was organized and effective; she had a positive flair for scheduling and seemed to know instinctively when problems would arise, and was generally able to shift gears before anything became seriously delayed. Nor did he have much luck undermining her organization. With the exception of Lundgren, all her subordinates seemed fiercely loyal, and the manpower cuts he'd mandated had been handled with minimal disruption, largely through attrition. The work rules had been tightened, and the more rigid schedule had caused some unrest, but she had been able to keep it under control, probably by blaming him for the changes.

It wasn't until December that Nicholson felt he could take the issue to Wheeler. Stock outs had been unusually high this year and there had been some lost sales. Most of this could be attributed to an unforecast late-year surge, but there had also been some slight errors in initiating production runs and ordering the proper subassemblies. Nicholson was counting on Wheeler's lack of manufacturing experience; he had doctored a couple of reports to exaggerate the effect of these errors, then asked for an appointment with Wheeler, at which point he presented the documentation, along with selected notes from his private file on Rose's personal clashes with him.

Wheeler sat quietly at his desk, read the report fairly thoroughly, then set it aside and picked up the second document. Nicholson could tell by the expression on his face that Wheeler was mightily displeased; the man positively blushed when he was angry. Nicholson sat back further in the chair, striving to look reluctant and sympathetic rather than combative. It would be best if the other man took the offensive.

After another few minutes, Wheeler set the second paper aside as well, then leaned forward, took off his glasses, and placed them carefully on the desk. "I assume that you didn't bring these to me just to provide some reading matter. What course of action are you proposing?"

This was the moment where Nicholson had to be careful

not to overplay his hand. "Well, sir, it is evident that Cindy's job performance has deteriorated. I don't think it's sabotage," he let that idea sink in, "but I do think that she's still upset about the transfer of her department into manufacturing. That's why I showed you the notes about some of our arguments."

"That's understandable. It wasn't meant as a demotion, but I can certainly see how she might have interpreted it that way. Status seems to be a rather high priority in this company; it often interferes with getting the job done."

"Yes, sir, but she had to have known that she could not continue reporting directly to the president of the company. She's just not the right sort of person for a position at that level of management."

"More precisely, James, the reason for the change was that the Materials Department properly belongs in manufacturing and should never have been taken out of that division in the first place. The change had nothing to do with her personality or abilities."

"Yes, of course." Back off that tack immediately, he thought. It would not do to suggest, however obliquely, that Wheeler had made a decision for nonprofessional reasons. "But clearly she has lost a degree of interest and attention because of the change. I have heard rumors that she is seeking other employment. There is also an obvious animosity directed toward me," he nodded to the paper, "and it may well be best for all concerned that she leave Eblis and find herself a new position."

"Are you suggesting that we fire her? For what reason? The errors here," he tapped the first report with his glasses, then put them back on, "are hardly sufficient to justify such an extreme action. The shortfall in the sales forecast this year and the lack of information about the

November bubble of orders are at least as serious, and I have no intention of shaking the sales department up with such a radical move."

"No, nothing like that. But it might be best to have her in, explain to her that we feel a change would be in the best interests of both parties, and request that she resign."

"Have you spoken to her about this?"

"No, sir. To be quite honest, I doubt very much that she would respond favorably to anything I said on the matter. I very much fear I misunderstood her personality when the transfer was first made, and once I was on her wrong side, there was nothing I could do to salvage the situation. I've made a few overtures, but she seems unwilling to meet me halfway."

"So you think I should talk to her?"

"If you believe that would be best. It certainly couldn't do any harm."

Wheeler sat back, his face still flushed, then replaced his glasses. He turned to one side, gazing out through the window that overlooked the recently expanded parking lot. Nicholson could almost see the wheels turning in his head. James did not particularly like his boss; the man was not easily intimidated except by superior knowledge, and while it was possible to marshal the necessary facts—or manufacture the "facts" as required—it was a time-consuming process. Wheeler also had an annoying habit of mulling things over, sometimes for several minutes, and keeping his subordinates waiting while his thought processes completed themselves, particularly when he was called upon to make a decision. Staff meetings had occasionally run quite long, with a good portion of the time having passed in relative silence.

Finally, Wheeler turned to meet Nicholson's eyes again,

and the latter recognized that the man's mind was made up.

"James, this," he picked up the report on stock outs, "is superficial and misleading. If anything, our ability to fill orders this year was outstanding under the circumstances. You have reduced the manpower in the Materials Department by fifteen percent despite an increase in business activity of almost the same percentage in the other direction."

"But there is no direct correlation between staffing and production levels in a service department."

Wheeler raised his hand, brushing aside the argument. "I said nothing about those cuts because I transferred that department to you, and I back up my managers' actions, even if I happen to disagree with them. And I don't reverse their decisions or even question them, even when I do disagree with them, unless my reason for doing so is compelling."

"The staff level has nothing to do with those errors, sir. The errors were made in the scheduling and raw material functions, but the cuts were made entirely in expediting, labor reporting, and the warehouse."

Wheeler did not flinch when Nicholson sat abruptly forward. "Don't play me for a fool, James." His words were sharp and unfriendly. "I know as well as you do that the expediters provided the information to the schedulers, and now the information is delayed at least an additional day while the data is sifted through the computer. And the warehouse personnel you eliminated were the ones who did the revolving inventory checks, as well as their normal duties. I do know what cycle counting means, and I did listen when you and Cindy argued about eliminating it three months ago. As a matter of fact, I have no quarrel with your move to cut personnel here. The unfortunate consequences were the result of inadequacies in other departments. If data processing had completed the bar code inventory system as scheduled, we wouldn't even have noticed the loss of the warehouse personnel."

Nicholson thought furiously. Should he press the attack, or was this a good time for a tactical retreat? He had rarely seen Wheeler this determined before; the man always played everything so low-key. But Wheeler was speaking again, and Nicholson forced himself to pay attention.

"This other report," he picked up the summary of their personal interactions, "is illegal and trivial." He tossed it into his waste basket without glancing in that direction. "I am ordering you to immediately destroy any other copies or records containing this information when this interview is concluded." The man's face was bright red now, but his voice was firm, under control. For the first time in many years, Nicholson felt concern. He may have misread the situation and committed a major blunder.

"I am aware of your sentiments toward Ms. Rose, James. I was aware of them at the time of the transfer, just as I know what Ms. Rose and others think of you. Although the depth of animosity is stronger than is perhaps usual, it is understandable. You are a controversial man. Your methods are sometimes extreme, but in general you perform, and the bottom line is, if you help this company to become more profitable, you ultimately do more good for the employees than the relatively small degree of harm you may cause by some of your rather arbitrary decisions. I am also aware that you keep your staff terrified of you, and that even if they were being ordered to load trucks full of merchandise for delivery to your home, I would probably never hear of it from anyone who worked for you."

"It is not uncommon for people to be loyal to their bosses, Mr. Wheeler. I think I have been a steadfast employee of this company over the years."

"Drop the act, James. You have no sense of loyalty to this company except that you intend to guarantee a steady paycheck. I'm not critical of that attitude. Most successful businesses nowadays seem to lack any sense of disinterested obligation to their employees, so it is merely a matter of balance for them to reciprocate. Employment today is a matter of selling one's time and abilities, just as it always was, but with far less of a factor of personal trust than in the past. For that reason the successful employer must have a conduit, a way to penetrate through the spheres of influence of subordinates. I know that you use Lundgren to get through the layer of secrecy that surrounds Rose; it's a necessary if somewhat unpleasant need."

A sudden realization struck Nicholson. He spoke aloud, for the first time not considering his words beforehand. "Are you saying that you have Rose spying on me?"

Wheeler's mouth jerked into a faint smile which immediately disappeared. "No, not exactly. If I ever approached her in that regard, she'd do you an enormous favor and resign on the spot, I suspect. It's not her style. She has, frankly, some rather old-fashioned virtues that will not help her career, particularly in the corporate world. She's too honest and above board. But in this context, it works out the same way." Wheeler opened his desk drawer, took out his pipe, and began tamping it. "I know damned well that if something happens within manufacturing that I need to know about, it will come up at a staff meeting.

349

I don't mean to imply that she's spying on you or anything like that. I suspect she'd consider that beneath her dignity. But she is absolutely frank and straightforward, and I can find out more by casually asking her how things are going than by reading twenty pounds of computer printouts."

At this point Nicholson wanted nothing more than to leave, to escape with as much dignity as possible. Later he could mull the conversation over, decide where and how seriously his defenses had been breached. "Well, under the circumstances, I suppose I should apologize for wasting your time." He started to rise.

"One thing more, before you go." And now there was the taste of fire in his words. "I expect that you will administer the materials department in the same fashion as any other. There will be no further reduction of personnel unless it can be justified financially. You will not in anyway retaliate against Ms. Rose. Any unofficial personnel records on her, or any other employee of this company will be destroyed today, whether they are kept here or elsewhere. Is all of this understood?"

He had to try three times before he could answer. "Yes, sir."

"I realize that it is sometimes difficult to accept that the business world is no longer an exclusively male club. I'd be less than candid if I didn't admit that I am sometimes discomfited myself. I grew up believing that women had no head for business matters, and it's hard to change at my age." Wheeler removed his pipe. "But there is a difference between being conditioned into regressive patterns of behavior and actively attempting to destroy others simply because they don't fit our picture of what they should be. If you're having a problem with Rose as a co-worker, then the problem is yours, James, not hers. She can be a caustic person to deal with, but so can you. If she can put up with you, then you ought to be able to put up with her. If you're as good a manager as you would like me to believe, that is."

His departure from Wheeler's office was as close to a panicky retreat as he had ever made in his life.

Supper that night was unsatisfactory. Dolly spotted his mood right from the moment he stepped into the house and kept as low a profile as possible. Several times during dinner he snapped at her, but she responded meekly on each occasion. Frustrated, full of rage that could not find an outlet, Nicholson drove downtown and made one of his infrequent visits to Pirelli's Bar. The alcohol helped to dim the fury, but there was still no release. At one point he was jostled by another man, but when Nicholson rounded on him, his hand already clenched into a fist, the man apologized profusely and hastened off.

Nicholson drank at a slower pace as the hours advanced, but shortly after eleven o'clock, he stumbled on his way to the rest room. The loss of physical control disturbed him, and he left the bar shortly thereafter. It was unusually warm for October, but still cool enough to counteract some of his insobriety. Not for one moment did he believe that he could drive safely, however, and he resolved to walk a bit and try to clear his head. It really wasn't much of a surprise when, about twenty minutes later, he discovered that he was standing in front of the Sheffield Library.

Almost independently of his own volition, Nicholson found himself turning to enter between the two stone posts that marked the entrance to the driveway. The grounds were in terrible condition, grass and shrubbery untrimmed, litter gathered in every available corner where the wind could send it, the darkness mercifully hiding all but the very worst of it. As Nicholson rounded the corner of the building, he noticed a faint glow ahead, down at the far end, originating somewhere just this side of the rear tower.

His thoughts tumbled over one another as he struggled to throw off the effects of his drinking, and a primitive sense of caution caused him to advance as quietly and circumspectly as possible. The light flickered occasionally, as though something were moving back and forth in front of it. Something or someone, he realized.

Minutes later, Nicholson stood just outside the circle of light cast by a flickering lantern which had been set on the ground snug up against the tower. A woman stood in front of him, close enough now that she would have seen his figure if she had turned in the right direction. Fortunately, she was staring directly up into the eyes of the gargoyle, whose face was lowered in her direction, hanging about a foot above her own eye level. Even as he watched, she moved forward, ran both hands lasciviously up the sides of its carved body, then across the chest. When they reached its muscular shoulders, she clasped them, used the leverage to pull herself up on tiptoes, pressed her own lips against the cold stone mouth. Nicholson was stirred by a renewal of his earlier rage, now reinforced by what he saw as the desecration of something that had become important to him, an integral part of his life. He was about to step forward and call out angrily when she stepped back and did something even more outrageous.

Despite the chill of the evening, the woman was disrobing. Nicholson stood immobile, shocked beyond measure. She moved with ease, efficiently removing sweater and pants, bra and panties, tossing them to one side. Once again he wanted to call out, but he was still held silent by something within him that wanted to understand what was going on.

What happened next was even more perplexing. Without a sound, moving to a music that was audible to no one but herself, the woman began dancing slowly and suggestively within an area about two meters in diameter, directly in front of the gargoyle. It was during this dance that she turned so that the light from the lantern fully illuminated her face, and Nicholson recognized her. It was Valerie Meredith, whom he remembered from his high school years, although he couldn't recall ever having seen her since their graduation. They had never been close, had dated only twice, and Nicholson had not quite fit into the circle of people she had gathered about her. But Valerie still looked much the same as she had many years ago, and he had no difficulty recognizing her.

She danced slowly, a series of figure eights that moved her naked body gradually closer to the gargoyle. Then, when she was less than a meter away, Nicholson noticed something else, a feature of the statue that he had never seen before. From the hollow between the lower limbs, a gigantic male organ protruded, tumescent, thrust upward at a sharp angle from the rest of the body. But just as he noticed it, Valerie obstructed his vision, placing her hands on the shoulders of the gargoyle once more, this time raising her entire body, positioning hips and pelvis to impale herself in some strange parody of coitus with the gargoyle.

"No!" Nicholson didn't know what compelled him to intervene at that point, but there was no question in his mind that he had to act now, that if this upstart woman had her way, something would be lost to him, lost forever.

353

He stepped out into the circle of light, shouted at her again. "Leave it alone! You have no right, you bitch!"

Valerie had frozen at the first shout, but made no move to release her hold on the statue. "Go away, asshole," she hissed, head turned back to look over her shoulder. "Leave now. You don't know what's going on here. You don't want to know."

He hesitated at the quiet tone of authority in her voice but pushed forward once more. There was no way James Nicholson was going to be thwarted again, not now, and particularly not by a woman. Not here, not in his place of refuge. "Get down from there!" Within seconds he was close enough that he could have reached out and touched her.

This time she did move, jumping lightly to the ground and turning to face him. "Go away now!" Her eyes flashed at him, holding his gaze, although he wanted to stare lower, to where her breasts were visible in the flickering light. "I won't warn you again. You cannot understand what is happening here, and it's none of your business."

Infuriated, Nicholson stepped forward, one hand reaching out to grab her arm. His motive was uncertain even to himself. Perhaps he meant to shake her, perhaps to push her away. Whatever his intention, she interpreted it as a threat and responded instinctively, striking at him with the palm of her hand. The slap pushed Nicholson over the edge, and the pent-up fury exploded in a blind wave. He struck out, a closed fist rather than a slap, which Valerie ducked away from with only partial success. His first struck her shoulder as she tried to duck and she stumbled, almost falling. Nicholson stepped forward, arm already cocked for a second blow, when she leaned forward, raising her knee at the same time, aimed at his crotch. At the last second he turned partially away, but pain lanced through his thigh. Memories of the night he had come here with Barbara Howell surfaced, a bitter nostalgia.

Nicholson tried to hit her again, and she danced nimbly out of his way, laughing now. "Okay, big man, you want to play in my league, you better be prepared to take what comes to you." And she danced in suddenly, feinted a kick at his groin. When Nicholson dropped his hands to catch her leg, she lashed out with one hand and her nails caught his cheek. Lines of pure pain burned on one side of his head and he tried to swat her hand to one side, but already Valerie had slipped away. She stood there, naked, taunting him by the posture of her body even more than by her words.

"Had enough yet?" She threw back her head and laughed loudly. "What's the matter? Haven't you ever seen a woman's body before?" She thrust her pelvis forward. "Bet you'd like to look at this one a little closer, wouldn't you? But I've got a better lover." And she turned and looked up at the gargoyle again. "He never poops out at the end."

Her inattention proved her undoing. Nicholson almost ran to where she stood, grabbing her upper arms and lifting her from her feet. Valerie tried to kick out at him, but he slammed her back against the tower wall and there was no room for her to swing her legs. She snapped her head forward, trying to bite him, but he evaded her teeth, then threw her to one side. Valerie fell to one knee, was already rising as he stepped forward. This time his fist connected with the side of her head and she went sprawling onto the ground.

"Goddamned bitch!" He stood over her, shaking with rage.

Valerie rolled over onto her side, looked up at him. There was no fear in her eyes and she was smiling. "What's next, kiddo? Rape? Do you think you can get it up?"

There was no thought of sex in Nicholson's mind at all. Sex was a form of power that he had outgrown, at least that was how he thought of it, when he bothered to think of it at all. Even with Dolly, sex was an intermittent affair, resorted to only periodically when he felt it was necessary to reassert his rights in the matter. But Dolly had surrendered to him long ago, and there was no point in wasting a display of power where none was needed. Valerie misjudged him badly when she tried to tempt him with sex, and again when she thought to impair his judgment by implying that he was sexually inadequate. Nicholson quite simply didn't care.

But he did care that she was in his private place, that she was dirtying something he considered important. He lashed out with his foot, aiming for the rib cage. Valerie threw herself back at the last instant, but the blow still landed solidly, and she rolled away in pain. But now there was rage within her mind as well as his, and she sprang to her feet despite the piercing blaze of fire in her side and charged. Nicholson's own fury had turned to a cold singlemindedness of purpose. He fended off a series of slaps and slashes, a few of them penetrated ineffectively, as he no longer felt the pain, any pain. All he could feel now was a cold determination to make certain that this woman never infringed upon his life again. Choosing the time carefully, he swung back, hitting her on the jaw. Valerie fell back against the wall just beneath the gargoyle's still figure, stunned into immobility.

Nicholson took advantage of the opportunity and

grabbed her by the upper arms again, lifting her into the air. It was not certain what he planned to do as he took two steps backward, perhaps throw her into the bushes, but she twisted in his grasp, kicking out at him again as she tried to free herself. Perhaps he meant to slam her into the wall again, at least that's what he told himself later, but instead he drove her back into the outstretched arms of the gargoyle.

Valerie's face altered into an expression of complete surprise, even consternation, and Nicholson felt much of the tension go out of her muscles. Puzzled, he released her and retreated a step. And that's when he saw the tip of the stone phallus, where it had burst through her body just above the navel. His eyes traveled up from that glistening tip to her face, and her features twisted into a mask of sudden rage. Valerie placed one hand on each of the gargoyle's arms and levered her body forward. The tip of the phallus disappeared and she abruptly dropped to her feet. A red line of blood ran across her abdomen and down one thigh.

"You fucking pig!" She tried to scream the words, but her voice came out shaky. When she took a step, it was wobbly, but she stayed on her feet and Nicholson backed away from her advance. "I'll get you, you bastard! You can't do this to me! I was chosen, do you hear? Chosen!"

"No!" Nicholson protested. "Not you! Never you! Never anyone but me!" Rage overpowering every other emotion, Nicholson pressed forward again, his arms a flurry of blows as he drove her back. Valerie clawed at him, spitting and hissing in her frenzy, but she had been too badly damaged. When the fog lifted and Nicholson finally desisted, she knelt on the ground just beneath the gargoyle, looking up at him through a mask of blood.

"You aren't worthy," she said weakly. "I'm still the one who ..."

But whatever else she might have said at that point was never spoken. The gargoyle's right arm moved slowly but deliberately down. She had time only for a startled glance upward before those razor sharp claws ripped out her throat. Valerie had known somehow that the choice would be made tonight, but she had not known that the gargoyle had left it to his two protegés to make that decision. The stronger, the more worthy, had prevailed.

Somehow, in that moment, Nicholson was beyond reality, beyond everything he had ever believed up to that moment, beyond anything human. There was not a tremor in his hand or a doubt in his mind as he sidestepped the still warm corpse of Valerie Meredith and reached to accept the outstretched hand of the gargoyle.

The hand closed around his own.

CHAPTER FIFTEEN
NIGHT OF THE GARGOYLE

The contact between those two hands was almost sexual in its intensity—certainly it was a consummation of something more than anything James Nicholson had ever before experienced. There was almost an electric tingle, but it was one which spread throughout the man's entire body with a perceptible excitation. What the gargoyle may or may not have undergone at the same moment is perhaps something no human being could ever know, but the closest we might approximate is that it was a sense of achievement, fulfillment, the culmination of decades of painstaking preparation. The essence which separates life from nonlife was being leached out of Nicholson's body, and he felt himself stiffening into immobility, even as mind registered the gargoyle stepping out from the wall, fully independent, muscles rippling, joints and extra joints bending with fluid animation. The eyes were alight with savage joy as it drew what it needed from the man, the contact of their two hands the conduit for its passage. In just seconds, the gargoyle would be fully articulated, the man a bizarre statue of no particular artistic merit, but of minutely executed detail.

But the gargoyle had underestimated the strength of human evil, just as Nicholson had failed to anticipate its own malice and self-interest. Along with the life force that flowed from his body, there also came a substantial portion of Nicholson's spirit, a living essence of self-interest that would not allow itself to be snuffed out, no matter how inhuman and unprecedented the opposition to its continued existence, and when at last the union was complete and the grotesque homunculum stepped free, its mind was fogged with conflicting emotions and personalities. Its limbs, while workable, were not as supple as one would expect from an organic life form. Similarly, the statue of Nicholson did not remain erect; the knees bent just slightly, and it slumped slowly to the ground. The transfer had not taken place as intended. Something more and something less had passed between the two, and neither was any longer a discrete entity.

The gargoyle took a tentative step away and swayed dizzily. A human observer would have seen the creature shake its head in puzzlement. Its thoughts were a confused mixture of its original plans and bits and pieces of Nicholson's life. The dominant emotion was its unceasing hatred of the human race and of all animate life, and the need to destroy that which it so despised. But there was now an overlay of very specific and personal feelings which were strong enough to capture the attention of the conscious mind. The amalgam of James Nicholson and the gargoyle hated people, specific people, all those Nicholson had encountered in life who'd thwarted or annoyed him in any fashion. They were spread through time and space, from his childhood to the present, all equally reprehensible in his distorted view.

Faces appeared in the gargoyle's mind, faces from

Nicholson's life. There was Mickey Palatto and Jason Richards and Ron Joslin and Barbara Howell. There was Mr. Gotlieb, who had sprayed him with the garden hose, and Mr. Parkinson, who had caught him shoplifting, and Mrs. McKenzie, who had given him an unsatisfactory grade in biology. There were people from the union and people from management, John Paruti, Stuart Hansen, Gordon Wheeler, Cynthia Rose, Harry Rollins, and Oliver Moore. The faces of his wife and children appeared—Dolly, Margery, and Eric—and some of his neighbors, particularly those who refused to socialize with the Nicholsons . . . and a host of bartenders, cab drivers, store clerks, policemen, teachers, and service personnel. He hated them all, and therefore the gargoyle hated them all and desired their immediate destruction. But there were practical limits to its powers, and it cast about for those nearest to its present location, sensing them with an ability never known to any mere mortal. And immediately it picked up the spoor of three of its enemies, two men and one woman, all within easy reach. Those three would be the first, but far from the last. Far, far from the last.

Mickey Palatto was not happy with his life. He would never admit it to anyone, not even to himself, but everything he'd touched since childhood seemed to self-destruct. His first marriage had ended within two years; his second wife hadn't even bothered with the formality of a divorce. She'd just cleared everything out of their small bank account, packed her clothes, and disappeared while he was at work one day. He'd never heard from her, and he often informed drinking buddies that he felt he had gotten off cheap. Lacking a high school diploma, he had no opportunity for really good employment, and the chip he'd carried on his shoulder throughout his twenties had cost him several jobs. As a consequence his reputation was that of a troublemaker, and that had made it even more difficult for him to find work. Now in his forties, overweight, balding on top, perhaps a bit too fond of the bottle, still heavily muscled, but softer, he lived alone in an apartment in the low-income housing development, wondering what the future might hold for him.

He was sitting watching television, the late movie, not paying much attention to the story but enjoying himself because he thought the female lead attractive, and when she wasn't on screen, he kept busy washing down nacho chips with cold beer. Mickey was on vacation this week, and television was just about his only leisure activity. He used to bowl from time to time, but the few friends he'd kept since high school had mostly moved away, and he'd never really been any good at it.

Mickey was just beginning to nod off, another of his habits, when he heard the sound of glass breaking on the balcony. Each apartment in the complex had a narrow balcony with sliding glass doors, barely big enough for two people to sit and look out. In Mickey's case, the view was of the town cemetery, not one he chose to contemplate very often, and the drapes had remained drawn for months. It sounded very much as if a door had been shattered, perhaps by a rock.

Mickey roused himself, perpared to go out and yell down at those responsible, probably kids who would by now be halfway across the cemetery, far beyond even the sound of his voice. But before he could take another step, he heard a sound as though something heavy were moving on top of the broken shards. Apparently someone had climbed up onto his balcony, probably a burglar, although

Mickey couldn't imagine why any thief would want to break into the units in the complex. All the residents combined would probably be unable to come up with enough valuables to be worth such an effort, let alone a single apartment.

But for the first time in months, perhaps years, Mickey felt truly alive, felt the way he had in school, when he'd commanded a small but devoted legion of followers, when everyone else walked warily in his presence, when he'd been someone important, a force to be reckoned with. Carefully, quietly, he crossed to his tool box, lifted out the crowbar, and turned toward the short hall leading to the balcony. Whoever it was, they were in for a surprise. Mickey Palatto might be getting older, might be a bit thick around the middle, but he was still no pushover. He could still deal the blows when the need arose.

He held the crowbar in his right hand, the forked tip lying across his left palm, and moved slowly through the darkened hall. There were no lights on in the apartment; he kept it unlighted whenever possible, to save on electricity. Besides, his aging television was losing its sharpness and looked better in the dark.

He reached the corner and paused. A right turn and he would be only a meter from the inside door that opened onto the balcony. The intruder could not have come this far yet without being seen, but Mickey couldn't remember if the inside door was shut. He used the balcony as a storage room for dirty laundry, trash he had not yet bothered to carry downstairs, and anything else he wanted out of his way. Well, he thought, either way I have to round that corner if I want to know what's going on. Within a few seconds, someone is going to have a very big surprise ... and maybe a sore head as well. He tapped the end of the crowbar against his free hand several times as he worked up the nerve to make his move.

Mickey inhaled deeply, then took two quick steps and turned. In the shadows just this side of the balcony doors, stood a figure—not tall, but heavily built, completely motionless. Somehow Mickey knew that he had not surprised the other, that it had been waiting for precisely this move, had known he was there all the time. There was a sense of imminent menace about the shape and posture that made his skin crawl.

"All right, you motherfucker." He spoke softly, refusing to be intimidated. "You broke into the wrong damned apartment this time. Come out here into the open here where I can see you, real slow now, you hear me, or you're gonna hurt like you've never been hurt before."

There was no movement at all, no hint of any intention to comply, or flee, or anything else. Mickey wondered if he had some kind of psycho to contend with. But he felt confident so long as he held the crowbar. Although, come to think of it, what if the intruder carried a gun? Suddenly he could not bear not seeing his opponent more clearly, not knowing precisely what he was up against. Keeping the shape centered in his vision, he felt along the wall for the light switch, located it, and flipped it up.

Mickey's first thought was that this had to be some sort of practical joke. The figure that stood there was a statue of some kind, a monster, human only in the grossest of terms. But then the ugly face lifted and the eyes blinked, and he knew beyond any shadow of a doubt that it was real, not an illusion, not a trick, not a costume. And now it took a step toward him.

"All right, you motherfucker," he said softly. "Come and get it."

364

The gargoyle moved toward him, its limbs articulated in a strange parody of human locomotion, the double-elbowed arms flexing in an indescribably bizarre manner. It wanted to see fear in Palatto's eyes, it needed to recognize in its foe the utter panic in the face of his enemy before the body could be sent into oblivion. The gargoyle had nothing to fear; it lacked any understanding of that emotion. It wanted only to destroy, both physically and mentally, those individuals whom the Nicholson part of its personality had hated.

When it had moved within arm's reach, the mouth opened in a malevolent grin. Mickey raised the crowbar, aiming a blow directly at the head. Nicholson's instincts had survived the transfer, and the gargoyle unthinkingly flinched from the descending crowbar so that it struck the left shoulder instead of landing squarely on the furrowed brow. And for the first time in its existence, the gargoyle felt pain, a bright flame of agony, nothing like a mere human would have experienced taking that powerful a blow, but unpleasant enough to be avoided in the future, damaging enough that it had difficulty raising its arm to brush away the man's makeshift weapon.

Enraged at its own vulnerability, at the weaknesses which had been inflicted upon it by the Nicholson personality, the gargoyle dropped all thought of protracted revenge. It fairly leaped forward now, the uninjured right arm flashing out to rip four deep cuts through the filthy undershirt that covered Mickey's paunch. He dropped back a step, his eyes wide, while blood poured out of the deep wounds, then raised the crowbar, shouted out a meaningless monosyllable, and rushed forward again. The gargoyle caught his descending blow, twisted and snapped the forearm, and the heavy tool fell to the floor. One leg rose and the clawed foot flashed outward and down, raking across the man's thighs and groin. Mickey stumbled and would have fallen, but he was still held by one arm. He tried to swing a punch then, but he was off balance and fell forward instead, body half-turning, and the crippled left arm smashed into his ribs, the claws cutting through flesh and bone alike. Nearly senseless, he offered no resistance as the creature shifted its grip and threw him up against the far wall. Mickey slid down into a sitting position, watching his blood flow out onto the carpeting. With three quick steps the gargoyle came to stand directly in front of him again, and one foot flashed upward, this time smashing into his chin, breaking his neck, and scraping bloody flesh from the lower half of his face. He never moved again, but the gargoyle stood looking down on his body for a long time afterward, trying to remember just what it was that this man had done to him.

Ron Joslin had remarried in 1981, and while he had to admit that Peggy was not as interesting and spontaneous a person as Barbara, she was certainly prettier and much more willing to cater to his whims. His marriage to Barbara had broken up because each had too many interests and neither was willing to surrender them; they'd respected each other's rights and recognized the problem soon enough to end the partnership before they were at each other's throats. He was still fond of her, though, and he knew that she'd filled some gaps in his life that Peggy would never be able even to understand. Nevertheless this new arrangement seemed much more likely to last a long time, and his new job was paying rather well. All things considered, he hadn't done too badly.

Peggy had money as well, a not inconsiderable inheritance, though not enough to provide them with a life of luxury. Ron would have worked even if there had been enough money to enable him to quit simply because he needed something to do, but there was nowhere near that kind of security in the money left to Peggy by her parents. Nevertheless they lived in one of the better parts of Managansett, just east of the cemetery, a quiet neighborhood with newer homes and not many children yet. It was convenient to downtown and there were persistent rumors of a highway extension to lead south toward the interstate. It was a two-story house; Ron abhorred ranch-style homes and told Peggy he didn't feel right sleeping on the ground floor.

The Joslins owned a cat, a haughty Siamese named Tamur, who pretty much had the run of the place, although she preferred to spend the night in the kitchen. It was Tamur who first realized there was a prowler on the premises. She didn't see anything, and her cautious sniffing failed to detect any unfamiliar odor, but with some sense unavailable to humans, she knew something was amiss. Springing onto the counter, she peered out through the darkness into the backyard. There was no movement except the slight swaying of a limb from the tree around the corner of the garage. Tamur curled up on the windowsill and watched for a long time, but when nothing happened she eventually relaxed and began grooming herself.

Thus it was that the cat's head was turned away when one clawed hand punched through the window with such speed and force that most of the pane remained intact. Most of Tamur remained intact as well, but not enough to sustain life. And then there was no one left to notice as the window was unlocked and opened and something entered the darkened house, something that had no legitimate business there at all.

Ron Joslin had always been a light sleeper and was often wakened simply by the sound of a car passing on the street. He didn't know what had disturbed him this evening, but there had been some kind of noise from downstairs and he would not be able to go back to sleep until he identified it. Probably, he thought, Tamur has knocked something off the kitchen table again. Sometimes the cat did it just because she wanted attention. He glanced at the bedside clock and noticed it was only one in the morning.

"I'll give her some attention she doesn't want," he muttered softly, so that he would not wake Peggy. With exaggerated caution he slipped out of bed, donned slippers and robe, then moved around to the bedroom door, opening it only partway so that it wouldn't creak. Much of this care was unnecessary; Peggy was a sound sleeper.

He was less cautious outside the room, walking briskly down the stairs to the ground floor. The thought of a burglar never entered his head, and he was totally unprepared when he was grabbed by the hair from behind, his head tilted back, and something sharp and hot and icy touched his throat and everything became very vague and there wasn't much pain and pretty soon there wasn't anything at all.

The gargoyle held the man by the hair until the last blood pumped from his torn throat, then let the body slump to the floor. It had learned caution at its first encounter. These flimsy humans could inflict damage upon it now, could cause it discomfort and perhaps even kill it. And that would never do. The gargoyle must survive, must go on forever. But first it must kill all the Nicholson enemies, because that had somehow become one of the imperatives of its existence, something that it must accomplish before it could attempt to sort out the conflicting desires in its own consciousness. It felt around for the next enemy now. The woman, yes. She was only a few blocks away. She would be next . . . then the others. All of them would die soon.

The gargoyle left by the front door.

It was Barbara's birthday and the mailman had brought a large package, almost too large for her to carry easily. She signed for it and carried it into the kitchen, dropping it on the table. Presumably it was a present, but there was no indication who had sent it, no return address, no identifiable postmark. Mystified, she used a paring knife to cut the strings that bound it and slice through the packing tape. Then she pried the top flap loose, peeling it back to reveal a gift-wrapped parcel. It was far too awkward to lift out, so she cut the ribbon and ripped through the brightly colored paper, revealing the inner box. She was just reaching to open that as well when the table began to shake. Barbara stepped back just as the top of the carton burst open and a horrible face rose into view.

She stumbled back, retreating as quickly as possible, but slipped and fell to her knees. With one hand braced on the counter she started to rise, but she froze in position as more and more of the dark-skinned creature rose into view. It was utterly impossible; the box was not large enough to have contained anything this size. Two enormous batlike wings unfurled and flapped spasmodically as it got free of the carton and jumped down from the table to stand beside her, almost her height and much bulkier.

Eyes glowed as the mouth opened, saliva dripping from its fangs as it reached down toward her throat.

And Barbara woke up. Her bedroom was dark, lit only by a diffuse glow from streetlight on the corner. The house was silent and she could almost hear her own heart beating. She was drenched with perspiration, her muscles knotted. This was the second time she'd dreamed of the gargoyle this week; she'd dreamt of it once the week before. It seemed to have become an obsession with her, and she had no idea why this should have happened to her, nor why at this particular time. She was aware of its connection with two unpleasant scenes from her childhood, and certainly it was ugly enough to cause nightmares, but why was it rising from her subconscious after a gap of so many years?

She didn't feel that sleep would come easily for the rest of the night, at least until she'd had a chance to calm down. She thought about having some warm milk; that was supposed to be the cure for this sort of thing, but warm milk had always nauseated her unless it had cocoa in it, and she didn't keep any in the house. Perhaps a cup of tea would help. She slid out of bed and found some slippers, then made her way down to the kitchen.

The kettle was on when she thought she heard something moving outside. She stood at the rear window, but the small fenced yard was cloaked in darkness, and if there had been anything there, either it was where she couldn't see it, or it had left. Ordinarily she would have dismissed it as a cat almost immediately, but the memory of her dream made her jumpy and she was unable to throw off the feeling that she was being stalked. It was too cold to go outside without heavier clothing than her nightdress, but she turned on the rear porch light, which illuminated

370

about two-thirds of her field of vision. Still nothing. Thoughtfully, she left the light on, telling herself she was being silly and jumping at shadows, but without for a single instant considering turning the light back off.

The kettle whistled, so she poured herself a cup of hot water, dropped in a teabag, and waited for it to steep. A car drove past and she jumped, almost knocking the cup from the table. That did it, she thought, glancing at the clock. It was just after three. Tomorrow was Saturday and she had no plans. There was no way she could go back to sleep just now; she would stay up until dawn, catch up on some reading, perhaps. She could always nap later on, during the daylight, if she felt sleepy. This had better not become a habit, she thought. Am I getting neurotic in my middle age? Afraid of the dark? Falling prone to the hysterical fears of spinsters?

The stairway light blew out when she turned it on this time. Great, she thought ... just what I needed. Can't change that bulb without a stepladder. She climbed the stairs in darkness, almost tripping over a wrinkle in the runner, but she reached the landing without incident and had soon dressed in a pair of jeans and a pullover. She kept the thermostat set fairly high, but it was still chilly at night. The house was old enough that the insulation wasn't as efficient as it might have been, and there were quite a few drafts.

It was even darker as she headed downstairs, carefully picking her way down each riser. She was perhaps halfway when she realized that there was something wrong. The glow from the kitchen light easily reached this far; the bottom of the staircase should be at least murkily visible. That meant that the fluorescent light in the kitchen was no longer on.

Barbara hesitated on the stair. Of course, it was possible that the fluorescent tube had also burned out. It was a pretty big coincidence, of course, but she hadn't replaced the fixture in at least a year. But something else bothered her as well, something subliminal. For no apparent reason, she felt she was no longer alone. Something or someone had intruded upon her home, something that was waiting for her to walk in unawares. It was irrational, but there was no way to shake the feeling.

Barbara ran through a catalog of items in the house that might be useful as weapons. The telephone was in the kitchen, naturally, and there was no way that she could call the police without something more substantial than a vague feeling that someone might be in the house with her. Frightened or not, she was not about to make a spectacle of herself. Barbara was not about to sacrifice her dignity now. The front door was at the foot of the stairs, and she supposed she could make it outdoors before anyone could reach her, but that still left her with the problem of where to go and what to do. She was loathe to be driven out of her house, particularly when she had no evidence that there was any real threat in the first place. To the right was the door to the garage, where her car was parked. She couldn't recall offhand where she had left the keys, probably in her purse. But where was her purse? On the floor near the front door, perhaps ... that was where she usually dropped it. But the darkness at the foot of the stairs was too impenetrable for her to confirm or deny this theory. There were some tools in the garage, left by her uncle when he had died over two decades ago, but she had never even looked at them other than to bring a hammer and screwdriver inside for use on minor repairs. It wasn't clear that she could have wielded any of them in such a manner as to cause more damage to an opponent than to herself. Barbara had never cast herself as the heroic type.

To the left was the living room, which opened up into the kitchen and pantry at the far left, and back under the stairway to the dining room and the downstairs lavette. There was a small sewing room behind the garage, opening onto the dining room, which Barbara's aunt had used as her bedroom during her last years, when she was frequently too ill to climb the stairs unaided. The back door of the kitchen opened out onto the porch, the side door into the pantry.

Barbara strained to hear anything out of the ordinary, any clue as to the location or even the existence of any other living being in the house. Finally, cautiously, she descended the rest of the way to the ground level, but paused again. She had just remembered the baseball bat. It was in the hall closet, under the staircase, way in the back. Barbara wasn't sure she could swing it hard enough to do any real damage, but at least it was better than nothing.

It was only a matter of seconds to tiptoe across the darkened room and remove the bat from the closet. Holding it in front of her with both hands, she moved slowly to the archway leading into the kitchen. There was a switch just inside the door; if the light had been turned off rather than blown out, she ought to be able to turn it right back on. Holding the bat in her right hand now, she extended her left hand forward, slid it along the wall, found the switch, and pressed it up. The room beyond was flooded with light and she heard the faint, familiar hum of the fluorescent tubes.

Barbara couldn't stand the suspense any longer. Raising the bat high above one shoulder, she stepped around the entranceway, staring directly down into the small kitchen.

Nothing seemed amiss, nothing out of place, no stranger lurking in the corners.

The cup of tea was still sitting on the table, steaming slightly, an appetizing golden color. Still unable to shake the feeling of another presence nearby, Barbara looked under the table, behind the wastebasket, every place that even a small animal might hide. The kitchen was as empty as it had been when she'd left it. Could she have turned the light off herself without thinking about it? Could it be just her overactive imagination and the unreality that often lingered after a particularly vivid dream?

"You're losing it, woman," she said softly, setting the baseball bat down in a corner. She spent the next few minutes drinking the tea, willing her jangled nerves to relent. Stubbornly her mind insisted that there still was danger. She lifted the telephone, pressed the receiver to her ear, heard the reassuring dial tone. "Listen," she told herself, "the telephone line has not been cut, there's no one lurking in the house, the doors and windows are all locked...." And she stopped. Were they? She was rather careless about security, and when she had put the trash out on the back porch earlier the night before, had she bothered to relatch the door? She started for the entranceway to check it, paused long enough to retrieve the bat from its resting place, and walked over to examine the lock. The inner door was not secured, but the storm door might be. She opened the first, leaned over to see if the locking pin was in the closed position. It was not.

"All right," she told herself as she locked it, then as an afterthought, locked the inner door as well. "So someone

374

might have come in. I'll just have to be more careful in the future. But that doesn't mean anyone came in tonight."

She turned and walked back around to the table and was just reaching for her tea cup when the gargoyle stepped out of the pantry into clear view, his face distorted into a humorless smile.

Oddly enough, despite the unreality of what stood before her, Barbara never believed she was dreaming. She knew instantly that this was a real creature that confronted her, that it meant her harm, and she knew where it had come from. Later she might sit down and think through the implications of a statue that could climb down from the top of a building and enter her home, but in that endless moment, the only thoughts that surfaced in her mind were how to escape or, alternatively, how to injure or kill this monstrous evil thing. She would also wonder later how it was that her unconscious mind had known all along that this day was to come, sending dreams to prepare her, for there was no doubt at all that the recurring dream image had been a warning of this reality.

Raising the bat above her head with both hands, Barbara advanced, her lips curving into a snarl that the gargoyle itself might have been proud of. "You get out of my house!" she shouted, and swung the bat at its head.

The gargoyle was unimpressed by the woman's bravado, but the learned responses of the Nicholson personality responded to the descending bat, and the creature flinched, knowing that it could be hurt. The bat struck it a glancing blow along the shoulder that had already been hurt, and that reminder of the now rapidly dissipating pain drove the gargoyle into a rage. It slashed first with one arm, then the other, the second time catching the bat and knocking it from Barbara's grasp. She fell back against the table in reaction while her erstwhile weapon smashed into the wall clock, then fell behind the refrigerator. Barbara braced herself with both hands against the table and pushed off, hoping to run past the gargoyle, but it jumped sideways to block her path, the fangs lifting as it smiled horribly. She shrank back a step, looking about for something else to use as a defense.

A hiss came from the gargoyle's mouth and it looked surprised for a moment, as though it expected human speech to have issued forth, as indeed it had. But the gargoyle had no lungs or vocal chords, and what little sound did emerge was purely the product of its discharge of psychic energy, more mental than physical in nature. But the pause was long enough for Barbara to move sideways to the stove. She grabbed the still steaming tea kettle and swung it around, hot water spraying ahead of her and landing on the gargoyle in a broad swath of steam.

The results were gratifying, if short-lived. Each drop of water hissed and sputtered, and the gargoyle would have cried out in pain if it had been capable of sound. The burning sensation was beyond all its previous experience, and it retreated, slapping at the tiny droplets of water. Barbara didn't hesitate for a second, slipping past the flailing arms and running for the front door. But something caught her feet as she reached for the knob and she fell headlong. Her purse had been there after all.

The car keys! She grabbed the purse and started to reach into it, but looked up suddenly as a dark form interposed itself in the light from the kitchen. She scrambled back to her feet, opened the garage door instead, and ran through, slamming it behind her. Unfortunately she couldn't lock the door from this side. With the palm of her hand, she slammed the "Up" button on the automatic garage door opener and climbed into the car, dumping the contents of her purse out onto the seat beside her. She had just picked up the keys and slipped them into the ignition when the door to the house exploded off its hinges, slamming down onto the hood of the car and then falling off to one side.

The engine started up the first time and she shifted into Drive just as a dark shape flew at her. Her side window exploded into thousands of tiny particles as the gargoyle drove its fist through it. Barbara closed her eyes and pressed on the gas, and the accelerating car broke out into the open. For a second, a cold, hard hand brushed her cheek as she pulled clear. She opened her eyes as her head was pulled to one side, losing control of the steering wheel for a split second. The left front wheel went over the edge of the driveway and across the lawn, and she hit the front lamppost with her headlight and bumper. The car came to a stop, but luckily the engine didn't stall.

Behind her the gargoyle rose from where it had been thrown to the floor of the garage, more furious than ever. Once again injury had been done to its left arm. Already stiff because of the flawed transfer process, it was now sending out continuing messages of dull pain. That bitch, came the thought. All my life she and others like her have been causing me pain. Now it's my turn to return the favor. She can run, she can save a few minutes, but she cannot hide. No matter where she goes or how fast she runs, I'll find her sooner or later. I'll find all of them. The gargoyle emerged from the garage just as Barbara was backing the car away from the mangled lamppost.

Even as Barbara turned the wheel toward the driveway entrance, a shape flashed past the car to the right, moving to block her way. She spun the wheel back, bypassing it, but this time she hit the stone wall glancingly and heard the sound of metal tearing. Briefly the car's front quarter hung up and she feared she would be unable to advance further.

"No, damn it!" She stepped on the gas again and, with a double bump as the rear wheels cleared a part of the wall that had fallen in their path, she drove out into the street and started to turn. There was a loud thump as the gargoyle sprang into the air, landing with both splayed feet on the roof of the car, but her sudden acceleration unseated it and it toppled into the road behind her as she sped down the block.

The gargoyle rose to its feet, staring after her. So the bitch would escape this time, it thought. It doesn't matter. There will be another opportunity. That chance was to arise a lot sooner than it ever imagined.

At the end of the street, Barbara hit the brakes and the car screeched to a halt. "No!" She wasn't sure to whom she was talking, maybe just herself. "I will not be driven out of my own home." She glanced up into the rearview mirror, saw the gargoyle standing in the street in front of her house, visible in a pool of light from the streetlamp overhead, looking almost wistful as it stared after her. Lips set, she made a sudden U-turn, cutting across a neighbor's lawn as she did so. The car handled sluggishly because of the damage to the front end, but she was past caring.

At first the gargoyle could not credit what it was seeing. She was coming back. It would have another opportunity to finish this now. But then it realized that the automobile was coming quite quickly, accelerating rapidly, and it remembered that it could also be hurt in its present form, perhaps seriously. At the last moment it knew what might even be called fear as it turned and leaped to one side. The left fender, already crumpled by the collision with the lamppost, caught the gargoyle at thigh level, sending its body spinning through the air to land in the hedges. Momentum carried the car past, and Barbara was four houses away before she brought it to a near halt, then made another one-hundred-and-eighty-degree turn.

The gargoyle climbed up out of the hedge with great difficulty, since its left hip joint did not appear to be working properly. For the first time it unfurled its wings, planning to escape by means of flight, to mend itself, to bide its time for another day, another place. It had already bided its time for centuries; a slight delay now would be but a minor inconvenience. But James Nicholson knew he could not fly, knew it beyond any shadow of a doubt, knew it so absolutely that no matter how actively the gargoyle flapped its wings, it could not leave the ground. And then it heard the car bearing down again.

It couldn't fly but those muscular legs could still generate a powerful leap, even with a crippled hip. It almost cleared the hedges and would have landed successfully on the other side if the left leg hadn't buckled on impact, sending it rolling over the lawn. Barbara drove past again, hitting the brakes hard, then swerved up onto her lawn, carefully avoiding the remains of the lamppost, then accelerating back along the line of houses toward her adversary, churning up grass and flowerbeds with reckless abandon. Along the street several lights snapped on as people were stirred from their sleep.

The gargoyle turned to face her, cocking an arm back, timing itself, then leaping forward at the windshield of her car. Barbara flinched this time as one clawed fist smashed through the center of the safety glass, but she kept her foot firmly on the gas pedal. The gargoyle's body slewed sideways on the hood, and it tried unsuccessfully to grab the dashboard before falling off on the passenger side. Barbara turned right at the next driveway, turned again when she reached the street, and started back. Her knuckles were white where she gripped the steering wheel and her mouth was set in a rictus of hate that would have shocked her had she taken a moment to glance into the rearview mirror.

The gargoyle burst out of the darkness, crossing the street in front of her, angling away. Barbara never hesitated for a moment. She turned the wheel to follow, up over the curb, narrowly missing a fire hydrant as she did so, then across one lawn, two, three, while at least one angry man stood on his porch in a bathrobe, shaking his fist and shouting imprecations. She was beyond caring, beyond anything but the destruction of this abomination that she pursued. It could not be allowed to survive this encounter.

It disappeared around the side of a house, and she suddenly became concerned that it would go someplace where she could not follow in the car. Certainly even limping as badly as it was, it would be more than capable of killing her if she approached it outside the safety provided by the vehicle. But there was plenty of room between the houses, and her one remaining headlight spotlighted the dark figure as it clambered over a fence. No time to stop and think ... she pressed down hard on the gas pedal and the fence flew to pieces in front of her. She was successfully through, but the impact had torn the wheel from her hands, and lacking control she skidded into a vegetable garden, stopping only a couple of feet from the back porch of the house beyond. The engine stalled this time.

Frantically Barbara glanced around, but no attack seemed imminent. The gargoyle seemed to have disappeared. Still, she'd better try the engine right away. The first time the starter whined and nothing happened. "Come on," she said softly. "Let's go!" No success on the second attempt either. More lights were going on with every passing second and she could hear people shouting. She turned the key again and this time the engine coughed and started. Backing out into the clear, she shifted to Drive and pulled across the lawn to the street.

But where to now? Although she looked in both directions, there was no sign of that hunched, grotesque figure. Where would it go? How could she find it? And then she realized the answer at once.

The gargoyle was running as fast as its misshapen limbs could carry it, even with the damaged hip. There was no question about its attitude now: fear had replaced hatred. It had no experience of the emotions of weakness, fear, pain, the possible end of existence. But now it knew them all, and it was not prepared for such a change in its view of itself and its environment. Had it not been for the Nicholson personality, it might well have frozen into gibbering immobility, but for the first time it was glad that the transfer had been flawed. It could still function, still move, drawing upon Nicholson's ability to live with the fact of its own mortality. Now it was seeking that most essential of commodities, security. And where would it be more secure than the wall of the Sheffield Library, where it had remained for the past several decades, untouched and untouchable? There would be another time, but right now it needed sanctuary, to mend its wounds and consider what it had learned.

It reached Main Street and turned right. Had it not

been early, the sight of the knobby, malformed creature running through the shopping district would have caused an uproar. As it was, no living being except a prowling dog even saw it pass, and the dog wasn't particularly happy about the encounter. Twenty blocks to go and it would reach the entrance to the Sheffield estate, then fifteen, ten, five.

And a one-eyed dragon suddenly appeared from a side street ahead, turning in the gargoyle's direction. It froze in place, its mouth curling into a snarl, its wings rustling behind. The oncoming car picked up the gargoyle's form in the circle of light from the remaining headlamp, and it swerved up onto the sidewalk, bearing down rapidly. Undecided which way to jump, the gargoyle waited a fraction too long before darting out into the middle of the street, and one wheel caught an ankle. There was a sound like shattering stone as the car passed, and the gargoyle fell to the pavement, rolling over onto its back. When it tried to rise this time, it fell back, staring down in surprise at the stump at the end of its leg where one four-clawed foot had previously been. Carefully it tried again, this time placing the injured limb down like a pirate with a wooden leg. It seemed almost as if it were moving in slow motion, its reactions dulled with the shock. There was no bone, of course. Statues don't have bones. Or blood. But neither do they heal.

Barbara had turned the car and was roaring back down the road, fighting to keep control as one tire blew loudly and disappeared in rags of rubber from the rim. The gargoyle rose from the street in front of her, turning slowly in her direction. She caught one final look of rage on its face as it stared into the windshield and thought for just one second that it looked an awful lot like James Nicholson, and then the wings unfolded as it reared up in front of the hood and she struck it head on travelling at something over forty miles an hour. There was a thud and the car swerved completely out of control. For a second the sign at Pirelli's Bar flashed in front of her eyes, then the car hit the front of the building and everything flashed brilliantly for a few seconds before turning black.

Chief Dowdell was never happy about his investigation of the events of that evening. When they had pulled Barbara Howell out of the car wreck, she was bleeding profusely from several wounds to the head, although most of them subsequently proved to be superficial. The hospital confirmed that she had a severe skull fracture and, as it turned out, three weeks would pass before he could question her. The bizarre story she told of an animated statue trying to kill her was probably the result of the head injuries, but if so, what had caused her to go on a driving spree at such an ungodly hour in the first place? The doctors hinted that she was under a lot of strain because of the remarriage of her divorced husband, with whom she appeared to be still in love, and that she might be suffering from a nervous disorder. Her insurance company agreed to pay for most of the damages, and she'd indicated her willingness to pick up the tab for the rest. There seemed to be no purpose in pressing charges so long as all the aggrieved parties were satisfied, but Dowdell didn't like the loose ends.

For one thing, it had been discovered that the statue mounted on the roof of the Sheffield Library had, in fact, been removed. No one knew how or why exactly, but state police said it was professionally done and must have required extensive equipment. How thieves could erect scaffolding and winches during the night, chisel a statue off a wall, and removed it, all without anyone noticing it, was a mystery.

If anyone did know the answers, thought Dowdell as he replaced the file in his drawer, they aren't coming forward. He donned his uniform cap and left the office, stepping out into the bright sunlight. Winter was only a few weeks away and already the sun felt colder. Mysterious deaths, walking statues, mild-mannered women going on wild driving rampages through their neighbors' yards—all these things seemed from some alien world. Nothing like that could ever happen here. Managansett was a nice, quiet town.

Yes, he thought again, standing on the doorstep now. A nice, quiet town.